ACCLAIM FC

"*Seasons of an Amish Garden* follows the year through short stories as friends create a memorial garden to celebrate a life. Revealing the underbelly of main characters, a trademark talent of Amy Clipston, makes them relatable and endearing. One story slides into the next, woven together effortlessly with the author's knowledge of the Amish life. Once started, you can't put this book down."

—SUZANNE WOODS FISHER, BESTSELLING
AUTHOR OF *THE DEVOTED*

"[*A Seat by the Hearth*] is a moving portrait of a disgraced woman attempting to reenter her childhood community . . . This will please Clipston's fans and also win over newcomers to Lancaster County."

.—*PUBLISHERS WEEKLY*

"This story of profound loss and deep friendship will leave readers with the certain knowledge that hope exists and love grows through faith in our God of second chances."

—KELLY IRVIN, AUTHOR OF *THE BEEKEEPER'S SON* AND
UPON A SPRING BREEZE, ON *ROOM ON THE PORCH SWING*

"This heartbreaking series continues to take a fearlessly honest look at grief, as hopelessness threatens to steal what happiness Allen has treasured within his marriage and recent fatherhood. Clipston takes these feelings seriously without sugarcoating any aspect of the mourning process, allowing her characters to make their painful but ultimately joyous journey back to love and faith. Readers who have made this tough and ongoing pilgrimage themselves will appreciate the author's realistic portrayal of coming to terms with loss in order to continue living with hope and happiness."

—*RT BOOK REVIEWS*, 4 STARS, ON *ROOM ON THE PORCH SWING*

"A story of grief as well as new beginnings, this is a lovely Amish tale and the start of a great new series."

—*PARKERSBURG NEWS AND SENTINEL* ON *A PLACE AT OUR TABLE*

"Themes of family, forgiveness, love, and strength are woven throughout the story . . . a great choice for all readers of Amish fiction."

—*CBA MARKET MAGAZINE* ON *A PLACE AT OUR TABLE*

"This debut title in a new series offers an emotionally charged and engaging read headed by sympathetically drawn and believable protagonists. The meaty issues of trust and faith make this a solid book group choice."

—*LIBRARY JOURNAL* ON *A PLACE AT OUR TABLE*

"These sweet, tender novellas from one of the genre's best make the perfect sampler for new readers curious about Amish romances."

—*LIBRARY JOURNAL* ON *AMISH SWEETHEARTS*

"Clipston is as reliable as her character, giving Emily a difficult and intense romance worthy of Emily's ability to shine the light of Christ into the hearts of those she loves."

—*RT BOOK REVIEWS*, 4$\frac{1}{2}$ STARS, TOP PICK! ON *THE CHERISHED QUILT*

"Clipston's heartfelt writing and engaging characters make her a fan favorite. Her latest Amish tale combines a spiritual message of accepting God's blessings as they are given with a sweet romance."

—*LIBRARY JOURNAL* ON *THE CHERISHED QUILT*

"Clipston delivers another enchanting series starter with a tasty premise, family secrets, and sweet-as-pie romance, offering assurance that true love can happen more than once and second chances are worth fighting for."

—*RT BOOK REVIEWS*, 4$\frac{1}{2}$ STARS, TOP PICK! ON *THE FORGOTTEN RECIPE*

"In the first book in her Amish Heirloom series, Clipston takes readers on a roller-coaster ride through grief, guilt, and anxiety."

—BOOKLIST ON *THE FORGOTTEN RECIPE*

"Clipston is well versed in Amish culture and does a good job creating the world of Lancaster County, Penn. . . . Amish fiction fans will enjoy this story—and want a taste of Veronica's raspberry pie!"

—PUBLISHERS WEEKLY ON *THE FORGOTTEN RECIPE*

"[Clipston] does an excellent job of wrapping up her story while setting the stage for the sequel."

—CBA RETAILERS + RESOURCES ON
THE FORGOTTEN RECIPE

"Clipston brings this engaging series to an end with two emotional family reunions, a prodigal son parable, a sweet but hard-won romance, and a happy ending for characters readers have grown to love. Once again, she gives us all we could possibly want from a talented storyteller."

—RT BOOK REVIEWS, 4½ STARS, TOP
PICK! ON *A SIMPLE PRAYER*

". . . will leave readers craving more."

—RT BOOK REVIEWS, 4½ STARS, TOP
PICK! ON *A MOTHER'S SECRET*

"Clipston's series starter has a compelling drama involving faith, family, and romance . . . [an] absorbing series."

—RT BOOK REVIEWS, 4½ STARS, TOP
PICK! ON *A HOPEFUL HEART*

"Authentic characters, delectable recipes, and faith abound in Clipston's second Kauffman Amish Bakery story."

—RT BOOK REVIEWS, 4 STARS ON *A PROMISE OF HOPE*

SEASONS

OF AN

AMISH GARDEN

OTHER BOOKS BY AMY CLIPSTON

THE AMISH HOMESTEAD SERIES

A Place at Our Table

Room on the Porch Swing

A Seat by the Hearth

A Welcome at Our Door (available May 2019)

THE AMISH HEIRLOOM SERIES

The Forgotten Recipe

The Courtship Basket

The Cherished Quilt

The Beloved Hope Chest

THE HEARTS OF THE LANCASTER GRAND HOTEL SERIES

A Hopeful Heart

A Mother's Secret

A Dream of Home

A Simple Prayer

THE KAUFFMAN AMISH BAKERY SERIES

A Gift of Grace

A Promise of Hope

A Place of Peace

A Life of Joy

A Season of Love

NOVELLA COLLECTIONS
Amish Sweethearts

NOVELLAS
A Plain and Simple Christmas
Naomi's Gift included in *An Amish Christmas Gift*
A Spoonful of Love included in *An Amish Kitchen*
Love Birds included in *An Amish Market*
Love and Buggy Rides included in *An Amish Harvest*
Summer Storms included in *An Amish Summer*
The Christmas Cat included in *An Amish Christmas Love*
Home Sweet Home included in *An Amish Winter*
A Son for Always included in *An Amish Spring*
A Legacy of Love included in *An Amish Heirloom*
No Place Like Home included in *An Amish Homecoming*

NONFICTION
A Gift of Love

SEASONS

OF AN

AMISH GARDEN

Four Stories

AMY CLIPSTON

ZONDERVAN®

ZONDERVAN

Seasons of an Amish Garden

Copyright © 2019 by Amy Clipston

This title is also available as a Zondervan e-book.

Requests for information should be addressed to:

Zondervan, *3900 Sparks Dr. SE, Grand Rapids, Michigan 49546*

ISBN: 978-0-310-35430-7 (trade paper)

Library of Congress Cataloging-in-Publication
CIP data is available upon request.

All Scripture quotations, unless otherwise indicated, are taken from The Holy Bible, *New International Version*®, NIV®. Copyright © 1973, 1978, 1984, 2011 by Biblica, Inc.™ Used by permission. All rights reserved worldwide. www.zondervan.com

Any Internet addresses (websites, blogs, etc.) and telephone numbers in this book are offered as a resource. They are not intended in any way to be or imply an endorsement by Zondervan, nor does Zondervan vouch for the content of these sites and numbers for the life of this book.

Publisher's Note: This novel is a work of fiction. Names, characters, places, and incidents are either products of the author's imagination or used fictitiously. All characters are fictional, and any similarity to people living or dead is purely coincidental.

Printed in the United States of America

19 20 21 22 23 / LSC / 5 4 3 2 1

CONTENTS

SPRING IS IN THE AIR. 1

HOME BY SUMMER 95

THE FRUITS OF FALL. 189

WINTER BLESSINGS 281

SPRING IS IN THE AIR

For my amazing editor Jocelyn Bailey, with love

GLOSSARY

ach: oh
aenti: aunt
appeditlich: delicious
bedauerlich: sad
boppli: baby
brot: bread
bruder: brother
bruders: brothers
bruderskinner: nieces/nephews
bu: boy
buwe: boys
daadi: grandfather
danki: thank you
dat: dad
dochder: daughter
dochdern: daughters
Dummle!: Hurry!
fraa: wife
freind: friend
freinden: friends

3

froh: happy
gegisch: silly
gern gschehne: you're welcome
Gude mariye: Good morning
gut: good
Gut nacht: Good night
haus: house
Ich liebe dich: I love you
kaffi: coffee
kapp: prayer covering or cap
kichli: cookie
kichlin: cookies
kinner: children
krank: ill
kuche: cake
kuchen: cakes
kumm: come
liewe: love, a term of endearment
maed: young women, girls
maedel: young woman
mamm: mom
mammi: grandmother
mei: my
naerfich: nervous
narrisch: crazy
onkel: uncle
schee: pretty
schmaert: smart
schweschder: sister
schweschdere: sisters
sohn: son
schtupp: family room

GLOSSARY

Was iss letz?: What's wrong?

Wie geht's: How do you do? or Good day!

wunderbaar: wonderful

ya: yes

Family Tree

Featuring *The Christmas Cat* novella characters from
the collection *An Amish Christmas Love.*

Thelma m. Alfred Bender

Mandy   Rhoda

Leona m. Marlin Blank

Darlene m. Uria Swarey   Ephraim   Katie Ann

Emma m. Henry (deceased) Bontrager

Hank the Cat

Darlene m. Uria Swarey

Savannah   Rebekah

Marietta m. Roman Hertzler

Clara

Gertrude m. Elvin King

Wayne

Feenie m. Jeptha Lantz

Arlan   Christian

Saloma m. Floyd Petersheim

Jerry   Biena

CHAPTER 1

Katie Ann Blank's stomach tightened as she marched up the steps leading to Emma Bontrager's back porch. When she reached the door, she squared her shoulders and swallowed a deep breath. The brisk April breeze sent the ties of her prayer covering fluttering over her shoulders, and the crisp air seeped through her black sweater, black apron, and blue dress.

Today was an exciting day, and the thoughtlessness of her older brother, Ephraim, wouldn't tarnish it.

Or would it?

Shoving the thought away, she knocked on the storm door and then did her best to force her lips into a smile. The door opened, and Emma stood before her.

"Katie Ann!" Emma pushed the door open wider. "I was beginning to wonder if you were going to join us." Her warm brown eyes sparkled in the late afternoon sunlight as she stepped out onto the porch. Although Emma was in her late sixties, Katie Ann had always thought she looked a decade younger because of her smooth skin and the dark hair that revealed only a hint of gray.

"I was delayed, but I'm here now." Katie Ann held up the plate of peanut butter cookies she'd baked yesterday. "I brought *kichlin*."

"*Danki*." Emma pointed toward the inside the house. "I have barbecue meat loaf in the oven."

"My favorite." Katie Ann smiled. "Did the meeting start?"

When Emma nodded, Katie Ann felt her shoulders deflate.

"But you haven't missed much," Emma added quickly as she beckoned her to enter the house. "*Kumm.*"

Katie Ann followed Emma into the house and set the plate of cookies on the mudroom bench before removing her sweater and hanging it on a peg. The aroma of the meat loaf filled her senses, and her stomach growled its approval.

As voices filtered in from the kitchen, renewed disappointed buzzed through her veins. How could her own brother have forgotten to pick her up for the meeting? After church, Ephraim had taken his girlfriend, Mandy, home to visit with her family. But before going to the Benders', he'd promised to pick up Katie Ann on his way to Emma's house. Katie Ann had waited and waited for Ephraim's horse and buggy to appear in the driveway. When he was more than thirty minutes late, the truth hit her like a thousand bales of hay falling from the loft in her father's largest barn— Ephraim had forgotten her. And the oversight cut her to the bone. Her brother had never left her behind before.

Surely he'd apologize as soon as he saw her, and then everything would be okay—more like it was four months ago, before he began dating her best friend and everything changed.

Mandy's voice sounded from the kitchen. "Now we need to make a list of what we want to plant in the community garden."

Katie Ann followed Emma to where Ephraim and Mandy sat at one end of the table. Mandy was writing on a notepad while their friends Wayne King and Clara Hertzler looked on. Another young man, someone she didn't think she'd ever seen, sat beside Wayne.

"Katie Ann!" Clara waved her over and pointed to the empty chair between her and the young man Katie Ann didn't know. "I was wondering where you were, but Ephraim thought you'd be here soon."

"Did he?" She shot her brother a glare, and he shifted in his seat as his golden-blond eyebrows lifted, a question in the honey-brown eyes they'd both inherited from their mother. At twenty-three, he might be two years older than Katie Ann and much taller than her at six feet, but he had to know when his little sister wasn't happy with him—even when he didn't seem to know why.

"Katie Ann." Mandy's bright-blue eyes sparkled as she smiled. "I'm so glad you made it."

"*Ya*, I am too." Katie Ann divided a look between her brother and her best friend. Surely Ephraim had told Mandy he was supposed to pick her up.

Katie Ann set her plate of cookies on the counter, and then she walked around the table and sank onto the empty chair. She set her tote bag on the floor and began to dig through it for her notepad and pen. When something soft and furry rubbed against her leg, she looked down at Emma's fat, orange tabby cat and grinned. Hank the cat had invited himself to move in with Emma on Christmas Eve during a snowstorm, and despite her efforts to shoo the cat away, Hank had stayed, becoming the widow's sweet companion. Emma had named Hank after her late husband, Henry, using the nickname Henry's friend Urie sometimes called him.

"Hi, Hank." Katie Ann rubbed the cat under his velvety-soft chin.

He responded by closing his eyes as he purred. Then he tilted his head to the side so she could rub his cheek.

"He likes you."

Katie Ann looked up, and her gaze collided with the mysterious young man's dark eyes. His handsome face lit up in a kind smile, and an adorable dimple appeared on his left cheek. She was speechless for a moment, stunned by his friendliness. His thick dark hair complemented his eyes. Who was he? And how had he found out about their meeting today to plan the special garden they were going to plant in Henry's memory?

She dismissed her questions and shrugged while continuing to rub the cat's cheek. "He likes everyone."

The young man shook his head as a sheepish expression overtook his strong jaw. "No, he hissed at me when I tried to pet him."

Katie was surprised. "Really? He might need to get to know you before he'll let you pet him."

"Maybe you can introduce me to him after the meeting."

"Okay." *But I'll have to know your name first.* Katie bit back a grin as she turned to the cat and rubbed his ear. As if he suddenly had become bored with the attention, Hank sauntered off toward Emma's family room.

Gathering up her notepad and pen, she sat up straight, opened her notebook, and prepared to take notes.

"I've drawn a map of the garden," Mandy continued, "and I have suggestions on what we can plant where." She held up her diagram. "Carrots here, cucumbers here, corn over here, lettuce here, and melons over here."

Katie Ann glanced down at her notepad. Last night she'd spent two hours mapping out where she thought they should plant the vegetables and fruit. Beside the diagram, she'd listed some issues they needed to tackle, such as putting up fencing. She held her breath for a moment and stared at her notepad as Mandy continued reciting her plans.

Suddenly, a wave of confidence overwhelmed her. She had to interject her thoughts. After all, this garden had been her idea. When she and her friends visited Emma on Christmas Eve, Emma talked about how much she missed her late husband. Together, they decided to plant the community garden to both keep Henry's memory alive and help Emma navigate her grief. They would donate their crops to the Bird-in-Hand Shelter for the homeless.

"I have a suggestion," Katie Ann said.

Mandy stopped speaking, and Katie Ann felt everyone's gaze hone in on her. Her cheeks heated.

"What is it?" Mandy asked.

"We need to put some sort of fencing in. Otherwise our crops will be destroyed by animals, such as rabbits and deer."

"That's a *gut* point," the young man beside her said.

"Oh." Mandy's eyes widened as she glanced at Ephraim. "I hadn't thought of that."

"I can work on finding fencing," Wayne offered.

Clara rubbed her hands together. "I can't wait to get started."

"Does this all sound *gut* to you, Emma?" Katie Ann turned to her friend, who stood at the kitchen counter, filling the cat's food bowl while he walked in circles at her feet and rubbed at her shins.

"*Ya.*" Emma set the bowl on the floor beside Hank's water bowl. "Whatever you all want to do is fine with me."

"Great." Ephraim grinned at Mandy.

"I have another idea." Katie Ann sat up a little taller. "We could have a stand down by the road to sell our vegetables and fruit. Here's why: I found out we can't donate food to the shelter, but we can sell what we have and then give the money to the shelter in memory of Henry. Emma, I remember you told us Henry always made a donation at Christmas."

"Really?" Mandy's eyes were wide again. "I didn't know shelters needed money instead of food donations."

"I was surprised, too, but I'm glad I asked. We can also use the stand to sell baked goods, such as pies and cookies. We'll donate all the proceeds to the Bird-in-Hand Shelter. We'll have to get our parents' permission to use our own supplies for the first round of sales, and then we can use some of the money we make for supplies as well as any costs associated with keeping the grounds running."

"I can talk to our local grocery store owners about getting some baking supplies donated," Clara said.

"That would be fantastic." Katie Ann wrote down the idea.

"The bake stand sounds great." Wayne pointed to the other young man. "Chris and I can build the stand, right, Chris?"

"*Ya*. That's no problem at all." Chris leaned back in his chair and folded his arms over his wide chest. "And I can get wood and supplies from *mei dat's* cabinet shop."

Katie Ann turned toward him. *So his name is Chris and his* dat *is a cabinetmaker.*

"Great!" Katie Ann wrote on her notepad. "That helps if the supplies are donated. Now we just have to buy the seeds for the vegetables."

"I can help with that too," Clara said. "*Mei onkel* owns a nursery. I can get the seeds from him. He might even donate them."

"Fantastic. When do you think you can get them?" Katie Ann asked.

Clara shrugged. "I can go to his store tomorrow."

"That means we can start planting Tuesday afternoon," Ephraim said, chiming in. "I'll bring our gardening tools. And I'll see if I can get someone to plow the area. Our neighbor has a plow." He pointed to Mandy's notepad. "Write that down, okay?"

"*Wunderbaar.*" Mandy wrote on her notepad and then tapped her pencil on the tabletop. "I think that's all we had to discuss." She turned to Ephraim. "Did I forget anything?"

Ephraim tilted his head and looked up at the ceiling. "I think the only other issue was inviting other youth groups to help us. We decided the six of us would have our meetings with Emma on Sundays, like today, and workdays with a bigger group will be on both Tuesdays and Saturdays. Right?"

"That's right!" Mandy snapped her fingers. "I knew I was

forgetting something. We need to invite the members of our youth group and then ask them to invite people they know."

"I brought my cousin." Wayne gestured toward Chris. "Does that count?"

Cousins! Katie Ann looked at both men. While they both had dark-brown hair, the similarities ended there. Wayne's eyes were dark blue, and Chris's reminded her of melted milk chocolate.

"*Ya*, that counts, but we need more people to help with the planting and the harvest." Ephraim tapped the table. "Let's all plan to invite at least one person to join us at our next meeting."

"I will." Clara held up her hand as if answering a question in school.

"I don't have any other *freinden*," Wayne joked, and Chris chuckled.

Katie Ann looked down at her notepad. She was thankful she'd made a list since Mandy hadn't mentioned the fencing and hadn't known about not being able to donate the food they were going to grow.

"The meat loaf and potatoes are ready," Emma announced. "Do you all want to eat now?"

"*Ya*," Ephraim said, and the rest of the group agreed. "*Danki.*"

Mandy stood. "Emma, let me set the table."

"I'll get the drinks." Clara followed her to the cabinets.

"I'll help serve," Katie Ann said as she pushed her pencil and notepad into her tote bag.

"Katie Ann," Chris said.

"*Ya?*" She looked up at him.

"I haven't had a chance to introduce myself." He held out his hand. "I'm Christian Lantz."

"Hi. I'm Katie Ann Blank. Ephraim is *mei bruder*." She shook his hand, and when his skin touched hers, she felt a strange fluttering in her chest.

"It's nice to meet you." Chris smiled.

"You too." Katie Ann's cheeks heated as she hurried to the counter and scooped pot holders from a drawer.

"I'm so glad you got here okay," Mandy said as she gathered a stack of dishes from the cabinet. "Ephraim and I were worried about you."

"What?" Katie Ann turned toward her. "Are you joking?"

"Why would I joke?" Mandy blinked as she looked up at her. Although they were the same age, Katie Ann was nearly five inches taller than Mandy's five-foot-two, petite stature.

Katie Ann paused and glanced toward the table, where the three young men talked about plans for the bake stand. Did her brother truly not remember that he'd promised her a ride? If so, what did that say about their relationship? She and Ephraim had always been close. Did Katie Ann not matter in his life anymore now that he was dating Mandy?

Mandy took a step toward her. "Why did you ask me if I was joking?"

Katie Ann turned back toward her friend. "Ephraim was supposed to pick me up on your way to Emma's."

"We were?" Mandy's forehead pinched.

Katie Ann rested her hand on her hip. When had Mandy and Ephraim become a *we*? They weren't married. They weren't even engaged!

"I discussed it with Ephraim after church," Katie Ann continued. "He was supposed to drop by the *haus* and pick me up at four. When he wasn't there by four thirty, I realized he had forgotten me."

"I'm sure he didn't mean to." Mandy touched Katie Ann's arm. "We were visiting with my parents and *mei schweschder*, and we lost track of time. We didn't leave *mei haus* until after four."

The excuse sounded so ridiculous that Katie Ann just turned back to the counter, picked up the pot holders, and lifted the meat loaf pan. "I'll take this to the table."

Emma rushed ahead of her. "Let me put a trivet on the table for you."

Katie Ann delivered the meat loaf and side dishes to the table, and Clara poured glasses of water while Mandy set out plates and utensils. Then Katie Ann took a seat between Clara and Chris. Ephraim brought a folding chair from the utility room and squeezed in between Mandy and Emma.

After a silent prayer, they filled their plates, and conversations popped up around the table. Katie Ann peeked at her brother and found Mandy whispering to him as his lips pressed into a thin line. Was she telling Ephraim he'd forgotten his sister?

"Emma, you make the best barbecue meat loaf," Clara said after swallowing a bite. "What's your secret?"

"It's all in the barbecue sauce," Emma responded before revealing the recipe.

"How's your family, Wayne?" Clara asked a minute later.

Katie Ann stabbed a forkful of meat loaf. As she chewed, she pushed around the pile of green beans on her plate.

"Do you like to cook and bake?"

Katie Ann's head whipped up, and she found Chris looking at her. "What?"

His dark eyebrows lifted. "I asked if you liked to cook and bake."

"Oh." Katie Ann nodded. "*Ya*, I do."

"Will you make pies and *kichlin* to sell at the stand?" he asked before taking a bite of meat loaf.

"I will." She studied his handsome face. Was he always this friendly with girls he'd just met? She ignored the question as the urge to know him better piqued her curiosity. "Are you a cabinet-maker like your *dat*?"

"*Ya, mei dat* owns a shop, and *mei bruder* and I work there." He buttered his baked potato.

"Is your *bruder* older or younger?"

"He's three years older than I am. He's married, and he and his *fraa* live just a mile away." He finished buttering his potato and then offered her the butter.

"*Danki.*" She began to butter her own potato.

"I think the plans for the garden sound really *gut*," Chris said.

"I do too." She tried to smile, but her disappointment in her brother continued to nip at her.

"I can't wait to see it when it's harvesttime," he added.

"*Ya*," she said, agreeing.

They made small talk while they ate. When everyone had finished, they drank coffee and ate the cookies Katie Ann brought and the chocolate pie Clara brought.

After dessert, the three young women helped Emma clean the kitchen, and the young men went outside to continue talking on the porch. Katie Ann kept her head down as she washed the dishes and set them in the drying rack. Mandy worked beside her, drying the dishes and setting them back in the cabinets, while Clara wiped down the table and swept the floor. No one said much.

"*Danki* for supper, Emma," Clara finally said when the kitchen was clean. "I'll see you Tuesday."

"*Gern gschehne*," Emma said. "Be safe going home."

Mandy looked at Katie Ann, and her expression clouded with what looked like concern. "Are you going outside now?"

"I'll be there in a minute."

Mandy hesitated and then nodded. "All right. *Gut nacht*, Emma. *Danki* for supper."

"*Gern gschehne*." Emma gave her a little wave before Mandy disappeared through the mudroom. Emma turned to Katie Ann. "*Was iss letz?* Why didn't you walk out with Mandy?"

"Nothing is wrong." Katie Ann busied herself by folding the damp dish towels. "I just wanted to make sure you weren't left with a mess."

"Katie Ann." Emma touched her shoulder. "I've gotten to know you very well during the past few months, and I can tell when something is bothering you. I don't mean to pry, but you can always talk to me."

"I know." Katie Ann bit her lower lip as she debated how much to share. "I'm just upset because *mei bruder* forgot to pick me up today. He and Mandy visited with her family after church, and they were supposed to get me on the way here. That's why I was late. When Ephraim didn't show up, I had to ask *mei dat* if I could use his horse and buggy."

"I'm sure it was an honest mistake."

"It's not just that." Katie Ann could hear her voice thicken. "Everything is different now that he's dating Mandy. I'm invisible when they're together. I feel like I'm losing *mei bruder* and my best *freind*."

"They don't mean to ignore you." Emma smiled. "They're just all wrapped up in each other right now. The relationship is new, and they're getting to know each other. I'm certain Ephraim would never want to hurt you."

Katie Ann looked down at the worn tan linoleum as doubt swirled through her mind.

"You should just talk to Ephraim alone and tell him that he hurt your feelings. Then he'll apologize, and everything will be fine."

Katie Ann forced a smile as she looked at Emma. "Okay. I will."

"*Gut.*" Emma gave her a quick hug. "You get on home now before your parents start to worry. I'll see you Tuesday."

"Okay." Katie Ann thanked Emma for supper, and then she shoved her cookie plate into her tote bag and retrieved her sweater from the mudroom. She walked outside and shivered as she made her way down the porch steps.

Her feet slowed when she spotted Ephraim and Chris standing in front of what she assumed were Chris's horse and buggy. Chris laughed, and his laughter was loud and boisterous, causing her brother to join in. She was intrigued by Chris's contagious laugh, and for a brief moment, it brightened her dark mood. But when Ephraim and Chris looked at her, she nodded, frowning, and kept walking.

"I'll see you at home," Ephraim said.

"Bye, Katie Ann!" Mandy called from inside Ephraim's buggy.

Katie Ann gave her a halfhearted wave before untying her father's horse and climbing into his buggy.

As she grabbed the reins, she looked at the two men one last time. When Chris gave her a big smile, her pulse galloped. Why did a man she barely knew cause her heart to react that way? Something had to be wrong with her.

~

A knock drew Katie Ann's attention to her bedroom door later that evening. She looked up from the Christian novel she'd been reading on her bed. "Come in."

She felt her lips press together in a scowl as her brother entered.

"Can we talk?" Ephraim's tall stature filled her doorway.

"*Ya.*" She closed the book and set it on her nightstand as her stomach clenched. "What do you want?"

He stopped at the footboard of her double bed. "Mandy told me you were upset because I didn't pick you up on our way to Emma's today." He rubbed the back of his neck. "I completely forgot I was supposed to give you a ride."

Katie Ann sat forward as her temper flared. "How can you say that? We talked about it after church, when I said good-bye to you before I went home with *Mamm* and *Dat*. I asked you if you'd stop by the *haus* and get me, and you said yes."

He gave her a palms up. "I'm sorry. I forgot."

"So you weren't listening to me." A heaviness settled in the center of her chest.

Ephraim swiped his hand down his face. "I don't know, but I'm sorry, okay?"

She studied him as a thought occurred to her. "When did Mandy tell you I was upset?"

"While we were eating at Emma's *haus*. Why?"

"So you've known for three hours, and you're just now apologizing?"

"I wanted to earlier, but you were talking with *Mamm*. I thought I should wait until we were alone."

Katie Ann leaned back on her headboard as she continued to study her brother. He'd waited three hours to apologize to her. Did that prove how insignificant she now was in his life? The question sent hurt and anger swirling through her.

"Look, I made a mistake." He tapped her footboard. "Will you forgive me?"

"You've never forgotten me before. I feel like I'm invisible when you're with Mandy."

He blew out a puff of air. "I didn't mean to make you feel that way. Mandy is important to me, but you'll always be *mei schweschder*."

"Do you love her?"

A smile turned up his lips and spread across his face. "*Ya. Ya,* I do." He jammed his thumb toward the doorway. "I need to take a shower. *Gut nacht*."

As Ephraim disappeared into the hall, Katie Ann reeled at the information her brother had just shared. He was in love with Mandy. He was in love with her best friend!

Katie Ann wanted to be happy for him, and she knew she *should* be happy for him. But instead, her heart seemed to break a fraction. Nothing would ever be the same. And she missed the way things used to be.

CHAPTER 2

C hris glanced at the clock on the wall in his father's shop as he wiped his hands with a red shop rag. He smiled as his plans clicked into place in his mind. It was almost three, the time he'd hoped to leave so he could meet up with Wayne and head to Emma Bontrager's house for their first Tuesday meeting. He'd finished all his tasks in record time today. Now he just had to convince his father to allow him to leave early.

The familiar sweet scent of wood and stain filled his nostrils as he crossed the shop lined with workbenches, all cluttered with an array of tools. The soft yellow light from lanterns perched around the large former barn illuminated the shop. A pile of wood sat beside cabinets in various stages of development that were perched on the benches in the corner.

He passed a workbench where his older brother, Arlan, sanded a cabinet as a diesel generator hummed. Then Chris came to a stop at the doorway of his father's office. Leaning on the doorframe, he waited for him to look up. He was sitting at his desk, peering at a large ledger, with his reading glasses perched on his long, thin nose. But when *Dat*'s attention remained on the numbers in the ledger, Chris knocked on the door, pushing it open wider.

"Christian." *Dat* removed his glasses and tossed them onto his desk as Chris stepped inside. "I didn't realize you were standing there. Is it suppertime already?"

"No." Chris sank onto a nearby stool. "But all my work is done. I was wondering if I could leave early today."

"Leave early?" *Dat's* dark eyebrows lifted. "You never leave early. In fact, I normally can't get you to come in for supper on time. Where are you going?"

"I have plans with Wayne." Chris wiped the wood dust off his dark trousers. "I finished sanding those cabinets, and I can stain them first thing tomorrow. I'm ahead of deadline, so may I please leave?"

Dat touched his graying brown beard as he studied Chris. "What sort of plans do you have with Wayne?"

"We're going to Emma Bontrager's *haus* again to make more plans for the community garden project. You remember I told you about that, right? Wayne and a few of his *freinden* are building a community garden in memory of Emma's husband. I'm going to help build the stand to sell the baked goods, fruit, and vegetables with the spare wood you said I could have."

"Right." *Dat* nodded as he crossed his arms over his chest and leaned back in his chair. "You're awfully excited about this community garden project."

"*Ya.*" Chris shrugged. "I enjoy spending time with Wayne."

"Is that the only reason you're so eager to help with this garden?"

"No. I just think it's a great project to benefit the Bird-in-Hand Shelter, and I want to be a part of it. It's a *wunderbaar* charity. That's what Jesus told us to do, right? We're supposed to help each other."

Chris hoped his expression didn't betray his words. While he did believe in the project and wanted to spend time with his favorite cousin, those weren't the only reasons he was excited to go to Emma's house. He wasn't exactly lying, but he wasn't ready to tell his *dat* about the pretty blond he'd met at the meeting on Sunday. He'd spent the past two days thinking about Katie Ann Blank and wondering why she looked so sad when she left Emma's house. For some unknown reason, he longed to find out what had upset her. He just hoped she also planned to be at Emma's house tonight.

"All right." *Dat* nodded toward the doorway. "Go on and have fun. Tell Wayne I said hello. Just be sure to get those cabinets stained tomorrow morning. We need to install them on Friday."

"*Danki, Dat.*" Chris waved at his brother before heading out of the shop.

He breathed in the crisp spring air and strode past the two additional buildings that were part of his father's business. A large building closer to the road served as a showroom, complete with a tall sign reading Lantz & Sons Cabinets. A smaller building beside it was the shop they used for staining. Chris started helping his father work on cabinets when he was old enough to hold a sanding block. Someday his father would retire and he and Arlan would take over the business. But surely *Dat* had many more years of work to complete.

Chris quickened his steps as he approached the back porch of their house. He had thirty minutes to shower and change before he had to head out to Emma's. He'd love a chance to talk to Katie Ann alone. He'd been wondering if she had a boyfriend, although he didn't want to ask Wayne. If she didn't, then maybe, just maybe, Chris had a chance to win her friendship—and then her heart if she was the girl he thought she was.

Katie Ann pressed down on the lid of the large container with the taco casserole she'd made for everyone at Emma's house today. Then she glanced up at the clock.

"You're not late yet," *Mamm* said. "It's only three fifteen."

"*Gut.*" Katie Ann had been rushing around all day, eager to complete her chores before it was time to go.

Will Christian Lantz be there again today?

Her cheeks burned at the silent question, and she quickly dismissed it. Why was she wasting a thought on a man she didn't even know? Besides, he most likely had a girlfriend and would never be interested in someone as ordinary as her.

Returning her attention to *Mamm*, she pointed to another casserole dish on the counter. "I made an extra casserole for you and *Dat*. You just have to warm it up."

"*Danki.* That was sweet of you. You know your *dat* loves your taco casserole."

"Do you need me to do anything else before I leave?"

"No, but *danki* for offering."

Katie Ann retrieved her notepad and tote bag from her bedroom and then hurried down to the kitchen. Ephraim stood talking to *Mamm*. Katie Ann slowed her steps as a frown overtook her mouth. Her anger from Sunday persisted despite Emma's advice to forgive her brother.

Ephraim turned toward her and pointed toward the back door. "I loaded all our gardening tools into the buggy. Are you ready?"

Katie Ann shrugged as she fingered the strap on her tote bag.

Ephraim's eyes narrowed. "Are you still angry with me?"

Katie Ann shrugged. "I'm just a little hurt."

He blew out a loud sigh as he started for the back door. "I'll be in the buggy. If you're not outside in five minutes, I'm going without you." Then he disappeared through the mudroom.

Mamm lifted her eyebrows as she turned toward Katie Ann. "Why are you being so rude to your *bruder*?"

"We had an argument on Sunday." Katie Ann shifted her weight on her feet as embarrassment ignited her cheeks.

"Why did you argue?" *Mamm's* honey-brown eyes seemed to peer right into Katie Ann's soul.

"He forgot to pick me up. That's why I had to take *Dat's* horse and buggy to Emma's."

Mamm was silent for a moment. The ticking of the clock above the sink seemed somehow louder as Katie Ann awaited her mother's assessment of the situation.

"You're still upset about a mistake your *bruder* made two days ago?" *Mamm* asked.

Katie Ann nodded as guilt tightened the knots in her back. "He forgot about me."

"It's our way to forgive, Katie Ann. You know that."

Katie Ann nodded.

"Besides that, you don't realize how blessed you are to have your older *bruder* in your life. Mine moved to Ohio twenty-five years ago, and I miss him." *Mamm's* expression warmed. "You need to forgive Ephraim. We all make mistakes because we're human and we fall short of the glory of God." She gestured toward the mudroom. "Go before he leaves. And make sure you tell him you forgive him before this gets blown all out of proportion."

"*Ya, Mamm.*" Katie Ann gave her a quick hug before grabbing the casserole dish from the counter. "See you later."

In the mudroom, Katie Ann pulled on her sweater and then rushed outside to her brother's waiting buggy, where she found him scowling. Her mother's warning rang in her ears as she climbed into the back.

"I didn't think you were going to come out," he grumbled as he guided the horse down the driveway toward the road.

"I'm here." She stared out the windshield. As much as she longed to clear the air between them, her pride strangled her words.

The *clip-clop* of the horse hooves and the whirl of the wheels filled the buggy as they made their way to Mandy's house. Katie

Ann hoped someday she and Ephraim would find their close sibling relationship again. Until then, she'd feel like the fifth wheel on his buggy.

~

Chris glanced around the large field behind Emma's house, where a young man he didn't recognize plowed the designated garden area with a team of horses. A group of young folks, including Mandy, Ephraim, Wayne, and Clara, stood together and talked. Chris searched the faces for Katie Ann's, and his excitement dissolved when he didn't find her.

You're here to help your community, not find a girlfriend.

He gritted his teeth as guilt filled his chest. But when he spotted movement in his peripheral vision, he turned to his right and found Katie Ann sitting at a card table on Emma's back porch. She had her head bent as she concentrated on something on the table.

She's here!

He smiled as he made his way toward her. She was pouring seeds into a canvas bag. She stopped working and pushed back an errant tendril of golden hair that had fallen out from beneath her prayer covering. She turned, and when her gaze entangled with his, her pretty pink lips turned up. Her beautiful face seemed to glow.

"Hi, Chris," she said as he climbed the porch steps. "*Wie geht's?*"

"I'm great. How are you?"

"*Gut.*" She gestured toward the garden. "Earl Smucker was able to bring his father's plow over. Clara brought the seeds, so we're going to start planting as soon as he's done. I'm just putting them in canvas bags to get them ready. It's supposed to rain tonight, so it's the perfect time."

"Fantastic." He rubbed his hands together. "Can I help you?"

"*Ya*." She gestured to the chair beside her, and then she handed him a canvas bag and a bag full of seed packets. "You can empty these packets into that bag."

"Okay."

They worked in silence for several minutes, and he couldn't keep his eyes from finding their way over to her. He took in her attractive face—her high cheekbones, her gorgeous honey-brown eyes, and her long, slender neck. Did she have any idea how pretty she was?

"How was your day?"

Her question caught him off guard for a moment, but he quickly recovered. "*Gut.* I got all my work done early so I could come help. How about yours?"

"The same." She kept her eyes focused on the packets of seeds. "I helped *mei mamm* with the cleaning, and then I made a casserole to bring for supper." She looked up at him. "Do you like taco casserole?"

"I'm sure I do."

"You're sure you do?" Her brow furrowed. "Does that mean you've never had it?"

He shook his head. "I haven't, but I like tacos."

"Oh, *gut.* I hope you can stay for supper and try it." She returned to her work.

"I'd love to."

"Great. Did you build cabinets today?"

"No, but I finished sanding some. I have to stain them tomorrow."

"What do they look like?" She looked up, and her eyes sparkled.

He shrugged. "Well, they're oak cabinets. They're going in the kitchen of one of our *Englisher* clients."

"They sound nice." She ripped open another packet of seeds

and dumped them into her bag. "How long have you been building cabinets?"

"All my life. *Mei dat* took over the business from *mei daadi*, and then he taught *mei bruder* and me how to build them. I think I started sanding when I was around four. What does your *dat* do?"

"He's a dairy farmer."

"That's hard work."

"*Ya*, it is. There's always something to do on a farm."

They worked in silence for a few more minutes, and his thoughts wandered back to Sunday and the sad expression on her face when she left Emma's house. If he asked her what was wrong, would she feel comfortable enough to tell him?

"Has everything been okay?" he asked.

"What?" She pushed one tie from her prayer covering behind her shoulder as her brow pinched once again.

"You looked upset on Sunday when you walked out to your horse and buggy. I hope everything is okay."

She studied him for a moment as her eyes widened and then went back to normal size. He'd crossed a line, and he longed to take back the comment. Now she'd never trust him.

"I'm fine. *Danki* for asking." To his surprise, her expression was kind. Perhaps he hadn't missed his chance to build a friendship with her.

"*Gut.* I know we just met, but if you ever need someone to talk to, I'm available."

She smiled. "I appreciate that."

"You two are getting a lot done."

Chris looked up at Mandy, who was standing on the steps with Ephraim. He glanced at Katie Ann as her smile faded and her pretty face clouded. Could Mandy and Ephraim be the source of her sadness? But Ephraim was her brother. Why would he upset her?

Mandy pointed to Katie Ann's canvas bag. "Which seeds are we going to plant first?"

"I'm starting with lettuce seeds," Katie Ann explained. "I have a book on gardening, and it recommended planting lettuce this time of year."

"Oh." Mandy nodded. "I hadn't thought to research what to plant first." She looked up at Ephraim. "We should have picked up a book on gardening when we were out shopping the other day."

"You're right." Ephraim nodded. "I hadn't thought about it."

Katie Ann pointed toward the field, remembering the plan Mandy laid out at their first meeting. "We want the lettuce planted in that section over there."

"That's right," Mandy said.

Ephraim nodded at Chris. "It's *gut* to see you. I'm glad you could come back today."

"I am too." Chris held up his canvas bag. "I'm helping Katie Ann get the seeds ready."

Mandy turned to Ephraim. "Why don't we ask everyone to come over here to help with the seeds? We don't want to run out of daylight."

"*Ya.* Let's go tell them." Ephraim took her hand in his as they walked down the steps and toward the group of young folks standing by the barn, watching the plow.

Chris was certain he heard Katie Ann sigh, and he opened his mouth to ask her what was wrong. Changing his mind, he closed his mouth. He'd already told her he was happy to listen if she wanted to talk. If she felt the urge to share her feelings with him, he had to allow her to do it when she was ready.

As he continued to empty seed packets into his bag, Chris was certain of one thing: something was bothering Katie Ann, and he was determined to find out what it was so he could help her.

CHAPTER 3

"What kind of *kichlin* do you want to bake?" Katie Ann asked Mandy as they stood at the counter in her kitchen Friday morning.

"Hmm." Mandy tapped her chin as she turned a page in *Mamm*'s favorite cookbook. "How about cinnamon roll *kichlin*?"

"Ooh! My favorite!" Katie Ann clapped her hands and smiled as happiness bubbled up inside her.

For the first time in a while, she felt as if she had her best friend back. When she invited Mandy over to bake, she at first thought she would refuse. Instead, Mandy sounded just as eager to spend time with Katie Ann as Katie Ann was to spend time with her. Maybe they could get their relationship back to where it used to be, when they would spend hours together baking and talking. Mandy had always been like the sister Katie Ann never had.

Katie Ann crossed the floor to the pantry. "I'll get the ingredients. You read the list to me."

"Let's see," Mandy said. She called out each ingredient—eggs, butter, vanilla, sugar—and Katie Ann brought them to the counter.

As Katie Ann began assembling the ingredients in a bowl, Mandy stared out the window and fingered the ties on her prayer covering.

"Are you going to help?" Katie Ann asked as she cracked an egg.

"What?" Mandy spun toward her, and her cheeks flushed bright red. "I'm sorry. I was looking to see if Ephraim was outside."

Katie Ann swallowed a retort. "He's probably in the barn with *mei dat*."

"Oh." Mandy gave a little smile. "Do you think I could go visit him?"

Katie Ann stilled. "You want to go see him now? Aren't you going to help me?"

Mandy shrugged as her smile widened. "Only one of us can mix the ingredients, right?" She pointed toward the back door. "I'll only be a minute."

Before Katie Ann could respond, Mandy slipped into the mudroom, and the sound of the storm door clicking shut came behind her.

Anger, sharp and swift, sliced through her. Today was supposed to be their day, but Mandy had chosen Ephraim over her once again. Furious tears stung her eyes as she mixed the batter with an aggressive strength. Once again she felt invisible and insignificant, instead of like Mandy's best friend. While she was working hard to rebuild their friendship, Mandy didn't seem to make any effort.

Pushing away her self-pity, Katie Ann began preparing the dough. She peered out the window above the sink and spotted Mandy and Ephraim talking outside the barn. Ephraim looked mesmerized as Mandy spoke to him. When she finished talking, they both laughed, and their smiles were nearly as brilliant as the morning sunlight.

Envy wrapped around Katie Ann like an itchy blanket as she watched Ephraim take Katie Ann's hand in his and then steer her toward the house. Would Katie Ann ever find a man who would care for her the way her brother cared for Mandy?

She'd dated two young men from her youth group in the past, and neither of them had looked at her the way Ephraim looked at Mandy. Her relationships had been insignificant and short, lasting barely two months each. What did it feel like to have a man pay attention to your every word and hold your hand as you walked together? She'd never known that feeling. Would she ever be blessed with a relationship like that?

Guilt nipped at Katie Ann as she began to flatten the dough. Giving in to jealousy was a sin. Wouldn't *Mamm* be disappointed if she heard Katie Ann's thoughts?

"I found an assistant," Mandy sang as she stepped into the kitchen with Ephraim in tow. "Ephraim wants to help me make the filling for the *kichlin*."

"She's going to teach me how to be an expert baker." Ephraim kept his eyes focused on Mandy as he grinned down at her.

Katie Ann felt her lips twist downward. Once again she was a third wheel, the odd person out when her brother and Mandy were together. "Do you want me to leave?" The question leapt from her lips without any forethought.

"What?" Mandy's gaze swung to Katie Ann's as her forehead puckered. "Why would we want you to leave?"

"If I left, you and Ephraim could bake alone." Katie Ann gestured between them. "You'd have privacy."

Mandy's mouth worked, but no words escaped.

"Don't be *gegisch*." Ephraim shook his head as he walked to the sink. "We'll all work together."

"*Ya!*" Mandy joined Katie Ann at the counter. "It will be fun. What do we do first to start the filling?"

Katie Ann tried to smile, but her day was ruined. She'd looked forward to baking with Mandy, but instead, she'd wound up serving as their chaperone. Would she ever get her best friend back?

"Would you like a *kichli*?" Katie Ann held up a tray of cinnamon swirl cookies as she stepped into Emma's kitchen the following afternoon.

"Look at those!" Emma gasped as she reached for one. "Did you make them?"

"*Ya.*" Katie Ann shook her head. "Well, more accurately, Mandy, Ephraim, and I made them."

Emma held up the cookie. "How fun."

Katie Ann swallowed a sarcastic snort.

Emma took a bite and then groaned as she closed her eyes. "Katie Ann, these are *appeditlich*. You all did a great job."

"*Danki.*" She set the tray on the counter and then crossed her arms over her chest. Yesterday's events filtered through her mind. She'd felt like an intruder as Mandy and Ephraim laughed and flirted while they made the cookies. She found herself regretting inviting Mandy over for a "fun day" together. It wasn't fun for anyone but Mandy and Ephraim.

"*Was iss letz?*"

Katie Ann looked up at Emma's kind eyes. "What do you mean?"

"Something is always wrong if *appeditlich kichlin* are in the room and you're not smiling." Emma pointed to the kitchen table. "Let's sit. Tell me what's upsetting you."

Katie Ann sat down as Emma placed the tray of cookies in the center of the table and then sat down across from her.

"What's on your mind?" Emma lifted another cookie from the tray as she put the rest of the first cookie in her mouth.

Katie Ann ran her fingers over the table as she contemplated her words. "When I invited Mandy over yesterday, I thought we could bake together and that it would be like old times. We used to bake for hours, and we'd talk about everything from the *buwe* we liked to our favorite books. But now it seems like we can't spend time together unless we include *mei bruder*. I want to have time with her, too, you know? I feel like I'm not *gut* enough to be with her now. She'd rather be with Ephraim than me, and it hurts. I just miss how things used to be." She longed to erase the whine in her voice, but her frustration was real.

Emma reached across the table and touched Katie Ann's hand. "I understand you miss Mandy, but you haven't lost her. Your relationship has changed, but you still have her as your *freind*. I know she still cares about you."

Katie Ann nodded as her suddenly tight throat trapped her words. Why was she so emotional?

"You've known her since you were seven years old, and that's a special friendship. Mandy wouldn't just give that up. Relationships change. That's just part of growing up. But you'll always have Mandy in your life. I told you about *mei freind* Sally. She and I have known each other since first grade, just like you and Mandy. Our friendship has changed over the years, but we're still close."

Emma pointed toward the window. "If she left me a message on my voice mail today, I'd call her back, and we'd pick up where we left off during our previous conversation. She's still my best *freind* after all these years."

Katie Ann nodded, but doubt filled her mind. How could she and Mandy remain close if Mandy never wanted to really talk to her? It just didn't make sense. She needed to change the subject before it broke her heart.

"I saw a lot of young people working outside when I came in." Katie Ann forced her lips into a smile. "It looks like the planting is just about done."

"*Ya.*" Emma took a napkin from the holder in the center of the table and began to mop up the crumbs from the cookies she'd eaten. "We've had a lot of help. I think word about this project has spread throughout the community."

"What a blessing." Katie Ann's thoughts turned to Emma's late husband. "What would Henry say if he were here to see it?"

Emma's eyes glistened in the sunshine pouring through her kitchen windows. "He would be honored, just like I am."

As if on cue, Hank hopped up on the chair beside Emma and rubbed his head against her arm.

"*Ach.*" Emma smiled down at him and scratched his ear. "You always know when I need a hug, don't you, Hank?"

Katie Ann laughed as the cat continued to rub Emma's arm.

"Katie Ann," Clara announced as she walked into the kitchen from the mudroom, "I didn't see you arrive. How long have you been hiding in the kitchen?"

Katie Ann shrugged as she looked at Emma. "I don't know. Maybe twenty minutes?"

"Oh! Did you make these?"

"*Ya.* Have one."

Clara reached for a cookie, took a bite, and then moaned. "Oh. So *gut!*"

"I'm glad you like them." Katie Ann pointed toward the back of the house. "I was just telling Emma I was surprised to see all the help we have."

"*Ya.* I told one of my cousins, and she invited her whole youth group to come. The planting is almost done. We're going to start watering now." Clara finished eating the cookie. "You should take a few of these out to the barn. I bet Wayne and Chris would love them."

"Chris is here?" Warmth filled Katie Ann's chest as her pulse kicked up.

"*Ya*. He and Wayne are building the stand out in the barn." Clara pointed to the tray. "You need to sell these at the stand."

Katie Ann stood. "Let's take this tray of cookies to the barn."

Chris hammered another nail into a piece of wood while Wayne cut another piece with a saw. They must have been working for more than an hour now, and he found himself repeatedly checking the doorway to see if Katie Ann had arrived to work in the garden today too. Earlier he'd asked Clara if she'd seen Katie Ann, and Clara told him she wasn't certain if Katie Ann had planned to come to Emma's today. His happy mood deflated like a balloon when he heard that. He'd made plans to start building the stand today, but he'd also hoped to spend some time with Katie Ann.

He couldn't seem to get her off his mind. Her pretty smile had floated in the back of his thoughts since he'd talked to her on Tuesday. Had she thought of him too?

"This is coming together really well," Wayne said. "I think the *maed* will be *froh* with it."

"I hope so," Chris said. Who was he kidding? He wanted to impress only one *maedel*—

"Do you need a snack?"

Chris pushed his sweaty hair off his brow and turned toward the barn doors. His heartbeat quickened when he found Katie Ann smiling at him, holding a tray of cookies. Was he dreaming? Clara stood beside her, holding up two bottles of water.

"That sounds perfect." Wayne set the saw on the ground and walked over to the two young women. "Wow. What kind of *kichlin* are those?"

"Cinnamon swirl." Katie Ann kept her eyes focused on Chris as she spoke. "I made them yesterday. I hope you like them."

Chris set down his hammer and started toward her. "They sound amazing."

Katie Ann lifted her chin as if proud of her creation. She was adorable.

"Uh-uh," Clara said as Wayne reached for a cookie. "Wait a minute, Wayne." She held the bottles in one hand and pulled a small bottle of hand cleaner from the pocket of her apron. "Clean those hands first."

Wayne sighed, followed her instructions, and then took a cookie.

Chris followed suit and cleaned his hands before approaching Katie Ann. "*Danki.*" He took a cookie from the tray. "These look and smell *appeditlich.*"

"I can't wait for you to taste one." Her eyes sparkled as he took a bite. "What do you think?"

"Fantastic." He shook his head as he leaned back on the barn wall. "You made these?"

She nodded. "*Mei bruder* and Mandy helped, so I can't take all the credit."

"I told her she should sell these at the stand." Clara handed Chris a bottle of water.

"*Danki.*" Chris nodded. "I agree. These would sell out."

Katie Ann's gaze moved to their project. "How's it going?"

He swallowed the last bite of his cookie and took another one. "Pretty well. We've only just started."

Katie Ann walked around it, touching the pieces of wood he'd hammered together. "What will it look like?"

He held up the drawing he'd created Monday night. "It's going to have eight shelves on the front and storage on the back. It will take us a couple of weeks to build, and then I'll have to sand it and stain it."

"It looks perfect. It will be nice and big, so we'll have plenty of room." She looked up at him. "It was kind of you to offer to help build it."

"I'm *froh* to help. *Mei dat* donated the wood and supplies." He popped the last of the second cookie into his mouth.

"Please tell him *danki*." Katie Ann turned toward him and held up the tray. "Only two left."

"I want one." Wayne grabbed one cookie and Chris took the other. "You have to make these again," Chris said.

Katie Ann laughed. "I will."

"I'll take the tray in." Clara took it from her. "I want to see if Emma needs any help in the kitchen." She headed out of the barn through its large doors.

"Is Ephraim coming today?" Wayne asked Katie Ann.

She shrugged. "I'm not sure. He was working on a project with *mei dat* in one of the barns when I left to come over here."

"Oh." Wayne nodded.

Chris glanced at Wayne, and an idea gripped him. If he could find a reason to send Wayne out of the barn, then he could speak to Katie Ann alone. His looked at the tools and noted that the container of nails was almost empty.

"Wayne, would you please look in my buggy to see if I have more nails? I'm almost out."

"Sure." Wayne took a long drink of water as he headed out of the barn.

Chris held back a sigh of relief as he turned to Katie Ann. "How have you been?"

"Fine." She sank down onto a hay bale. "How about you? Have you had a *gut* week?"

"*Ya.*" He sat down beside her.

"Did you finish staining those cabinets you were working on?"

"I did." He smiled. She had remembered their discussion on Tuesday. "I stained them on Wednesday, and we installed them yesterday."

"That's great." She seemed genuinely interested in what he shared. "Are you working on a new cabinet project now?"

"*Ya*, I am." He recalled what she'd said earlier about her brother. If her brother hadn't come today, would she need a ride home? If she accepted a ride from him, they'd have more time alone. The thought of taking her home in his buggy made his heart seem to trip over itself. "Did you bring your *bruder*'s horse and buggy today?"

"No." She shook her head. "I got a ride from *mei dat*'s driver. I'm going to call him to come and get me when I'm ready to head home."

"I have my horse and buggy here," he said. "Would you accept a ride from me?"

"Oh, I wouldn't want you to go out of your way for me." She waved off the offer.

"How far away do you live from here?"

"Just a couple of miles."

"Do you live in Bird-in-Hand?"

She nodded.

"That's not out of my way at all. I'd love to give you a ride home, if you'd like one." He took a breath as he awaited her response, hoping he hadn't come on too strong.

"I'd like that."

"Great." Chris could hardly wait to get to know Katie Ann better.

~

"Tell me about your family." Katie Ann hugged her sweater against her chest as she sat beside Chris two hours later. After talking with him in the barn for a while, she had watered a few sections in the garden and then swept Emma's porch before helping store the gardening tools in the barn.

When Chris had asked her if she was ready to go home, excitement hummed through her at the thought of riding with him in his buggy. She was thrilled to spend more time alone with him and get to know him better. She was certain she'd developed a crush on him, and she hoped he liked her too.

"Well, I've already told you *mei bruder* is married and lives about a mile away." He gave her a sideways glance.

"What's his *fraa*'s name?"

"Mary."

"Do they have any *kinner*?"

"They will soon."

Katie Ann clasped her hands. "They're expecting?"

"*Ya*, their first." He smiled, and his dimple came out to play as he guided the horse through an intersection.

"Your parents must be thrilled."

"They are." Chris nodded. "It's all *mei mamm* talks about. She's been sewing for months. I don't think the *boppli* will need any clothes or blankets for at least a year."

Katie Ann laughed. "That's *wunderbaar*. How long have they been married?"

"Almost three years." He kept his focus on the road ahead as he spoke. "They had hoped to start a family sooner, but God's plan was different."

"Oh." Katie Ann fingered a button on her sweater.

"How about you?" he asked. "Tell me about your *dat*'s farm."

"Well, there's not much to tell. We have horses, cows, a couple of donkeys, chickens, and a few dogs. And kittens in the barn. I like to play with them."

"It's nice that your parents support your helping Emma."

"*Ya*, I'm thankful they allow both Ephraim and me time to help her out. It all started on Christmas Eve. Emma was supposed to come for supper, and when she didn't arrive, we were worried about her. Ephraim, Mandy, Wayne, and I went to check on her, and we wound up baking with her."

"Wayne told me you were snowed in, and that you had to sleep in her *schtupp*." He grinned, and she enjoyed how his handsome face lit up.

"*Ya*." She chuckled. "That was unexpected. It's rare that we have a blizzard here on Christmas."

"That's true." He pointed to the street sign. "Do I turn here?"

"*Ya*."

A comfortable silence fell over the buggy, and Katie Ann settled back against the seat. She couldn't remember a time when she'd felt so comfortable with a young man other than Ephraim.

"The garden looks great," Chris finally said.

"*Ya*, it does. I'm so excited to see it come together. It seems like just yesterday we decided to plant it." The idea of the garden had been hers, but Ephraim and Mandy had helped turn her dream into a reality. Katie Ann's chest tightened as she recalled how much had changed since Christmas Eve, when Mandy and Ephraim had first seemed to show interest in each other, and the disappointment and frustration of the past four months.

She turned toward Chris, and the urge to share the feelings that had been troubling her heart for months overtook her.

He gave her another sideways glance. "Are you okay?"

"*Ya*." She took a deep breath. "Are you close to your *bruder*?"

"*Ya*, I'd say we're close."

"Did your relationship change when he met Mary?"

Chris paused as if contemplating the question. "*Ya*, it did."

"How?"

"Well, we didn't talk as much as we used to, and he wasn't around as much since he spent a lot of time with her and her family." He looked over at her. "Why?"

"Ephraim started dating Mandy right after Christmas," she

began. "Mandy has been my best *freind* since we were *kinner*, and now she's always with Ephraim. I hardly ever see her now, and if she comes to see me, *mei bruder* is always there too. I always feel like I'm in the way."

Chris nodded. "I remember how that felt when Arlan always had Mary with him."

"How did you adjust to it?"

He shrugged. "I guess I just got used to it." He smiled at her. "You'll get used to it too."

"Oh." She bit back a frown. She'd hoped he'd offer her a solution that would solve all her problems, but she was thankful to get some of her troubles off her chest. She pointed to her driveway. "This is my farm."

Disappointment wafted over her as Chris guided his horse up the long rock driveway that led to the two-story, white farmhouse that had always been her home.

When he halted the horse, he turned toward her. "I enjoyed our time together today."

"I did too." *And I don't want it to end.* "Would you like to meet my family?"

His expression brightened. "*Ya.* That would be nice."

Katie Ann climbed out of the buggy and led him up the path to the back porch. Inside, they stepped into the kitchen and found her mother taking baked chicken from the oven. Her father and brother already sat at the table.

"Katie Ann," *Mamm* said. "You're home."

"*Ya*, Chris gave me a ride. *Mamm* and *Dat*, I'd like you to meet *mei freind*, Chris Lantz." Katie Ann introduced Chris to her parents. "Chris, these are my parents, Marlin and Leona Blank."

Dat stood and shook Chris's hand. "Welcome to our home."

"It's nice to meet you," Chris said. He greeted her brother and then turned to her mother and shook her hand. "How are you?"

"I'm fine, *danki*." *Mamm* smiled. "Would you like to join us for supper?"

"Oh no, but *danki*. *Mei mamm* is expecting me." Chris turned to Katie Ann. "I hope to see you soon."

"*Ya*." Katie Ann smiled up at him. "*Danki* for the ride home."

Chris said good-bye to her parents and Ephraim and then headed out to his waiting horse and buggy.

Katie Ann turned to her mother, who grinned at her. "May I, uh, help you set the table?"

"It's all set." *Mamm* folded her arms over her chest. "Have you been keeping secrets from me?"

"No." Katie Ann shook her head.

"Is he your boyfriend?" Concern colored her father's question. "He needs to ask permission before he can date you."

"No, no." Katie Ann held up her hands. "He's just a *freind*. He's Wayne King's cousin, and he's helping us with the garden. He offered me a ride home, and I accepted so *Dat* wouldn't have to spend money on a driver. That's all. We're not dating."

"I think he does like you, though," Ephraim said.

Katie Ann gaped as his words filtered through her mind. Could Ephraim be right?

Mamm lifted her eyebrows as if to indicate she wanted more information later when they were alone.

"Let's eat," Ephraim said.

After helping her mother bring the rest of the food to the table, Katie Ann slipped into her usual chair across from Ephraim and bowed her head for a silent prayer. As she began to fill her plate with baked chicken and macaroni and cheese, she wondered if Ephraim was right about Chris liking her. And if he did, would he eventually ask her to be his girlfriend? The question sent the heat of anticipation crawling up her neck to her cheeks.

CHAPTER 4

Happiness bubbled up inside Katie Ann as she stepped into Emma's barn, her shoes crunching the hay on the floor. For the past two weeks, she had relished seeing Chris on Saturdays, Sundays, and Tuesdays as they worked to make their community garden a reality.

She had enjoyed getting to know Chris as they took time to chat each time they were at Emma's house. He had given her a few more rides home, and they'd talked while sitting on the porch or watering the budding lettuce, broccoli, carrot, tomato, and spinach crops. She hoped someday soon he would ask her to be his girlfriend. Adrenaline kicked up her steps at the thought, and the sweet aroma of stain filled her senses as she continued through the barn.

She gasped as the stand came into view. Just like Chris's drawing, it had a counter and then eight shelves for items to sell. He stood in front of it as he brushed a coat of stain on the wood, his face covered with a mask. He turned toward her, and his eyes widened.

Removing the mask, he grinned, revealing his adorable dimple. "Hi."

"Hi." She pointed to the stand as she approached. "It's so *schee.*"

"You think so?" He placed the brush and mask on top of a can of stain and rubbed his clean-shaven jaw. "I'm a little disappointed in it."

"Why?" She tilted her head.

"I see the imperfections." He pointed to the shelves. "They're not exactly straight."

She shook her head. "You're your own worst critic."

"Aren't we all?" He pushed his hand through his thick, dark hair.

"*Ya*, I suppose so, but I think the stand is *wunderbaar*."

"*Danki*." He picked up two bottles of water and handed her one. "I'm glad you like it."

"When will we be able to use it?" She walked around it, silently marveling at his expert skill. She couldn't find any flaws despite his criticism of his work.

"It needs to sit a few days."

"So we might be able to use it Saturday?"

"*Ya*." He nodded. "I think it should be ready on Saturday. I'll ask Wayne and a few of the other guys to help me haul it down to the road."

"Great! I'll tell the other *maed* we should start baking. Clara got some supplies donated, so we can start selling baked goods now. That will kick-start our fund for the Bird-in-Hand Shelter." She launched a mental list of what she would bake—a few varieties of cookies and maybe a pie. She couldn't wait to tell Emma, Clara, and Mandy that the stand was almost ready.

"Fantastic." He pointed to two large, upside-down buckets. "Would you sit with me?"

"*Ya*." She sank down on a bucket beside him and opened her bottle of water.

"How have you been since Sunday?"

"*Gut*." She took a sip. "How about you?"

"Fine." He fingered the top of his water bottle. "How are things with Ephraim and Mandy?"

"Okay." She shrugged. "I actually had a nice talk with Mandy on our way home from Emma's Sunday night. She was attentive, and it almost felt like old times."

"That's great." He nudged her shoulder with his. "I told you everything would be okay. Didn't I?"

She swallowed a gasp at the familiar gesture and their easy discussion. Did he like her as much as she liked him? Her heart seemed to flip-flop.

"Didn't I?" he asked again.

"*Ya*, you did." She enjoyed his gorgeous grin.

"Have you seen the crops?" He gestured toward the barn door. "They're starting to grow." He took a drink from his bottle.

She nodded. "I know, and the weeds are already out of control. I'm going to help pull some."

"*Ya*, those weeds sure are hardy." He pointed toward the stand. "I'm going to finish staining it and then clean up the mess."

"Okay." She stood. "*Danki* for the bottle of water."

"*Gern gschehne.*" He winked at her, and she marveled at the depths of his brown eyes. Then he capped his bottle and pulled on his mask.

"I'll see you later." She started for the barn doors.

"Hey, Katie Ann."

She spun toward him, and he pushed the mask up onto his hair as he pointed his brush at her.

"I'll be by later to check your weeding skills." He wagged the brush. "You'd better get all those weeds. I'd better not find any cheatgrass or bull thistle mixed in with our crops."

"I'll do my best." She laughed.

Chris echoed the laugh, sending his loud, booming mirth into the air. The contagious sound caused her to laugh even more.

When he put the mask over his nose and turned back to the stand, Katie Ann headed outside. She couldn't stop her smile as she made her way to the back porch and picked up a bucket. She waved at friends who were already working as she walked over to the garden, chose a row, and then began to weed. She enjoyed the feel of the moist earth on her fingers as she yanked up the pesky weeds and dropped them into the bucket.

She glanced down the row and spotted Hank trotting toward her, his orange tail standing straight up like a sail on a boat.

"Hey, Hank," she sang as he approached her. "How are you?"

He gave a short meow and then flopped down by her feet, rolling around in the dirt.

"You're so *gegisch*." She rubbed his belly, and he rolled onto his side before closing his eyes. "The sun feels *gut*, huh?"

She turned her attention back to the weeds, and the sun heated her neck as she bent down. Humming to herself, she recalled her conversation with Chris. She'd never felt such a close friendship with a man. Was she imagining their connection? Or did he feel it too? If he did feel it, did that mean they were meant to be together? Her hands trembled at the idea of having met a man she might spend the rest of her life with.

"Katie Ann. *Wie geht's?*"

Katie Ann tented her hand above her eyes as she peeked up at Mandy, who was smiling down at her. "Mandy. Hi." She stood and wiped her hands down her black apron.

Mandy pointed to the bucket. "You've pulled some big weeds."

"*Ya*. And I just worked on this row last Saturday."

"They sure do grow fast." Mandy pointed to where other young folks were weeding. "It looks like we have someone in every row."

"I know." Katie Ann pointed at the ground. "I saw that we still needed someone over here, so I chose this one." Suddenly, she thought of a way to keep Mandy talking to her. "Do you want to help me?"

Mandy glanced around the garden and then looked back at Katie Ann. "Sure."

"Great." Katie Ann bent and began pulling more weeds. "I talked to Chris earlier, and he's almost done staining the stand."

"I didn't realize that." Mandy stooped to work beside her.

"Have you seen it?" Katie Ann dropped a large, green weed into the bucket.

"No, not since last week. How does it look?"

"It's *wunderbaar*," Katie Ann said as she flicked dirt off her hands. "It has eight shelves on the display and then storage in the back. We can keep pies in coolers until we're ready to sell them."

"Really?" Mandy pushed back behind her ear a thick tendril of golden-blond hair that had escaped her prayer covering. She pulled another weed and dropped it into the bucket. "That's fantastic."

"I know. We could start selling baked goods at the stand now. Why wait until the harvest?"

Mandy stood up and nodded. "That's a fantastic idea."

"You think so?" Katie Ann hated the hopefulness in her voice. Why was she so determined to win Mandy's approval?

"*Ya*, I do." Mandy wiped her hands on her apron. "We can talk to Clara and Emma about what we want to sell at the stand."

"That's exactly what I was thinking." Katie Ann grinned as she stood. She and Mandy were on the same page for the first time in months. Did she have her best friend back?

She looked toward the barn and, when she spotted Chris talking to Wayne, the urge to tell Mandy how she felt about Chris overwhelmed her. She wanted to share the details of their conversation in the barn and tell Mandy how Chris seemed to really like her. She longed for Mandy's opinion on what Chris's attention meant, as well as for her advice on how to proceed without scaring Chris away.

"You look like you're dying to share something with me." Mandy lifted her eyebrows. "What is it?"

"I want to tell you about what happened in the barn earlier," Katie Ann began. "I went in to check on Chris and the stand, and he—"

"Mandy!"

Mandy spun toward the house. "Ephraim is calling me." She turned toward Katie Ann. "We'll talk later, okay?"

Before Katie Ann could respond, Mandy was gone, nearly jogging toward the porch. Anger, hurt, and irritation itched inside Katie Ann's skin as she watched her best friend climb the back steps to meet Ephraim.

When Mandy laughed at something Ephraim said, a wave of betrayal washed over Katie Ann, twisting her insides as the reality hit her—Ephraim had replaced Katie Ann in Mandy's life. Mandy didn't need her anymore, and Katie Ann would never be the same without her best friend in her life.

Chris wiped his hands on a red shop towel as he stepped out of the barn and into the bright afternoon sunlight. He glanced around the half-acre garden and took in the dozen young folks who worked there, weeding and talking in the rows.

When his gaze landed on Katie Ann, he stilled. He watched as she bent down, pulling weeds and dropping them into the bucket. She was working alone, and he tried to analyze her stiff posture. Was she concentrating on the weeds? Or was she upset about something? He couldn't tell since she was too far away for him to see her expression.

He considered their conversation earlier in the barn. She had seemed to enjoy talking to him as much as he enjoyed talking with her. He wanted to ask her if he could give her a ride home today, but he lost his courage before she left the barn. He didn't want to come on too strong, but he had enjoyed getting to know her during the past couple of weeks.

He longed to continue to get to know her, and he wanted to ask her father if he could date her. The thought of approaching her father filled him with both excitement and anxiety. Would he allow him to date her even if her parents didn't know him or his family? He'd considered asking his cousin for his opinion, but he hadn't had the opportunity to discuss it with Wayne.

Movement in his peripheral vision drew his attention to his left. Ephraim was walking toward him.

Chris swallowed a groan as worry crept into his mind. Had Ephraim caught him staring at his sister? If so, would he tell Chris to wipe away all thoughts of Katie Ann?

Clearing his throat, Chris stood up straighter and hid his worry behind a smile. "Hi, Ephraim." He shook his hand.

"Hi, Chris," Ephraim said. "I heard you're almost done with the stand."

Chris shoved the rag into his pocket. "I just finished staining it."

"That's fantastic." Ephraim's smile was wide. "Mandy mentioned that the *maed* want to start baking and selling items this weekend so we can begin raising money for the Bird-in-Hand Shelter. She, Emma, and Clara were just in the kitchen making a list of what they want to bake."

"I'm glad to hear it." Chris looked over at Katie Ann again. Why were Mandy, Clara, and Emma making a list without Katie Ann? He hoped they hadn't forgotten about her. Katie Ann was so excited about using the stand.

"You like *mei schweschder*." It was a statement instead of a question.

Chris swallowed a lump in his throat as he turned toward Ephraim. To his surprise, Ephraim smiled at him. He didn't find a trace of disapproval or animosity.

"It's okay." Ephraim patted his arm. "I'm not angry."

"Okay." Chris gave a nervous laugh. "*Ya*, I do like her."

"That's great." Ephraim crossed his arms over his chest. "I'm sure she likes you too."

"*Wunderbaar.*" Chris stood a little taller. "I was going to ask her if I could give her a ride home this afternoon."

"I'm sure she'd like that."

Chris's thoughts turned to their father, and he forced himself to ask his burning question. "Do you think your *dat* would let me date her?"

"*Ya*, I do." Ephraim nodded. "I think he'll approve of you. Katie Ann and I have told our parents about how much you're doing for the garden. I'm sure *Dat* will agree you're a *gut freind* to both of us."

"Great." Relief loosened the knots in his shoulders. "You and Mandy have been dating for a while now?"

Ephraim looked toward the house. "*Ya.* I asked her out right after Christmas. We've known each other nearly all our lives, but things changed between us about six months ago. She's one of the greatest blessings in my life. I'm so glad God brought us together."

Chris nodded. He understood what Ephraim meant.

~

"I'm so glad you asked me to ride home with you." Katie Ann smiled at Chris as he guided the horse toward her street.

"I enjoy every minute we get to spend together." He gave her a quick smile before guiding the horse through an intersection. "It looked like you got a lot of weeding done."

"I did. I believe I got most of that cheatgrass and bull thistle." She sighed as she settled back in the seat.

"*Was iss letz?* Are the weeds bringing you down?"

"No, it's not that." She ran her fingers over the velvety seat cover. "I was just disappointed when Clara told me she, Mandy, and Emma had started a list of baked goods to make for the stand. I wanted to help make the list. Instead, Clara told me what to bake."

"I'm sorry." His eyes seemed to fill with concern. "I'm sure they didn't mean it."

"I know." But she shook her head as she recalled how Mandy had made no effort to speak to her alone after their brief conversation in the garden. Why didn't Mandy miss their friendship as much as Katie Ann did?

"Penny for your thoughts."

She turned toward him and laughed when he gave her a puppy dog expression. "What's that look for?"

"I just hope you'll tell me what's on your mind."

"It's not that important." She continued to fiddle with the seat.

"If it's important to you, then it's important to me." His words made her heart seem to swell.

"I'm just disappointed. Mandy and I had started talking in the garden while we were weeding together, but we never got to finish our conversation."

"What were you discussing?"

"Nothing, really." Katie Ann's cheeks felt as if they had burst into flames.

Chris halted the horse at a red light and turned toward her. "From the look on your face, I get the feeling you were discussing something interesting."

She opened her mouth to respond, but her embarrassed words lodged in her throat.

When a car horn tooted behind them, Chris turned his attention back to the road again, and Katie Ann breathed a sigh of relief.

"What are you going to make for the bake stand?" Chris asked.

"Oh." Katie Ann sat up straight, surprised by the subject change. "Clara asked me to make some of my favorite *kichlin*."

"If you make those cinnamon roll *kichlin*, please save a few for me."

She grinned. "How about I make you your own batch?"

He touched his chest. "Oh, be still my heart."

She laughed, and they talked about all their favorite cookies the rest of the way.

When Chris halted the horse in front of her back porch, Katie Ann turned toward him. "Would you like to stay for supper? *Mamm* always welcomes company."

He nodded. "*Ya*, I would. *Danki*."

"Great." She pushed open the buggy door. "Come inside."

They walked up the back-porch steps together and entered the house. Ephraim and *Dat* were already seated in the kitchen, and *Mamm* and Mandy were bringing food to the table. The aroma of chicken and dumplings filled her senses, causing her stomach to gurgle.

"Katie Ann," *Mamm* said. "I'm glad you're here."

"May Chris stay for supper?"

"Of course." *Mamm* gestured toward the table. "Have a seat, Chris, and we'll set a place for you."

"*Danki*." Chris moved to the right of her father, shaking his hand as he sank into the chair.

"How are you, Chris?" *Dat* asked.

"Fine. How are you?"

"I'm well." *Dat* pointed to Ephraim. "Ephraim was just telling me about the stand you built for the garden project. I hear your *dat* runs a cabinetry business."

"That's right. Our shop isn't far from here in Ronks."

While *Dat* and Chris fell into a conversation about Chris's family's business, Katie Ann set Chris's place at the table and then helped her mother and Mandy serve the rest of the food. Then Katie Ann sat down beside Chris. Mandy sat across from her, beside Ephraim.

After a silent prayer and starting their meal, they discussed the garden's progress, the way the weather was cooperating, and their plans to make the roadside stand a success. While Katie Ann enjoyed her supper, she silently marveled at how well Chris fit in with her family. He talked to her father about woodworking and laughed at his silly jokes. When Chris laughed his contagious laugh, her family seemed to laugh even more. He seemed to enjoy being there, and Katie Ann relished having him beside her.

Did this mean God wanted them to be together? Did the ease of the friendship indicate God would bless their relationship if they dated? Her heart soared at what their future might hold.

Katie Ann looked across the table at Mandy as she and *Mamm* discussed a recipe for strawberry pie. As she studied her best friend's pretty face, disappointment swirled through her chest. She recalled the old times when she and Mandy would talk for hours. Would Katie Ann ever regain that kind of friendship with Mandy? How she longed to share her deepest feelings with her best friend. Would she ever have the opportunity to tell Mandy about Chris? And would Mandy care if she did tell her?

And why hadn't Mandy shared her feelings about Ephraim? Katie Ann found herself stuck on that last thought. They were best friends, but Mandy never discussed how she felt about Katie Ann's brother. Yet it might be awkward to hear Mandy talk about her brother in a romantic way. Was that part of the reason Mandy had pulled away from her and put so little effort into saving their friendship?

Still, Katie Ann couldn't deny how much her heart ached for the closeness she used to share with her best friend. She pressed her lips into a tight line.

"Hey." Chris's voice was soft in her ear, sending a chill dancing up her spine. "Are you okay?"

"*Ya.*" Katie Ann smiled at him. "I'm fine."

Chris lifted an eyebrow.

"Who would like brownies?" *Mamm* asked as she stood and began to gather the dinner plates.

"Oh, I don't know if I could eat anything else." Chris leaned back in the chair and touched his flat abdomen. "Dinner was so *appeditlich. Danki* for inviting me."

"You should make room for *mei mamm*'s brownies," Ephraim said. "They're the best."

"Okay. You convinced me," Chris said, and everyone chuckled.

Katie Ann and Mandy helped *Mamm* carry the dinner dishes to the counter, and then Katie Ann took the pan of brownies to the table while *Mamm* filled the percolator for coffee. Over dessert they discovered mutual friends in the community.

When the brownies were gone, Katie Ann helped clean up the kitchen while the men sat outside on the porch.

"Supper was *wunderbaar*, Leona," Mandy said as she dried the dishes. "*Danki* for inviting me to stay."

"You know you're welcome anytime, Mandy." *Mamm* glanced at Katie Ann as she scrubbed a pot. "I think Chris is enjoying himself."

"*Ya.*" Katie Ann nodded while wiping off the long kitchen table. "I think so too."

Mandy smiled at her. "You'll have to tell me about Chris sometime." She turned back to the counter and lifted a dish from the drying rack.

Katie Ann shook her head as disappointment rolled through her. If only Mandy had given her a chance earlier, she'd already know all about Chris.

⁓

"I had a *wunderbaar* time tonight," Chris said as he and Katie Ann stood beside his buggy.

"I did too." Katie Ann looked up at the sky, where the sun began to set, painting the horizon with vivid splashes of gold and orange. She hugged her arms over her sweater. "It's a *schee* night."

"*Ya*," he agreed. "Spring is in the air."

"It sure is." She looked at him. "I'm glad you stayed for supper."

"Your parents are great." Chris leaned back against the buggy wheel. "I especially enjoyed getting to know your *dat*."

"I think he liked you too."

He touched her shoulder. "You seemed a little tense at supper. Is there anything you want to talk about?"

She swallowed a sigh. She couldn't deny that Mandy had hurt her. It was healthier for her to share her feelings than to let them eat her up inside. "I told you about how Mandy hurt my feelings."

He stood up straight. "I remember."

"I was just thinking about it during supper. I really miss her. I miss our close friendship."

"Don't give up on her. I'm sure she didn't mean to hurt you. Maybe if you're honest with her and tell her how you feel, she'll make more of an effort to be a better *freind*."

"That's *gut* advice. *Danki*." Katie Ann prayed he was right.

"*Gern gschehne*. I want to ask you something." He took her hand in his.

When their skin touched, a spark sizzled up her arm, and she bit back a startled gasp.

"Okay." Her voice trembled.

"I talked to your *dat* earlier, and I asked his permission to date you." His brown eyes seemed to search hers. "So would you be my girlfriend?"

"*Ya*, I'd love to." Her pulse pounded as he grinned.

"*Danki*." He leaned down, and when he brushed his lips across her cheek, she sucked in a breath.

"*Gut nacht*," he whispered in her ear, sending chills shimmying up her spine. "I hope to see you soon."

"*Gut nacht*," she responded before he climbed into his buggy.

Katie Ann waved as Chris guided his horse down the driveway toward the road. As his buggy disappeared from sight, she bit her lower lip. Happiness, warm and comforting, fluttered through her as she hugged her arms to her chest.

For the first time, Katie Ann felt as if she'd met a man who truly cared for her. Maybe, just maybe, she had found someone who would love her and want to build a future with her. She looked up at the sky and smiled as she opened her heart to God.

"*Danki*, God, for bringing Chris into my life. Please guide him safely home and bless him. I'm so grateful for his friendship. Please let our relationship grow like the vegetables and fruit thriving in Henry's garden. Amen."

Katie Anne couldn't wait to see what God had in store for her and Chris.

CHAPTER 5

Katie Ann bent at her waist and hummed to herself as she pulled another thick, pesky bundle of ryegrass and dropped it into her bucket. The afternoon sun warmed her neck.

"Katie Ann!"

She tented her hand over her eyes as she turned toward the house. Clara was rushing over to her. "*Ya?*"

"It's your turn to run the stand." Clara pointed in the direction of the road. "I'll do your weeding."

"*Ya*, sure. That's fine." Katie Ann wiped her palms down her apron. "Has it been busy?"

"*Ya*." Clara nodded, and the ties for her prayer covering bounced off her slight shoulders. "I can't believe how much money we've raised since we opened the stand. It's only been a month."

"I know. It's been a blessing. Did Mandy get more baking supplies like she promised?"

"No. Mandy said she forgot." Clara's smile flattened. "I had to pick them up."

"But it was Mandy's turn to get them." Katie Ann's shoulders tensed with a mixture of anger and disappointment.

"It's okay. I think she was busy with Ephraim." Clara waved it off. "Anyway, I went ahead and got more donated, and then I purchased the rest of the supplies with some of the money we had set aside for the stand. It's all in Emma's pantry."

"*Danki* for taking care of that." Katie Ann did her best to set aside her frustration with Mandy, but it seemed to keep festering at the edge of her thoughts. She gestured toward the house. "I'll wash my hands and then go out to the stand."

"Great!" Clara bent and began weeding.

Katie Ann waved at friends who were weeding and watering the vegetable beds as she made her way to the house. Inside, she said hello to Emma and a few others who were busy baking cookies in the kitchen. After washing her hands in the bathroom, she walked down the rock driveway to the stand, where Rosalyn and Ellen Beiler stood behind the counter.

"Hi," Katie Ann said as she approached them. "I'm here to relieve you."

"Oh, *danki*," Rosalyn said. "We wanted to take our turn weeding."

"Don't worry." Katie Ann pointed in the direction of the garden. "Plenty of weeds need to be pulled."

"*Gut.*" Ellen followed her sister out from behind the stand.

"The money box is on the second shelf." Rosalyn pointed to the coolers. "More pies are there in case you sell some."

"It's been busy." Ellen tilted her head. "I thought Mandy was going to help too."

Katie Ann shrugged. "I haven't seen her."

"She's probably too busy with Ephraim." Rosalyn rolled her eyes. "They never seem to have time for anyone else lately."

Katie Ann tried to hide her surprise at the statement. So she wasn't the only one who had noticed how Mandy and Ephraim were behaving.

"We'd better start weeding." Ellen pointed behind Katie Ann. "I think you have your first customer. There's a car now."

"Oh. I'd better get ready." Katie Ann scooted behind the stand and waved good-bye to Rosalyn and Ellen as they started up the driveway.

The gray sedan stopped in front of the stand, and three women dressed in jeans and T-shirts climbed out.

"Look, Charlotte," one of the women said. "I told you this was an Amish bake stand."

"You were right, Lois," Charlotte said.

"How are you?" Katie Ann sat down on a stool behind the counter.

"We're fine, sweetie," the third woman said. "What are you selling?"

Katie Ann gestured toward the shelves of baked goods. "We have cookies—chocolate chip, peanut butter, macadamia nut, oatmeal raisin, butter, and sugar. We also have shoo-fly, apple, lemon meringue, pecan, and sweet potato pies. All the proceeds from this stand are for the Bird-in-Hand Shelter for the homeless."

"Really?" Lois said. "That's really neat." She looked at the other women. "Let's get some goodies to take home."

Ten minutes later, each of the women had left with three trays of cookies and two pies, and Katie Ann unloaded the coolers to refill the shelves.

Chris approached the stand as she set the last shoo-fly pie on a shelf.

"How's business?" He rocked back on his heels, lifting his straw hat and raking his hand through his thick, dark hair.

"Business is *gut*. Three tourists just cleaned off the shelves." Katie Ann pointed to the storage shelf behind her. "I had to unload the coolers. It's a *gut* thing Clara picked up more baking supplies."

"That's fantastic." Chris tapped the counter. "I'm glad the stand is working out."

"It's perfect." Katie Ann perched on the stool. "We've already raised nearly two hundred dollars for the Bird-in-Hand Shelter, all in a few weeks."

"Wow. What a blessing."

He smiled at her, and her heart fluttered. The past month had been a whirlwind since they'd started dating. She'd had supper with his parents, and she'd also met his brother and sister-in-law. She'd enjoyed spending time with Chris at Emma's house as well as at her house and at his. But something was still missing—her best friend.

Katie Ann still hadn't had the opportunity to share her excitement about Chris with Mandy. Every time she'd tried to talk to her, Mandy had been distracted or Ephraim had interrupted them. Just as Clara said, Mandy was busy with Ephraim. Sorrow coursed through her, squeezing her heart and tightening her throat.

But Katie Ann pushed it away as she looked up at Chris's warm brown eyes. She couldn't allow her sadness over her best friend to ruin her time with her boyfriend.

He cocked his head to the side and seemed to assess her. "Is everything all right?"

"Everything is fine." Katie Ann brightened. "How is your day going?"

"*Gut.*" He nodded. "I'm working with the guys on a few projects for Emma. Are we still going to ride home together this afternoon?"

"I wouldn't miss it for anything." Happiness zipped through her as he smiled, and his dimple made yet another grand appearance.

"*Gut.*" Chris picked up a stack of chocolate chip cookies wrapped in plastic wrap. "How much for these?"

"Two dollars." She leaned forward on the counter.

"That's a fair price." He pulled his wallet out of his back pocket. "I'd like to purchase these, please."

"*Danki*, sir." She gave a little laugh as she took the money from him. Their fingers brushed, sending heat to the places their skin touched.

She put the cash in the money box. Chris opened the plastic wrap and held up a cookie, offering it to her.

"No, *danki*." She shook her head. "They're for you."

"All right." He shrugged, took a bite, chewed, and swallowed with a sigh of appreciation. "So good. Well, I need to get back to the barn. Wayne and I are repairing the horse's stall, and then we're going to fix the fence at the back of her pasture." He winked at her and started up the driveway. "See you later. Sell lots of baked goods."

"I'll try." As Katie Ann watched him walk away, she was so grateful for her boyfriend.

"Hi, Emma!" Katie Ann stepped into Emma's kitchen the following Sunday and held up a Pyrex portable dish and three frozen loaves of bread. "I made lasagna for supper tonight. I also picked up some garlic bread. I hope everyone brings their appetites."

Emma clapped her hands. "Oh, that's *wunderbaar*. I think everyone will love it." She looked up at the clock on the wall. "You're early."

"*Ya*, I asked *mei dat* to bring me over now. I want to finish preparing the food and spend some time with you before everyone else gets here." Katie Ann set the dish on the counter. "Would it be all right if I preheated the oven?"

"Of course." Emma laughed. "You know you don't have to ask permission to use my oven."

"*Danki*." Katie Ann flipped the dial to the appropriate temperature and then turned to Emma. "I'll put the lasagna in as soon as the oven timer buzzes." She felt something brush her leg, and she looked down as Hank circled around and rubbed her legs. "Hi, Hank. How are you?"

The cat sat back on his haunches and blinked up at her.

"It's nice to see you too." Katie Ann laughed. "He looks like he's in a *gut* mood."

"He's always in a *gut* mood. Aren't you, Hank?" Emma leaned down and rubbed his ear. The cat responded by tilting his head and closing his eyes as he purred. "He's such a lovable guy."

Katie Ann smiled. She was thankful Hank had chosen Emma as his companion on Christmas Eve.

"How's Chris doing?" Emma asked as she turned her attention back to Katie Ann.

"Oh, he's fine." Katie Ann's cheeks heated. She was taken by surprise at the direct question. "He should be here in a little bit."

"You two seem *froh*." Emma leaned back on the counter. "I've noticed how you both smile as you talk together. You remind me of Henry and me when we first dated."

"You think so?" Katie Ann couldn't stop a smile now.

"*Ya*, you do. Henry always knew how to make me smile, even on the worst of days. I remember the day we found out *mei dat* had had a heart attack. He had collapsed, and we got him to the hospital as quickly as we could." Emma got a faraway look in her eyes as she gazed across the room. "I was certain I would lose *mei dat*, and I was distraught. Henry came to the hospital with me, and he held my hand and kept talking to me. He told me *gegisch* jokes and rubbed my back while we waited for news from the doctor."

Katie Ann gasped. "Was your *dat* okay?"

"*Ya*." Emma nodded. "He had to take it easy, and he had to change his diet, but he made a full recovery. It was a miracle."

"Oh, *gut*." Katie Ann breathed a sigh of relief.

"Henry was a tremendous help to my family and me. He took care of *mei dat*'s chores, and he made sure *mei mamm* and I had what we needed. He was such a *gut* man." Emma leaned forward. "You know, Chris reminds me of him."

"Really?" Katie Ann heard the thread of hopefulness in her voice.

"*Ya.* Chris is so kind and thoughtful." Emma pointed toward the windows. "He and Wayne repaired my horse's stall last week, and now they're working on the pasture fence. They said they'll paint it after they have all the broken pickets and rails replaced. That's something Henry would have done for an older neighbor when we were younger."

Pride filled Katie Ann's chest. "*Ya,* Chris is a *gut* man."

"I'm so *froh* you found him." Emma touched Katie Ann's cheek. "I think he'll make you very happy." She tilted her head as her expression filled with concern. "How are things with Mandy and Ephraim?"

Katie Ann shrugged. "Ephraim and I are okay. I guess. We haven't really talked."

"Why not?"

"I suppose I don't know what to say." Katie Ann's throat felt as though it were thickening. "We used to talk about nearly everything, but these days I don't know what to say to him. It's as if he's changed."

"Has he changed? Or have you both changed?"

Katie Ann contemplated Emma's question, but the answer escaped her. "I don't know."

"Have you truly tried to talk to him?"

Katie Ann shook her head as shame nipped at her. "I guess not."

"What about Mandy?"

"I'm going to try to talk to her today, to ask her if she wants to come over to bake or sew one day this week."

"That's a great idea." Emma turned toward the cabinets. "Let's find pans for your bread so we'll be ready to put it in the oven when it's time."

As Katie Ann turned her attention to the food, she had a new thought. If she could fix her relationship with Mandy, maybe she could also improve her relationship with her brother.

～

"The lasagna was fantastic." Chris leaned over and bumped his shoulder against Katie Ann's as they sat at Emma's table.

"*Danki.*" She smiled up at him as she inhaled his familiar scent—moist earth mixed with sandalwood and soap. "I'm glad you enjoyed it."

"You had me in mind when you made it, right?" His gorgeous eyes sparkled with mischief. "You knew I'd like this."

"*Ya.*" She laughed. "You like food, and you seem satisfied with whatever I make, so of course you were on my mind when I put it together."

"It was *appeditlich.* You're a great cook." He touched her hand, and she relished the feel of his warm skin against hers.

"*Danki.*" Katie Ann stood and gathered their plates, along with Wayne's and Clara's. She carried them to the counter.

"Dinner was great." Mandy sidled up to her and set a pile of utensils next to the dishes. "*Danki* for cooking."

"I'm so glad you liked it." As Katie Ann looked at Mandy, a surge of confidence bubbled up inside her. "Could I talk to you later?"

"*Ya,* of course." Mandy's smile faded. "Is something wrong?"

"No." Katie Ann shook her head. "I just want to talk."

"I look forward to it." Mandy's smile was back, but it seemed to wobble. Was she nervous?

"Okay," Clara said as she approached them with the remainder of the dishes. "I'll start washing. Who wants to dry?"

"I'll dry," Mandy offered, taking dish towels from one of the cabinet drawers.

When the dishes were done—although they'd soon have to wash coffee mugs and dessert dishes—Katie Ann stepped over to the counter, where Mandy sorted utensils into a drawer. "Do you have a minute to talk now?"

Mandy looked up at her and nodded. "*Ya*, that would be *gut*." She dropped the last of the knives into the drawer. "Do you want to go outside on the porch?"

"*Ya*, that would be perfect." Katie Ann turned to Emma, who was arranging a plate of cookies. "We're going to step outside for a minute."

"*Gut*." Emma gave her an encouraging smile.

As Katie Ann walked toward the mudroom, she caught Chris's gaze. He gave her a nod and a thumbs-up, which ignited a tiny flame of hope deep in her chest. He had suggested she try to talk to Mandy again, inspiring her to give her best friend another chance. She followed Mandy out to the porch, where they both stood at the railing. The sweet smell of moist earth filled the warm May evening air.

"What do you want to talk about?" Mandy asked.

"I was wondering if we could make plans to get together—just the two of us." Katie Ann leaned back on the railing. "We haven't really talked in a while, and I've missed you."

Mandy's expression warmed. "I've missed you too."

"You have?" The question slipped past Katie Ann's lips without any forethought.

"Of course I have." Mandy gave a little laugh. "You're my best *freind*. Why wouldn't I miss you?"

Relief spilled over Katie Ann. Maybe she hadn't lost Mandy's friendship! "I'm glad to hear it. I was thinking maybe we could get together for a sisters' day. We can bake some things to sell at the bake stand or we can sew. Whatever you'd like to do would be great."

"Okay." Mandy touched her chin. "Maybe we can plan for Tuesday? We can get together at your *haus*, and then Ephraim can bring us over here to work in the garden and at the stand."

"That sounds *gut*."

The back door opened, and Ephraim appeared in the doorway. "Mandy. Are you coming back in? We're having *kaffi* and dessert. Clara made her amazing sugar *kichlin*."

Mandy's expression brightened. "I'll be right there."

Ephraim nodded at Katie Ann and then disappeared inside the house.

"We'll have a *gut* time on Tuesday," Mandy said. Then she hurried after him.

Would they? Katie wondered if Mandy could stay away from Ephraim long enough to have even one meaningful conversation with her.

CHAPTER 6

Katie Ann turned the pages of her mother's favorite cookbook with anticipation. This afternoon she and Mandy would bake items to sell at the stand, and they would finally talk. She'd been so excited last night that she'd had difficulty falling asleep.

She looked up at the clock and then walked to the windows that faced the driveway.

Mamm stepped into the kitchen. "She should be here any minute."

"I know." Katie Ann looked over her shoulder at her mother. "I'm just eager to get started. We haven't really talked for so long."

"I'm sure you two will have a great time." *Mamm* picked up a bag of material from the counter. "I'll be in the sewing room if you need me."

Katie Ann returned to the counter and flipped through the cookbook, taking in the possible recipes they could make for the stand. She perused the variety of cookies, and when she settled on one, she mentally checked off the ingredients. She moved around in the pantry and gathered what they'd need. She was taking a mixing bowl from a lower cabinet when she heard the storm door open and click shut.

"Hi!" Mandy called as she stepped into the kitchen. She set a bag on the table.

"*Wie geht's?*" Katie Ann pointed to the cookbook. "Are you ready to get started? I checked, and I have all the ingredients to make chocolate crinkle *kichlin*. Doesn't that sound *gut?*"

"*Ya.*" Mandy jammed her thumb toward the door. "I need to go tell Ephraim something, but I'll help you in a minute when I get back." She started toward the mudroom.

"What?" Katie Ann crossed the kitchen, her blood pressure ticking up higher with each step.

Mandy turned around. "I said I need to go tell Ephraim something." Her forehead puckered. "Why do you look so confused? I'll be right back."

"I'm not confused. I'm upset." Katie Ann's voice rose. Her breath scorched a hole in her chest, and she tasted rancid jealousy. "You came here to spend time with me, not talk to *mei bruder.*"

"I just have to tell him something. It will only take a few minutes."

"But you're here to see *me.*" Katie Ann jammed her finger in her chest. "Today is supposed to be my day. You can talk to him later when we're on our way to Emma's."

Mandy blinked as she studied Katie Ann. "Why are you acting this way?"

"Because I'm tired of being the third wheel." Katie Ann could hear the tremor in her voice as her body vibrated with a mixture of heartache and fury. "You've ignored me for months now, and I've had it. I'm done trying to gain your attention."

"Ignored you?" Mandy shook her head. "When have I ever ignored you?"

Katie Ann gave a sarcastic laugh. "Are you kidding me?"

"No." Mandy shook her head. "Tell me when I ignored you."

"Too many times to list." Katie Ann gestured widely as anger swirled in her chest like wasps. "Countless times during the past couple of months I've tried to talk to you, and you've either ignored me or walked away because Ephraim called you or interrupted us. Ever since you started dating *mei bruder*, you've completely forgotten about me."

"I'd never forget you, Katie Ann. You're my best *freind*." Mandy's cornflower-blue eyes sparkled with tears. "We've been *freinden* since we were *kinner*. Just because I've fallen in love with your *bruder* doesn't mean you don't matter to me."

"That's not how it feels." Katie Ann pointed at her, her hands trembling. "I've been trying to talk to you about Chris for more than a month. I wanted to tell you about how he and I were getting to know each other, and about how he asked me to be his girlfriend. But every time I tried to tell you, you walked away. I've worked so hard to try to save our relationship, and you haven't tried at all. You act like I'm not worth the effort."

"What are you talking about?" Mandy's eyes narrowed to slits. "That's not true."

"*Ya*, it is. I tried to tell you one day while I was weeding the garden about a month ago. As soon as I started talking, Ephraim called you and you left. You promised we'd talk later, and we never did."

Mandy shook her head. "I don't remember that."

"Really?" Katie Ann jammed her hands on her hips as a violent volcano erupted inside her, unpredictable and severe as her fury boiled over. "I tried a few other times, and each time you had to go talk to Ephraim. We used to talk about everything, Mandy. Do you remember that? Before you started dating Ephraim, we'd tell each other our secrets, but that changed when you started dating him. It's like you can't be his girlfriend and my best *freind* at the same time. You have to do one or the other."

Mandy's face twisted into a dark glower. "Are you asking me to choose between you and Ephraim?"

"No." Katie Ann shook her head. "But I have to believe that

you can be a better *freind* to me. I deserve it after all these years. I don't understand how you could just throw me away like an old, useless toy."

Tears trickled down Mandy's pink cheeks. "I can't believe you're saying all this. I've never ignored you, and I've never thrown you away. I think you're just jealous."

"What?" Katie Ann's voice rose again. "You're not listening to me at all."

"*Ya*, I am listening to you." Mandy sniffed as she brushed away tears with her hand. "You're accusing me of ignoring you and of forgetting our friendship. That's not true at all. You're just being cruel."

"I'm not the only one who's noticed this change in you."

"What do you mean?"

"Not long ago, Clara told me you forgot to get the baking supplies when it was your turn. She had to get supplies donated and then buy the rest herself. She said you seemed too busy with Ephraim to remember to get them." Katie Ann gestured around the kitchen. "Other people have commented that you and Ephraim have alienated the rest of us. It's like you're in your own world, and none of the rest of us exist anymore."

Mandy took a step toward the door. "I didn't come today to be criticized. I thought we'd have a fun time, but that's not what you had in mind at all. You just invited me over here to make me feel bad."

"You're missing the point," Katie Ann insisted, holding her hand up to stop her from leaving. "I want our friendship back. I want things to be the way they used to be, before you were completely smitten with *mei bruder*. I want to be able to share things with you. I want to tell you all about Chris and how *froh* I am with him. You haven't had any interest in hearing about my life, and I have a lot to tell you."

"So tell me." Mandy threw up her arms. "Tell me now."

Katie Ann gaped.

"Well?" Mandy pointed at her. "You were so determined to get me to listen. Now I'm listening. What is so important that you can't wait for me to go out and say hello to your *bruder* before we start baking?"

Katie Ann shook her head. "This isn't how I wanted this discussion to go."

"Maybe you should have thought about that before you started yelling at me." Mandy scowled. "You seem to think everything is my fault." She pointed to her chest. "Maybe it's partially your fault that we haven't been talking. Have you ever considered that our relationship has changed because we've both changed?" She wiped more tears. "You're so quick to blame me for everything. All I did was fall in love with your *bruder*. Aren't we all supposed to fall in love and get married?"

"*Ya*, but we don't have to drop our *freinden* along the way!"

"I never dropped you!" Mandy yelled back.

They stared at each other as tears burned Katie Ann's eyes. She could feel the rift between Mandy and her expanding into a great chasm.

Mamm appeared in the doorway. "What's going on in here?"

Mandy made a sweeping gesture toward *Mamm*. "Why don't you tell her? Tell her how you've done nothing but criticize me since I arrived here. Tell her you're jealous because I spend time with your *bruder*."

"That's not what I said." Katie Ann ground out the words as her temper flared.

"I'm going out to see Ephraim." Mandy turned and started toward the mudroom.

Katie Ann pointed after her. "If you walk out that door now, don't bother coming back in."

"Don't worry," Mandy said without looking back. "I'm not interested in coming back in." Her footsteps echoed in the mudroom before the storm door opened and slammed shut.

"What just happened?" *Mamm*'s eyes focused on Katie Ann. "What did you say to her?"

"I told her how I felt." Katie Ann sniffed as tears poured from her eyes. Her hurt ran so deep she feared she might drown in it. "She said she was going to go see Ephraim, and I said today was supposed to be my day." She pointed to her chest. "I told her I've missed her, and that I've felt ignored since she and Ephraim started dating. I explained that other people have noticed the change in her and Ephraim too. They've also said they've alienated their *freinden*."

Katie Ann's words came in a rush. "I explained I just wanted time with her. I told her that time and again she's chosen Ephraim over me. I've tried so hard to save our friendship, but she hasn't given it any effort at all. It's as if she doesn't care. She said I'm making it all up, but I'm not. All she's done is ignore me since she started dating Ephraim, and I'm tired of it."

"Just calm down." *Mamm* rested her hands on Katie Ann's shoulders. "You two can work this out if you just listen to each other. Maybe you shouldn't have come on so strong."

"How did I come on strong?" Katie Ann grabbed a napkin from the holder in the center of the table and wiped at her eyes and nose. "I just told her the truth."

"I know you did, but I heard you yelling. Sometimes you have to be gentle when you tell people what's difficult to share." *Mamm* touched her cheek. "I'm sure you didn't mean to hurt Mandy, but I think you needed to take her feelings into consideration too."

"Her feelings?" Katie Ann's lip trembled. "What about my feelings?"

"I know you're hurting, *mei liewe*, but I'm sure Mandy is hurting now too. You said some upsetting things to her."

Katie Ann shook her head as she stepped away from her mother, betrayal choking back her words. "How can you say that? She's the one who ignored me and pushed me away. I didn't do anything wrong."

"Katie Ann!" Ephraim's voice shouted from the mudroom. "Where are you?"

Katie Ann spun toward the mudroom doorway as Ephraim stomped in. Tension rolled off him like a fourth entity in the room.

"What did you say to Mandy?" Ephraim walked over to her and wagged a finger just millimeters from her nose. The intense look in his eyes stole Katie Ann's breath.

"Ephraim," *Mamm* began, "please calm down."

"*Mamm*, let me handle this." He turned back to Katie Ann, his hand vibrating as he pointed at her once again. "Mandy is out on the porch and can't stop crying. What did you say to her?"

Katie Ann blanched, and unease blossomed at the base of her spine. She couldn't remember ever seeing her brother so angry. "I told her I'm tired of feeling like I don't matter. I just told her how I felt." She gave him a brief explanation of what she'd already shared with *Mamm*.

Ephraim shook his head and swiped his hand down his face. "How is it that you always make everything about you?"

"What do you mean?" Katie Ann's body quivered as pressure clamped on her chest like a vice, squeezing tight.

"Have you ever considered how Mandy feels?" He pointed toward the back door. "You made your best *freind* cry because you felt ignored. You could have discussed this with her instead of yelling at her and making her feel criticized. You never put anyone else's feelings before yours."

"That's not true!" Katie Ann couldn't stop herself from yelling as her anger spiked. "I've tried over and over to talk to her, but every time you call her away or she decides she needs to see you instead of finishing her conversation with me. I'm tired of being left behind. I need a best *freind* who truly cares about me."

"Is that so?" Ephraim lifted his chin as he glared at her. "Maybe you're not *gut* enough to be her best *freind* anymore."

Katie Ann gasped.

"Ephraim!" *Mamm* snapped. "Don't talk to your *schweschder* like that."

"I'm just telling her the truth, *Mamm*. No one has the right to make Mandy cry that way. Katie Ann is being selfish and only thinking of herself."

"No, that's not true." Katie Ann shook her head. "I'm not being selfish. I'm just trying to save my relationship with my best *freind*."

Ephraim snorted. "Yelling at someone and accusing them of being cruel is not how you save a friendship."

"Everything was fine until you stole her away!" Katie Ann gave her brother a push, and he stepped away from her.

He gave a sarcastic laugh. "Really, Katie Ann? I didn't steal Mandy away from you."

"*Ya*, you did." Katie Ann brushed away more tears as they streamed down her face. "If you hadn't butted in, we'd still be best *freinden*."

"I didn't butt in." Ephraim glared at her. "Mandy and I fell in love. Where is the fault in that?"

"You should have found someone else." Katie Ann sniffed. She knew she was being immature, but she couldn't help herself. The rift between her and Ephraim and the rift between her and Mandy were both tearing her heart to pieces.

"You can't help who you love," Ephraim said. "Don't you love Chris?"

Katie Ann blinked, the question knocking her off balance for a moment.

"You don't choose who you love," Ephraim continued. "God puts who you're supposed to love in your life so you can find that person." He scowled. "I'm so disappointed in you. I thought you could handle my falling in love with Mandy, but it's obvious you couldn't." His eyes seemed to glimmer with fury . . . and hatred? "You're not *mei schweschder*, and you're not Mandy's *freind*," he spat. "You're someone I used to know, but I don't know you now."

Katie Ann winced as if he'd physically hurt her. Her soul was crushed.

"Ephraim!" *Mamm* yelled. "Stop it. You're going to say something you regret."

"Don't worry, *Mamm*," Katie Ann whispered through her tears. "I'm leaving."

She hurried up the stairs to her room. After slamming her door, she flung herself onto her bed and sobbed into her pillow. She'd lost both Mandy and her brother, and everything was ruined.

CHAPTER 7

Chris hurried up Emma's back-porch steps as a grin tugged at his lips. He wanted to see Katie Ann and find out how today went with Mandy.

Katie Ann had been in his thoughts all day long as he'd sanded a set of kitchen cabinets for a customer. He'd sent up prayers, asking God to bless her day and help repair her fractured relationship with Mandy. While he prayed, he analyzed his feelings for Katie Ann, and he realized he was in love with her. He truly loved her, and he couldn't wait to tell her.

After completing all his chores, he had cleaned up his work area, showered, put on fresh clothes, and then rushed over to Emma's house. He longed to tell Katie Ann he loved her after he found out how the day had gone. He just hoped she loved him too.

When he didn't see her at the bake stand, he had hurried up the driveway to the garden. He found a group of young men and women weeding and watering the crops, but he didn't see Katie Ann or Mandy. Most likely, Katie Ann was helping in the kitchen, baking more goodies to sell at the stand.

Chris headed into the kitchen through the mudroom, where he found Mandy and Emma sitting at the table.

Mandy wiped her eyes and as she looked up at Chris. "Hi. How are you?" Her smile wobbled.

"I'm fine, *danki*. How are you?"

When Mandy shrugged, concern filled Chris as he took in her expression. She didn't look happy. Did that mean her afternoon with Katie Ann hadn't gone well? Or had she and Ephraim broken up?

"Where's Katie Ann?"

Mandy and Emma shared a look, and then Mandy looked back at him. "She's not here. She's at home."

He crossed the kitchen and came to stand by her. "Is she *krank*?"

"No."

"So why isn't she here?"

Mandy hesitated, and worry washed over him.

"Please tell me what's going on," Chris said, nearly pleading with her.

"We had an argument, and she didn't come with Ephraim and me." Mandy ran her finger over the wood grain as she stared down at the table.

"Oh." Chris nodded as understanding filled him. Their conversation hadn't gone the way Katie Ann planned. "I'm sorry to hear that."

"*Ya*, I am too." Mandy sniffed, and then she wiped at her eyes again as Emma rubbed her shoulder.

"It will be okay, *mei liewe*." Emma's voice was soft and comforting.

"I hope so. I don't know what to do without her friendship."

"Just give her time," Emma said. "She'll calm down and realize she needs you both."

Chris turned toward the door just as Ephraim walked in. "Ephraim. Hi."

"Hi." Ephraim shook his hand, and Chris took in the lines on his forehead.

"Mandy just told me Katie Ann stayed home today."

"*Ya.*" Ephraim blew out a deep breath.

"I told him we argued with her," Mandy said, her voice shaky.

"You both argued with her?" Chris divided a look between them.

"*Ya.*" Ephraim's frown deepened. "It was pretty bad."

Tears rolled down Mandy's cheeks.

Alarm sliced through Chris. If Katie Ann had argued with both her brother and her best friend, she must have felt so alone. She needed him. She needed him *now*.

"I'm going to go." Chris started for the door. "I'll see you all soon."

He almost tripped over Hank as he rushed to his waiting buggy. He climbed in and guided his horse down to the road, his heart pounding with worry.

When he arrived at Katie Ann's house, he guided the horse up the driveway and halted it in front of her back porch. Leaping from the buggy, he tied the horse to a nearby fence and then took the back steps two at a time. He knocked on the back door and held his breath as he awaited an answer.

The door opened, and Katie Ann's mother greeted him. "Hi, Chris."

"Hi, Leona." Chris removed his straw hat and fingered it in his hands. "I'm concerned about Katie Ann since she didn't come to Emma's like she always does on Tuesdays. I wanted to check on her."

Leona frowned as she pushed the door open wide. "*Ya*, come in. I'm not sure if I can get her to come downstairs. She's been up there all afternoon and refuses to leave her room."

Knots of unease formed in Chris's stomach as he followed

her into the kitchen. "Mandy and Ephraim said they argued with her."

Leona heaved a deep sigh that sounded as if it had bubbled up from her toes. "It was terrible." She shook her head as her frown deepened. "I've never heard Katie Ann and Ephraim argue like that."

"May I ask what happened?"

Leona hesitated, and he regretted the intrusion.

"I'm sorry. You don't need to tell me."

"No, it's okay. I'll tell you."

As he listened to Leona's account of the argument, dread unfurled in his chest like a noxious weed. With all his praying during the day, he'd never imagined it would turn out this way. He had expected Katie Ann and Mandy to have an amicable conversation that would end in a renewing of their friendship. He'd never thought she would lose Mandy's friendship and destroy her relationship with her brother.

"I've tried to talk to her," Leona continued, her eyes wet with unshed tears. "I've gone to her room four times and begged her to talk to me. Each time, she asked me to leave. I just don't know what to do. I never argued like this with *mei bruder*. I'm not sure how to help them work it out."

"Would you like me to talk to her?" Chris offered, hoping he could be a blessing to Katie Ann and her family.

"*Ya.*" Leona stood. "Maybe you can talk some sense into her and encourage her to apologize to both Mandy and Ephraim. I can't stand to see the three of them in such pain. I hoped *mei kinner* would always remain *freinden*."

"I'll try my best to get through to her."

"*Danki.*" Leona disappeared, and soon her footfalls sounded from the stairwell.

As he waited in the kitchen, Chris scrubbed his hand down his face and silently prayed that he could somehow reason with Katie Ann. A few minutes later, he heard footsteps on the stairs, and then Katie Ann appeared.

His heart felt twisted as he took in her red, puffy eyes and the sadness etched in her face. She looked as if she had cried for hours, and he longed to take her into his arms and comfort her.

"Chris." She walked to the table and sat down across from him. "What are you doing here?"

"I was worried. I've been thinking about you all day, and when I got to Emma's . . . I wanted to talk to you." Chris reached across the table for her hands. "How are you?"

She stared at his hands for a moment, and then she set hers on the table, allowing him to take them in his.

"I guess you know what happened." Her voice was soft, her tone unsure.

He nodded. "*Ya.*" He forced a smile. "You can fix all this. Just tell Mandy and Ephraim you're sorry, and everything will be fine."

Her eyes narrowed as her lips pressed together into a thin line. "Why should I apologize? I didn't do anything wrong."

Chris squeezed her hands as he contemplated how to convince Katie Ann she'd been wrong. "I know you're hurting right now, but I bet you all could have handled the situation differently."

"How could you possibly know that, or how I feel? You weren't there." She pulled her hands out of his grasp and sat up straight, lifting her chin.

Losing the contact of her skin left a coldness in its wake.

"I understand you better than you think." He ran his fingers over the wooden tabletop as he spoke. "*Mei bruder* and I were always close, and we spent a lot of time together. We used to go hunting and fishing, and we'd talk for hours while we were on those trips together. Then it all changed when he met Mary—probably more than I let on when we talked about this before."

Scowling, she crossed her arms over her chest as she studied him.

"Arlan didn't have much time for me anymore once Mary became part of his life," Chris continued, despite her sour expression. "I remember one time I asked him to go fishing with me, and he said he couldn't because he was having supper at Mary's parents' *haus*. Another time he had to cancel his plans with me because he was going to take Mary to spend the day at a lake. I was angry, and I was hurt. In fact, I was jealous of Mary."

Her expression warmed slightly, and he was certain he spotted tears in her eyes.

"But then I realized I had overacted." He did his best to keep his words measured and not accusatory. "I knew in my heart that it was natural for Arlan to fall in love and to pull away from me and our parents. We're expected to meet someone, fall in love, get married, and start a family. It's a difficult transition, but it's what we're expected to do. Now Arlan is married, and Mary comes first in his life. But I know he loves our parents and me. And he's still my best *freind*. We see each other at work and church, and sometimes we still go fishing. I'll cherish the time we had together when we were younger. Our relationship has changed because we're older now, but we're still close. And he's still *mei bruder*."

He finished speaking, and a heavy silence filled the kitchen. Pressure built in his chest as he awaited her response.

Her eyes narrowed again as she leaned forward, her pretty face expressing more anger than before.

"What did I say wrong?" he asked.

"You think I overreacted?" She nearly spat the words at him.

He paused, uncertain how to respond.

"If I overreacted, then why have other people also noticed the change in Ephraim and Mandy?" Katie Ann's voice rose. "Rosalyn Beiler commented that Ephraim and Mandy never have time for anyone else lately. Clara had to get the baking supplies even though it was Mandy's turn because, she said, Mandy was too focused on Ephraim to remember them." She pointed to her chest. "How am I the bad person when others have said the same things I'm saying?"

"I think it's more complicated than that. I think this is just what happens when two people fall in love."

Her angry expression remained as she stood. "You should go."

"What?" He was stunned.

She pointed at him. "You don't understand how I feel."

Her furious words punched him in his gut.

"I do understand." He sank back into his chair. "Katie Ann, I came to see you because I was worried about you. I thought about you all day, and I prayed for you all day. I care about you." He took a deep breath. It was time to tell her how much he cared. He reached deep inside himself and found all the courage he could muster.

His hands trembled as he looked into her beautiful eyes. "In fact, I wanted to tell you that I love you."

Her eyes widened for a fraction of a moment, and then they narrowed one more time.

He sucked in a breath, awaiting a response, but she remained silent. He'd made a huge mistake. From her reaction, it was apparent the feeling wasn't mutual. The betrayal paralyzed him for a moment as he tried to recover.

He pushed back the chair and stood. "I'm sorry I came. Goodbye."

She stared up at him, a tear tracing her pink cheek.

He started for the door, his heart heavy and the weight of his disappointment and hurt bogging his steps.

When he'd made it outside, Chris looked up at the sky and shook his head. Not only had he misinterpreted Katie Ann's feelings for him, but he'd also stuck his nose in where it didn't belong.

He'd pushed Katie Ann away by telling her she'd overreacted, and the pain of her rejection crushed him.

Chris climbed into his buggy and guided his horse toward the road. Maybe somehow Katie Ann would realize he truly loved her. All he could do was pray for her and beg God to fix what had broken between them.

~

Katie Ann covered her face with her hands as sobs choked her. She'd lost three of the people she most cared for—Ephraim, Chris, and Mandy—in just a matter of hours. She folded her arms on the table and tried to calm herself as her tears continued to flow. Her mother's and Chris's words echoed through her mind, and soon guilt became a snake that twisted her insides.

What is wrong with me?

Maybe she had been too harsh with Mandy, and perhaps she had overreacted. But if that were true, why had her angry feelings overcome her? Didn't her feelings matter too?

As her tears subsided, she began to whisper a prayer. "I don't know what to do, Lord. I'm afraid I've lost three of the people I love the most in this world. Please help me figure out how to fix these broken relationships. Guide my heart, Lord, and help me make things right."

A calmness covered her heart, and she knew that with God's help, she'd fix things—somehow.

~

Katie Ann stepped into Emma's empty kitchen. She set a container of chocolate chip cookies on the counter, and when she felt Hank rub on her leg, she bent and rubbed his head.

"Katie Ann," Emma announced as she walked into the room. "It's so *gut* to see you. How are you? Have you worked things out with Mandy and Ephraim? They haven't said."

Katie Ann shook her head as tears filled her eyes. "No. I've wanted to apologize to them ever since we argued a few days ago, but they've been avoiding me, and I don't know what to say anyway." Her throat had thickened so much, her words barely squeezed out. "I'm so embarrassed. I realized Chris was right when he told me I overreacted, and now I'm afraid they'll never forgive me. It took all my courage just to come here today, assuming they would be here." She sniffed as a tear slipped down her cheek.

"Of course they'll forgive you." Emma led her to the table. They sat down on opposite sides, and Emma leaned in to take her hand. "They love you. They'll forgive you as soon as you tell them you're sorry."

"But what if they don't?" Katie Ann hated the whine in her voice. Ephraim was right. Too often she thought of herself before anyone else, and that had to change.

"They will." Emma squeezed her hand. "When I first started dating Henry, my best *friend*, Sally, was jealous too. She and I had a falling-out, and we didn't talk for about a week. Then she apologized, and I told her she'd always be my best *freind*. As I told you a few weeks ago, we're still close to this day." She smiled. "Mandy loves you. She won't give up on you. And neither will Ephraim."

Katie Ann wiped away her tears with the back of her hand. "You think so?"

"*Ya*, I know so." Emma pointed to the back door. "They're already out working in the garden. Go talk to them now."

"Okay." Katie Ann walked out to the porch and saw where Ephraim and Mandy were, side by side. Taking a deep, shuddering breath, she walked down the steps and to the garden. When she approached their row, she slowed her steps, silently hoping Emma was right.

Ephraim stood up straight and faced her, his expression warmer than she'd expected. Had he missed her as much as she'd missed him these past few days?

"May I please talk to you?" Katie Ann fingered her black apron as she came to a stop in front of him and Mandy. Her heart seemed caught in her throat as she studied them.

"*Ya*." Ephraim glanced at Mandy and then back at Katie Ann.

"I want to apologize." Her voice sounded shaky as guilt chewed on her stomach. "I was wrong to yell at both of you, and I'm really sorry. I've been immature, selfish, and mean. I'm *froh* that you found each other, and I realize that I need to back off and give you both space. I miss both of you, and I hope you can forgive me."

"I'm sorry too," Ephraim said. "I was too hard on you, and I was thoughtless. I'm sorry for all the terrible things I said."

"You are?"

To her surprise, Ephraim smiled. "Of course I am. You're my baby *schweschder*. I don't want to lose you. You're important to me." He pulled her in for a quick hug.

"You're important to me, too, Ephraim." Then Katie Ann turned to Mandy. "I really miss you."

"I miss you too." Mandy hugged her. "I'm sorry for being a bad *freind*. I'll try harder." Mandy sniffed and wiped her eyes. "And I realized you were right. I have alienated our *freinden*, and I haven't done my part with the garden. I've been too focused on Ephraim, and I need to find some balance. Also, I did ignore you, and I promise I'll do better." She smiled through her tears. "I want to hear all about Chris. Let's get together tonight and talk, okay? Just us *maed*. No *buwe*."

Katie Ann shook her head as dread poured through her. "There's nothing to talk about. Chris is upset with me."

"What happened?" Mandy's eyes widened.

"I argued with him too. I think it's over between us." Katie Ann bit back the bitter taste of regret.

"I think you're wrong." Mandy pointed past her. "He's watching you right now. Look."

Katie Ann spun and spotted Chris standing by the porch. He raised his hand and waved, and she returned the gesture.

"Go." Mandy gave her a little nudge. "Talk to him. We'll talk later. I promise."

"Okay." Katie Ann's heart thumped as she hurried across the porch. "Hi."

"Hi." Chris nodded toward the barn. "Can you talk?"

"*Ya.*" Anxiety curdled in her stomach as she walked beside him. She followed him inside the barn and then faced him. "I'm so sorry about what I said."

"It's okay." He touched her arm. "I'm sorry for coming on too strong."

"It's not you." She shook her head. "I was immature and self-ish. Everything you said was right. I did overreact, and I'm sorry." She looked into his kind eyes. "I understand if you want to break up with me, but I can't stand the thought of losing you. Please forgive me."

"Of course I forgive you." He cupped his hand to her cheek, and she leaned into his touch. "I'm just sorry that I hurt you. I only wanted to help."

"You did help." She blinked back tears. "You made me realize how wrong I've been about everything. I apologized to Ephraim and Mandy, and they forgave me. Mandy said she's going to make time for me, and we're going to talk more later. *Danki* for making me realize that my relationship with her and Ephraim will change, but I won't lose them. I guess relationships are like gardens. We need to water them and weed them to keep them healthy, and then they'll continue to grow. It takes dedication and work, but it's worth it."

He smiled as he rubbed her cheek. "That's very true."

She studied his handsome face as she recalled their last conversation. "Did you mean what you said?"

"Did I mean what?"

"When you said you loved me?"

He nodded. "Of course I meant it."

"*Gut.*" She smiled. "Because I love you too."

Leaning down, Chris brushed his lips against hers, and the butterflies in her stomach crashed together. She closed her eyes and enjoyed the feel of his kiss, his warmth wrapping around her like a comfortable blanket.

"*Ich liebe dich,*" he whispered in her ear, and his breath stirred the tiny hairs on her neck.

"I love you too," she said. "*Danki* for believing in me."

~

On Sunday afternoon, Katie Ann smiled as she sat on a grassy hill next to Mandy while Chris and Ephraim played volleyball with youth group members.

"It's the perfect day." Mandy tented her hand over her eyes.

"*Ya*, it is." Katie Ann looked at her. "I'm so *froh* we worked things out. I really did miss you."

"I missed you too." Mandy touched Katie Ann's arm. "I promise I won't let anything come between us again. If you start to feel like I'm pulling away, let me know, okay?"

"I will." Katie Ann looked at the makeshift volleyball court on the Beiler family's meadow. Chris served the ball with a perfect flourish.

Mandy scooted closer to Katie Ann. "How are things with Chris?"

"Great." Katie Ann felt her smile widen. "I've never been happier." Her thoughts turned to Mandy's relationship with her brother. Even if it might be awkward, she should ask. "How about you and Ephraim?"

Mandy shrugged and then laughed. "Perfect."

"Great."

They talked about their boyfriends for a few minutes until the volleyball game broke up and the men joined them.

Chris dropped down beside Katie Ann on the grass. "Were you impressed by my volleyball skills?" He took a drink from the bottle of water she'd kept for him.

"Of course." She rested her head on his shoulder, and Chris kissed the top of her head.

She smiled up at him and then glanced at Mandy and Ephraim, who were so obviously in love.

Closing her eyes, she silently thanked God, not just for the opportunity to serve her community with the special garden, but because he'd used it to bring her and Chris together.

DISCUSSION QUESTIONS

1. Katie Ann feels invisible when Ephraim and Mandy are together. Think of a time when you felt lost and alone. Where did you find your strength? What Bible verses would help?

2. Chris tries to encourage Katie Ann to accept how her relationship with her brother is changing by sharing a story of how his relationship with his brother changed when Arlan started dating and then got married. Can you relate to his story? Share this with the group.

3. The youth in Emma's community started a garden in memory of her late husband and to raise money for the local homeless shelter. Have you ever been involved in a local community project? What was it?

4. Which character can you identify with the most? Which character seemed to carry the most emotional stake in the story? Was it Katie Ann, Mandy, Chris, or someone else?

5. Emma tells Katie Ann a story about how her friend Sally was jealous when she started dating Henry. Then she encourages Katie Ann to apologize to Mandy, Ephraim, and Christian. Do you agree with Emma's assessment of the situation? Why or why not?

6. Katie Ann realizes at the end of the story that she overreacted when she yelled at Mandy, Ephraim, and Chris. What do you think caused her to change her point of view throughout the story?

ACKNOWLEDGMENTS

As always, I'm grateful for my loving family, including my mother, Lola Goebelbecker; my husband, Joe; and my sons, Zac and Matt.

Special thanks to my mother and my dear friend Becky Biddy, who graciously proofread the draft and corrected my hilarious typos.

I'm also grateful for my special Amish friend who patiently answers my endless stream of questions. You're a blessing in my life.

Thank you to my wonderful church family at Morning Star Lutheran in Matthews, North Carolina, for your encouragement, prayers, love, and friendship. You all mean so much to my family and me.

Thank you to Zac Weikal and the fabulous members of my Bakery Bunch! I'm so grateful for your friendship and your excitement about my books. You all are awesome!

To my agent, Natasha Kern—I can't thank you enough for your guidance, advice, and friendship. You are a tremendous blessing in my life.

Thank you to my amazing editor, Jocelyn Bailey, for your friendship and guidance. I'm grateful to each and every person at

HarperCollins Christian Publishing who helped make this book a reality.

I'm grateful to editor Jean Bloom, who helped me polish and refine the story. Jean, you are a master at connecting the dots and filling in the gaps. I'm so happy we can continue to work together!

Thank you most of all to God—for giving me the inspiration and the words to glorify you. I'm grateful and humbled you've chosen this path for me.

HOME BY SUMMER

For my wonderful agent, Natasha Kern, with love

GLOSSARY

ach: oh
aenti: aunt
appeditlich: delicious
bedauerlich: sad
boppli: baby
brot: bread
bruder: brother
bruders: brothers
bruderskinner: nieces/nephews
bu: boy
buwe: boys
daadi: grandfather
danki: thank you
dat: dad
dochder: daughter
dochdern: daughters
Dummle!: Hurry!
fraa: wife
freind: friend
freinden: friends

froh: happy
gegisch: silly
gern gschehne: you're welcome
Gude mariye: Good morning
gut: good
Gut nacht: Good night
haus: house
Ich liebe dich: I love you
kaffi: coffee
kapp: prayer covering or cap
kichli: cookie
kichlin: cookies
kinner: children
krank: ill
kuche: cake
kuchen: cakes
kumm: come
liewe: love, a term of endearment
maed: young women, girls
maedel: young woman
mamm: mom
mammi: grandmother
mei: my
naerfich: nervous
narrisch: crazy
oncle: uncle
schee: pretty
schmaert: smart
schtupp: family room
schweschder: sister
schweschdere: sisters
sohn: son

GLOSSARY

Was iss letz?: What's wrong?
Wie geht's: How do you do? or Good day!
wunderbaar: wonderful
ya: yes

Family Tree

Featuring *The Christmas Cat* novella characters from
the collection *An Amish Christmas Love*.

Thelma m. Alfred Bender
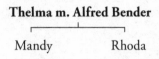
Mandy   Rhoda

Leona m. Marlin Blank
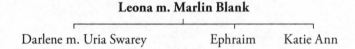
Darlene m. Uria Swarey   Ephraim   Katie Ann

Emma m. Henry (deceased) Bontrager
Hank the Cat

Darlene m. Uria Swarey
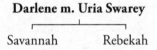
Savannah   Rebekah

Marietta m. Roman Hertzler
Clara

Gertrude m. Elvin King
Wayne

Feenie m. Jeptha Lantz
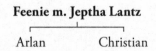
Arlan   Christian

Saloma m. Floyd Petersheim
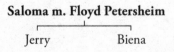
Jerry   Biena

CHAPTER 1

"Oh no!"

Clara Hertzler dropped another ripe red strawberry into her basket as she looked toward Emma Bontrager's house. The Beiler sisters were standing by the water spigot near the back porch, staring at it. Clara wiped her hands down her black apron, lifted her full basket, and headed their way.

The hot early June sun beat down on her neck as she caught up to Rosalyn and Ellen.

"Try it again," Ellen said as she pointed to the faucet.

"I did try it," Rosalyn snapped. "It doesn't work."

"Is the faucet broken?" Clara asked as she set the basket on the edge of the porch.

"*Ya*, I think so. What are we going to do now? How are we going to water our crops?" Rosalyn gestured toward the half-acre garden their area youth tended so they could raise money for charity in memory of Emma's late husband, Henry.

"We'll carry the water cans into the kitchen and fill them there," Clara said. "We'll just have to make do until we can get a plumber here."

"Why do we need a plumber?" Ephraim Blank asked as he approached with his girlfriend, Mandy Bender, in tow.

"The spigot stopped working." Ellen pointed to it.

"When did that happen?" Ephraim bent down and began to examine it.

"Just a few minutes ago," Rosalyn said. "I was going to fill my can and start watering the lettuce beds."

"Have you ever fixed a spigot?" Mandy asked Ephraim. A smile tugged at her lips.

"No." Ephraim shook his head as he fiddled with the handle. "But it can't be too difficult, can it?"

"*Ya*, it can be." Mandy crossed her arms over her black apron. "You don't want to make it worse and then cause a big plumbing mess for Emma, do you? Remember, this is Emma's *haus*, not yours."

Clara held back a snort as Ephraim glared at his girlfriend.

"I'm going to go wash these strawberries and get them ready to sell at the stand." Clara glanced at Mandy. "You might want to ask Wayne if he knows a plumber. His *dat* seems to have a lot of contacts in the community."

"That's a *gut* idea." Mandy tapped Ephraim's shoulder. "Why don't we find a professional?"

Ephraim heaved a loud sigh. "You have very little faith in me, *mei liewe*."

"I do have faith in you, but I think we should find the right person to fix the spigot." Mandy grinned, her face lighting up.

Clara smiled as she carried the basket up the porch steps. She could see how Ephraim couldn't resist Mandy, with her gorgeous hair the color of sunshine and her beautiful eyes a striking blue. She wasn't exactly jealous of Mandy and Ephraim's relationship, but she often wondered if she'd ever find someone who would love her the way Ephraim obviously loved Mandy.

It seemed as if love was in the air. Her close friend Katie Ann, Ephraim's younger sister, had met and fallen in love with Chris Lantz in the spring.

Pretty soon I'll be the only maedel *in my baptism class who isn't engaged or married.*

Clara stepped into the kitchen and made her way to the sink. God would reveal his plan for her soon enough. In the meantime, she would enjoy these days of fun and friendship.

"Look at those *schee* strawberries!" Emma clapped her hands as she appeared beside Clara. Her warm brown eyes sparkled as she picked up a bright-red strawberry and examined it. Although she was in her late sixties, Clara and Katie Ann frequently marveled that Emma looked much younger with her youthful face and the dark hair that revealed only a hint of gray. "We've been blessed with such a *wunderbaar* crop this summer."

"I know." Clara nodded as she began to wash the strawberries. "I don't think we'll have any trouble selling these at the roadside stand. After subtracting our expenses, we've already raised more than six hundred dollars to give to the Bird-in-Hand Shelter. I'm so thankful the garden has been such a success."

"I am too." Emma pulled out the drainboard. "Let me help you. We can put these in the plastic containers and then take some of them down to the stand right away."

"*Danki.*" Clara's thoughts turned to the outside spigot. "The faucet outside isn't working. We need a plumber."

"Really?" Emma turned toward her.

"*Ya.* Rosalyn and Ellen were trying to fill their watering cans, but there was no water pressure." When Emma's forehead pinched, Clara added, "The garden committee will take care of the cost."

"Oh, I'm not concerned about that." Emma waved off the comment. "I just hate the inconvenience."

"We'll manage. We can just bring our watering cans in here to fill them." As Clara washed another strawberry, she felt something soft rub against her leg, and she looked down at Emma's fat, orange tabby cat and grinned. "Hi, Hank."

Hank invited himself to move in with Emma on Christmas Eve during a snowstorm, and despite her efforts to shoo him away, Hank had stayed, becoming the widow's sweet and constant companion.

"I'm surprised Hank isn't outside helping with the weeding," Clara said.

"He was outside earlier, but he came in for a snack. Sometimes I wonder if he likes to come inside to check on me." Emma smiled down at the cat before she began drying the strawberries and setting them in the clear plastic containers they used to sell them.

"I'm sure he does check on you." Clara opened her mouth to make another comment about the cat, but then the loud put-put-puttering sound of an engine blasted through the kitchen windows. "What on earth is that?"

Clara moved to the far window and peeked out as an older-looking, mint-green pickup truck stopped at the top of the driveway. The engine died with a loud sputter before the driver's side door opened, and a tall man with sandy-blond hair, mirrored sunglasses, tan cargo shorts, and a blue T-shirt emerged from the truck's cab.

"Emma," Clara said, tossing the words over her shoulder, "do you know an *Englisher* who drives a mint-green pickup truck?"

"No, I don't think I do." Emma sidled next to her. "He doesn't look familiar."

Wayne King, Ephraim, and Mandy all walked over to the truck, and the men shook the driver's hand. Clara stared at the mysterious guest. He looked familiar to her, but she wasn't sure why.

When Biena Petersheim came around from the other side of the truck and stepped toward Mandy, Clara gasped in recognition. "Oh, my goodness! It's Jerry Petersheim!"

"Jerry Petersheim?" Emma asked. "You mean Saloma and Floyd's *sohn?*"

"*Ya*. He looks so different from when we went to school and youth group together. I know he isn't Amish anymore, but it still feels strange to see him dressed like an *Englisher*." She leaned forward on the windowsill as she took in Jerry's appearance. He was taller—much taller. He used to match Clara's five feet seven, but now he stood just under Ephraim's six feet. And he seemed more muscular as he leaned against his truck and crossed his arms over his wide chest.

Although Clara saw Jerry's parents and younger sister in church every other week, she hadn't seen him there in five years. When she had occasionally spotted him around town dressed like an *Englisher*, she'd longed to understand what had caused him to leave the faith and abandon the culture into which they had both been born and raised.

She marveled once again at how *English* he looked. Jerry wasn't dressed like Ephraim and Wayne, with their broadfall trousers, plain button-down shirts, and suspenders. And while Ephraim and Wayne both wore their hair in a traditional bowl cut, Jerry sported a fancier *Englisher* hairstyle, long on top and short on the sides and in the back.

New confusion washed over Clara as she studied her old friend. Why had Jerry left their faith? He'd seemed happy enough when they were in school, but when his younger sister joined the church two years ago, he wasn't even there. Why would Jerry choose to be *English*? His parents and Biena never said.

"Clara?" Emma touched her arm. "Are you okay?"

"*Ya*." Clara forced a smile as she looked at Emma. "I'm just surprised to see Jerry here. I've spotted him in town a few times, but we were never close enough to speak."

The storm door opened and clicked shut before Biena stepped into the kitchen. "Clara!" She rushed over and hugged her. "How are you? I told you at church that I'd come today." At nineteen, Biena was four years younger than Clara, and the sandy-blond hair that peeked out from her prayer covering reminded Clara of Jerry's. But her eyes weren't as bright blue as Clara remembered his eyes were.

"*Ya*, you did. I'm so glad you could make it."

"How are you, Emma?" Biena turned to the older woman and hugged her too.

"It's nice to see you," Emma said. "Are you here to help with the garden?"

"*Ya*, I am." Biena's smile widened. "I heard a few other members of my youth group talking about it, and I wanted to come out." She pointed toward the back door. "Mandy said I might be able to help you with the strawberries. She said we can package them up and then take them out to the stand."

"That's a great idea." Clara motioned for Biena to join them at the sink. "We'll have this done in no time at all." As she washed more strawberries, Biena and Emma dried them and put them in the containers. Her mind spun with questions about Jerry. "I'm so surprised to see your *bruder* here."

"*Ya*. He agreed to drop me off." Biena closed a full container of strawberries. "When he saw Ephraim and Wayne were here, he decided to visit with them."

"What's he doing these days?" Clara washed the last strawberry.

"He started working for our *onkel* Saul's plumbing business about four years ago."

"He's a plumber?" Clara spun toward her. "He's here just in time, then."

Biena shrugged. "Why?"

"I wonder if he can fix the outside spigot." Clara pointed toward the window. "It stopped working."

"Oh." Biena nodded. "You should go ask him before he leaves. I'll carry these down to the stand for you."

"*Danki.*"

Once outside, Clara saw Jerry was still leaning against his truck and talking to Ephraim and Wayne. He had his head bent back as he laughed at something someone said, and Clara felt transported back in time, to when they were in school. Jerry's laughter still seemed larger than life. A smile tugged at her lips as she approached him. When his gaze met hers, his own smile widened.

"Clara." Jerry stood up straight. "How long has it been?"

"Too long." Clara smiled. "Biena mentioned you're a plumber."

"I am." He rubbed the stubble on his chin. "Are you looking for one?"

"*Ya*, we are." She pointed toward the house. "Our outside spigot stopped working. Would you please look at it?"

"Sure." Jerry climbed up into the bed of his truck, opened a large toolbox, and pulled out a tool bag.

Ephraim turned to Clara. "I'm glad you thought to ask him. We were too busy reminiscing."

Jerry hopped down from the truck and walked over to her. "So where exactly is this spigot?"

"I'll show you." As they walked together, Clara admired how grown up Jerry looked. His hair was thicker and his jawline stronger, making him seem more mature. He wasn't a skinny teenager anymore.

"The garden is incredible." He gestured toward the rows of crops, where several groups of young people were weeding or harvesting the early fruits and vegetables. "Ephraim and Wayne were telling me how this project came about. It's really amazing."

"*Ya*, I'm thankful to be a part of it." She looked up at him. "It was nice of you to bring Biena by."

He nodded, and she longed to read his mind. Why had he turned away from their church?

When they reached the back porch, she pointed to the spigot. "There it is."

"All right." He leaned over and began to fiddle with it. After a few moments, he had it off and turned it over in his hands. "Looks like it needs to be replaced."

"Can you do that?"

"It's not difficult. All I need to do is—" An electronic ring sounded, and he reached into his shorts pocket and pulled out a cell phone. "Hello?" He nodded while listening. "Yeah, I'll be there. I just need about an hour or so to help a friend. All right. Bye." He disconnected the call and slipped the phone back into his pants pocket.

Clara shook her head as she stared up at him. "What happened to you?" The question slipped from her lips without any forethought.

Jerry's lips flattened into a thin line for a fraction of a second, and then his smile returned. "I need to run to the hardware store for supplies, but I'll be right back. It won't take me long to fix this."

"Wait." She reached for his arm but then pulled back her hand. "Do you need money?"

"No. It won't cost much at all." With a quick nod, he walked away.

Clara stared after him, her mind still spinning with questions.

"Clara!" Biena called from the porch, balancing six containers of strawberries in her arms. "Would you please help me carry these strawberries out to the stand? We have a lot more than I thought."

"*Ya.*" Clara hurried up the steps and took three of the containers from Biena's arms.

"*Danki,*" Biena said as they started down the steps together. "Did Jerry look at the spigot?"

"*Ya.* He says he can fix it, but he had to go buy supplies. He'll be back." Clara looked toward Jerry's truck, where he was again talking with Ephraim and, this time, with Chris as well.

Jerry said something to Ephraim as he nodded toward the

house, and then he climbed into his truck. The pickup roared to life, and then he backed it down the driveway and soon disappeared down the road.

"May I ask you something?" Clara said as she and Biena walked down the rock driveway.

"Of course." Biena smiled at her.

"Why did Jerry leave the church?"

When Biena's smile faded, regret tightened Clara's throat. "I'm sorry. That was too personal."

"No, it's okay." Biena's smile was back, but it seemed to wobble a bit. "I don't know why he decided to become *English*. My parents used to try to encourage him to join the church, but it always ended in an argument. When he moved out and started renting a room from our *onkel*, my parents stopped trying to change his mind. They wanted him to at least visit us, and he does. He also runs errands for *mei mamm* nearly every week to help her out."

"Oh." Disappointment filled Clara's chest. She'd last spent any time with him at a youth gathering when they were both seventeen. And now she hardly recognized the man he had become.

"But he's *mei bruder*, and I still love him." Biena's happiness somehow seemed forced. Clara assumed she was disappointed in his decision to be *English* too.

They approached the stand, where Katie Ann Blank stood selling to two *English* women. One of the women looked at Clara and Biena and gasped. "Blanche! Look at those strawberries."

The other woman echoed the gasp. "They're lovely! We have to take some of those home too." She turned to Katie Ann. "How much are they?"

Clara and Biena set the strawberries on the counter while Katie Ann quoted the price. After the women paid for their purchases, they thanked Katie Ann and left in a red SUV.

Biena rubbed her hands together. "I'm ready to work."

"Okay." Katie Ann laughed. "Do you want to help me with the stand?"

"You're not ready for a break?" Clara asked.

"No." Katie Ann waved off the question. "I'd rather be here than weeding." She gave a little laugh, her cheeks reddening. "Is it bad to admit that?"

"No." Clara smiled. "I'd honestly rather work in the garden than sit down here at the stand."

"How about I help Katie Ann and you pick more strawberries?" Biena suggested.

"Sounds great. Come and get me if you need me." Clara waved good-bye and headed back to the garden.

She had nearly filled another basket with strawberries by the time Jerry's truck pulled back into the driveway. When her basket was full, she carried it toward the house, keeping her gaze trained on Jerry. He was squatting next to the spigot, and he seemed to be rebuilding it. She set the full basket on the porch and walked over to him.

"How's it going?" She pushed her prayer covering ribbons behind her shoulders.

He looked up at her. "All right. I'm almost done."

With his sunglasses off, she had a full view of his cobalt-blue eyes. She'd forgotten just how blue they were. The urge to get reacquainted took hold of her. She grabbed an empty bucket, turned it over, and sat down beside him.

"So how have you been?" she asked.

"*Gut.*" He gave her a sideways glance. "How about you?"

"Fine." She needed to pull him into a conversation. "How's your family?"

His lips quirked. "I think you know the answer to that. You see them every other Sunday at church."

"Right." She gave a little laugh as her cheeks heated.

"How are your parents, Clara?"

"Fine." She shrugged. "*Mei dat* still builds sheds with his *bruders*. Mei mamm* still has her seamstress business. They're both still as ornery as ever."

He chuckled. "Glad to hear it."

"I heard you're working for your *onkel*."

"*Ya*. I work full-time for *mei onkel* Saul and rent a room from him. I'm saving to move out. I haven't decided if I'm going to rent a place or buy one."

"Why did you go to work for your *onkel* when you always worked for your *dat*'s farm?"

"I guess I needed a change." He shrugged. "*Mei onkel* offered me the job, and *Dat* told me to take it. He hired someone else to help him."

She studied his easy expression, searching for any sign of a lie. Did his father tell him to do that because his uncle isn't Amish? She pushed the thought away. It wasn't her concern.

"Do you like being a plumber?" she asked instead.

"*Ya*, sure. It's challenging. I seem to learn something new every day, and there's always something to be fixed."

"Oh." She felt the urge to ask him if he had a girlfriend, but that seemed too personal and pushy. Still the question echoed through her mind.

"I suppose you're not married yet," Jerry said.

His directness caught her off guard, and her mouth dropped open.

He laughed. "I'll take that as a no."

"If I were married, I'd be too busy to spend my Saturday afternoon working here." She gestured toward the garden.

"That's true."

She tilted her head. "How about you?"

"Married?" He shook his head as he put the new spigot on. "No. I don't even have time to date."

So that answered her question.

"What about you?" he asked, his focus on his task.

"I'm not dating anyone." She gathered the folds of her blue dress in her hands as she watched him work. She wanted to know why he hadn't joined the church when they were eighteen as she had, along with their friends. But asking something so personal would be even more rude and pushy than asking if he had a girlfriend.

He finished fiddling with the spigot and then turned the handle. When water began flowing, she clapped.

"*Danki,*" she said. "Let me pay you."

"That's not necessary."

"At least let me pay for the materials."

"No. It really wasn't a big deal." He began packing up his tools. "I have to get going. *Mei onkel* called me earlier about an emergency job out in Strassburg."

"Oh." She longed to find a reason to keep him there. What was wrong with her? "Are you coming back to help us with the garden?"

"Maybe." He stood and picked up his tool bag. "I guess I'll see you soon."

"Okay."

As he walked to his truck, she realized she'd like to see him again very soon.

⁓

"I saw Jerry Petersheim today," Clara told her mother as she dried the supper dishes later that evening.

"Really?" *Mamm* looked up from washing a platter. "Where did you see him?"

"At Emma's. He dropped off Biena, and then he stayed to fix Emma's outside spigot." Clara set a stack of three dinner plates in a cabinet. "I know he left the faith, but it still seems strange to see him dressed as an *Englisher*."

"*Ya*, I know. I've seen him around town." *Mamm* rinsed the platter and set it in the drying rack.

"He rents a room from his *onkel* and works for his plumbing business. He has a cell phone and drives a pickup truck. I was so surprised, since we were such *gut freinden* in school." Who was she kidding? She'd had a crush on him for years and had even dreamt of dating him after they were both baptized. But that didn't happen.

"Unfortunately, some Amish people do make that decision." *Mamm* shook her head as she turned her attention to washing a large serving bowl.

"What was it like when your *bruder* left the church?" Clara asked.

Mamm's shoulders sagged. "It was terrible. My parents were so upset."

"Did they try to convince him to stay and join the church?"

"*Ya*, we all did, but our efforts just pushed him further away. As I've told you, he moved to Maryland and married a woman he met at work." *Mamm* kept her gaze fixed on the bowl. "I still send him a Christmas card every year and hope he'll respond. He hasn't, but the cards have never been returned to me. I assume that means he still lives in the same *haus*."

"Do you think you could have eventually convinced him to stay in the church if he hadn't moved away?"

"I don't know." *Mamm* rinsed the bowl and set it in the rack. "Sometimes I wonder if I should have tried harder, but then again, I pushed him away as it was."

As Clara put away the dried platter, an idea filled her mind. What if she could find the right words to convince Jerry to return to the Amish church? He couldn't be happy divided from his family. And maybe she could get to know him again in the process.

CHAPTER 2

R elief flooded Jerry as he stared at his mother's shopping list
and crossed off the last item. He was happy to do her a favor.
She'd always bent over backward to take care of both his sister and
him. But he despised grocery shopping and would rather be anywhere else than the market.

He glanced at the lunch meat counter as he pushed his grocery
cart toward the cashier. When his eyes fell on a young woman who
looked like Clara, he stilled. She said something to the Amish man
behind the counter and then laughed.

Jerry grinned. Yes, that was Clara. He'd never mistake her
laugh. He adored the sweet, rich sound that seemed to fill the
room with warmth, and it tugged at his heartstrings.

He leaned forward on the cart and continued to study her.
She looked radiant in a cranberry-colored dress that complemented
her gorgeous coffee-colored eyes and the dark-brown hair he could
glimpse from beneath her prayer covering. She was always pretty
when they were growing up together, but she seemed somehow
different now—more mature with her long, slender neck and high
cheekbones.

He'd imagined the eager young men in her youth group would
jump at the chance to date someone as beautiful, sweet, and funny

as she was. A few of his friends had even confessed they wanted to date her after they were baptized.

Jealousy was a bitter taste in his mouth.

He mentally shook himself. Why should he care if Clara dated his friends? He'd met lots of pretty girls in the bars his *English* friends invited him to. Besides, he wasn't even Amish. Any relationship with her beyond friendship was forbidden. In fact, she would be shunned if she dated him.

Not that she would even be interested in him.

In a flash, she turned toward him. He'd been caught.

"Jerry!" She waved. "How long have you been standing there staring at me?"

"Staring at you?" He straightened and clicked his tongue. "What makes you think I was staring at you? I was looking for roast beef, but you were blocking my way." He pushed the cart toward her.

She laughed, and he enjoyed the sound once again. "What brings you here today?"

He pointed to the shopping cart. "*Mei mamm* gave me a list."

"Shouldn't you be at work?"

"I finished a job early, so I thought I'd be a dutiful *sohn* and see if *mei mamm* needed anything at the market." He rolled his eyes. "I think she was waiting for my call."

"Well, that was nice of you." She set a bag in the shopping basket hanging on her arm. "I had to get lunch meat and rolls to share at Emma's today. It's my turn to bring the snack."

"Let me take that." He reached for the basket, and when his hand brushed hers, he felt a flare of heat. Had she felt it too? Her eyes didn't show any reaction, so he must have imagined it. He set her basket in his cart.

"*Danki.*" She walked beside him toward the cashier. "It's hot out there today, huh?"

"*Ya.*" He nodded. "It feels like summer."

"It sure does." She fingered her black apron. Was she nervous? They never had any trouble talking at school or youth group.

"Is Biena coming to help at the garden today?" she asked.

"*Ya.* I'm supposed to drop her off a little later."

"Great. She's *gut* help." She paused for a moment. "Maybe I'll get to see you for a minute or two when you drop her off."

"That sounds *gut.*" Did she want to see him as much as he wanted to see her?

When they reached the cashier, Clara put her items on the counter and paid. Then she turned to him and gave him another wave. "It was *gut* seeing you."

"You too." He smiled at her. "Take care."

"Hopefully I'll see you later at Emma's."

"*Ya.*"

As she disappeared through the doors, he longed to ask her to wait for him. He quickly paid for his groceries and then hurried out to the parking lot. He loaded his bags into his toolbox and then motored across the lot, where he spotted Clara heading toward the road. Had she walked to the grocery store? If so, this was the perfect opportunity to spend more time with her.

"Hey there," he said through the cab's open window as he drove alongside her. "Need a ride to Emma's?"

She touched her chin as if debating her answer, and her brown eyes sparkled with mischief. "*Mei mamm* told me not to accept rides from strangers."

"What if I tell you my name before you get in?"

She laughed as he stopped the truck.

"Please get in," he said.

"Fine." She jogged around the front of the truck, wrenched open the door and climbed into the passenger seat before pulling the door shut. She glanced around the cab as she fastened her seat belt. "This is a nice truck. I like it."

"*Danki.*" He steered through the parking lot. "I bought it from *mei onkel.*"

"What year is it?"

"It's a 1964 Chevrolet."

"Wow. It's a lot older than we are, huh?" She ran her hand over the dashboard.

"I needed a truck, and the price was right." He pulled onto the road.

"Why don't we stop at your parents' *haus* first and pick up Biena? Then you can drop both of us off at Emma's."

"That's a *gut* idea." He turned toward the road that led to his parents' house and glanced at her. "Why did you walk to the market instead of calling a driver?"

The breeze from the open window caused the ties on her prayer covering to flutter over her slight shoulders. "It's a *schee* day, and it's not far from *mei haus* to the market and then to Emma's. I couldn't justify wasting money on a ride on a day like this." Her smile faded. "You're not going to charge me, are you?"

"Are you serious?" he deadpanned.

"No." She laughed, and then her expression became almost pensive. "Tell me, Jerry. You told me you live at your *onkel's haus* and work for his plumbing business, but other than that, where have you been for five years?"

"Why? Have you been looking for me?"

"No." She shook her head, and he was almost certain she blushed. "I just wonder what you were up to. When I asked your family how you were, they said you were fine, but not much else. And I didn't want to pry."

She asked about me? The notion took him by surprise for a moment, trapping his words in his throat.

"So where were you hiding?" She leaned forward, her eyes almost flirty.

"I wasn't hiding anywhere," he insisted. "I told you, I've just been living with my *onkel* and working."

"Huh. It's funny that I haven't run into you before now, although I saw you from a distance around town a few times." She tilted her head. "We had a lot of fun in school, didn't we?"

"Yeah, we did," he agreed with a grin. "You always made me laugh with jokes during class. We got in trouble more than once thanks to you making a funny face when we were supposed to be listening."

"*Ya*, but *mei mamm* didn't think it was funny when we had to stay after to clean because Teacher Marian said we were 'disruptive.'" She made air quotes with her fingers as if to quote the teacher. "But we thought it was hilarious."

She looked out the window and then at him once again. "I always appreciated how you defended me on the playground when Roy Zook used to make fun of how I threw the softball or missed a hit." She rolled her eyes. "He made recess a nightmare for me."

He frowned. "I never could stand him after that."

"But you took care of him, didn't you?" She leaned over again, and he caught a whiff of her flowery shampoo.

Why did the aroma make his pulse race?

He did a mental headshake.

"Didn't you?" she repeated the question.

He shrugged as if it weren't a big deal that he had, in fact, found a way to stop the bullying.

"What did you do?" She poked his arm.

"I simply told Roy if he didn't leave you alone, I would tell everyone in class about the time he cried like a baby after falling out of a tree when we were six."

Her grin widened. "What happened?"

"You already know his farm is located on the same street as *mei dat's*," he began, and she nodded. "We decided to climb that big cherry tree in my yard. He fell out and skinned his knees, and then he sobbed for his *mamm* for nearly an hour. He made me promise I would never tell anyone because he was afraid his three older *bruders* would harass him."

He signaled and steered onto the long dirt road that led to his father's place. "One day when he made you cry, I'd had enough. I followed him home and told him if he ever teased you again, I would tell the details of that day not just to his *bruders*, but to the entire class."

She gasped. "You didn't!"

"I most certainly did."

"This is why I declared you my best *freind* when we were ten."

He felt a strange stirring in his chest at her words. Why was he so emotional today?

As if oblivious to his inner turmoil, Clara gazed out the windshield as his father's brick, two-story farmhouse came into view. She smiled at him. "I spent a lot of time here as a kid. I still remember playing softball with you, Biena, and our *freinden* in your *dat's* big field. We had so much fun."

"Yeah, we sure did." He parked the truck by the back porch and pushed open his door.

She hopped down from the truck and went around to his side. "Is your *mamm* home?"

"She should be." He retrieved the grocery bags from the toolbox. "Let's see."

He followed her up the porch steps and into the house. When they stepped into the kitchen from the mudroom, they found his mother standing at the counter, flipping through a cookbook.

"Hi, Saloma!" Clara rushed over and gave her a hug.

Jerry grinned as he set the grocery bags on the table. Clara had never been shy with her affection.

"Clara!" *Mamm* exclaimed. "What a nice surprise." She turned to Jerry, her eyebrows lifted. "I didn't expect you to bring Clara home with the groceries."

Clara chuckled. "We ran into each other at the market, and he offered to give me a ride to Emma's *haus*."

"Isn't that nice." *Mamm*'s expression seemed to hold something other than mirth, giving him pause. What was she planning?

Clara moved to the table and began opening the bags. "Why don't I help you put your groceries away?"

"Oh no." *Mamm* waved off the offer. "You can get on to Emma's *haus*. I think Biena is ready to go too. She just went upstairs to get something."

"I'll get her." Jerry went to the hallway and stood at the bottom of the stairs. "Beanie! Are you ready to go to Emma's?"

"I've told you not to call me that!" Biena growled from the second floor.

Jerry snickered as he leaned on the banister.

"Are you still teasing her?" Clara appeared in the kitchen doorway.

"Isn't that my job as her big *bruder*?"

"No, it's not!" Biena snapped as she started down the stairs. "He should respect his younger *schweschder*."

"You know I love you." He smirked at Biena, and she rolled her eyes. "Hey, I came by to pick you up, didn't I?"

"You had to come anyway since you picked up *Mamm*'s groceries." Biena reached the bottom stair and smiled at Clara. "Clara. I didn't realize you were here."

"Your *bruder* found me at the market and dragged me here." Clara bumped his shoulder, and he enjoyed the easy teasing.

"Yup. I threw her into the truck as she kicked and screamed." He motioned toward the back of the house. "We should go."

He followed the women into the kitchen, where Biena hugged *Mamm*.

"I'll be back for supper," Biena said.

"Have fun." *Mamm* waved at Clara. "It was nice seeing you."

"You too." Clara waved back. "I'll see you at church." As she left the kitchen with Biena, Jerry started to follow.

"Jerry," *Mamm* said, and he spun to face her. "It's *gut* seeing you with Clara again. It's been a long time since you two used to spend time together. I'm *froh* you've reconnected because of Emma's garden."

So she wasn't just happy to see Clara. She was thrilled to see *him* with Clara.

Jerry couldn't keep his lips from pressing into a flat line. His mother hadn't brought up his lack of commitment to the Amish church for a very long time, yet he could tell the familiar lecture was forming in her mind.

"You and Clara were always such *gut freinden*, and you can't deny that you care about her. Obviously, she hasn't married, and I don't remember hearing that she's ever dated anyone for long. If you came back to the church, maybe that friendship could turn into something more." *Mamm*'s bright-blue eyes glittered with hope.

He swallowed back the frustrated words that threatened to jump from his lips. His parents would never understand why he didn't feel the same connection to the church they did, that he'd never felt God calling him to join the church. And he didn't want their lectures to start again. They just added to the guilt he already felt.

But yelling at his sweet mother would be a sin, and he would never want to hurt her. Instead, he took a deep breath.

"*Mamm*." He held up his hand. "Please don't get your hopes up. I'm just giving Clara and Biena a ride to Emma's *haus*. There's no romance here. Now, I need to get going. We'll talk later, okay?"

She nodded and sniffed. Was she going to cry? Oh, he could never stand to see her cry. The idea made his heart fracture a little.

He was such a disappointment to his parents, but he couldn't force himself to be someone he wasn't.

He forced his lips into a smile. "I'll see you later, *Mamm.*"

Before she could respond, he hurried out the back door. Biena and Clara sat on the bench seat in his truck. When he saw his sister was sitting in the middle, disappointment curled through him. He'd hoped Clara would sit next to him.

Stop it! She's Amish, so don't waste your time thinking about her!

"Ready?" He climbed into the driver's seat and brought the rattling engine to life.

"We've been ready," Biena snapped. "You're the one who took forever to get out here."

Clara snickered beside her.

"Right." He steered the truck down the driveway to the main road.

"I was thinking we should work on the last of the strawberries this afternoon," Biena said as they drove down the road. "Rosalyn told me they're all ripe now, so we need to get them to the stand as soon as possible."

"That's a *gut* plan." Clara looked out the front window.

Biena continued. "I hope we have enough of those little plastic baskets."

His sister's discussion about strawberries served only as background noise as he drove to Emma's house. Considering his mother's words, he couldn't wipe the image of her hopeful face out of his mind. But no, he wasn't ready to give up his *Englisher* life yet. He might never be ready, not even for a beautiful woman like Clara. Besides, was being attracted to her a good reason to join the church?

His heart raced as he contemplated asking Clara on a date. They'd never discussed being more than friends, so how could he even assume she'd be interested in him that way, even if he were Amish? The thought haunted him as he halted the truck by Emma's barn.

"Hello!" Biena slapped his shoulder. "Are you even listening to me, Jerry?"

"What?" He put the truck in park and turned toward his sister.

She harrumphed as she folded her arms at her waist. "I asked you when you're going to pick me up."

"Oh." Jerry sighed. "What time do you want me to pick you up?"

They settled on a time, and then the women climbed out of the truck.

Biena left, but Clara walked around to the driver's side door and looked up at him. "You don't want to stay and help, huh?"

He looked toward the sectioned-off areas of the garden, where groups of young people worked, and he shook his head. "I'd be a liar if I said I enjoyed gardening."

"You could fix Emma's leaky kitchen sink along with her toilet that never stops running."

He looked down at her as she tilted her head and gave him a look of feigned disappointment.

"You don't want to help an older *freind* in need?" she asked.

"You're really *gut* at guilting people, aren't you?"

"The best." Her gorgeous grin was back.

"Fine." He blew out a sarcastic sigh.

"Yay." She clapped and took a step back as he climbed out of the truck.

"You always win." He shut the truck door.

She shrugged. "I do my best." Then she started toward the house with her grocery bag in hand. She swiveled toward him and waved. "I'll see you later."

CHAPTER 3

"Thank you for your purchase." Clara smiled at the two *Englisher* customers.

After handing the women their change, Clara loaded their strawberries and cookies into plastic bags. "Enjoy the rest of your day." She waved as they climbed into their car and drove off.

Clara turned to Katie Ann. "I can't believe how many pints of strawberries we've sold." After helping pick and clean strawberries for more than an hour, Clara had taken a turn at the stand.

"I know." Katie Ann rubbed Hank's chin as he sat on a stool beside her. "It's been busy. We've raised a lot more money for the Bird-in-Hand Shelter today."

"*Ya*, we have." Clara leaned on the counter in front of her and smiled. It was a perfect day—the sun was shining, she was working at Emma's house, and she'd managed to convince Jerry to help too. She stood up straight as the last thought echoed through her mind. How was she going to convince him to do something far more important—join the church?

"Hi." Biena approached them. "I was sent to relieve one of you."

"Oh." Katie Ann looked at Clara. "Would it be okay if I went? I haven't been able to talk to Chris all day."

"Sure." Clara gestured toward the barn. "Tell him hi for me."

"*Danki.*" Katie Ann rushed off, as if fearing Clara might change her mind.

Biena hopped onto the stool beside Clara and caressed Hank's ear. His purr grew louder as he tilted his head and closed his eyes. "You really have a gift with *mei bruder.*"

"What do you mean?" Clara blinked, stunned by the comment.

"This morning when I asked Jerry to drop me off here, I also asked him if he would stay and help. He had every excuse in the book. He even said he was going back to our *onkel's haus* to clean his room." She rolled her eyes. "I've never seen his room messy. He's always kept it neat and tidy."

She shifted her hand to Hank's other ear. "I was surprised when I went into Emma's kitchen and found him there working on the sink. He said you asked him to fix both the sink and the toilet, and that did the trick. You definitely know how to get him to do what you want."

"It's no big deal. I just guilted him into using his skills to help Emma." Clara tried to dismiss the comment as she sat down on the stool beside Biena.

"I think it's more than that." Biena smiled at her. "You and Jerry were always *gut freinden.* I'm not surprised he stayed when you asked."

"Right." Clara's cheeks burned as she looked toward the road. She needed to change the subject before Biena saw right through her confusing emotions.

The truth was she hadn't stopped thinking about Jerry since he first dropped Biena off at Emma's house. And she was overcome with excitement when she'd turned around in the market and found him watching her. She was even more thrilled when he offered to drive her to Emma's house.

When she turned nineteen, and had lost hope that Jerry was ever coming back to the church, she assumed she'd find an Amish man, fall in love, and eventually get married. But none of the young men who asked her to date them had warmed her heart. Her limited relationships had each lasted barely a month. But her heart had awakened since she'd reconnected with Jerry, and the realization scared her to the depth of her soul. How could she allow herself to be attracted to a man who wasn't Amish—and might never be? She couldn't bear to think of the hurt it would cause her family.

A car stopped in front of the stand, and she swallowed a sigh of relief. She needed the distraction from her thoughts of Jerry.

A tall woman clad in shorts and a pink T-shirt climbed out of the driver's seat. "I heard you're selling the best strawberries in all of Lancaster County."

"Yes, ma'am! We sure are!" Biena exclaimed.

The woman pulled a wallet from her purse. "I'd like to buy them all."

"All of them?" Clara asked.

"Yes. I'm planning a big party, and I want to make some strawberry shortcakes." The woman leaned on the counter. "How many containers do you have?"

Clara looked down on the shelves and counted. "Ten pints," she said.

"Great." As the woman began to glance around the shelves, Clara and Biena looked at each other, wide-eyed. "I'll also take ten trays of your cookies. A variety is fine. How much for all of that?"

Clara calculated the price, and the woman paid before Clara and Biena helped load all the items into her car.

"I'll go up to the *haus* for more strawberries," Clara said after the woman left. "We also need more *kichlin*. We're completely out of chocolate chip and macadamia."

"Okay." Biena pointed to Hank, who was happily napping on the third stool. "Hank and I will handle business while you're gone."

Clara laughed as she started up the driveway. She waved at

friends working in the garden before entering the house. When she stepped into the kitchen, she found Emma, Mandy, and Katie Ann washing cucumbers. Baskets of vegetables and fruits lined the kitchen table.

"We're out of strawberries and chocolate chip and macadamia *kichlin*," Clara announced.

"I'll have to make more *kichlin* in the morning," Mandy said. "It's too hot to turn on the oven now."

"And we're out of baskets for the strawberries," Katie Ann said. "We can't sell more until we get some."

"I'll take you to the store."

Clara turned to see Jerry standing in the doorway to the mud-room. He seemed larger than life with his wide shoulders and tall stature, and his dark-blue T-shirt accentuated his bright, intelligent eyes. She swallowed against her suddenly bone-dry throat.

Stop it! He's not for you! Not unless he joins the church.

"Aren't you busy?" Clara did her best to add an edge of annoyance in her voice to hide her surging attraction to him.

"I need to get a rebuild kit for the toilet." He pointed in the direction of the downstairs bathroom. "We can stop at whatever store you need."

"Let me give you some money." Emma started walking toward the family room.

"No, no." Jerry shook his head and held up his hand. "I can get it."

"Don't be *gegisch*." Emma rested her hands on her hips. "I don't expect you to pay for the parts to fix my toilet."

"It's only a few dollars. I can cover it, Emma." His voice was gentle but firm.

Emma folded her arms over her chest. "You *buwe* are so stubborn. I'll find another way to pay you. What's your favorite kind of *kichli*?"

"I've never met a *kichli* I didn't like."

As Jerry grinned, Clara's admiration for him swelled. He didn't want to come to Emma's, but now he was paying for the supplies to fix her plumbing. He was such a good man.

"Let's go." Jerry held up his keys and jingled them, as if to signal to Clara that he was ready. Then he turned back to Emma. "We'll be back soon."

"*Danki.*"

Clara walked beside him to his truck and then climbed into the passenger seat and buckled her seat belt.

"I thought we'd go to the hardware store first." He turned the key and the engine roared to life.

"Okay." She folded her hands in her lap as he drove out to the road. "Did you fix the kitchen sink?"

"Yeah." He kept his eyes focused on the traffic ahead. "It wasn't difficult. The toilet will be fixed soon."

"That was nice of you to insist on paying for the parts."

He shrugged as he gave her a sideways glance. "It's not much at all." He turned back to the road.

"Still, it's nice." She paused and studied him, taking in his handsome profile as questions danced through her mind. "Jerry, why did you stop coming to church and youth group?"

Something unreadable flashed over his features, but then it disappeared. "It's difficult to explain."

"I'm listening." She leaned toward him, and he laughed. "What's so funny?"

He nodded at her. "You've never been subtle."

She gaped at him, and he laughed again.

"You can trust me," she said.

"I know that."

The compliment sent warmth swirling through her chest. "If you know you can trust me, then tell me."

He drove in silence for several moments, his eyes trained on the road once again. She held her breath, hoping he'd finally open up to her.

When he drove into the parking lot at the hardware store, her shoulders wilted. They were at their destination, and she'd missed her chance for a real conversation with him. She unbuckled her seat belt and began wrestling with the heavy door.

"Wait." He touched her shoulder, but then he pulled back his hand as if her sleeve had bit him. "I want to answer your question."

"Okay." She angled her body toward him.

He looked down at his lap as if gathering his thoughts. "I don't know how to explain it, but I've never felt God calling me to join the church." He peeked up at her.

She scooted closer to him. "But you were an active member of our youth group, and you always seemed attentive in church. Why would you suddenly turn your back on our culture and beliefs?"

"That's not what I mean." He turned toward her and leaned back on the door. "While everyone else was looking forward to making a commitment to the Amish community, I felt awkward. I always thought I would feel God calling me to be baptized, but I never have."

She tried to digest his words, but she just couldn't understand them. "God loves you. He loves all of us, and we're all called to be his baptized disciples."

"Forget it." He pushed his door open. "Let's buy our supplies and get back to Emma's *haus*."

Disappointment filled Clara as they walked toward the hardware store. She longed to encourage Jerry to open his heart to her, but she feared pushing him away with too many questions. Inside, she kept the conversation light, asking him only about his purchases.

After he'd gathered the supplies and paid for them, they climbed back into his truck and headed to the bulk food store.

"So what do we need here again?" he asked as she led him down an aisle.

"Containers for strawberries and trays for *kichlin*." She found the containers and began to fill their shopping cart.

"Let me help you." He reached for the stack of containers in her hands.

When their fingers brushed, heat zipped up her arm, and her pulse skittered at the contact. She bit back a gasp as she released the containers. Her cheeks burned, and she turned back toward the shelf, hoping to hide her reaction to his touch.

"I think we need three more stacks." She busied herself with gathering more containers and handing them to him, careful to avoid physical contact.

After filling the cart with the trays for cookies too, they headed to the cashier. Jerry took his wallet from his pocket and handed the cashier a stack of bills.

"What are you doing?" Clara held up her own wallet. "I was going to pay."

"I've got it." He took his receipt and change. "Thank you." Then he pushed the cart toward the exit.

"Jerry!" Clara trotted after him. "Why did you pay?"

"Because I wanted to." When they reached the truck, he hopped into its bed as if it were effortless and opened a large plastic container. "Hand me the bags."

"Why did you pay?" she demanded again.

"I already told you. Because I wanted to." He reached down. "Now, hand me the bags."

"I was going to be reimbursed," she continued. "We have a fund for all garden expenses. You need to turn in your receipt to get reimbursed."

He frowned. "If I agree to that, will you please hand me the bags?"

"*Ya.*" She nodded. "I will."

"Fine." He rolled his eyes. "Now hand me the bags so we can get back to Emma's *haus.*"

Satisfied with his response, she handed him the bags and he stowed them in the large container. Soon they were on their way back to Emma's house.

"*Danki* for taking me to the store," she said as the truck puttered its way down the road.

"*Gern gschehne.*" He slowed to a stop at a red light.

She glanced at him. Maybe she could just ask him one more thing. "You said you don't feel the call to join the church, but you still speak in Pennsylvania Dutch."

He shrugged. "I hear it all the time at my parents' *haus,* and that's what many of our customers speak. So why wouldn't I speak it?"

"That's something else." She angled her body toward him. "If you truly are *English,* do you have a television and access to the internet?"

"Who said I'm *English*?" His blue eyes challenged her.

She extended her hands, palms up. "Well, your fancy haircut, your phone, your clothes, and your truck give it away."

He opened his mouth and then closed it again. When the light turned green, he took his foot off the brake and the truck lurched forward. An awkward silence filled the cab like a thick, choking fog.

Clara regretted her words, and she racked her brain for something else to say.

"Why aren't you dating anyone?" he asked.

"What?" She turned toward him.

"I thought for sure you'd be engaged by now."

"Why would you say that?" She searched his face for any signs of a joke.

"A few of my *freinden* admitted they wanted to date you."

"When did they say that?"

"Before I left."

Stunned by the information, she paused, gathering her thoughts. "What did you tell them?"

"I didn't say anything, but I assumed they would pursue you. I always imagined one of them would have the confidence to ask you to marry him." He turned his head to look at her. "You haven't dated anyone since I left?"

"I've had a couple of boyfriends, but the relationships didn't last very long."

"Why?"

"I don't know. I guess we just weren't compatible."

"Did you end the relationships?"

She nodded.

"That's what I thought."

"What does that mean?" Frustration nipped at her. Was he accusing her of something?

"No man in his right mind would end a relationship with you." He slapped on the blinker and then merged onto the road that led to Emma's house.

Oh.

His words twirled through her mind as confusion taunted her. Why would Jerry say such a thing?

She fingered the door handle as he steered into Emma's driveway. When the truck came to a stop, she pushed open the door and started to climb out.

"Clara. Wait."

She looked over her shoulder at him.

"I didn't mean to upset you." His face was lined with what looked like contrition. "I'm not Amish, but I hope we can still be *freinden.*"

"We'll always be *freinden*." Her heart tugged at the possibility of being more than his friend, but because he wasn't a baptized member of the church, she'd be shunned if that happened.

"*Gut*." He smiled. "Let's unload the supplies so I can finish fixing the toilet."

As she climbed out of the truck, her thoughts turned to her uncle who'd left the community and cut off all communication with their family. Maybe her mother could help her figure out a way to bring Jerry back to the church—before it was too late, before he decided there was no turning back.

⌒

"*Mamm*, may I ask you a question?" Clara turned to her mother as they sat on the back porch drinking iced tea that evening.

"You know you can ask me anything." *Mamm* ran her fingers over her glass as she pushed her rocking chair into motion.

"What did you say to *Onkel* Norman to try to convince him to stay in the church?"

"I begged him to stay. I told him he was my only *bruder*, and I didn't want to lose him. I told him it would break *Mamm* and *Dat*'s hearts if he wasn't Amish." *Mamm* shook her head. "But it didn't work. I wound up alienating him instead of keeping him in my life."

The pain in her mother's eyes nearly broke her in two.

"You must miss him," Clara said.

"I do. Very much." *Mamm* smiled at her, but it was a sad smile. "You would love him. He's friendly and funny. He loved to tell jokes, no matter how *gegisch* they were." She got a faraway look in her eye. "One time *mei dat* was trying to tell him something serious, and Norman kept cracking jokes. *Dat* was angry, but then he just started laughing." She chuckled.

"He sounds *wunderbaar*."

"*Ya*. I'd love to get to know his *fraa* and *kinner*." She turned to Clara once again. "And I would love for you to know your cousins."

"*Ya*, I would too." Clara sipped her iced tea as she worked up the courage to ask her next question. "Do you think there's any way I can convince Jerry to join the church?"

Mamm looked at her a moment before answering. "It's a very personal decision, Clara."

"I know."

"And if you try to push him, you might alienate him, just like I alienated *mei bruder*."

Clara stared down at her glass. If she didn't try to convince Jerry to stay, she could lose any chance of being more than a friend to him, just as she had five years ago when he first stepped away from the church. But if she did try to convince him, pushing too hard, she could lose him even as a friend.

"*Was iss letz?*" *Mamm* asked.

Clara looked up at her mother. "What do you mean?"

"You seem upset."

Clara hesitated as her thoughts spun. While she wanted to tell her mother that her feelings for Jerry worried her, she didn't want to upset her too.

"You care about him, don't you?"

Clara gritted her teeth. *Mamm* could tell the truth just by looking at her face. She was in trouble now!

"It's okay." *Mamm*'s expression was warm, and that loosened some of the anxiety in Clara's tense spine. "Jerry has always been a *gut freind*, and it must be exciting to reconnect with him. But he's not Amish. Don't get too caught up in your emotions or you'll wind up with a broken heart. You can't force him to join the church, but you can be his *freind* and gently encourage him. Maybe you can invite him to come to a church service and then let God do the rest."

"That's a really *gut* idea." Hope rose in Clara's chest as she took another sip of tea. Maybe if she invited Jerry to church and he went, he would feel inspired to be baptized. And if he was baptized, maybe, just maybe, she had a chance to be his girlfriend.

As she looked out toward her father's barn, she sent a prayer up to God, asking him to bring Jerry back to the church for good. Maybe Jerry's heart would turn toward the church the way the flowers in Emma's garden, snuggled next to Henry's, turned their faces toward the morning sun.

CHAPTER 4

"Y̶ou're staying to help, right?" Biena pinned Jerry with one of her serious stares. "You've finished your work for the day, and it's a beautiful Saturday afternoon."

"What makes you think I don't have things to do at *Onkel* Saul's *haus*?" Jerry shifted his truck into park and leaned on the steering wheel.

Biena's lips turned up in one of her mischievous smiles as she pointed toward the garden. "Because Clara is here."

Jerry bit back a groan. How could his little sister read him so well? He looked out toward the garden, where Clara sat on a bucket and worked in the soil. Then his gaze moved to the back porch, where Ephraim, Chris, and Wayne seemed to be working on the storm door. He recalled that Ephraim mentioned it.

"I could help the guys replace Emma's door."

"There you go." Biena smacked his arm. "That's a *gut* excuse to stay." Then she pushed open the truck door, stepped out, and slammed it shut. "I'll see you later," she called before hurrying toward the garden.

Jerry climbed out of the truck and walked up the path to the porch. As he moved past the garden, he spotted Biena talking to Clara, who'd looked up with her hands tented over her eyes. Clara glanced over at Jerry and waved.

Jerry waved back and then jogged up the porch steps. "You three look like you need some expert advice."

"*Ya?*" Wayne looked around. "Do you see an expert anywhere, Ephraim?"

"No. I can't say that I do."

"Did we call for an expert?" Chris chimed in.

"Uh-huh. I see how it is." Jerry leaned back against the porch railing. "I'll just stand here and keep my mouth shut as you drop that door on yourselves."

Ephraim lifted a blond brow. "Really?"

Jerry laughed. "Let me help you. I've replaced a few doors in my day."

Wayne turned to Ephraim. "Let him help. We'll laugh when he drops it on himself."

"That's a *gut* idea." Ephraim made a sweeping gesture toward the door they planned to replace. "Go right ahead."

Jerry stepped over and picked up a screwdriver. Soon he was taking the door off its hinges.

"So other than being a plumber for most of the last five years, what have you been doing?" Wayne stood close by, looking ready to help.

"Not much. Just working." Jerry nodded toward the door. "Help me lift it." He and Wayne removed the door and leaned it against the railing.

"We've all been working," Wayne said. "But you came to youth group one day and disappeared the next. You haven't even come to church."

"Have you joined a different church?" Ephraim pulled out a pocketknife and began to remove the packaging from the new door.

"No." Jerry looked out toward the garden, where Clara and his sister now worked side by side.

"Then what kept you away?" Wayne asked. "You never gave us any indication you'd be leaving, let alone not coming back."

For a moment Jerry regretted allowing his younger sister to guilt him into staying today. But his friends had a right to know more about him. After all, he'd abandoned them.

"I don't think he wants to discuss it." Chris opened the packaging, revealing a storm door that included a full-view glass front.

"Why did Emma choose a door with a full glass front?" Jerry asked.

"You really have to ask?" Wayne deadpanned. "So Hank can look outside."

"I should have known." Jerry grinned as he shook his head. He looked toward the garden again and spotted Hank giving himself a bath in the sun. "That cat has a *gut* life here, huh?"

"*Ya*, he sure does," Chris said.

"So why have you stayed away from us for five years, Jerry?" Wayne asked again. "You could have at least come around once in a while."

Because I didn't want any lectures? Because I wouldn't have known what to say?

"I really don't know." Jerry grabbed one side of the door. "Ready to lift?"

"That's not a *gut* answer."

"No, it's not, but it's the truth." Jerry helped Ephraim lift the door and carry it to the frame.

"Well, whatever your mysterious reason is, we're glad you're back." Ephraim swiped his hand over his sweaty forehead.

"I am too," Jerry said. And he was.

"How did you convince your *bruder* to help today?" Clara stopped weeding the cucumber bed and looked toward the porch, where Jerry helped Ephraim and Wayne adjust the newly installed door for Emma while Chris handed them tools.

Biena pulled another weed and dropped it into the bucket beside her. "I pointed out that you were here."

Clara felt as though her heart had tripped over itself as she looked at her friend.

"Don't look so surprised," Biena said. "It's obvious you two like each other."

Clara gasped as she leaned close to Biena. "Please don't say that out loud."

"Why?" Biena's eyes widened. "Do you have a boyfriend?"

"No, I don't, but your *bruder* isn't baptized. I don't want to get in trouble with the bishop." Clara paused. "I do like your *bruder*, but we can't be anything other than *freinden* unless he comes back to the church, okay? Please don't tell anyone I care about him."

"Okay." Biena lowered her voice. "Maybe you can help him decide to come back to the church."

"I hope so." Clara looked back toward the house as a yellow taxi pulled into the driveway and stopped next to Jerry's truck. A young woman stepped out. "Who could that be?"

"Oh, it must be Tena." Biena stood and wiped the worst of the dirt off her hands with a rag from the pocket of her apron. "Emma said her great-niece was coming to visit from Indiana."

"Her great-niece?"

"*Ya*. Emma said Tena's fiancé broke up with her, and she's heartbroken. Emma invited her to visit for the summer, to help get her mind off what happened."

Clara clicked her tongue. "That's so *bedauerlich*."

Emma appeared on the back porch, and then she rushed down

the steps and to the taxi. She hugged the girl and then paid the driver.

"Let's go meet her," Biena said.

Clara wiped a few more cucumber beetles off the crops and then stood, trying to get the dirt off her hands too. She fell into step with Biena, and they made their way past the rows of fruits and vegetables toward the driveway.

Emma saw them coming. "Clara. Biena." She gestured for them to join her. "Come and meet my great-niece."

Clara and Biena quickened their steps.

"Tena, this is Clara Hertzler and Biena Petersheim. And this is my great-niece, Tena Speicher."

"It's nice to meet you." Tena smiled, and her pretty face lit up.

"Hi. Welcome. We'd shake your hand, but ours are still too dirty from working in the garden." Clara wondered why Tena's fiancé would break up with her. She looked to be in her early to midtwenties, and she had beautiful fiery-red hair under her prayer covering and gorgeous chestnut eyes.

"It's nice to meet you," Biena said. "Emma speaks highly of you."

"*Danki.*" Tena blushed. Besides being attractive, she seemed sweet and kind.

"Is your luggage in the trunk?" Emma asked, and Tena nodded. Emma turned to the porch, where the men were now picking up tools. "*Buwe!* Would a couple of you please help Tena with her luggage?"

All four men dropped what they were doing and came down, and Emma made introductions. Clara felt a twinge of jealousy when Jerry shook Tena's hand.

The driver had popped open the taxi's trunk, and Ephraim and Wayne retrieved Tena's suitcase and zippered tote bag. Emma, Tena, and Biena headed into the house. Chris, Ephraim, and

Wayne went back to collect the tools and old door, but Jerry stayed behind.

Clara looked up at him. "You decided to help again today, huh?"

"Yeah, well, it's a *gut* cause." He shrugged. "And I didn't have anything else to do."

"You were bored, then." Clara grinned, and he did too. "It looks like you four did a *gut* job installing the new door."

"It was easy, really. I did it myself." He threaded his fingers together and then cracked his knuckles as if to prove his strength. "I'm kidding. It went quickly with four of us working together."

"I saw." She crossed her arms over her chest. "Are you coming back next Saturday?"

"Do you want me to?" He raised his eyebrows, and she hesitated. "I'll take that as a yes."

"Will I see you in church tomorrow?" she asked, and it was his turn to hesitate. "I hope I do," she added.

His bright eyes locked on hers. She shivered, despite the hot June sun.

"I should get back to work," she said. "The cucumber bed is full of crabgrass and cucumber beetles."

"I need to help clean up the mess over there." He jammed his thumb toward the porch.

"Don't leave without saying good-bye to me," she told him. Then she turned and strolled back to the cucumbers.

~

Clara tried in vain to suppress a frown as she dropped into the chair beside Katie Ann at Emma's house Sunday afternoon. She glanced around the kitchen table at the familiar faces of her friends, but her heart sank when she didn't find Jerry sitting beside his sister. Biena had wanted to join their weekly garden committee meeting this afternoon, and Clara had hoped Jerry would bring her and decide to stay too. He hadn't.

Worse, he hadn't come to church that morning.

Disappointed, she looked down at the tabletop as Mandy reported the success of the past week's sales.

He never promised you he would come to church!

She ignored the voice in her head. She'd prayed her words of encouragement would inspire Jerry to be there. But they hadn't. Her mother's warning about pushing him away echoed in her mind, but after Biena telling her Jerry liked her too, she was determined to convince him to join the church. How could she let today hold her back from the dream of welcoming him home? From the dream of being more than his friend?

When she heard a meow, she looked down at the floor. Hank sat staring up at her, blinking.

"Hi, Hank," she whispered as she stroked his head. "How are you today?"

"I think that covers everything on our agenda," Mandy said. "We'd like to welcome Tena to our group. Tena is Emma's great-niece, and she's visiting from Indiana for the summer."

"Hi, everyone." Tena smiled. "I'm excited to be here."

"We'll serve the meal now," Mandy said after everyone had greeted Tena. "Let's eat."

Clara followed the rest of the young women to the kitchen counter, and when she opened a drawer to grab a stack of utensils, she felt a hand on her arm.

"Are you okay?" Mandy whispered in her ear.

"*Ya.*" Clara shrugged. "Why?"

"You seem upset." Mandy's blue eyes studied her. "Tell me what's bothering you."

Clara glanced over her shoulder to where Biena spoke to Emma and Tena. She leaned closer to Mandy and lowered her voice. "I was hoping Jerry would come to church today, and even here. I'm just disappointed."

Mandy was silent for a moment, and Clara bit her lip, awaiting her friend's assessment of her confession.

"So you *do* still have feelings for Jerry. I was afraid of that."

Clara stilled. If she admitted she did—had everyone in their youth group seen through her?—would it get back to the bishop?

"*Was iss letz?*" Katie Ann sidled up to Mandy with wide eyes.

Clara bit back a groan. How could she admit to her two best friends that she had feelings for an *Englisher*? It was bad enough that she'd admitted it to Biena. But this wasn't just any *Englisher*—he was Jerry Petersheim, her lifelong friend!

Mandy spun toward Biena and Tena. "Biena, would you please finish setting the table? I need to talk to Katie Ann and Clara for a minute."

"*Ya*, of course." Biena walked over and took the utensils from Clara.

"*Danki*," Clara said.

"We'll be right back," Mandy told Emma as she took Clara's arm and steered her out to the porch with Katie Ann in tow. Then she led Clara down the steps and out to the garden. She stopped at the end of one row and looked up at Clara. "You still have feelings for him."

"Feelings for whom?" Katie Ann looked at Clara's face. "Oh. Jerry."

Clara groaned and placed both palms on her cheeks. "Is it that obvious?"

"Most everyone thought you liked each other as more than *freinden* before he left the church, but you know it would be wrong to date him now," Mandy said with a warning tone.

"You'd be shunned," Katie Ann added.

"I know, I know!" Clara threw up her hands. "That's why I told him I hoped to see him at church today, and I prayed he would be there. I thought if I encouraged him to come back to the church, he might join, and then we could date. That is, if he wanted to."

Katie Ann gave her a sad smile. "That's really sweet, but it has to be his choice to come back to the church."

"I know that too." Clara kicked a stone with the toe of her black shoe. "*Mei onkel* Norman left the church before I was born. *Mei mamm* still misses him. I was hoping to get Jerry to come back, not just for me, but for his family too. And I can't believe he really wants to live as an *Englisher*."

"Just keep encouraging him." Katie Ann patted her arm. "But also keep your distance. You can't risk being shunned."

"Katie Ann is right," Mandy said. "You can be his *freind*, but don't let your heart get too involved. If he doesn't join the church, you'll get hurt."

Clara nodded as tiny knots of worry invaded her stomach. "*Danki*."

"Hey," Ephraim called from the porch. "Are you *maed* coming in to eat? If not, I'll eat your egg salad for you."

Mandy laughed. "We'll be right there."

Ephraim disappeared into the house, the new storm door clicking shut behind him.

Mandy gestured inside. "Let's go."

～

"We missed you at church today," Clara told Jerry as she rode beside Biena in his truck later that evening.

"You missed me, huh?" He grinned at her as he steered the truck through an intersection.

"*Ya*, I did." Frustration nipped at her as she studied his coy grin. "I thought you might actually show up."

"I think he slept in today," Biena said.

"It would have been nice to see you at your home church," Clara said. "Your church family misses you."

His smile flattened, and he stared straight ahead. A dense silence filled the truck's cab, and it stayed.

Clara ran her finger over the top of the metal window frame as she watched the farmhouses seem to zoom by. A summer breeze came through the window, and the ribbons on her prayer covering fluttered around her face.

"Tena is nice," Biena said, her voice finally shooing the silence away. "She said she's going to be here through the fall now."

"That's *gut*." Clara kept her gaze focused on the scenery. "I'm sure Emma enjoys the company."

"*Ya*, they seem close. I'm glad Emma will have someone there to help around the *haus*," Biena continued. "Tena can help her cook and do laundry. Maybe help with her flower garden."

Biena started talking about her favorite flowers, but Clara lost herself in disappointment. She stole a glance at Jerry, leaning forward slightly so she could see him around Biena. With a muscle flexing in his tense jaw, he sat ramrod straight, and his focus ahead never changed. She was sure she felt intensity radiating off him.

Had she pushed him too hard?

Worry replaced her disappointment. *Mamm*, and Katie Ann, and Mandy had all warned her not to pressure him, but she'd done just that. The notion of losing him forever stole the air in her lungs. He was her friend, her very good friend. She couldn't lose him after just reconnecting with him! Guilt, hot and searing, sliced through her chest.

Folding her arms over her middle, she settled back in the seat and tried to ignore the tears that threatened her eyes.

When her farm came into view, she sat up straight and searched her mind for something to say that would encourage him to come back to Emma's again. She couldn't give up on him just yet.

"Here we are." Jerry stopped the truck by the porch, keeping it in gear.

"*Danki* for the ride." Clara pushed open the door and then turned to him. His expression had relaxed slightly, but she still saw intensity in his jaw. "Are you planning to come to Emma's again?" She froze in place, awaiting his rejection.

"*Ya.*" He leaned on the steering wheel. "The guys asked me to help paint her front door and trim."

"Oh. She'll appreciate that." Clara felt her body relax. "I guess I'll see you both soon, then."

"You will." Biena smiled. "Tell your parents hello for us."

"I will." Clara looked back at Jerry and saw something new flash over his face. Was it regret? Did he wish he hadn't promised the other men he'd help? "*Gut nacht.*"

"Take care," he said, but his tone was anything but encouraging.

She climbed out of the truck, walked to the back porch, and then waved as the truck backed out of the driveway. She stood rooted to the ground.

Would she and Jerry have dated years ago if he'd joined the church then? The thought of what might have been haunted her. Or was she kidding herself, imagining they would ever have been more than friends?

～

Jerry lifted his hand and waved at Clara before taking the truck back to the road. He gripped the steering wheel with such a force he feared it might snap. All his confusion and frustration swirled in his gut as he recalled her words.

It would have been nice to see you at your home church. Your church family misses you.

She made it sound as if every Amish person had the same

relationship with God, leading to the same commitment to the church. But he'd always struggled to feel connected to God. That was why he hadn't joined the church with his friends.

"Clara asked me where you were today. She really missed you." Biena's words broke through his thoughts. "It's obvious she cares about you."

Jerry sat up straighter, and his heart warmed at the notion of someone as special as Clara caring about him. Could it be true?

"You care about her, too, don't you? You always have."

He didn't look at her, even as he slowed to a stop at a red light. "What would it matter if I did? I'm not Amish."

"Oh, please. You can't deny you care about her. It's written all over your face when you two are together. It *is* a shame you can't be together, though. You'd have to join the church."

He frowned as he looked at her. "Now you sound like *Mamm*."

"Well, it's the truth." She shrugged as if deciding to join the church was the easiest decision in the world. "I think you and Clara would make a great couple. I never understood why you didn't join the church and then date her when you were in youth group."

"Really?"

She snorted. "Please. Everyone talked about how you two liked each other, and some of us thought you were meant to be together. Don't act like you didn't know that."

He ignored her assumption as he turned onto their street. He hadn't known.

"I just adore Clara. She's so sweet and funny. And I'm sure you've noticed she's *schee*," Biena continued.

Jerry had noticed how pretty Clara was, years ago, but that still wasn't a reason for him to join the church. He turned the truck into their driveway and parked in his usual spot behind the barn. When he bought the truck, *Dat* had insisted he park back there so their Amish neighbors couldn't see it from the road—as if the neighbors weren't already aware of *Dat*'s non-Amish son. Only when he had to load or unload supplies for his mother did he park near the house.

Jerry climbed out and met Biena at the back bumper.

"You should seriously think about it." Biena wagged a finger at him. "If you joined the church, you'd not only make *Mamm* and *Dat froh*, but you could date the *maedel* you've cared about since you were a *bu*."

"I appreciate your input, Beanie, but that's enough lecturing for one day, okay?"

She opened her mouth as if to protest his use of her despised nickname, but then she closed it.

"Okay," she said before moving toward the house.

Later that evening, Jerry walked upstairs to the bedroom he rented in his uncle's home, his mind still spinning with Biena's words about how easy it would be to join the church and make everyone happy. He crossed the room to his closet and opened the door.

As he ran his fingers over his old Amish trousers and shirts, memories assaulted his mind—sitting in church between Ephraim and Wayne and talking to his friends at youth gatherings, yes, but then laughing with Clara while playing volleyball, sitting on the grass and talking to Clara, and watching Clara mingle with her friends.

All his memories of being Amish featured Clara's beautiful smile, her adorable laugh, and her bottomless, coffee-colored eyes. But caring about an amazing woman wasn't a reason to join the church. Didn't he need to feel the call from God to justify asking the bishop's permission to become a member? Wouldn't he wind up resenting the church if he joined only to date Clara? The problem was he didn't feel a call to any church—Amish or otherwise. He didn't feel a call from God.

Renewed confusion and frustration dug their claws into his shoulders as he slammed his closet door shut. If he hadn't driven Biena to Emma's house that day, he never would have found himself stuck in the middle of this quandary.

He lowered himself onto the corner of his bed, and it creaked in protest of his weight. He had to stop torturing himself. He had a good life and a job he enjoyed. Soon he'd have enough money to buy a house of his own and move away from his Amish roots.

But if he was so determined to shed his Amish roots, why did he feel a tiny thread of longing beckoning him back to the church?

CHAPTER 5

C lara smiled as she put two cantaloupes and a watermelon on
the counter. "Would you like anything else?"

"Hmm." The middle-aged woman tapped her finger against
her chin. "Those cookies look awfully good. And I'm thinking
about those strawberries." She waved off her own comment. "I'll
just take them both." She set two trays of oatmeal raisin cookies
on the counter, along with a container of strawberries. "How much
will that be?"

Clara pulled out a calculator to add up the items, and then the
woman handed her the cash. "Have a good afternoon," Clara told
her after she'd bagged all the purchases and helped her load her car.

"You too, honey. You might want to go inside soon. It smells like
rain." The woman waved before climbing into her dark-blue van.

Clara took a deep breath as she looked at the gray clouds clogging the previously blue sky. It did smell like rain, and she was
certain she heard a rumble in the distance. She looked toward the
house, where Jerry, Ephraim, Chris, and Wayne had been replacing
the rotten wood in Emma's front steps and porch, but it looked like
they'd already moved their supplies inside somewhere.

For the past two weeks, before tackling the rotten wood today,
Jerry and his three friends had been painting Emma's front door

and all the trim on her house. He'd been a dedicated member of their group, helping with all the projects Ephraim suggested.

They'd spoken each time he came, and he'd given her a ride home at the end of the day. They hadn't discussed his lack of attendance at church again, but their discussions had been cordial.

If only he were Amish . . .

Clara pushed the thought away as a clap of thunder exploded even closer than the last rumble, and then a mist of rain kissed her cheeks.

When another sudden boom of thunder shook the ground, she gasped and hopped off the stool. She had to get all the food inside the house before the threatening rainstorm ruined it. She began to pack packages of cookies and slices of pie and cake into a nearby cooler. Once they were stowed, she moved on to the strawberry containers.

But then the sky opened, and rain poured down, drenching her prayer covering, clothes, and shoes within seconds. She whipped off her black apron, but she couldn't do anything about her favorite green dress.

"Oh no," she groaned as she worked faster to load the remaining food.

"Let me help you."

The voice was warm in her ear, sending chills dancing down her spine. She looked over her shoulder to where Jerry stood, his hair soaked and sticking up in odd directions, making him look younger and even more adorable.

"*Danki*," she said.

"We need to hurry." He looked up, blinking water out of his eyes. "I think it's going to get worse."

Another clap of thunder stunned her, and she jumped.

"Right." She finished packing the strawberries and moved on to the carrots and celery.

Soon they had all the fruits and vegetables packed up. Chris, Ephraim, and Wayne, along with Mandy, Katie Ann, and Tena, joined them. The men carried the heavy coolers and boxes while the women followed with the money box and assorted items that couldn't fit in the coolers. They all ran as fast as they could.

When they reached the house and entered the back door, they stored the baked goods in the refrigerator and freezer and the coolers in the mudroom. Emma was waiting with towels, and Clara grabbed two.

"You're soaked." Jerry grinned down at her as she wiped a towel over her face.

"You are too." She handed him the other towel.

"Could I give you a ride?"

"That would be nice. I don't want to walk home in this."

"As if I would ever let you walk in a storm."

"Let me?" She challenged him with her hand on her hip.

He rolled his eyes. "You're incorrigible, Clara Hertzler. I'll go get my truck."

"*Danki.*"

As he went out the back door, she dropped the towel in the hamper in Emma's utility room, wrung out her soaked apron, and then said good-bye to everyone. Chris insisted on standing by the back door with her until they saw the truck pull up. Then they both rushed down the porch steps and through the rain under Emma's umbrella, and she climbed into the passenger seat. She shivered as she waved a thank you to Chris and then pulled on her seat belt.

"Biena was *schmaert* to stay home today and help your *mamm* with that quilting project." She rubbed her hands together.

"But she missed out on all the fun," Jerry quipped, putting the truck in gear and steering out of the driveway.

"That's true." The truck bounced down the road with rain drumming on the roof above them and peppering the windshield. "How is the porch project going?"

"Pretty well. The porch had more rotten boards than we thought, so it's going to take a bit longer than we anticipated."

"It's *gut* that you're doing it."

"*Ya*, it is." He gave her a sideways glance. "I think we're going to repair the roof next. She showed us a couple of stains in the ceiling, and Ephraim says he knows how to replace the tiles."

"I think Ephraim knows how to do everything."

Jerry chuckled. "I do too. Or he acts like he does to impress Mandy."

Clara laughed. "I could definitely see that."

They rode in a comfortable silence for a few minutes, and Clara enjoyed the sound of the rain on the roof. She felt completely at ease with Jerry, as if the tension between them had evaporated.

When they arrived, he maneuvered the truck near the path leading to her back door and shut off the engine. The rain intensified and fiercely pelted the metal roof of the truck.

"I don't think this is going to let up." He scanned the floor. "I'm sorry I don't have an umbrella."

"I'll be fine." She looked down at her soaked apron and dress and then shook her head. "I don't think I could get much more drenched. My shoes will take forever to dry out."

Her gaze collided with his, and they laughed. "We're a sight, huh?"

"*Ya*, we are." He angled his body toward her, resting his bent elbow on the back of the seat as he looked at her.

She tilted her head to the side and studied him. Memories of their days in youth group filled her mind, and she smiled. Everything was so simple back then.

"Penny for your thoughts." He shoved the fingers of his left hand through his wet hair, causing it to stand up in a wild blond mess.

"I was just thinking about youth group." She turned and rested her shoulder against the dark-green vinyl seat. "We had a lot of fun."

"*Ya*, we did."

"What do you miss about being Amish?"

He looked out the windshield and then back at her. "I miss the community. I miss feeling a part of something." He looked down at his fingers as he brushed them over the back of the seat. "I miss not being a disappointment to my parents."

Her heart squeezed at the sadness she was certain she heard in his tone. "Why don't you come back?" She whispered the question and hoped he heard it over the roar of the rain.

He looked up at her.

"Come to church tomorrow," she said.

Instead of responding, he reached over and traced the tip of his finger down her cheek with a light, butterfly touch, and then he dropped his hand. Her breath caught in her throat as her cheek burned where his skin had been.

"You had a raindrop there." His look was intense as his eyes locked with hers.

Heat flooded her body from her head straight to her toes. Sitting this close to him was dangerous. She had to get out of the truck before he touched her again.

"*Danki* for the ride." She gripped the door handle. "I hope to see you in church tomorrow."

Before he could respond, she thrust open the door, hopped out of the truck with her wet apron in hand, shut the door hard, and ran to the house through the angry raindrops.

"*Gude mariye.*" Jerry stepped into his mother's kitchen the following morning, and the aroma of eggs, bacon, and freshly baked bread filled his senses and caused his stomach to gurgle.

Mamm and Biena looked over from the counter, and their eyes widened in unison.

"What are you doing here so early on a Sunday?" *Mamm* asked.

"I thought I'd go to church with you." He slipped into the chair next to his father, who stared at him with the same confused expression his mother and sister had.

"What did you say?" *Mamm* set a platter of scrambled eggs on the table.

"I said I'd like to join you for church . . . if that's okay." Jerry smiled at her.

"*Ya.*" *Mamm*'s smile could have lit up a darkened room. "That would be *wunderbaar.*"

"Are you serious?" *Dat* looked unconvinced. "You're really going to go to church with us?"

"*Ya*, I am."

Biena set a plate and utensils in front of him. "Are you going just to see Clara?" She set a filled coffee cup next to him.

"*Danki*," Jerry said. "And, no, I'm not going to see Clara." He'd spent most of last night analyzing his sudden urge to go to church, and he realized he wanted to worship, especially with his former district. He was almost certain he'd heard a tiny whisper from God calling him to the church, yet a thread of uncertainty remained along with the thread of longing he'd experienced for weeks.

"You're not dressed appropriately." *Dat* pointed to Jerry's blue short-sleeved polo shirt and khaki trousers. "You don't look Amish."

Jerry shifted in his seat. "I don't have any Amish clothes that fit. I'm taller than I was the last time I went to church. And I'm not ready to dress Amish yet."

Dat rubbed at his graying light-brown beard and stared. Jerry could feel the disapproval coming in waves.

Will I ever stop disappointing him?

"Let's eat," *Mamm* said. "We'll need to get on the road before we know it."

As Jerry bowed his head in silent prayer, he asked God to guide his heart.

⁓

Clara's heart seemed to trip over itself as she carried a coffee carafe to the table where Jerry sat in the Esh family's barn. She'd been so shocked when she spotted him at the back of the barn during the church service that she'd rubbed her eyes to make sure she wasn't imagining him. Yes, she'd told him she hoped he'd be there, but she didn't really think he would come. Then when he waved to her, she'd almost fallen off the bench. She wanted to talk to him alone, but they wouldn't have a chance during the noon meal. Maybe he would join them at Emma's house later.

Moving down the long table, she filled men's coffee cups as she made her way to Jerry, who sat next to his father and across from Ephraim and Wayne. She took in how his blue polo shirt made his eyes seem bluer somehow. Also, his clean-shaven face and strong jaw looked even more handsome without the stubble she'd noticed there yesterday.

She did a mental headshake. Why was she torturing herself? Just because he was at church didn't mean he was going to be baptized.

"Would you like *kaffi*?" She held up the carafe and forced her lips into a smile.

"*Ya*, please." Floyd, Jerry's father, lifted his cup, and she filled it. "*Danki*."

Then she reached across the table and filled Wayne and Ephraim's cups before turning to Jerry. Warmth cascaded through her as her gaze tangled with his. She felt as if everyone else in the barn had faded away and they were the only two people left—alone.

"*Kaffi?*" she asked.

"*Ya.*" He smiled. "*Danki.*"

She filled the cup and then handed it to him. When their fingers brushed, she swallowed a gasp. "It's *gut* to see you here."

"It's *gut* to be here."

She lost herself in the depths of his eyes for a moment.

"Clara," a man called, snapping her out of her trance. "Could I get a refill?"

"Excuse me," she said to Jerry before turning away.

She felt a twisty pang in her chest—a mixture of yearning and panic. She was falling too deep into her emotions for Jerry. She needed to ask someone for advice, and she trusted only one person to listen without judgment.

～

"Clara. You're early," Emma said as Clara stepped into her kitchen later that afternoon.

"I need to talk to you." Clara wrung her hands as she looked at the table. "Could we sit before anyone else gets here?"

"Of course, *mei liewe.*" Emma cupped her hand to Clara's cheek. "You look so distraught. Tell me what's wrong."

Clara sank into a chair as Emma sat down beside her. She paused for a second, debating how much to share. Then she shook her head and started from the beginning. "You know Jerry and I were *gut freinden* in school and in youth group."

Emma nodded.

"He was like my best *freind*, really. Well, he was my best guy

157

freind. He defended me on the playground when we were *kinner,* and we were close even after we finished school."

"You care about him." Emma's smile was warm.

"Right." Clara cleared her throat. "Well, it broke my heart when he stopped going to church and youth group five years ago, and I was shocked the day he dropped Biena off here. Since he started helping here last month, we've talked, and I've encouraged him to come back to the church. I assume you saw him today, right?"

"*Ya,* I did. And it's so *wunderbaar* that you've done that." Emma clasped her hands together.

"I'm not so sure." Clara lifted a paper napkin from the holder in the middle of the table and began folding it into a smaller square. "He was still dressed like an *Englisher.*"

"I did notice that." Emma frowned.

"He sat in the back of the barn, too, instead of with the other unmarried young men."

"I know, but he came to church." Emma patted her hand. "That's what you wanted, right?"

"*Ya,* it was." Clara pushed the napkin away. "But that's not what's bothering me."

"You can tell me. I'll listen to you, and I'll keep your secrets."

"I know, and I appreciate it." Tears stung her eyes, and she unsuccessfully tried to blink them back. "I care about Jerry, Emma, and that scares me."

"*Ach, mei liewe.*" Emma rubbed her shoulder.

"I'm afraid I'm going to become too attached to him, and then I'll be crushed if he doesn't join the church." Clara grabbed another napkin and dabbed tears from her cheeks. She heard a thump and saw movement out of the corner of her eye. Then she felt something velvety soft on her arm. She smiled as Hank sat beside her on the table, rubbing his head against her.

"He knows you're upset. Don't you, Hank?" Emma asked.

"He's so sweet." Clara touched the cat's ear.

"*Ya*, he's sweet, but not when he wakes me up at five thirty in the morning to fill his food bowl." Emma clicked her tongue. "Clara, you care for Jerry, and I think he cares for you too."

"You do?" Clara thought she felt her heart perform a giddy flip. Hearing that from Biena was one thing. Hearing it from Emma was another.

"It's obvious with the way you two seem to gravitate to each other, but I don't have to tell you it's risky to allow yourself to develop deeper feelings for him. You said it yourself—he's not Amish, and he hasn't made any promises to join the church, has he?"

Clara's heart sank, and she shook her head.

Hank moved to Emma, and she rubbed his chin.

"Years ago, an *Englisher* joined the church and married an Amish woman. They had six *kinner* together, and then one day he left and never came back." Emma's expression was grave. "His *fraa* was devastated when he divorced her, and of course she never remarried. But I think the heartbreak was too much for her anyway. She could never trust another man."

"That's so *bedauerlich*."

"*Ya*, it was." Emma shook her head as Hank jumped down to the floor and sauntered off toward the family room. "I'm not implying Jerry will join the church and then leave. I'm just trying to caution you. He went to church today, and that's a big step in the right direction. But you can't force him to become baptized, and you can't hang all your hopes on the possibility he will. If you allow yourself to get too emotionally involved with him, you might find yourself alone and shunned."

Emma gave Clara's hand a gentle squeeze. "I don't want that for you. Why don't you give Jerry some space? Let him figure out his feelings toward the church. Then if he joins, you can explore what the future might hold for you."

"*Danki*." Clara forced a smile that felt brittle. As much as Emma's words made sense, Clara didn't know how she was going to let go of her growing feelings for Jerry.

⁓

"It was nice to see you at church today," Clara told Jerry as they sat on Emma's back porch later that evening. She pushed the rocking chair into motion with her toe as she stared out toward the garden. The aroma of moist earth filled her nostrils as a warm breeze fluttered over her skin.

"And surprising?"

She nodded.

"My family was just as surprised as you were. Maybe more." He rested his elbows on the armrests of his chair.

"Do you think you'll come again?"

"*Ya*." He nodded. "I do."

"Did the bishop talk to you?"

"He said it was nice to see me too."

"That's *gut*." She looked out toward the rows of cornstalks reaching toward the sky. Her mind spun with Emma's words of caution and her confusing emotions for Jerry. How could she release him when she'd already invested so much of her heart into their friendship? Why would God lead her to Jerry if they weren't meant to be together?

"Clara?"

"What?" She turned her head toward him.

"I asked you if you'd like a ride home." His mouth quirked. "You seemed lost in thought. What were you thinking about?"

"Oh, nothing." She waved it off and stood. "*Ya*, I'll take that ride."

"Not until you tell me what was on your mind."

Oh no!

She tried to think of some excuse for her distraction, but her mind went blank.

The storm door opened and Biena appeared on the porch. "*Mamm* is going to worry about us if we don't leave soon. Are you ready to go?"

Relief flooded Clara. *Saved by Biena!*

"*Ya*, let's go. We'll drop Clara off at her *haus*." Jerry stood.

As Clara walked toward Jerry's truck, she wondered if someday she'd be able to ride with him in a buggy he owned instead.

Dread bogged Jerry's steps as he made his way up the path to his parents' back porch. *Dat* was sitting in a rocking chair, and he had a deep frown on his face.

"Hi, *Dat*," Jerry said as he climbed the steps. "I thought I'd say hello before going home."

"Have a seat. I want to talk to you."

Jerry sat down in the rocking chair beside him. A heaviness filled his chest as he looked out toward the sunset and the cicadas serenaded the evening. He and his father rarely had deep conversation, so something had to be wrong.

"What are you doing?" *Dat* asked.

"What?" Jerry turned toward him and felt his brow pinch.

"Why did you go to church with us today?"

"I thought you'd be *froh* that I went."

Dat studied him, and Jerry fought the urge to cringe. "No, that's not it. If you truly wanted to be Amish, you'd dress like it." He pointed to Jerry's khaki shorts. "You'd get rid of that truck, and you'd buy a horse and buggy."

Jerry held up his hands as if to calm his father's boiling frustration. "Going back to church today was a step toward a decision."

"A step toward a decision?" *Dat* said. "You either want to be Amish or you don't. You can't have it both ways." He pointed toward the barn. "You can't drive that truck while you consider what you want to do. It's one or the other."

"Why are you so angry with me?"

"Because you're going to break your *mamm's* heart again," *Dat* snapped. "You already hurt her when you stopped going to church, moved out, started dressing *English,* and bought that truck." He gestured widely. "Now you're going to attend a few services, make her believe you're coming back, and then change your mind. I know you, Jerry. You need to make up your mind."

He flinched at the accusing words. Did *Dat* know him—really know him? And what would his father know about his dilemma? Nothing.

When his phone buzzed, he pulled it from his pocket.

"This is exactly what I'm talking about," *Dat* continued. "You can't go to an Amish church service and then read texts on your phone."

"It's for work, *Dat.*" Jerry glanced at his uncle's text with instructions for when and where to report for work tomorrow, and then he pushed the phone back into his pocket.

"So what's it going to be? Are you going to come back to the church or not? You can't leave your mother in limbo like this."

"I don't know." Jerry settled back in the chair as waves of unease stirred in his gut.

"This is about Clara Hertzler, isn't it?"

Jerry's gaze cut to his father.

"Don't look so surprised. I'm not deaf, and I'm not blind. I heard your *schweschder's* question about why you were going to church this morning, and I saw how you and Clara interacted today." *Dat* leaned toward him. "If you decide to join the church, it can't be just for her. It has to be for God. And if you aren't going to join the church, you shouldn't string her along. You know you can get her shunned, right?"

Jerry bit back bitter-tasting guilt.

Dat stood. "You need to figure out what you're doing before you hurt yourself and everyone who cares for you."

As his father disappeared into the house, Jerry leaned his head back against his chair and closed his eyes. Tension burned in his chest as *Dat*'s words echoed in his head. He was stuck between two worlds—Amish and *English*—and he had no idea where he belonged. Where was his true home?

CHAPTER 6

C lara pushed her potato salad around on her plate with her fork as envy ran through her veins.

Across from her at Emma's large picnic table, Katie Ann and Chris sat close together and talked, and Mandy and Ephraim leaned against each other and whispered. She turned toward Wayne and Tena, who had been sitting and talking beside her for nearly an hour. They had struck up a friendship, and they gravitated to each other every time Wayne was at Emma's house. They were both baptized, and most likely they'd be the next couple brought together by Emma's garden.

Her mouth twisted into a frown, and she rubbed her forehead where a headache throbbed. Jealousy was wrong. Letting it take over was worse. But she couldn't deny how it had overtaken her. Jerry had seemed distant during the past two weeks, and then he hadn't shown up at church today, let alone at Emma's house. Perhaps he'd realized once and for all that he didn't want to be Amish and thought it best to stay away from her—from all of them.

Humidity stole her breath. The hot, late-July air hadn't seemed to move at all today. She looked over at the path leading to the porch and spotted Hank asleep under a bush, curled up in a ball. He was probably too hot as well.

"Clara," Ephraim called, and she looked over at him. "Would you like a ride home?"

"*Ya.*" She nodded. "*Danki.*"

"Could I get one too?" Biena asked.

"Of course," Ephraim said. "We have room for both of you."

"We can leave right after we clean up the kitchen," Mandy said.

"Sounds *gut.*" Clara stood and began to gather their plates. As she carried them into the kitchen, she wondered when—and if—she'd see Jerry again.

~

"Thank you for coming in today," *Onkel* Saul said as he and Jerry reloaded supplies in his company van. "I hated to have to call you on a Sunday, but we have to do what we can when there's an emergency."

"I'm happy to help." Jerry put the last tool bag inside and shut the door. "I'm glad you called me." While he was grateful for the extra hours and pay for the emergency call, Jerry had hated missing the opportunity to go to church and see his friends today. And although he'd done his best to keep his distance from Clara for the past couple of weeks, heeding his father's warning that he could hurt her if he didn't, he'd spent the day wondering if she missed him as much as he'd missed her.

"Listen. I want to talk to you about something." *Onkel* Saul faced him, and Jerry couldn't help but think how much he looked like *Dat* with his graying light-brown hair and blue eyes. They were both in their midfifties now, but unlike *Dat,* *Onkel* Saul had decided not to join the church in his early twenties.

"Okay." Jerry leaned against the van's bumper.

"You're my hardest working and most loyal employee. That's why you were the one I called in today." *Onkel* Saul paused and took a breath. "I've been thinking about this for a while, and now is the time. You're ready for more responsibility, and I want to make you my assistant manager. I also want you to take over my business when I'm ready to retire."

Jerry swallowed, his throat suddenly dry.

"I'll double your salary, and I want you to start taking on your own jobs. I trust you to represent me well. What do you think?"

Jerry sank onto the bumper as the weight of his uncle's words knocked him off balance.

"Jerry?" *Onkel* Saul's eyebrows lifted. "Are you all right?"

"*Ya.*" Jerry gave a nervous laugh. "I'm just a little stunned."

"Don't you want to become my assistant manager and learn more about running the company?" *Onkel* Saul sat down on the bumper beside him. "You're like the son I never had. I want to retire someday, and I'd be honored to turn the company over to you."

Emotion clogged the back of his throat. "Thank you," he managed to say.

"Is that a yes?" *Onkel* Saul sounded hopeful.

"This is a lot to take in." Jerry's words were measured in the wake of his sudden confusion. "Could I have a week or so to think about it?"

"That's fair." *Onkel* Saul patted his shoulder. "Let me know when you're ready to talk about it."

"All right. Thank you." Jerry shook his uncle's hand, and then he walked to his truck as he tried to fully comprehend what his uncle had just offered.

He wasn't certain if he was ready to become his uncle's assistant manager, but he was certain he needed a good meal and a comfortable chair to rest his aching feet.

When Ephraim guided his horse into Biena's driveway, Clara's heart lurched. She could see Jerry's truck parked behind the barn.

"*Danki* for the ride," Biena called as she climbed from the back of the buggy. "I'll see you soon."

Clara leaned forward on the bench seat. "Could I have a minute to talk to Jerry?" she asked Ephraim.

"*Ya*, of course. I'm not in a hurry." He turned to Mandy beside him. "Are you?"

"No," Mandy said, although she looked at Clara with obvious curiosity.

Clara walked over to the truck as Jerry came around to the front of it. "Hi."

"Hi." His brow furrowed. "What are you doing here?"

"Ephraim is giving me a ride home." She jammed her thumb toward the house. "We dropped off Biena first. Where were you today?"

"I had to work." He leaned against the truck's fender. "There was an emergency. Pipes burst at a nursing home, and *Onkel* Saul asked me to help him take care of it. I just had to stop here to pick up something from *mei mamm* before I head back home."

"Oh." She nodded slowly, and suddenly she saw Jerry in a new light. According to their beliefs, it was a sin to work on Sundays. If Jerry intended to be baptized, he wouldn't be breaking that community rule. He wouldn't be acting like an *Englisher* at all.

A heavy sadness enveloped her. Jerry wasn't going to join the church, and it was time she faced the truth.

They stared at each other, and the silence stretched her nerves thin as tears threatened her eyes. She had to leave before they broke free.

"I'd better go." Her voice sounded thick to her own ears. "I'll see you."

"Yeah." He smiled, but the smile seemed weak.

Clara hurried to the buggy and climbed into the back. Tears streamed down her face, and she couldn't hold back a sob.

"Clara!" Mandy turned and reached over the seat to touch her arm. "What happened?"

"I can't do this anymore!"

"What do you mean?"

"I can't hold on to him. It's ripping me apart." Clara hugged her arms to her chest as if to hold her heart intact.

"You love him," Mandy said. Ephraim stayed quiet.

Clara nodded. "*Ya,* I think I do, but he's not going to join the church. I'm kidding myself. I've been kidding myself for two months now, and I can't do it anymore. I just can't."

"Shh," Mandy cooed. "Everything will be okay."

"I don't know how." Closing her eyes, Clara spoke through the rawness. "It hurts so much. I thought I was stronger than this."

"We'll get through this. You're not alone."

As her tears fell, a sharp pain slashed through her chest. Her heart was broken, and she had no idea how she would ever recover. How could she move on without Jerry?

~

"What's the plan for today?" Jerry asked as he stepped into Emma's barn the following Saturday afternoon and rubbed his hands together. Ephraim, Chris, and Wayne relaxed by the horse's stall.

"We were just talking about painting the inside of Emma's *haus,*" Chris said. "She told Katie Ann she wanted to have it painted, but she doesn't have the money to pay anyone to do it."

Ephraim turned to Chris and Wayne. "Why don't you go ask her where she'd like us to start after we finish all the other projects we're planning? I'll be there in a minute." They both nodded, and Ephraim turned to Jerry. "I need to talk to you."

"Okay." Jerry rested his hand on the stall door as Wayne and Chris exited the barn. "What do you need?"

Ephraim's expression darkened. "What are you doing with Clara?"

"What does that mean?" Jerry stood up straight.

"She's in love with you."

Jerry blanched as if he'd struck him. "What?"

"You remember talking to her on Sunday? When I dropped Biena off?" Ephraim asked, and Jerry nodded. "She sobbed the whole way home."

"Why? Because I had to work that day and didn't go to church?" His chest ached at the thought of having inadvertently hurt her.

"It's more than that." Ephraim's frown deepened. "She believes you're never going to join the church. What are you waiting for, Jerry? Just join the church so you can be with her. It's obvious you love her too."

"Whoa." He held up his hand. "I don't need you telling me how to lead my life." He eyed Ephraim with suspicion. "Did she ask you to talk to me?"

Ephraim shook his head. "I just want to help. I told you, she sobbed the entire way home." He rubbed at the back of his neck. "Mandy tried to calm her, but Clara was inconsolable. This is tearing her apart. It's obvious that you care about each other and want to be together. You know you can make this work if you join the church. I think you'll both be *froh* if you do."

"It's not that easy." Jerry leaned back on the horse's stall as confusion, guilt, regret, frustration, and loneliness all spiraled through him. "I do care about her, but I'm not sure if God is calling me to the church. I'm really confused right now."

"Why are you confused? You came to church a few weeks ago. Don't you feel like you've come back home to the community?"

Jerry stared at him. Did he? He didn't know. But he did know he didn't need Ephraim pressuring him too. And maybe Clara had put him up to it. He hadn't actually denied it.

"Jerry, you need to talk to Clara. She's really hurting, and I think you want to work things out."

"*Ya.* Maybe it's time I had an honest conversation with her." Jerry spun and headed for the barn doors.

"That's been long overdue," Ephraim called after him. "Remember, she cares about you. Don't make this worse."

Once outside, his head spinning with frustration, he scanned the garden for Clara. When he didn't find her, he went inside the house. She was in the kitchen, drying dishes as Emma washed them.

"Jerry." Her smile seemed like an effort as she looked over her shoulder. "How are you?"

"Could I please talk to you alone?" he asked, taking in her cautious expression. Maybe she knew very well what she'd done and was smart enough to know he'd be upset when he figured it out.

"*Ya*, of course." Clara pointed toward the family room. "Let's go into the *schtupp*."

Jerry nodded at Emma, and then he followed Clara into the next room.

"What do you want to talk about?" She fingered her apron as she looked up at him. Irritation whipped through him, and he ignored the anxiety he saw in her eyes.

"Did you ask Ephraim to talk to me?"

"No." Her nose scrunched as if she smelled something foul.

"He's pressuring me to be baptized and join the church. Did you put him up to it?"

"Why would I do that?" she said, her voice rising. She backed away from him.

"You've been pressuring me about this ever since I first ran into you here two months ago. Why wouldn't I assume you asked Ephraim to pressure me too?"

"I didn't." She shook her head as her eyes sparkled with moisture. "He did that on his own."

Guilt diluted his anger as she wiped away a tear, but he fought it.

"Why can't anyone let me make my own decisions?" His chest felt tight as anger won out. "I have *mei onkel* telling me he wants me to be his assistant manager, *mei dat* insisting I choose either the Amish or *English* world, and then you and Ephraim pressuring me to get baptized. Why does everyone want to run my life?" He jammed a finger in his chest. "This is my life, not yours."

"No one is telling you what to do." She sniffed as she wiped the back of her hand over her eyes. "We just want you to be part of our community. Is that so bad?"

His jaw worked as he stared at her. A sliver of panic moved through him, and something inside him broke open. "I can't do this. I'm sorry."

He rushed out the front door, ignoring her as she called his name.

~

Clara sank onto the sofa behind her as new pain hit her in the chest. Was that her heart ripping apart? She dissolved into tears and covered her face with her hands. She'd finally pushed Jerry away for good. The hurt was unbearable.

"Shh." Warm arms pulled her into a hug. "It's all right, *mei liewe*." Emma's sweet voice was a balm to her soul. "Everything will be all right."

"No. No, it won't." Clara rested her cheek on Emma's shoulder. "I pushed him away, just like *mei mamm* pushed away her *bruder* when she tried to get him to join the church. She alienated him, and he won't speak to her. I've never even met him or my cousins."

Emma rubbed her back. "I could see the conflict in Jerry's eyes. He's confused, but I think he'll come back home to the church and you. Just give him time."

"I hope you're right," Clara whispered as more tears streamed down her cheeks.

~

A knock on Jerry's bedroom door jarred him awake. He got out of bed, pulled on a T-shirt, and went to the door.

He yawned as he opened it. He hadn't slept well all week, ever since his confrontation with Clara. He hadn't even made an appearance at Emma's to work yesterday because he didn't know how he'd handle seeing Clara again. How could he have yelled at her like that? But he had to stay away from her, for her sake.

Then he was wide awake because his parents were standing in the hallway. "*Mamm? Dat?* What are you doing here, and on a Sunday?"

Mamm looked him up and down, her brow puckered. "I expected you to come to the *haus* and have breakfast with us before church today. Aren't you coming to church? You don't have to work for your *onkel* on a Sunday again, do you?"

"Not today, but I'm not going to church today either." He yawned again as he leaned on the doorframe.

"Why?" She gasped. "Are you *krank?*"

"No. I'm just not sure about church . . . or about anything."

"I don't understand." *Mamm* spoke slowly and cautiously.

"I'll talk to him, Saloma." *Dat* touched her shoulder. "Why don't you go wait in the buggy with Biena? I'll be right there."

Mamm divided a confused look between them and then nodded. "Fine." She turned to Jerry. "I hope to see you again soon."

"You will," Jerry said. "It's a promise."

As *Mamm* headed for the stairs, *Dat* said, "May I sit for a moment?"

"*Ya*, of course." Jerry opened his door wider and then sat down on the edge of his bed. *Dat* took his desk chair.

"You look terrible, Jerry."

"Thanks." Jerry gave a snort.

"Did you sleep at all last night?"

"Not much." Jerry rubbed at a knot in his shoulder. "I tossed and turned. I still have a lot to figure out."

"Do you want to talk about it?" *Dat*'s expression invited him in.

"I don't know." Jerry looked down at the floor. A familiar unease coated his throat, and he drew in a stuttering breath as the pain in Clara's eyes came to mind. He'd hurt her, and he thought he might suffocate on his guilt and regret. An ache opened somewhere inside and seeped through him.

"I haven't been completely truthful with you," *Dat* said.

Jerry's gaze snapped to his father's.

"I told you joining the church for Clara was wrong, but I never told you why I joined the church." *Dat* paused as Jerry held his breath. "I joined for your *mamm*."

"You did?" Jerry leaned toward his father, resting his elbows on his thighs.

"Your *onkel* and I discussed not joining the church. We both wanted to go to trade schools and make money." *Dat* shook his head. "I know it sounds greedy—and believe me when I tell you your grandparents weren't *froh* when we told them. Saul went to school and started his plumbing business, and I thought I was going to do something similar. But then I met your *mamm* and everything changed."

Dat gave him a sheepish smile. "I quickly figured out God's plan for me was different from what I'd had in mind. At first I felt like I was sinful becoming a member of the church because that was the only way to be with your *mamm*. But I soon figured out my heart was there for the right reason. Your *mamm* may have drawn me to the church, but God had called me there all along. I just wasn't listening hard enough to hear him."

Jerry swallowed as he tried to digest his father's confession.

"I'm sorry I didn't tell you this before." *Dat* paused, and then he leaned toward him. "Jerry, I think you need to open your heart to God and listen closely. He might be using Clara to call you."

He stood. "Are you sure you won't come with us today?"

Jerry couldn't face Clara and his friends. "*Danki*, but I'll stay home."

"Okay." *Dat* walked to the doorway and then turned back. "Don't stay away too long."

As his father disappeared down the hall, Jerry threw himself back onto his bed. He stared at the ceiling as his hurt ran so deep he thought he might drown in it.

He closed his eyes and contemplated his father's words. Then he opened his heart and began to pray:

God, I need you. I'm so lost and confused. I don't know where I belong. Am I supposed to be English, or am I supposed to be Amish? I think I might be in love with Clara, but I don't know if that's a strong enough reason to join the church. Please send me a sign telling me where I'm supposed to go. I'm listening.

CHAPTER 7

The August sun warmed the back of Clara's neck as she pulled another weed out of the zucchini bed and dropped it into the basket beside her. She wiped the back of her hand over her sweaty brow before reaching for another one.

"Do you need some help?"

Clara tented her hand over her eyes and looked up at Biena. "*Ya*, that would be nice."

"Great." Biena dropped her basket beside Clara and began pulling up weeds.

They worked in silence for several minutes, and Clara couldn't keep her thoughts from moving to Jerry. She hadn't seen him since he accused her of asking Ephraim to pressure him. That was two weeks ago, and her heart still ached for him. She'd worried about him and prayed for him, hoping their relationship could be repaired. She couldn't accept that even a friendship between them wasn't part of God's plan—unless because of her impatience, that had crashed and burned along with her hope for a future with Jerry.

Clara's curiosity got the better of her, and she couldn't stop herself from asking Biena the question on her heart. "How's Jerry?"

"He's okay." Biena kept her eyes focused on the zucchini plants. "He's been working a lot."

"Oh." Clara pulled another thick, hardy bundle of cheatgrass and dropped it into the bucket.

"I think he misses you."

Clara stilled, her lungs frozen.

"He's very mopey," Biena clarified.

"Mopey?"

"*Ya.* When he stops by our *haus*, he never smiles, and he just kind of paces around." Biena looked up at her. "You miss him, too, don't you?"

Clara nodded. "I do, but I'm not going to pressure him anymore. I'm here if he changes his mind."

"I think he will." Biena pulled another weed.

Clara shook her head. She wished she could believe he'd come back to her, that he could forgive her. But it had been two weeks. She'd missed her chance with him.

Yet Jerry Petersheim would always have a piece of her heart.

～

"You're all set. Just give me a call if that sink leaks again." Jerry set his tool bag in the toolbox in the bed of his truck and then jumped down next to his old school friend.

"*Danki* for coming today." Ivan Smucker shook his hand. "It was *gut* seeing you again. It's been too long."

"It has been a long time." Jerry took in Ivan's big, two-story farmhouse and the sixty acres that encompassed his dairy farm. Just like him, Ivan was only twenty-three, yet he already had his own house and a farm.

"Jerry!"

Jerry turned as Lorene, Ivan's wife, appeared in the driveway.

"Lorene," Jerry said as she approached. "It's so nice to see you. How are you?"

"I'm doing great. *Danki*. I was just visiting our neighbor. She had her fifth *boppli* last week, and I wanted to take her a little gift." She beamed as she went to stand by her husband, who put his arm around her shoulders. "You look well."

"I am." Jerry shook her hand. "I'm staying busy working for *mei onkel* Saul's plumbing company."

Lorene rested one hand on her protruding abdomen. "It's been a long time since we were all playing in the schoolyard."

Jerry nodded. "*Ya*, it sure has."

"Ivan and I will have one in school soon enough." She looked up at Ivan. "I can't believe we're going to be parents. It seems like we were just *kinner* ourselves."

"Time passes quickly." Ivan's face lit up with a smile.

"What about you, Jerry?" Lorene asked. "Are you going to get married and have a family anytime soon?"

Jerry swallowed as his thoughts turned to Clara. What if he *could* have a family, with her? What if he opened his heart to everything God had for him?

Without warning, all the questions haunting him evaporated. He loved Clara, truly loved her. His heart seemed to swell with excitement as he envisioned what his future could be. His love for Clara was godly, and she'd been trying to tell him he needed to come home. He could accept his uncle's offer of a promotion. He could have love, marriage, and if God willed, children.

Even more important was how he felt God's presence. Jerry had expected to hear a trumpet call with God's invitation to the church, but now he realized he'd been whispering in his ear all this time. Jerry just hadn't been listening close enough. *Dat* was right.

Now he heard God's call, and everything made sense. His throat thickened with the realization. His community, the community of his birth, was where his heart had been all along.

God wants me here.

I belong in this church.

This is my home!

He was supposed to be baptized and be Amish. But first he had to meet with the bishop and ask for permission. What was he waiting for?

"You know," he said to his friends, who were looking at him as though he'd forgotten they were even there, "I have to go." Jerry shook Ivan's hand and then Lorene's. "It was really nice seeing you. Call me if you have any trouble with your kitchen sink. Good-bye!"

He jumped into the Chevy and drove toward the bishop's house, his body vibrating with both excitement and anxiety. What if the bishop said no? What if Clara rejected him after the way he'd accused her?

He couldn't live in fear. He had to accept that God was calling him, and God's will was the law. Now he had to convince the bishop, Moses Chupp, that his intentions to join the church were sure and true. He prayed the Lord would give him the right words to convince the bishop that being Amish was the right path for him. This conversation would be life changing.

His heart felt as if it might beat out of his chest as he steered into the bishop's driveway. Moses was a dairy farmer, and Jerry expected him to be home. He parked his truck at the top of the driveway next to the bishop's two-story white house and climbed out.

As he approached the front door, he heard someone call his name. He turned and spotted Moses and his long, salt-and-pepper beard. The bishop was walking out of his barn—sprightly for a man in his midsixties, but a farmer got a lot of exercise.

"Hi, Moses." Jerry jogged over and reached out his hand to greet him. "Is now a *gut* time to discuss a personal matter?"

"Of course." Moses gestured toward a picnic table near the back porch. "Would you like to have a seat over there?"

"*Danki.*" Jerry followed him to the table, and they sat down across from each other on the worn wooden planks. "I appreciate your time."

"It's no problem," Moses said, folding his hands in front of him on the tabletop. "What can I do for you?"

Jerry paused for a moment, but then he decided to plow forward with the full story. "I've been doing a lot of thinking and praying, and I want to be baptized. I know I'm older than most of the folks who will be in your class next spring, but I've felt God call me. And I'm ready."

"Oh." The bishop's eyes flew open as if he were startled by an unexpected noise. "This is *wunderbaar.* I imagine your parents are *froh* to hear this."

"They don't know yet. I've been praying about it for some time, though, and I finally realized today that God is calling me to join the church. I came here as soon as I knew."

Moses nodded slowly, and his dark eyes seemed to study Jerry's. "Are you certain your reasons are pure?"

Jerry's thoughts turned to Clara, and he felt the overwhelming urge to be completely honest with him. "The truth is I'm in love with Clara Hertzler. I knew I cared about her as soon as I saw her again in June, but I also knew I couldn't be with her unless I joined the church. For months I've wrestled with this, afraid if I decided to be baptized, my reasons wouldn't be pure, that only my desire to be with Clara was calling me. Today I realized not only am I in love with Clara, but God has been calling me to the church all along. I just wasn't listening. Today I felt a part of the community again, and I want to commit my heart to God and this way of life."

The bishop rubbed his beard and was silent for a moment. "You truly believe God put this decision in your heart?"

"Absolutely," Jerry said, emphasizing the word. "I could never have decided this without his guidance."

"I believe you." Moses pointed toward the driveway. "What about your truck?"

"I was thinking about that as I drove over here. I'm going to talk to *mei onkel* about selling it to one of his other employees who wanted it before he sold it to me." Jerry yanked his cell phone from his pants pocket and set it on the table. "I'll donate my phone to the Bird-in-Hand Shelter." He gestured to his clothes. "And I'll ask *mei mamm* to start sewing for me too."

"You're ready to shed all your *Englisher* ways immediately?" Moses asked.

"*Ya*, I am. I'll start wearing Amish clothes as soon as *mei mamm* has them ready, and I'll be in church with my district. I'm ready to make a full commitment to this community and to my new life right away, and I'll be ready for my instruction in the spring if you'll accept me into the class." Jerry held his breath, his nerves thrumming as he awaited Moses's decision.

The bishop touched his beard once again, and then a smile broke out on his face. "I'm thrilled to hear you've made this decision. I'll welcome you in my class next spring, and you'll be baptized with the other young people in our district in the fall."

"Oh, *danki!*" He felt like a grinning fool, but he was so grateful. Jumping up, he shook Moses's hand with vigor.

Moses chuckled. "Go tell your parents. They're going to be thrilled."

"*Danki.* I will." Jerry jogged back to his truck, but he planned to tell someone else before he shared the news with his parents and sister.

As he drove to the Hertzler farm, he prayed Clara would not only forgive him, but wait for him to be baptized next fall.

Clara heard a knock on the back door as she chewed a mouthful of green beans. She swallowed and glanced at the clock on the kitchen wall. It was almost six o'clock. "Are you expecting company, *Dat*?"

"No, are you?" *Dat*'s gaze bounced between Clara and *Mamm*.

"No," *Mamm* said.

"I'll see who it is." Clara set down her fork and hurried through the mudroom to the back door. The air in her lungs stalled when her eyes met Jerry's. Had he forgiven her for pressuring him?

Maybe so, because his eyes seemed to plead with her as he folded his hands as if saying a prayer. "May I talk with you, please?"

"Hi, Jerry. *Ya*, of course." She slipped through the door and pointed to the rocking chairs. "Let's sit here." She sat down on her favorite one and turned toward him, her pulse quickening as she took in his expression full of uncertainty.

"I want to apologize." He angled his chair toward her and leaned forward with his elbows on his knees. "I've been terrible to you, and I hope you can forgive me."

"Of course. I forgive you. It's our way."

"I know that, but I really need your forgiveness."

"You have it, and I hope you've forgiven me too." She studied his handsome face. "What's wrong?"

"Nothing is wrong. In fact, everything is right. It's never been this right before."

"I don't understand."

"I realized something today, and I need you to hear me out."

"Okay." Should she be worried? Was he here to tell her goodbye?

"I went to Ivan Smucker's *haus* today to fix his kitchen sink. Did you know he married Lorene Fisher?"

Clara nodded. "*Ya*, I did. Why?"

"They're expecting a *boppli*, and they're really *froh*."

She scrunched her nose as worry gave way to confusion. "What's your point, Jerry?"

"I want everything they have. I want a *haus* and, if possible, children, and I want to have it all with you, Clara." He reached forward and took her hands in his. "I love you. I love you with my whole heart, and I'm sorry it took me so long to figure this out."

She gasped as tears pooled beneath her eyes. Was she dreaming? Had he truly told her he loved her? But what about the church? This couldn't happen if Jerry wasn't Amish.

"I realized you were right all along, Clara. I do need God in my life, and he's been calling me to join the church. I also realized he wants me to be a family with you! I just wasn't listening."

She wiped her cheeks dry as happiness swelled inside her.

"As soon as I left Ivan's *haus*," Jerry continued, "I went to see the bishop and asked him if I could join the next baptism class. He said yes. So I'm here to ask you to wait for me. I want to be baptized, and then I want to marry you and start a life together. *Mei onkel* asked me to be his assistant manager so I can take over the business when he retires. I struggled with that decision, too, but I've decided to accept his offer. I'll save my money so I can build you a *haus*. You just tell me what you want, and I'll do my best to give it you."

He paused. "You've been trying to tell me this is where I belong—here in this community. And you were right. This is my home."

Clara cupped a hand to her mouth as tears flowed.

His eyes searched hers. "Why are you crying? Are you angry with me?"

"No, I'm not angry." She chuckled. "I'm *froh*, Jerry. I've dreamt about this. I love you too."

"Does that mean yes? Will you wait for me?"

"Of course I will." She touched his cheek. "I'll wait as long as I have to."

"*Ich liebe dich. Danki* for helping me see the way."

Jerry pulled her closer for a kiss, and Clara closed her eyes and smiled against his lips. God sent him to Henry's garden so they would find each other and grow a life together, and she was filled with gratitude and joy.

DISCUSSION QUESTIONS

1. Clara is determined to encourage Jerry to join the church no matter the warnings she receives from family members and friends. Do you agree with how she approached the issue?

2. Jerry decided to step away from the church when he was a teenager because he didn't feel God's call to join the church and he didn't feel connected to God. Have you ever felt disconnected from your church or even God? If so, how did you overcome this feeling? Share with the group.

3. Clara's mother misses her brother, who left the community. She regrets pushing him to join the church, and she blames herself for their estrangement. Can you relate to her story?

4. Which character can you identify with the most? Which character seemed to carry the most emotional stake in the story? Was it Clara, Jerry, Jerry's father, or someone else?

5. Jerry's father hides the truth about why he decided to join the church. He doesn't tell Jerry how he first came to the church by marrying Jerry's mother until late in the story.

Do you agree with his decision not to tell Jerry the whole story from the beginning? Why or why not?

6. Jerry eventually realizes he belonged in the Amish community all along. What do you think caused him to change his point of view throughout the story?

Acknowledgments

As always, I'm grateful for my loving family, including my mother, Lola Goebelbecker; my husband, Joe; and my sons, Zac and Matt.

Special thanks to my mother and my dear friend Becky Biddy, who graciously proofread the draft and corrected my hilarious typos.

I'm also grateful for my special Amish friend who patiently answers my endless stream of questions. You're a blessing in my life.

Thank you to my wonderful church family at Morning Star Lutheran in Matthews, North Carolina, for your encouragement, prayers, love, and friendship. You all mean so much to my family and me.

Thank you to Zac Weikal and the fabulous members of my Bakery Bunch! I'm so grateful for your friendship and your excitement about my books. You all are awesome!

To my agent, Natasha Kern—I can't thank you enough for your guidance, advice, and friendship. You are a tremendous blessing in my life.

Thank you to my amazing editor, Jocelyn Bailey, for your friendship and guidance. I'm grateful to each and every person at

HarperCollins Christian Publishing who helped make this book a reality.

I'm grateful to editor Jean Bloom, who helped me polish and refine the story. Jean, you are a master at connecting the dots and filling in the gaps. I'm so happy we can continue to work together!

Thank you most of all to God—for giving me the inspiration and the words to glorify you. I'm grateful and humbled you've chosen this path for me.

THE FRUITS OF FALL

For my amazing friend and marketer,
Kristen Golden, with love

Glossary

ach: oh
aenti: aunt
appeditlich: delicious
bedauerlich: sad
boppli: baby
brot: bread
bruder: brother
bruders: brothers
bruderskinner: nieces/nephews
bu: boy
buwe: boys
daadi: grandfather
danki: thank you
dat: dad
dochder: daughter
dochdern: daughters
Dummle!: Hurry!
fraa: wife
freind: friend
freinden: friends

froh: happy
gegisch: silly
gern gschehne: you're welcome
Gude mariye: Good morning
gut: good
Gut nacht: Good night
haus: house
Ich liebe dich: I love you
kaffi: coffee
kapp: prayer covering or cap
kichli: cookie
kichlin: cookies
kinner: children
krank: ill
kuche: cake
kuchen: cakes
kumm: come
liewe: love, a term of endearment
maed: young women, girls
maedel: young woman
mamm: mom
mammi: grandmother
mei: my
naerfich: nervous
narrisch: crazy
oncle: uncle
schee: pretty
schmaert: smart
schtupp: family room
schweschder: sister
schweschdere: sisters
sohn: son

Was iss letz?: What's wrong?

Wie geht's: How do you do? or Good day!

wunderbaar: wonderful

ya: yes

FAMILY TREE

Featuring *The Christmas Cat* novella characters from
the collection *An Amish Christmas Love.*

Thelma m. Alfred Bender

Mandy   Rhoda

Leona m. Marlin Blank

Darlene m. Uria Swarey   Ephraim   Katie Ann

Emma m. Henry (deceased) Bontrager

Hank the Cat

Darlene m. Uria Swarey

Savannah   Rebekah

Marietta m. Roman Hertzler

Clara

Gertrude m. Elvin King

Wayne

Feenie m. Jeptha Lantz

Arlan   Christian

Saloma m. Floyd Petersheim

Jerry   Biena

CHAPTER 1

M ore thunder rumbled as rain splattered harder on the roadside stand where Tena Speicher frantically packed her wares
into coolers.

"*Ach*. No!" She groaned as she worked faster to clear the fruit
and vegetables lining the shelves. Then, just as the rain let up, she
grabbed the rest of the baked goods and shoved them into the last
cooler. Thank goodness they were wrapped. It was bad enough
that the burst had completely doused her clothes and shoes.

She swiped at the raindrops dripping from her prayer covering,
and a new clap of thunder caused her to jump.

Where was Wayne?

Tena glanced toward the road, where huge puddles had formed.
Movement out of the corner of her eye drew her attention to a man
walking along the side. Despite wet skin, the hair on the back of
her neck raised as she took in his disheveled appearance and slight
limp.

She could see what he was wearing beneath a billowing, clear
rain poncho. Clad in dirty blue jeans with holes in the knees, he
also wore a faded black T-shirt that looked streaked with mud,
sandals on his feet, and an olive-colored jacket tied around his
waist. His jaw was covered with a straggly brown beard, and his

brown hair looked as if it hadn't been trimmed in months. A large olive-green duffel bag was slung over his broad shoulder. As unshaven as he was, his face drenched with rain, she couldn't guess his age.

His dark eyes locked with hers, and her heart thudded in her chest.

She glanced toward her great-aunt Emma's house as her mouth dried. Why had she decided to pack up the stand by herself? Her friends rarely worked on their community garden on a Friday, preferring Saturdays. But a handful of them decided to care for their overabundance of ready-to-harvest crops today. They'd even decided to open the stand for business.

When they all decided to leave earlier than planned because of the threat of rain, she insisted she could pack up everything at the stand by herself so they could beat the storm. Wayne King stayed behind to help her carry it all to the house, but where was he?

"Excuse me, miss. Do you have anything I could eat?"

Tena spun as the stranger came closer. She took a step back and shook her head. "No."

He lowered the duffel bag, but he didn't let it fall to the already muddy ground. He gestured toward the empty shelves. "Don't you sell food here?"

"Yes," she said, making sure to speak English when with an *Englisher*. But if Wayne had been there, she would have told him how uncomfortable she felt in Pennsylvania Dutch. She gestured toward the dark sky. The rain was bound to come down again. "But I have to close up because of the rain."

"I would appreciate it if you could spare something first. I'm so empty my stomach hurts. Anything small would stop the hunger pangs." He pointed to the coolers. "Is there anything in there I could have?"

"I'm sorry, but no." She folded her arms over her soggy black apron as more thunder rumbled above her. She needed to get away from him, but how? He was standing in her way.

"Don't you have anything too old to sell now?"

"No. We'll store everything and sell it tomorrow. Our profits go to charity." She instinctively reached under the counter and placed her hand on the money box. Why hadn't Wayne hurried down to help her carry the food to the kitchen when it started to rain? Even if she could get past this strange man, he might try to follow her to the house.

Panic swelled inside her. He could be just like the *Englisher* who'd left her brother for dead.

"You're sure none of your food just got ruined?" The stranger leaned forward on the counter, his eyes trained on hers. "I would be happy to take it off your hands. Anything is better than nothing, and then you won't have to bother with throwing it away."

She shook her head. "Even if I did, I'm not permitted to give away the food. As I said, my friends and I run this stand to raise money for a local charity."

The man ran his hand down his face, displacing the rainwater in his beard. Tena was almost certain she spotted desperation in his eyes. Her heart pounded against her rib cage. What would he do? Hurt her?

"Hello there!"

Relief flooded her when she turned and found Wayne King walking up to the stand. *Oh, thank you, Lord!* She squelched the urge to hide behind him.

"I'm sorry to bother you," the stranger explained, "but I was wondering if you had any food to spare. I haven't eaten since yesterday. I can't pay you, but . . ."

"Of course we do." Wayne opened the closest cooler, retrieved a bag with three cookies, and handed it to the man. "Do you like chocolate chip?"

The man smiled, showing surprisingly white teeth. "That sounds amazing."

"Tena made them, so they *are* amazing." Wayne grinned down at her, his smile fading as she stared up at him. He raised his dark eyebrows as if to ask her what was wrong, although standing there dripping wet wasn't exactly great. She pressed her lips together and shook her head.

The man devoured the cookies and then set the plastic bag on the counter. "Those were delicious." He nodded at her. "So you're Tena."

"Yes." She touched one of the wet ribbons hanging from her prayer covering and cleared her throat. Why had Wayne told this stranger her name? She didn't want him to know anything about her. She just wanted him to go and leave them alone.

"Why don't we give you a real meal?" Wayne said. "Help me carry these coolers up to the house, and then Tena and her great-aunt Emma can whip up something for you. Well, after Tena gets out of those wet clothes." He turned to look at her again. "I owe you an apology for not getting down here sooner, but the storm spooked Emma's horse and she asked me to see to it."

Tena's eyes widened, and fear whipped through her as she gaped at Wayne. Had he lost his mind? Why would he invite this strange *Englisher* into her great-aunt's home? She had to stop him. He couldn't put them in danger like that!

"That would be fantastic." The stranger lifted his duffel bag, and then he came around the counter. "Which one would you like me to carry?"

Wayne pointed to a cooler and then gestured toward the driveway. "Just head up there and around the back to the porch."

When the man walked away, Tena grabbed Wayne's arm, but then she released it. Her cheeks heated as his vibrant blue eyes, the ones she thought of as sapphires, focused on her face.

She'd never been so forward with a man, but she had to get his attention.

Wayne stepped toward her and lowered his voice. "Are you all right?"

"No, I'm not." She pointed to the man making his way to *Aenti* Emma's home. "How could you invite him into *mei aenti's haus*? For all we know, he could be an escaped prisoner or a thief or . . . He could hurt us!"

Wayne's expression warmed, and he shook his head. "He's hungry, and we have plenty of snacks donated by the other members of our garden group. We also have lots of crops. We can offer him something to eat, and then he'll leave. I promise I won't go home until he's gone. I won't leave you and Emma alone with him, okay?"

She bit her lower lip as she looked up into his eyes. "Promise me."

"I promise." His easy smile turned up the corners of his lips. "Trust me."

Oh, how she wanted to trust Wayne, but trust didn't come easy to her.

He tilted his head. "What's going through your mind right now?"

"I'm just thinking about how the temperature is dropping because of the rain. It may be August, but I can feel a slight chill in the air." She picked up the cookie bag and shoved it into a trash can under the counter. Then she set the money box on top of the smallest cooler and lifted it into her arms. "We need to get inside. I don't think the rain will hold off much longer."

"Right. Let's go." Wayne picked up the remaining cooler, and she followed him up the rock driveway, dodging mud and puddles on her way to Emma's back porch. They made it just before more rain began to fall.

The stranger stood by the door with the cooler at his feet.

Hank, *Aenti* Emma's large, orange tabby cat, stood at the far end of the covered portion of the porch, watching the raindrops as they soaked the rows of fruits and vegetables Wayne and his friends had planted in the spring. The garden was established in memory of her great-uncle Henry.

The door opened with a squeak, and her great-aunt smiled as she looked at Tena and Wayne. Then she noticed the stranger.

"Hello there," *Aenti* Emma said. "May I help you?"

Her great-aunt was in her late sixties, but her flawless skin and dark-brown hair made her look much younger. Just last week, a woman at the market asked her if she was Tena's mother.

"Emma," Wayne began as he walked over to the man, "this gentleman hasn't eaten all day. I thought we could give him a meal."

"Oh, of course." *Aenti* Emma smiled and held out her hand, and the man shook it. "I'm Emma Bontrager. Welcome to my home."

"Thank you. I'm Alex McCormack. It's nice to meet you."

Tena shook her head at her great-aunt's response. Was she crazy too? Why wasn't she leery of strangers, especially *English* strangers?

"I'm Wayne King." Wayne shook Alex's hand and then gestured toward her. "As I said, this is Tena. She's Emma's great-niece, visiting from Indiana."

"Hi," Alex said.

Tena nodded, barely keeping a frown off her face.

"Let's get inside." Emma beckoned them in. The man set down his duffel bag, took off his poncho, and shook it free of rain. Then he and Wayne complied, moving past her into the mudroom with their coolers.

Tena, however, hung back, hoping for a moment to speak to her great-aunt alone.

"Hank," *Aenti* Emma called to the cat. "Get in here. It's raining, you *gegisch* thing."

The cat looked at her, yawned, and then sauntered toward the open door as if he had all the time in the world.

When Tena arrived for her visit and met this feline roommate in June, *Aenti* Emma explained that Hank had invited himself into the house last Christmas Eve during a snowstorm. Despite her efforts to shoo him away, the cat had stayed. And it seemed that *Aenti* Emma loved his company as much as he loved hers. Yet she didn't seem to mind when Hank decided to spend most of his nights on Tena's bed.

"Are you coming in, Tena?" *Aenti* Emma asked.

"*Ya*, but I want to talk to you first." Tena motioned for her to step out onto the porch, and then she lowered her voice. "I don't know why Wayne brought this man up here," she said after *Aenti* Emma let the door click shut. "He came to the stand and asked for food. Wayne gave him some *kichlin*, which I suppose was okay. But then he invited him to come into your *haus*. I tried to stop him, but I couldn't."

"It's okay." *Aenti* Emma rubbed Tena's arm. "I don't mind helping a stranger in need. That's what we're called to do, right?"

Tena gaped. "*Ya*, but we don't know anything about him. And he's an *Englisher*." She grabbed her arm. "What if he wants to see inside your *haus* so he can sneak back here and rob you?"

Aenti Emma chuckled. "What would he possibly want to steal from *mei haus*?" She gestured toward the door. "Would he want my book collection? Or maybe your *onkel*'s wood carvings?" She waved off Tena's concern. "You said Wayne offered him a meal. He didn't ask for it. That tells me he wasn't looking for a reason to see the inside of my home." She pointed to the door. "Stop being *gegisch*. Let's go inside so you can change, and I'll make this man something to eat."

Tena's shoulders tightened as *Aenti* Emma walked into the house. She wrung out the skirt of her gray dress and her black apron the best she could, but she was a mess. Then she picked up the money box and cooler and took a step before someone tall and wide blocked her way.

"Let me get that for you." Wayne took the cooler from her hands and gave her the money box. "I already stowed the other coolers in the utility room. I'll put some of the food in the refrigerator out there."

"You don't have to do that." She forced a smile. "I'll take care of it."

"I don't mind, and I know you want to get out of those wet clothes." He paused for a moment. "Are you sure you're okay?"

"I'm fine." She nodded toward the door. "Go."

"You're awfully pushy." When he gave her a lopsided smile, her heart surprised her with what felt like a somersault.

Tena stepped into the kitchen after shedding her wet shoes in the mudroom.

"What do you like to eat, Alex?" *Aenti* Emma was asking.

"Anything is fine. Thank you." He stood next to her at the counter.

"Would you like to wash up?" *Aenti* Emma pointed toward a doorway. "The bathroom is right through there, on the right."

"Go get changed, Tena," *Aenti* Emma said after Alex left the room. "I'll set the table for all of us. We'll have supper with our guest since it's almost time to eat anyway. I didn't plan a home-cooked meal since it's been so hot, but it will be filling." She pointed toward the stairs. "Go on."

Tena hesitated. "I don't want to leave you alone with—"

"Stop." *Aenti* Emma frowned. "Wayne is here, and I'm fine. Go get changed, and then you can help me get the meal ready."

Tena hurried into *Aenti* Emma's bedroom and hid the money box in her closet. Then as she climbed the stairs, she prayed Alex wasn't planning to hurt them.

CHAPTER 2

Tena hurried into the spare bedroom she'd made her own since her arrival at *Aenti* Emma's house two months ago. She removed her prayer covering and hung it on a peg on the wall to dry. Then she quickly peeled off her wet clothes, dried herself with a towel she'd grabbed from the upstairs bathroom, and pulled on a fresh blue dress and black apron.

She covered her bright-red hair with a blue headscarf and then rushed back down to the kitchen. *Aenti* Emma was placing a basket of rolls and a platter of lunch meat in front of Alex, who was already sitting at the table. He'd obviously washed his face and slicked down his wet hair, but she was sure he needed a shower under those filthy clothes.

Hank sat on a chair next to him and stared at the table as if he were waiting for someone to make a sandwich for his own supper.

"Tena, would you please get the lettuce, mustard, and mayonnaise?" *Aenti* Emma pointed toward the refrigerator.

"Of course." Tena gathered the requested items while *Aenti* Emma set a pitcher of water and four glasses on the table.

The door to the utility room opened, and Wayne entered the kitchen. "All the food is stowed." He crossed to the sink and began to wash his hands. "I put the lettuce in the refrigerator, but I left the other fruits and vegetables out."

"I appreciate it, but I would've helped you." Tena sidled up to Wayne as he leaned against the counter and dried his hands on a towel.

He shrugged. "It's no problem." His eyes moved over her, and she shifted her weight on her feet. "You look nice in blue."

"*Danki.*" She looked out the window to avoid his warm gaze.

"Alex, would you like some pretzels and potato chips?" *Aenti* Emma said. Before he could respond, she turned to Tena. "Would you please get them from the pantry?"

"Of course." Tena found them, and then she set them on the table next to the basket of rolls.

Alex seemed to study the food, and Tena was almost certain she saw tears in his eyes.

"Thank you for this." Alex's voice sounded small.

"You're welcome," *Aenti* Emma said.

Tena folded her arms over her chest as Wayne came to stand beside her. She supposed Alex was glad to have some food, but wariness prickled her skin as she observed him. Yet she found comfort in Wayne's presence. She hoped he would keep his promise and not leave before Alex did.

Aenti Emma sat down beside Alex, and then she looked at Tena and Wayne. "Join us. We're having supper a little earlier than usual, but I know I'm ready."

Tena jumped with a start when Wayne touched her arm.

"I'm sorry," he said. "I was just going to suggest we sit down." He made a sweeping gesture toward the table, and Tena took a chair across from Alex and her great-aunt.

Tena bowed her head in silent prayer, and when she looked up, Wayne and her great-aunt were still praying. Alex was politely waiting with his eyes cast down.

When everyone was ready, *Aenti* Emma handed Alex the plate of rolls, and Tena took some chips before handing the bag to Wayne.

When he had all the makings, Wayne opened a roll and put a pile of roast beef on it. "So, Alex, where are you from?"

"I'm from all over, I suppose." He was building a ham and cheese sandwich. "As I was growing up, I bounced around foster care homes not too far from here, and then I went into the military when I turned eighteen. I served in the Middle East and came back a few months ago."

"Do you work somewhere in this area?" Wayne asked.

Alex cut his sandwich in half as he frowned. "I wish, but I can't find a job."

Tena felt her eyebrows lift. "You can't?"

Alex shook his head. "I've had a difficult time finding one, but especially one that matches my skills." He took a bite of the sandwich, and then he wiped his scraggly beard with a napkin.

"Where do you live?" *Aenti* Emma added a pile of potato chips beside her turkey sandwich.

"I live all over the place. I look for places that are warm and dry." Alex took another large bite.

"Have you tried to stay at a shelter?" Tena picked up a potato chip and popped it into her mouth. "We donate the proceeds from our sales to the Bird-in-Hand Shelter."

Alex shook his head. "They don't want me there. I scare people because I have nightmares."

"You scare people?" Tena studied him. "I don't understand."

"Nightmares can happen when you've seen disturbing things. I wake up screaming sometimes, and it bothers the people trying to sleep."

Tena looked at Wayne. His deep-blue eyes focused on Alex as a warm expression cloaked his face. Didn't it bother him that the folks at the shelter didn't want Alex there? Were they afraid Alex would hurt them too?

"Do you have any family at all?" *Aenti* Emma asked.

Alex shook his head as he chewed.

Aenti Emma clicked her tongue. "I'm so sorry."

Alex shrugged. "That's just how it is. Sometimes those are the cards you're dealt, and you make the best of them."

"Did you travel a lot with the military?"

Alex nodded. "I did."

"Where did you go?" *Aenti* Emma leaned forward as her brown eyes sparked with interest.

"Mostly places in the Middle East, but I also saw a bit of Europe." Alex built a second sandwich, and between bites he shared stories about his experiences in the army.

Tena ignored her food and gripped the edge of the table. This man had been a soldier, trained to physically hurt someone if he needed to—or wanted to. A headache stabbed at the back of her eyes. If they hadn't opened the stand today, Alex never would have asked for food and then wormed his way into *Aenti* Emma's home. But Wayne and her great-aunt seemed to be riveted with his stories.

"Do you like chocolate cake?" *Aenti* Emma lifted Alex's empty plate after he'd finished his third sandwich.

"That sounds fantastic." Alex folded his hands on the table. "Thank you."

"I'm just happy we can help you." *Aenti* Emma turned to Tena. "Would you please get the cake out of the refrigerator?"

Tena retrieved the dessert she and her great-aunt had baked yesterday and set it on the counter. She cut two pieces, and then placed one in front of Alex and the other in front of Wayne. Once again, she was thankful Wayne had stayed this afternoon.

Rain continued to drum on the roof above them.

Tena looked at her great-aunt. "Would you like a piece?"

"No, thank you." *Aenti* Emma shook her head. "I ate too many potato chips. I think I've had enough for tonight." She gestured toward the empty chair next to Wayne. "Have a seat and eat a piece."

"No, thank you." Tena gathered up the condiments. "I'll start cleaning up."

"Let me help you." *Aenti* Emma stacked the rest of their plates and carried them to the counter before filling one side of the sink with soapy water.

Tena retrieved their utensils and glasses, and then prepared to dry the dishes as *Aenti* Emma washed them.

"So you grew up around here?" Wayne asked.

"That's right," Alex said. "I was born in Harrisburg, and I'm told my mother couldn't care for me. I tried to find her before I joined the military, but she had passed away. I don't know who my father is."

"Ach." *Aenti* Emma shook her head as she looked over her shoulder at Alex.

Tena kept her focus on drying the utensils. How did they know Alex wasn't just trying to gain their trust with these sad stories? *Aenti* Emma was obviously too tenderhearted not to believe them.

You were tenderhearted once.

She pushed away the voice in her head. She couldn't let down her guard.

Alex stood when he'd finished his cake. "Well, I thank you for this meal. It's getting dark, so I should be on my way." He pointed to the hallway. "May I use your bathroom before I head out?"

"Go right ahead," *Aenti* Emma said.

"Thank you." Alex disappeared through the doorway.

Wayne carried the rest of the dishes and utensils to the counter and then leaned back against it. "What do you think about letting Alex stay?"

"What?" Tena gasped. "Are you *narrisch*?"

"Hold on a minute." Wayne held up his hands as if to calm her. "I don't mean in the *haus*. I mean in the barn. And then I'll come check on you in the morning."

"That's a marvelous idea." *Aenti* Emma looked up at Wayne. "I have an air mattress, and I can give him a spare pillow and blankets. I bought the air mattress after you all spent the night Christmas Eve. I realized I needed something in case I had guests. Not until Tena called about an extended visit did I finally set up a guest bedroom."

"Have you both lost your minds?" Tena divided a look between them. "We don't know him." She gestured toward the doorway. "He's a total stranger." She looked up at Wayne's unconvinced expression. "You promised you would stay here until he left. Now you want to leave us alone with him?"

Wayne pinched the bridge of his nose, a gesture he seemed to make when he was frustrated. Well, she was frustrated too. "I'm needed at home, Tena, and he'll be in the barn. I'm not suggesting he sleep on the sofa in the *schtupp*."

"Still." Tena folded her arms over her apron. "He'll be here with us, and you won't. What if he tries to break in and hurt us? What if . . . ?" She pulled back her shoulders. "He needs to go back to the shelter. He's not our responsibility."

Wayne frowned and turned to *Aenti* Emma. "What do you think?"

"I think he can stay in the barn." *Aenti* Emma pointed to the window. "It's still raining, and I don't feel right sending him out there. It's not the Christian thing to do." She stepped across the kitchen floor. "Tena, come help me get the bedclothes."

Tena gritted her teeth as she followed her great-aunt upstairs to the spare room still used for storage. Boxes marked "books" littered the floor along one wall, and a stack of old quilts and a few bags of material had settled into corners. Tena wasn't sure what else was in here. She just knew *Aenti* Emma had cleared out the second spare room to make a bedroom for her, kindly using some furniture she already had.

Tena turned to her aunt. "How could you let him stay here? You know what that *Englisher* did to Micah. He almost died!"

"I know." *Aenti* Emma touched her face. "But not all *Englishers* are bad."

Tena shook her head. "I'm afraid of him."

"Let's give him a chance, okay?" *Aenti* Emma opened the closet door and struggled to reach the air mattress on the shelf.

"Let me get it," Tena grumbled as she reached for the box that included a battery-powered pump.

"Tena." *Aenti* Emma placed one hand on her arm. "Look at me."

Tena set the box on the floor and faced her.

"Everything will be fine." *Aenti* Emma's expression was warm, and her voice was gentle. "Alex just needs some help. He won't stay here forever."

Tena nodded despite her growing anxiety.

"I promise you we'll be safe." *Aenti* Emma pointed to the pile of quilts behind Tena. "Grab two of those in case it really cools off. I'll get a spare pillow."

Once they'd gathered what her great-aunt thought they needed, they returned to the kitchen. Alex stood by the table and scratched Hank's chin as the cat sat on a chair with his eyes closed.

"Alex has accepted our offer to spend the night in the barn," Wayne told them, and then looked at Alex. "Well, let's get you set up out there, and we'll settle Emma's horse for the night too." He took the box from Tena. "I'll come back before I leave for home," he told her.

"Okay."

Alex took the quilts and pillow from *Aenti* Emma. "Thank you for allowing me to stay."

"You're welcome." *Aenti* Emma smiled. "Sleep well." When the men started toward the mudroom, she added, "Use umbrellas so you don't get the pillow and blankets wet."

After the men had gone, *Aenti* Emma turned to Tena. "I'm quite tired. If you don't mind cleaning the kitchen alone this evening, I'm going to take a shower and head to bed."

"Of course. I don't mind at all."

"*Danki*. Don't stay up too late."

She left the kitchen, and Tena peered out the window to watch Wayne and Alex make their way to the barn. When she felt something soft against her legs, she looked down to see Hank walking in circles around her. She shook her head.

"You're a traitor, Hank. You're supposed to be on my side, but you seem to like Alex too."

The cat responded with a loud purr before sauntering over to his food bowl, where he began to loudly crunch his own meal.

Tena grabbed a wet cloth to wipe down the table.

She had just finished sweeping the kitchen floor when she heard Wayne come in the back door. She met him in the mudroom just as he set two umbrellas on the floor, still open so they'd dry.

"Alex is all settled in. Again, I'll be by early in the morning to make sure everything's okay."

"Don't you have chores to do on your *dat*'s farm first?"

"I'll let him know what's going on. He'll understand."

"Okay." She smiled at the thought of seeing Wayne again in the morning. Her heart gave a little kick as she studied his handsome face. She was grateful for his friendship.

He reached for her arm, but then pulled back his hand as if realizing that would be too forward. "You and Emma will be fine. I promise you. *Gut nacht.*"

"*Gut nacht.* Be safe going home."

He stepped out onto the porch, and she locked the door behind him.

She grabbed a lantern, turned off the propane-powered kitchen light, and made sure the front door was locked as well before starting up the stairs. Hank streaked ahead of her and scampered into her room.

The events of the day played through her mind as she changed for bed. She'd come to Bird-in-Hand hoping to leave her heartache back home in Indiana. But Alex had brought it all back to the forefront of her mind. She didn't want to think about Lewis and how he'd abandoned their plans to marry when he fell in love with an *Englisher*.

She also didn't want to think about what happened to her older brother, but she couldn't help it with Alex out there in the barn. Micah was walking through town when an *Englisher* high on drugs beat him with a baseball bat just to get the money in his wallet. Micah had been unconscious for nearly a week, and Tena and her parents feared he would die.

By the grace of God, he returned home after two months in the hospital and then a rehab facility, making a full recovery. But Tena would never forget the terror they faced when they thought Micah wouldn't make it.

As far as she was concerned, *Englishers* had no place in the Amish world, but now one was mere yards away in *Aenti* Emma's barn.

Meow.

Tena turned toward the bed, where Hank sat up straight, his purr loud as he stared up at her with his emerald eyes.

"I know. It's time to sleep." She turned off the lantern and climbed into the bed. As if on cue, Hank curled up at her feet, resting one paw on her ankle. "*Gut nacht*, Hank."

Tena smiled as she closed her eyes. How she loved sharing her bed with her great-aunt's precious cat. In fact, she loved everything about *Aenti* Emma's house and her new friends—especially Wayne with his kind blue eyes and lopsided smile.

No, no, no!

She had no room in her life for a boyfriend. She'd come to Bird-in-Hand only to spend time with her great-aunt and heal her broken heart.

She rolled onto her side and faced the window as her thoughts raced. She imagined Alex out in the barn, plotting to take advantage of them, and maybe even hurt them to do it. She couldn't— she *wouldn't*—let that happen.

CHAPTER 3

"G*ude mariye*," Wayne said when Tena unlocked and opened the back door. She looked relieved to see him. Had she been anxious about Alex all night?

"You're here earlier than I thought you'd be. It's only eight."

Then she smiled, her face lit like the midafternoon sun, warming his insides. The moment she arrived at Emma's that day in June, he was sure she was the most beautiful young woman he'd ever seen.

Today she wore the kelly green dress he'd decided was his favorite. It complemented her gorgeous red hair, which reminded him of a summer sunset. Ever since she'd told him she planned to stay only until after Thanksgiving, he'd prayed she'd change her mind, stay in Bird-in-Hand, and date him. The thought made his pulse flutter.

Tena's chestnut-brown eyes sparkled. "I know you said your *dat* would understand if you came back this morning, but I thought you'd have to do at least *some* chores before you came."

"I convinced him otherwise." He'd also promised his two younger brothers he'd do their chores on Monday if they covered for him today. "I was hoping you'd make me breakfast." He rubbed his flat abdomen. "I've been thinking about your pancakes ever since I got up."

"You're going to be *froh*, then." She gestured for him to come inside. "They're waiting for you."

His stomach gurgled with delight as he followed her into the kitchen. Emma was just setting a platter of pancakes into the oven. The table was set for three, so he assumed Emma was planning to invite Alex to eat breakfast with her and Tena.

"Wayne!" Emma moved to the counter. "Let me get another plate."

Tena turned to face him. "Did you check on Alex before you came to the *haus*, Wayne? We haven't seen him. *Aenti* Emma wanted to go to the barn to take care of her horse, but . . . Maybe he left?"

"No, I didn't. I'll go check now, and I'll take care of the horse too." He could tell Tena had tried to hide hope in her voice when she suggested Alex might have left. Was that why she'd seemed anxious? She was still concerned he might hurt her and Emma? Hadn't Wayne calmed her fears last night?

"Tell him we have pancakes ready," Emma said. "I just put them in the oven to keep them warm while I finish frying the bacon."

Tena turned away from him and moved to the refrigerator, obviously disappointed—and upset? He'd have to get her alone later so they could talk. Right now, though, he needed to see if Emma's guest would join them for breakfast.

"I'll be right back." Wayne stepped out the back door and into the humid August air. He made his way down the porch steps and past the rows of fruits and vegetables he and his friends had planted in the spring, in what they called Henry's garden. Henry was Emma's late husband.

The ground was soggy with the aftermath of the much-needed rain from last night—a blessing for their crops. The colorful array included some of his favorites: celery, lettuce, cantaloupe, watermelon, red and green peppers, radishes, squash, zucchini, and red tomatoes. Beyond the vast garden, cornstalks stretched toward the sky. Gorgeous blooms exploded in Emma's flower garden next to Henry's garden, giving another splash of vibrant color to her beautiful land.

The community garden project had come about last Christmas Eve, when Wayne; his best friend, Ephraim Blank; Ephraim's younger sister, Katie Ann; and her best friend, Mandy Bender, visited Emma. It was her first Christmas after Henry passed away. They found themselves snowed in, and they spent the night sleeping on the floor in Emma's family room.

During that same visit Katie Ann proposed starting a community garden in Henry's memory. They began planting in April, and with lots of hard work by multiple volunteers, the garden had flourished. The sales at their roadside stand had been brisk, making it possible to donate a good amount of money to the Bird-in-Hand Shelter, Henry's favorite charity.

Wayne stepped into the barn and found Alex packing. "Good morning. How did you sleep?"

"Fine, thanks." Alex tied his jacket around his waist and slung his duffel bag over his shoulder.

"Are you hungry?" Wayne pointed in the direction of the house. "Tena made us pancakes." When Alex remained silent, Wayne added, "They're the best pancakes in Lancaster County. Trust me."

"I appreciate the offer, but as you know, I don't have any way to pay for them."

"I didn't ask for money. I asked if you were hungry," Wayne said as he turned to tend to Emma's horse.

"Well, if you're sure." Wayne heard Alex let his duffel bag drop onto the barn floor with a thud.

"I am. Give me a hand here, and then we'll go get some of Tena's wonderful pancakes. We'll worry about the air mattress later."

Once he and Alex were in the house, the delicious aroma of pancakes, bacon, and coffee again made his stomach growl.

"Good morning, Alex." Emma greeted him with a wide smile. "I hope you slept well."

"I did. Thank you." Alex shifted his weight on his feet as he stared at the table and then looked over at Tena.

Tena nodded at Alex, her expression tentative as she filled four mugs with coffee.

"I think we're ready." Emma made a sweeping gesture over the table. "Why don't you two wash up, and then we'll eat."

Wayne washed his hands at the sink while Alex stepped out to the bathroom, and then he sat down beside Tena at the table. "Everything looks and smells *appeditlich*."

"*Danki*." Her smile wasn't reflected in her eyes. Was she upset with *him*? But what had he done since she smiled at him earlier?

When Alex returned, he sat down beside Emma.

Wayne bowed his head in silent prayer and then rubbed his hands together when Emma and Tena had finished praying too. "I've been thinking about these pancakes since I got up this morning."

Tena handed him the platter. "Help yourself."

"Thanks." He grinned at her, and then he set a pile of pancakes on his plate, ready to smother them in butter and syrup.

Tena took two and then passed the platter to Alex.

"I was thinking, Alex," Emma began. "You're welcome to take a shower here. I also have my late husband's shaving kit, if you'd like to use it. I'd be happy to wash all your clothes too. You can borrow some of Henry's clothes while you're waiting for yours to dry. I think they'll fit. He kept a youthful figure and was about your height."

Out of the corner of his eye, Wayne saw Tena still. She stared at Emma, obvious surprise flickering in her beautiful eyes.

"I don't want you to go out of your way," Alex said. "You've already done too much for me."

"Nonsense." Emma lifted her mug. "Would you like that shower?"

Alex hesitated, but then nodded as he chewed.

"And would you allow Tena and me to wash your clothes?" Emma gestured at Tena, who was still staring at her.

"That would be wonderful." Alex forked more pancake into his mouth.

"It's settled, then." Emma seemed satisfied with her declaration. "After breakfast, bring us your bag, and we'll start washing your clothes while you're cleaning up."

Tena's lips pressed into a flat line as she turned her attention to her plate. She'd taken only a few bites of her food, and now she merely pushed it around with her fork.

He leaned toward her. "Aren't you hungry?"

She shook her head. "Not really."

"Why?"

She shrugged and picked up her mug of coffee.

"How are your parents doing, Wayne?" Emma asked.

"Fine, thanks." Wayne speared a piece of bacon. "Dad is staying busy. He sold three horses last week, and we have customers coming up from New Jersey to look at a couple of horses on Tuesday."

"Your father owns a horse farm?" Alex asked.

"Yes." Wayne took a sip of coffee. "We breed, train, and sell them."

Wayne spent the rest of breakfast answering Alex's questions about his father's business. When they were all finished eating, Tena began clearing the table.

Emma turned to Alex. "Why don't you get your bag, and I'll find Henry's shaving kit."

"All right." Alex headed toward the back door, and Wayne again noticed his slight limp.

When Emma left the room, Wayne joined Tena at the counter. "*Was iss letz?*" he asked.

"Nothing." She kept her back to him as she began scraping a plate.

"Tena, look at me." He took her arm and gently turned her toward him. "Talk to me. What's bothering you?"

"It's nothing. I just didn't sleep well last night." She turned back to the sink, plate still in hand.

He reached for her shoulder but then pulled back. He'd already been too forward with her, but her silence was eating him up inside.

When she began filling the sink with water, he took a deep breath. He had to find the courage to ask her for a date. He would have to get her parents' phone number first and ask her father's permission. It was all he thought about. But right now he wasn't sure she'd accept.

"Tena, I just—"

The back door clicked closed and Alex reentered the kitchen.

Emma appeared holding a small zippered case and a stack of towels. "I found the shaving kit, and I also found a brand-new toothbrush you can have. Let me get you set up in the downstairs bathroom, and then I can show you where I keep Henry's clothes. I haven't been able to bring myself to give them away just yet."

She took him into the utility room to drop off the clothes in his bag, and then they both left the kitchen.

Tena's back had stiffened.

Wayne moved closer to her and lowered his voice. "Do you think we could talk later?"

"Wayne!" Ephraim Blank announced as he burst into the kitchen, followed by their friend Christian Lantz. "Why aren't you already outside to help us? We have to fix that broken fence today before we have ourselves some invaders." He looked over at Tena. "Hi, Tena."

"*Gude mariye.*" She tossed the words over her shoulder without turning around.

"*Gude mariye,*" Chris responded with a raise of his hand.

"I'll be right there," Wayne said. He'd forgotten all about the fence.

"We'll get started." Ephraim gave a wave, and then he and Christian disappeared through the mudroom.

Wayne swiveled toward Tena as disappointment rolled through him. He'd lost his chance to talk to her alone. "We'll talk later, okay?"

"Sure." She turned and gave him a forced smile before returning to the dishes. How were they going to work through this—whatever it was—so he could ask her to be his girlfriend?

~

As soon as the back door clicked shut, announcing that she was alone in the kitchen, Tena leaned forward on the sink and closed her eyes as frustration and disappointment itched beneath her skin. It was bad enough that an *Englisher* had spent the night in *Aenti* Emma's barn. But now he was showering in her great-aunt's bathroom and was going to use her uncle's shaving kit and wear his clothes!

A door clicked shut somewhere beyond the kitchen, and then the sound of running water filtered into the room. Tena tried to focus on the dishes and shove away her anxious thoughts. Why did *Aenti* Emma have to invite Alex into their home as if he were a long-lost relative? It just didn't make any sense. She knew how badly Micah had been hurt by that *Englisher*!

And Alex said he had nightmares after his service in the army. For all she knew, he could be taking drugs for that. He could be abusing them too.

"I'm going to fill this with the other clothes Alex took from his bag," *Aenti* Emma said as she returned to the kitchen carrying a basket with the dirty clothes he'd apparently left outside the bathroom door. "Then I'll start washing them."

"Do you want me to do it for you?" It was only proper for Tena to offer.

"No, no." *Aenti* Emma waved off the suggestion. "I'm sure your *freinden* will be here soon, and you have so many chores to do around the garden on Saturdays, especially today since the rain cut your work short yesterday. I can handle the laundry."

When the back door clicked open, Tena turned.

"*Gude mariye!*" Katie Ann Blank called as she entered the kitchen followed by Mandy Bender. "It's a *schee* day after that rain we had yesterday."

"*Wie geht's?*" Mandy waved and then bent down as Hank rubbed at her legs. "Hi there, Hank. How are you today?"

Hank looked up at her and blinked.

"It smells like pancakes in here." Katie Ann joined Tena at the sink. "Let me dry the dishes for you."

"*Danki,*" Tena said.

"Do you need help with that laundry, Emma?" Mandy asked. "Where did you get those clothes? They don't look Amish."

Tena braced herself as she waited for her great-aunt to explain.

"We have a guest staying with us," *Aenti* Emma said.

Katie Ann spun toward *Aenti* Emma. "What kind of guest?"

Tena scrubbed the syrup off forks and knives while Emma told them how Alex had come to stay with them last night.

"He slept in the barn?" Mandy asked.

"He's taking a shower right now?" Katie Ann chimed in.

"That's right. He needs our help, so we're helping him." *Aenti* Emma's words were calm despite Tena's festering anxiety at the situation.

"Wow. You're sure you don't need some help with the laundry?" Katie Ann said.

"I can handle it. I know you *maed* have things to do in the garden."

"Let me at least carry that basket for you." Katie Ann crossed the kitchen and took it before following *Aenti* Emma into the utility room, where the wringer washer and cleaning supplies were stored along with Hank's litter box.

Tena rinsed the last of the utensils and set them in the drying rack.

"I'll help you finish the dishes." Mandy appeared beside her. "Are you okay? You seem upset."

Tena bit her lower lip. Where should she even begin?

Mandy leaned on the counter and looked up at Tena. "Do you want to talk about it?"

"No, but *danki*." Tena shook her head. "I'm fine. I'd like to finish cleaning the kitchen and then go work at the stand. How does that sound?"

Mandy smiled, her bright-blue eyes sparkling. "That sounds *wunderbaar*."

CHAPTER 4

After they set up the stand with fruits and vegetables from the garden and a variety of fresh cookies and pies their friends had baked to sell, Tena hopped onto a stool and turned to Mandy beside her. "How are things with Ephraim?"

"*Wunderbaar.*" Mandy's eyes sparkled as she gave a dramatic sigh. "They couldn't be better." She ran her fingers over the counter as she seemed to lose herself in thought. "It's like I have another best *freind.* We talk for hours, and he's kind and supportive. He's just everything I'd always hoped I'd find in a boyfriend."

Tena nodded and looked toward the land across the road. She'd once felt that way about Lewis Yoder. He'd been her friend in youth group before he asked her to be his girlfriend.

For more than a year, he'd seemed like the perfect boyfriend, and he became her closest confidant. When he asked her to marry him, she was over the moon with joy. But that all changed when she learned he'd been seeing an *Englisher* woman behind her back.

Tena had been so overwhelmed with grief that she'd jumped at the chance to visit *Aenti* Emma when her mother suggested it. Getting away from Lewis and their community seemed like the best medicine.

"What about you and Wayne?"

"What?" Tena spun to face Mandy.

Mandy smirked. "Oh, come on, Tena. I'm not blind. I see how you and Wayne seem to gravitate to each other. You're so cute together."

"We're just *freinden*."

"Right." Mandy chuckled as she fished two bottles of water from the cooler by her feet. She handed one to Tena and then opened one for herself.

"I'm telling you the truth. I'm not looking for a relationship right now." Tena opened the bottle and took a long drink, enjoying the cool water on her parched throat. "Besides, I'm staying here only until after Thanksgiving. Then I'm going back home to Indiana." Why did those words make her sad? Bird-in-Hand wasn't her home.

"Don't say that." Mandy touched Tena's arm. "We're all going to miss you."

"*Danki*." Tena smiled. "I appreciate that."

"I know Wayne will miss you." Mandy grinned. "I've never seen him so interested in a *maedel*, and I've known him since we were in school together."

"Really?" Tena wanted to take back her question. She didn't want to encourage Mandy, but at the same time, she wondered what it would be like to date a man as kind as Wayne.

I thought Lewis was kind too!

"I don't think he's dated much either," Mandy continued.

Tena took another drink of water as she noticed a car slowing down on the road. "I think we have our first customers."

"Great." Mandy set down her water bottle and rubbed her hands together. "Let's make some money to help the homeless."

Tena squeezed mustard onto her cheeseburger and then added relish before taking a bite.

"These hamburgers are fantastic," Katie Ann said as she sat across the table from Tena. "*Danki* for bringing the beef for them, Clara."

Clara Hertzler shrugged as she sat beside Jerry Petersheim. "You're welcome. And I'm grateful Jerry and Biena brought the chips and beans."

"And I'm grateful Emma had enough buns." Jerry's cheeks blushed. "I forgot to put them on my list."

"I guess that's my fault," Biena, his sister, added. "When we were at the store earlier, I should have asked him if we were supposed to bring anything else."

"It's no problem," *Aenti* Emma said. "I had quite a few packages of buns left over from the last time you all decided to have a cookout."

"How's your burger?" Wayne asked the question close to Tena's ear, sending chills cascading down her spine. What was wrong with her?

"It's great." Tena smiled up at him. "I always love grilled hamburgers."

"I do too." Wayne smiled and then took a bite of his.

Tena gazed across the long table to where Alex sat between Ephraim and Chris. He looked like a new person with his hair washed and his beard and mustache shaved off. He was handsome in a rugged sort of way, despite a puckered scar on his chin. When he smiled, he revealed those white teeth, which also added to his attractiveness. She now guessed he was in his late twenties. She was relieved to see he was wearing his own clothes and that *Onkel* Henry's clothes were stowed away once again.

She'd been surprised earlier when she found him helping some of their friends weed the garden, and she'd been even more surprised when Clara invited him to stay for supper.

Why hadn't he moved on? Was he going to spend another night in the barn?

Despite that question causing a ball of nerves inside, she took another bite of her hamburger.

"Would you like to join us for church tomorrow, Alex?" Katie Ann asked.

Alex finished chewing, swallowed, and then took a drink from his glass of water.

"That's a *wunderbaar* idea," *Aenti* Emma chimed in. "You can ride to church with Tena and me."

Tena stilled and held her breath as she awaited his response. *Please say no! Please say no!*

"Thank you for the offer, but I don't think so." Alex shook his head and looked down at his plate. "I appreciate the invitation, though."

"Maybe next time." *Aenti* Emma turned to Clara. "How are your parents, Clara?"

Clara smiled. "They're fine, thank you."

Tena let out the breath she'd been holding as other conversations broke out around the table. When she felt someone watching her, she looked over at Wayne. His sapphire-blue eyes studied her rather intensely. She swallowed and then managed a smile.

"Do you like the beans?" she asked. "I love this honey flavor."

"*Ya*, it's *gut*," he agreed. "Let's talk later, okay?"

"*Ya*." As she took another bite of her burger, her stomach fluttered with the thought of being alone with Wayne.

~

Tena sat on the glider on her great-aunt's back porch and pushed it into motion as the cicadas serenaded her. The soft yellow glow of a lantern at her feet was her only light aside from the stars twinkling above her. She settled back in the seat and breathed in the warm air and scent of earth still moist from the rainstorm.

Footsteps crunched up the rock path, and Tena sat up. She leaned forward as the silhouette of a man approached the porch steps. She breathed a sigh of relief when Wayne's handsome face came into view.

"Hi," she said.

"Hi." He pointed to the glider. "May I join you?"

"Of course." She scooted over to the far side of the seat, and he sank down beside her, the glider shifting under his weight.

"I just said good night to Alex out in the barn."

She bristled at the mention of Alex's name. She had to change the subject—fast.

"Did you fix the fencing today?" She angled her body toward him.

"*Ya*." He rubbed his clean-shaven chin.

"Great."

"Alex was a *gut* help too. And it seemed like the weeding we did was calming for him." Wayne nodded toward the barn. "I think he likes it here with us."

Tena's smile faded as all-too-familiar apprehension churned inside her. She turned toward the barn as she imagined Alex sleeping on the mattress in there. Although all her friends seemed to trust him, she still couldn't stop that niggle of worry at the back of her mind. Alex might try to take advantage of her and her aunt.

"Were you upset with me earlier?" Wayne's question broke through her thoughts.

"No." She shook her head. Although she was annoyed with Wayne for inviting Alex to eat with them and then stay—even though *Aenti* Emma had insisted as well—she didn't want to argue with him before he went home. Not only did she enjoy spending time with Wayne, but she also felt safe when he was nearby.

"Okay." He shifted closer to her, and his leg brushed against hers. "I was worried I had done something to make you angry, and it was killing me that you wouldn't talk to me about it."

She blinked as she looked up at him. Why would Wayne be so concerned about her silence?

It didn't matter. She wasn't staying here long, and she wasn't interested in getting her heart broken again.

"You can always talk to me if something is bothering you," Wayne continued, oblivious to her thoughts. "You can trust me."

He touched her hand, and she jumped with a start, pulling her hand away from him.

"I'm so sorry." His eyes widened. "I didn't mean to be so forward."

"It's fine." Tena stood, her heart thumping as she cleared her throat. "It's getting late, and we have to be up early tomorrow for church. I really should head to bed."

"Oh. Right." He stood. "It was nice spending time with you."

"*Ya.*" She shook his hand, and when their skin touched, a tingle raced up her arm. "I'll see you in church tomorrow."

"*Gut nacht.*" He pulled a flashlight out of his pocket and then jogged down the steps and up the path toward his buggy.

She picked up the lantern and headed inside, locking the back door before making her way into the kitchen, where she ran her hands down her face as her head swam with confusion. Why had Wayne's touch affected her so much? She couldn't allow herself to have feelings for another man. She couldn't allow her heart to trust another man.

"Tena?" *Aenti* Emma called from somewhere in the house. "Is that you?"

"*Ya, Aenti* Emma." Tena stood up straight and squared her shoulders. "I just locked the back door. I'll check the front door before I go upstairs."

"Come in here before you go upstairs," *Aenti* Emma called.

Tena stepped into the doorway of *Aenti* Emma's first-floor bedroom, where she sat propped up on her bed, reading a book.

Aenti Emma set it on her nightstand before looking at Tena. "You've seemed distracted all day. Are you all right?"

"*Ya.*" Tena tapped her finger on the doorframe. "I'm fine."

Aenti Emma studied her for a moment, and Tena twisted one of the ribbons on her prayer covering around her finger.

"It's obvious to me that you're not happy Alex is still staying here," *Aenti* Emma began, her expression pleasant. "I know you weren't pleased when I let him wear your *onkel's* clothes, but I felt in my heart that helping him was the right thing to do. In fact, I believe your *onkel* Henry would have done the same thing."

Guilt, hot and searing, sliced through Tena, but she pushed it away. "What about what happened to Micah?"

"Not all *Englishers* are dangerous. You need to realize that. Also, Alex won't be here forever. He'll move on soon, but I'll sleep well knowing I did my best to help him. I just need you to be patient until he leaves. Would you do that for me?"

"Of course." Tena nodded. "This is your *haus*, so it's your choice."

Aenti Emma tilted her head. "While you're living here, it's your *haus*, too, *mei liewe*. Now get some rest. *Gut nacht.*"

"*Gut nacht.*"

As Tena got ready for bed, she hoped *Aenti* Emma was right that Alex would decide to move on soon. She wanted the reminder of how that *Englisher* had hurt her brother out of her sight for good.

⁓

Wayne smiled as Tena walked toward his table with a carafe of coffee after the church service. She looked radiant in a bright-yellow dress with her gorgeous hair peeking out from under her prayer covering. She was so beautiful.

"You're staring at her." Ephraim bumped his shoulder against Wayne's. "You really need to look away before it gets awkward."

"He's way past awkward," Jerry chimed in with a snort.

Wayne rolled his eyes and looked down at his plate.

"Have you told her how you feel?" Ephraim asked.

"No." Wayne shook his head. "I tried to last night, but she cut me off before I could get the words out." The truth was he'd chickened out. He had planned to ask her if she'd be willing to date him, but he just couldn't seem to form the right words. His courage had evaporated as soon as he sat down beside her on the glider.

"Oh." Jerry pretended to stab himself in the heart. "That's harsh."

"Be quiet," Wayne muttered. "Here she comes."

"*Kaffi?*" Tena held up the carafe.

"*Ya,* please." Wayne handed her his cup. "You look nice today."

"*Danki.*" Her cheeks blushed bright pink, and she looked adorable. She filled Ephraim's cup and then reached across the table and filled Jerry's. "I'll see you at *Aenti* Emma's *haus* later."

"I look forward to it," Wayne told her as she moved down the table.

"You need to ask her to date you," Jerry said.

Wayne nodded, but he had to find the courage. "I have an idea for the garden I want to run by you before I bring it up at the committee meeting today."

"What is it?" Ephraim took a sip of his coffee.

"I'm sure you noticed Alex worked hard in the garden yesterday," Wayne began, and Jerry and Ephraim nodded. "I was thinking maybe we could pay him with meals and a place to stay if he worked in the garden every day. He could keep up with the weeding we have a hard time doing since we're not there every day, and we'd be helping him by giving him food and a dry place to sleep. He could also do some of the watering Emma and Tena have been doing by themselves when we can't be there."

Jerry nodded slowly. "I think that's a great idea. We'd be giving him the chance no one else has. It would be great for his self-esteem." He tapped the table. "But you need to make sure Emma is okay with having Alex stay longer. It's her *haus* and barn."

Ephraim hesitated and then took another sip of coffee.

"I've known you since we were seven years old," Wayne told Ephraim. "I can tell when you're holding something back. What are you thinking?"

"I think you also need to discuss this with Tena before you bring it up at the meeting." Ephraim set his cup on the table. "Mandy said she got the impression Tena isn't too *froh* that Alex is living at her *aenti's haus*."

Wayne nodded. He couldn't assume Tena had let go her fear of Alex. "I'll get to Emma's early and talk to both her and Tena before anyone else arrives."

CHAPTER 5

Tena stepped to the back door when she heard a knock. Her heart skipped a beat when she found Wayne standing on the porch. "Hi, Wayne. You're early. Come on in."

"*Danki.*" He removed his straw hat and followed her into the kitchen, where *Aenti* Emma sat looking through a cookbook at the table.

She smiled up at him. "How are you, Wayne? I didn't have a chance to speak to you at church today."

"I'm fine. I was wondering if I could talk to you and Tena before everyone else gets here."

Tena sank into her usual chair and patted the chair beside her. "Sit."

"*Danki.*" Once seated, he folded his hands on the table. "I've been doing some thinking about Alex, and I want to get your opinions—and your permission, Emma—before I bring this up at the meeting this afternoon. I have an idea, but it will affect you two more than any of us on the garden committee."

Tena felt her lips turn down as apprehension unfurled like a flower. She'd barely managed to get over leaving Alex alone on *Aenti* Emma's property while they went to church. Now she had a feeling Wayne's idea was something she wasn't going to like.

"What are you thinking?" *Aenti* Emma asked him.

"Alex did a great job working in the garden yesterday," Wayne began. "Since he doesn't have a job, and the rest of us can't be here to help every day, I was thinking we could pay him to work in the garden by feeding him and letting him stay in the barn. This way he would have a safe place to live, we wouldn't have as much to do on Saturdays, and you two wouldn't have to do so much watering. We can use part of the profits from our sales at the roadside stand to pay for the cost of his food so it won't come out of your pocket."

"What?" Tena asked as anguish rolled through her. "You want him to stay, and you want to *pay* him?" She divided a look between her aunt and Wayne as her body began to tremble.

"That's right. Are you okay?" Wayne's face clouded with apparent concern. But if he were concerned about her, why would he suggest such a thing?

Tena glanced at *Aenti* Emma, whose eyes were focused on her. Then she looked back at Wayne.

"Alex makes me *naerfich*." Tena picked up a napkin and began to shred it as she tried to sort through her jumbled thoughts. "I'm not comfortable when he's around."

"Has he done anything to threaten you?" Wayne's words were slow and measured.

"No." Tena shook her head. "It's just a feeling I get."

"It's okay." *Aenti* Emma patted her hand. "I told you, he won't hurt us."

Tena tried to clear her throat past the knot of anxiety swelling there.

"I don't think he'll ever try to hurt you," Wayne said. "I've spoken to Alex quite a bit, and he seems like a *gut* man. I wouldn't suggest making this offer if I didn't feel you'd both be safe." Wayne toward *Aenti* Emma. "What do you think, Emma? Should we offer Alex the job if everyone on the committee agrees?"

"I think it's a *gut* idea," *Aenti* Emma said.

Tena's gaze snapped to her aunt's as distress weighed down her shoulders.

"I think Alex might appreciate the job." *Aenti* Emma stood. "You all need to vote on it and then decide, but I'll support whatever you want to do." She pointed toward the doorway. "I'm going to rest in my room until your *freinden* get here."

As *Aenti* Emma left the kitchen, Tena had the feeling she was giving her and Wayne a chance to talk alone. Hank scampered after *Aenti* Emma, his tail standing up as straight as a cornstalk.

Tena stood. "I should start getting our supper ready."

"Wait." Wayne followed her to the counter, and his eyes seemed to plead with her. "I want to talk to you. I need you to feel comfortable with this plan."

Tena leaned back against the counter and hugged her arms to her waist. "I've already told you how I feel. I'm not comfortable around *Englishers*, and I can't help it."

"Can you tell me why?"

While she longed to tell him what happened to her brother, she couldn't form the words. It felt too personal, too raw. She turned her head away.

"It's okay." He rubbed her arm, and she relished the chaste intimacy. "I'm glad you're being honest with me about how you feel." He paused. "But I feel in my heart that God is calling us to help Alex, and I can't shake that feeling. I prayed about it last night, and I prayed about it in church today. I got the same answer each time, so I believe I'm on the right path." He reached over and took her hands in his. "I need you to support me on this, Tena. I can't do this without your approval."

Her lower lip trembled as she looked into his eyes. How could she possibly tell him no when he believed he was doing God's work? Her voice stalled in her throat as tears threatened to spill from her eyes.

"Please, Tena." He gave her hands a gentle squeeze. "Will you support me on this?"

"*Ya*. On one condition." Her voice croaked.

"Anything."

"If I feel threatened by anything Alex says or does, you have to tell him to leave."

"Of course." He nodded. "I would never put you or Emma at risk."

"Then you have my support."

"*Danki!*" He pulled her toward him and wrapped his arms around her shoulders.

As she breathed in his spicy scent, she closed her eyes and lost herself in the moment, but then she pushed away from him. What was she doing? Asking for another broken heart?

"Did I do something wrong?" His eyes searched hers.

"No." She shook her head. "I made a casserole yesterday, and I need to turn on the oven to heat it up."

He followed her to the counter. "What can I do to help?"

"Why don't you get the plates and utensils ready?" She pointed to the cabinets.

~

Tena sat at the table beside Wayne during the meeting. She tried to keep a smile on her face as her friends discussed their weekly business. Then Wayne presented his idea.

When he was done, Tena glanced around the table, hoping at least one of her friends would agree with her point of view. But everyone nodded in agreement with Wayne.

"I think it's a *wunderbaar* idea." Mandy looked at Tena. "But does everyone agree?"

Tena nodded as she looked down at the table.

"Have you discussed it with Emma?" Ephraim chimed in.

"*Ya*, he has." *Aenti* Emma stepped into the room with Hank at her heels. "I'm fine with the idea as long as everyone else agrees." She looked over at Tena just as Mandy had, and Tena gave her a quick nod.

"Does anyone want to discuss it further?" Wayne asked, and no one responded. "Ephraim, I guess we can vote, then."

"Will everyone in favor of having Alex work on the garden in exchange for room and board please raise your hand?" Ephraim said.

When all her friends raised their hands, Tena lifted hers in solidarity.

"It's settled, then." Ephraim looked at Wayne. "Will you tell Alex the news?"

"I'll go now, and then he can eat with us." Wayne stood and left the room.

As Tena removed the casserole from the oven, she tried to convince herself that Wayne's confidence in Alex was warranted.

~

Alex had left a note in the barn saying he didn't want to disturb their meeting to let them know, but he was going for a walk. The group decided to go ahead with their meal when Emma said she'd save a plate for him.

Wayne was certain Tena's smile was disingenuous as the group talked and laughed during supper. She participated in the conversations swirling around the table, but her anxiety felt like a third person sitting between them. She told him she supported this plan, but her behavior said otherwise. He had to keep working on getting her to open up to him. She was holding something back, something that had to do with Alex. And he was determined to find out what it was.

After they'd eaten the meatball casserole and brownies she and Emma had prepared, the women began cleaning the kitchen and the men moved to the porch.

Outside, Wayne leaned against the railing while everyone else took a seat on the rocking chairs and glider.

"Are you going to go talk to Alex now?" Ephraim asked. "He's probably come back."

"*Ya.*" Wayne looked out toward the barn.

"Wayne." Mandy stood in the doorway holding a fork, a bottle of water, and a plate with a mountain of casserole and a large brownie. "Take this to Alex."

"*Danki.*" Wayne took what she'd offered and headed to the barn.

"I have supper for you," he said once inside.

Alex looked up from a book he was reading while sitting on the air mattress. "Thank you." He took the plate and fork, and Wayne sat the bottle of water on the floor.

"How has your day been?" Wayne sat on a nearby stool.

"Quiet." Alex ate a forkful of the casserole. "This is good."

"Tena is a great cook." Wayne couldn't stop a smile. What would it be like to date a woman like Tena? His heart seemed to swell at the thought. He had to find the fortitude to ask her if she would. "I want to discuss something with you."

Alex's expression fell. "I was planning on leaving tomorrow. I just wanted to ask Emma if I could stay one more night."

"I wasn't going to ask you to leave." Wayne rested his ankle on his opposite knee. "We're wondering if you'd like to stay indefinitely, in exchange for doing some work in the garden."

Alex studied Wayne with what looked like suspicion. "What do you mean?"

"If you work in the garden every day, we'll pay you with room and board." Wayne pointed out the barn doors. "You could do the weeding we can't possibly keep up with. No matter how much we do on the days we can be here, and no matter what Tena and Emma do on their own, the beds are overrun with dandelions, ryegrass, and bull thistle. The garden is just too big for our resources, and it needs a lot of watering too. You can also do any maintenance Emma might need when the rest of us aren't here. What do you think?"

"Are you sure this is a good idea?" Alex asked.

"Why do you ask that?"

Alex rubbed his chin, hesitating. "I don't think Tena wants me here."

Wayne nodded. "Maybe at first, but I've checked with her, and she's supportive of the idea. So what do you say? Would you like to stay here and help us?"

"I'd love it."

"Fantastic." Wayne leaned over and shook Alex's hand. "We all appreciate it."

"No, I appreciate it." Alex seemed to ponder something as he took a drink of the water. "I didn't think I'd wind up like this." He gestured around the barn. "When I joined the army, I thought it would be my career. Well, I thought it would be a stable job, but then I was injured." He pointed to his left leg. "I shattered my femur in combat, and when it didn't heal correctly, I was discharged. I thought I'd be able to rebuild my life, but things haven't turned out the way I thought they would."

Alex looked away as if shielding his emotions. "I'm thankful you and Emma believe in me, because it's been a long time since anyone has."

Suddenly Wayne felt a calm cover him like a warm, comfortable blanket. It was as if God were whispering in his ear. He was supposed to help this man, and he knew it deep inside. Asking Alex to stay was the right decision, despite Tena's hesitation.

"We're glad to help you," Wayne said. And he truly was.

Wayne smiled as he carried the empty plate and fork back to the house. As he sat and talked with Alex while he ate, the man must have thanked him at least ten times. If only Tena could see the appreciation in Alex's eyes, she would see one of the reasons Wayne wanted to help him. He prayed God would soften Tena's heart toward Alex soon.

He looked toward the porch and spotted her sitting with the other young women as they talked and laughed. She was radiant as she smiled at something Mandy said. He once again imagined what it would be like if they could be more than friends.

Ephraim came down the porch steps and met him. "Wayne, can we talk in private?" He nodded toward the garden. "Let's walk over there."

"Of course. Give me a minute." Wayne handed the plate and fork to Mandy, and then he followed Ephraim to the garden, near the tomatoes. They sat down on a bench in Emma's flower garden. "What's on your mind?"

Ephraim scrubbed his hand down his face and then blew out a sigh that sounded as if it had worked its way up from his toes. "I'm going to ask Mandy's *dat* for permission to ask her to marry me."

"Are you kidding me?" Wayne clapped his hands. "That's fantastic!"

"Shh!" Ephraim glanced toward the porch. "I don't want her to hear us."

"I'm sorry." Wayne punched Ephraim's shoulder. "I'm so *froh* for you."

"*Danki*." Ephraim shook his head. "I hope her *dat* will agree."

"I don't think you have anything to worry about. The Benders think the world of you."

"I also hope she says yes."

"Don't be *gegisch*. I imagine she's been waiting for you to ask." Wayne looked over at Tena. Would he ask her to marry him one day? The thought sent excitement ripping through his chest, surprising him. They'd never even been on a date!

"Did you talk to Tena earlier today?"

"*Ya*." Wayne slumped back on the bench. "I had to convince her to give Alex a chance. The truth is she's not just uncomfortable with him because, to her, he's a stranger. She seems to be afraid of him."

"Do you know why?"

Wayne's heart constricted as he recalled how she'd cried when he pressed her to tell him why. He couldn't bring himself to share the intimate details of their conversation. He was grateful she'd allowed him to hold her, but he also hadn't wanted the hug to end. She'd felt as if she belonged in his arms, as if they were meant to be together. But if that were true, why wouldn't she open up to him?

"I tried. I think she's afraid of all *Englishers*. She made me promise to ask him to leave if he said or did anything to make her feel threatened."

Ephraim's expression grew serious. "Do you think he would hurt Emma or Tena?"

"No. I truly believe he just needs someone to believe him in, and that's what I intend to do." Wayne angled his body toward his friend. "Now, tell me what you plan to say to Mandy's *dat*."

CHAPTER 6

"I can't believe September is almost over," Clara said as she rubbed Hank's chin. He was sitting on their spare stool inside the roadside stand.

"I know." Tena leaned forward on the counter and looked at the pumpkins sitting on the shelves Chris and Wayne had built the previous spring. "Next week is October."

"The month has flown by." Clara turned toward her. "Alex is working out well. He's done a great job keeping up with the weeding in the garden. Jerry told me he said he really likes working there because it calms him and he loves being outdoors."

"That's nice." Tena ran her fingers over the counter as she considered the past few weeks. She'd tried to get used to eating all her meals with Alex and seeing him around the garden and the house, but she couldn't stop feeling nervous around him.

She supposed he was pleasant enough and seemed respectful, and she no longer thought he would hurt them, at least physically. He was also hardworking, and he insisted on helping with the dishes even though she and *Aenti* Emma repeatedly told him it wasn't necessary. But he was still an *Englisher*. She wasn't willing to trust him like *Aenti* Emma and her friends seemed to, and she avoided him as much as possible. He could still be deceiving them.

Wayne had asked Tena several times if she felt comfortable around Alex, and each time she told him everything was fine. Still, she looked forward to the day when Alex decided to leave and find a new place to live.

"Everyone loves Alex." Clara returned to rubbing the cat's chin. "I heard Biena say he might work us all out of a job since he's so *gut* at gardening. He planted all Emma's spring flower bulbs before anyone else could offer."

Tena looked down at her fingernails. She'd bitten them to the quick.

"All right, Tena." Clara faced her. "I've known you for three months now, and I can tell when you're avoiding a conversation. What's going on?"

"Nothing." Tena shrugged and looked out toward the road. *Now would be the perfect time for a car full of* Englishers *to come and start buying all our goods.*

When no car appeared, she decided to change the subject. "How are things with Jerry?"

"They're *gut*." Clara's smile brightly. "We can't officially date until he's baptized next year, but we're enjoying spending time together."

"He's really nice."

"*Ya*, he is, and he's handsome too." Her cheeks flushed, and Tena laughed. "My parents really love him. I can hardly wait until he's baptized. We have so much to look forward to."

"*Ya*, you do." Tena drew circles on the top of the counter with her finger as memories swirled through her mind. She recalled how her heart had raced when Lewis proposed and how her mother had cried tears of joy when Tena told her the news.

Life was perfect back then—or so she'd thought. She believed she could never be happier, and then it all fell apart when she found Lewis kissing that woman behind his father's dairy barn the day she'd surprised him with one of his favorite pies—cherry. The ground seemed to collapse beneath her feet.

Lewis apologized for lying, but he also told her this Kendra Ramsey was his true love. He was going to leave the church and marry her.

Tena's world exploded in a million pieces, and she was certain she'd never love or trust another man.

"Are you really going to go back to Indiana after Thanksgiving?"

Tena's gaze snapped to Clara's, finding concern and possibly even disappointment there. "*Ya*, that's what I told my parents and *Aenti* Emma."

Clara frowned. "We're all going to miss you when you go, especially Wayne."

I'll miss him too.

Tena dismissed the thought. This wasn't her home, and she wasn't ready to trust any man. Her heartache was still too fresh.

A dark-colored SUV pulled up in front of the stand, and Tena and Clara sat up straight.

"Good morning," Clara sang as a young woman with long, wavy blond hair, bright-blue eyes, and a wide smile approached.

"Hi." She turned to the tall man with her. He had dark hair and eyes. "I think this is the place. I heard they have the best produce in Lancaster County."

As the woman came closer, Tena's stomach soured. With her flashy smile and fancy hair and purse, she reminded Tena of Kendra. She fought the urge to run to the house and barricade herself in her room to hide from her past.

"I heard you have the best corn," the woman said.

"Really?" Tena forced her lips to curve into a smile as she pointed to the display of corn ears. "Please help yourself."

"Great." The woman rubbed her hands together. "Do you have any bags?"

"*Ya.*" Clara pulled out a handful from under the counter. "We have a box too."

Ten minutes later, the *Englishers* left with a box full of vegetables.

"I think that was our best sale since we opened." Clara put the cash in the money box.

"*Ya.*" Tena looked toward her great-aunt's rock driveway and let out a sigh of relief when she spotted Mandy coming toward the stand. She was ready to get back to the house—away from the *Englishers* who visited the stand and everything they represented to her.

"Hi!" Mandy waved. "I'm here to relieve one of you."

"You can go," Clara told Tena. "I'm not ready to do more chores yet."

"Oh, come, Clara." Mandy bumped Clara with her shoulder. "Don't you just love stooping over and weeding?"

"I got my fill of weeding this morning." Clara looked down at the cat. "I'd rather stand here and rub Hank's chin for a while longer."

"I think he'll enjoy that." Tena started toward the driveway. "I'll see you two later."

When she reached the top of the driveway, she looked toward the barn. Wayne, Ephraim, Chris, Jerry, and Alex were all hard at work giving it a fresh coat of red paint. Wayne waved at her from atop a ladder, and she waved back.

As she walked toward the house, her thoughts turned to Wayne. He was handsome, kind, thoughtful, and generous. If she were ready to date again, she'd be blessed to have the chance to get to know him even better. But after what Lewis had done, she couldn't risk her heart.

Wayne sat in Emma's glider later that evening and breathed in the cool early evening air. In the distance, the sun was beginning to set, coloring the sky with gorgeous hues of red.

"Would you like some iced tea?" Tena sat down beside him and handed him a glass.

"*Danki.*" He took a sip and smiled at her. "It's *appeditlich.*"

This was his favorite time of the evening. All their friends had gone home, and he and Tena could sit on the porch together and talk—alone. Tonight, he'd decided, he would finally work up the courage to ask her to date him! Surely he'd waited long enough. She seemed to have forgiven his role in inviting Alex into her life.

"I'm glad you like it." She turned toward the barn. "You got a lot done on the barn today. It looks great."

"*Danki.*" He looked up at the sky and then back at her. "Your hair reminds me of the sunset."

"What?" Her chestnut-brown eyes widened as she gaped.

"Your hair." He pointed to the sky. "It reminds me of a gorgeous fall sunset."

She stared at him.

"What?" He laughed. "Why are you so stunned? No one has ever told you that?"

She slowly shook her head.

He set the glass on the porch floor and angled his body toward her. "Your hair is lovely, Tena. I can't believe no one has ever told you that."

"No, no one has." She shook her head and frowned. He was almost certain he spotted tears in her beautiful eyes.

"*Was iss letz?*" he asked as alarm shot through him. "Did I say something wrong?"

"No, it's not you." She took a deep breath. "I saw someone today who reminded me of her, and it brought it all back." She pulled a tissue from her pocket and wiped her nose.

"I'm sorry, Tena, but I'm confused. I have no idea what you're talking about."

"I'm not sure who *Aenti* Emma might have told. I was engaged last year. In fact, I was supposed to be married next month. Lewis and I had it all planned. We were going to live with his parents and eventually build a little *haus* on his *dat*'s dairy farm." She ran a finger around the rim of her glass. "Everything was perfect, or so I thought. One day I wanted to surprise him. I'd made his favorite kind of pie because it was exactly six months to the day before we were going to be married."

She paused and took a deep breath, her gaze still trained on her glass. "At first, I couldn't find him out in his barn, where he usually was that time of day. And his *dat* wasn't anywhere nearby. I saw a flashy little sports car in the driveway, but I thought maybe a customer had come to buy a quilt from his *mamm*.

"When I heard voices behind the barn, I walked back there and found him kissing a woman. She was an *Englisher* with long blond hair and fancy clothes. I gasped and dropped the pie, and Lewis ran over to me. He apologized and said he was going to tell me soon. He also said this woman, this Kendra, was his true love, and he was going to leave the church for her. I was crushed."

She looked up at him, and the pain in her eyes nearly broke Wayne apart.

"I'm so sorry," he whispered, his voice sounding thin to his own ears.

"I felt so stupid. I hadn't seen the signs there all along. He'd been withdrawing from me, distant. He hadn't told me he loved me in more than a month. I would say I loved him, but he'd just nod or say, 'Me too.' He told me he'd met her a few weeks earlier at a restaurant, and that he was going to leave the church and move in with her. She already had an apartment and a job lined up for him. I keep wondering what she had that I didn't. Why wasn't I *gut* enough?" Her voice cracked, and her tears broke free, streaming down her pink cheeks.

"Tena." Wayne pulled her against his side and took her hand. He was grateful she didn't pull away. "Lewis is the one who made the mistake. There's nothing wrong with you. He was misguided, and he didn't realize he already had the most amazing *maedel* he could have ever hoped to find. You're better off without him."

"That's what *mei mamm* said." She sat up straight and wiped her eyes and nose with another tissue. "But it still hurts, especially when I see someone who reminds me of Lewis or Kendra. When I saw that woman at the stand today, it was like reliving that horrible day. I came to Bird-in-Hand so I could forget it all and put it behind me, but it still hurts."

"Tena, you don't need Lewis. He didn't deserve you." Wayne longed to take away her pain, to help her forget. He had to tell her how he felt about her. He took a deep breath and took her other hand as well. "In fact, I care about you. When I first saw you, I felt something stir deep in my soul. You're the most beautiful *maedel* I've ever seen, and you're also a *wunderbaar freind.*"

He traced his finger down her cheek, and she shivered as her eyes went wide. "I love everything about you—your smile, your laugh, your sense of humor. I want to get to know you better and see where this relationship could lead. And I would be honored to date you."

"Wayne, I-I'm not ready," she stammered as she pulled away and stood. "I can't do this. I'm still working through everything Lewis did to me. I can't even think of dating right now."

"Okay." He shifted to the far end of the glider as disappointment gripped him. His cheeks burned with embarrassment, and he rubbed at the back of his neck. "I understand. I never meant to pressure you. I'm fine with just being your *freind* if that's what you need."

She bit her lower lip and studied him, and then she sank

back down on the glider. He longed to read her thoughts. Had he completely misread her feelings for him?

He swallowed a groan. How could he have been so blind as to assume she cared for him the same way he cared for her?

"You know I'm not going to stay here past Thanksgiving." She turned toward him. "You're wasting your emotions on me."

"No, I'm not," he said. "You're important to me."

She shook her head and looked down at the porch floor.

"Tena, please look at me."

She looked up at him and sniffed.

"Don't give up on yourself because of Lewis. He made the mistake, and you did nothing wrong."

"Let's talk about something else, okay?" She gave him a watery smile.

"Okay." He looked toward the barn. "A few folks have told me they're *froh* with Alex's work. He's done a great job in the garden, and he's really *gut* at keeping up with the maintenance around the *haus*. Emma told me he fixed that one window in the *schtupp* that kept going off the track."

Tena's spine went ramrod straight at the mention of Alex's name. Wayne was still befuddled by her feelings toward the man. He needed to know why she was so afraid of him.

"You're still disturbed by Alex being here. Did he do something to upset you?"

"No." She shook her head. "I just don't feel comfortable around *Englishers*. I've told you that."

He opened his mouth to defend the man, or at least ask her what it was about *Englishers* that prompted such as reaction. Surely it was more than her fiancé leaving her for an *English* woman. But he didn't want to argue with her after she'd finally bared her soul to him. They would discuss this further some other time. He took a long drink from his glass and then stood.

"I should get going." He held up his glass, and she took it. "No church tomorrow, but I'll see you soon."

"Okay. Have a safe trip home."

"*Gut nacht.* Sleep well." As he walked to his buggy, he prayed Tena would someday see the good in Alex—and open her heart despite what happened with Lewis.

Tena stood on the porch and watched Wayne lope down the rock path to his waiting horse and buggy. Confusion swirled through her mind and exhaustion through her body as she recalled their emotional conversation. She'd finally poured out her heart to him, and he'd listened and been supportive. And then he told her he cared about her. He even mentioned what he loved about her.

Did Wayne truly believe they could have a future?

Was that what she wanted?

She shook herself from her thoughts and carried the lantern and glasses into the kitchen. After washing the glasses and setting them in the drying rack, she locked the back door and walked into the family room. *Aenti* Emma sat in her favorite chair, reading a magazine. Hank sat beside her in *Onkel* Henry's favorite wing chair.

"Are you comfortable, Hank?" Tena asked with a laugh.

The cat simply lifted his head, blinked at her, and then snuggled deeper into the worn and faded blue fabric.

Aenti Emma set her magazine on the end table beside her. "Did you have a nice visit with Wayne?"

"*Ya.*" Tena sat down on the rocking chair across from her and set the lantern on the floor at her feet. "He told me he cares about me."

Aenti Emma smiled. "That's so nice. I had a feeling he did."

Tears filled Tena's eyes once again.

"*Was iss letz, mei liewe?*" *Aenti* Emma leaned forward and touched Tena's hand.

"I'm just so confused. How will I know when I'm ready to date again?"

"Well, I think you'll know when it feels right. If God puts that desire in your heart, you should give it a chance to grow and flourish, like our fruits of fall outside. You've seen how *schee* our pumpkins are? And the apples from my trees? God did that, just like he gives us relationships that grow with the seasons."

Tena sighed. "I just don't know what to do. I like Wayne. He's kind and listens to me, but I'm afraid of getting hurt again. I'm too scared to share my heart with anyone after what Lewis did to me. Also, I told my parents I'd be back before Christmas, and I don't want to wear out my welcome with you."

Aenti Emma clicked her tongue. "You can't let what Lewis did to you affect the rest of your life. Wayne is nothing like Lewis, and I believe he truly cares for you. When you're ready, you should give him a chance."

Tena nodded, but doubt continued to nip at her.

"And you're welcome to stay as long as you want," *Aenti* Emma said. "I love having you here. If you decide you want to stay permanently, I think your parents would understand. And they're welcome to come visit you." She pointed to the stairs. "You and I can clean out that second bedroom, and I'll get a double bed and a couple of dressers. We can make that another guest room for them."

Tena nodded, but it sounded too good to be true. Could she find true love with Wayne? But how could she just pick up her life and move to Bird-in-Hand when her parents and friends were back home in Indiana?

"I think I'm going to go to bed." Tena lifted the lantern and stood.

"Sleep well, *mei liewe*," *Aenti* Emma called after her.

"You too." Hank rushed past her on the stairs, and then he waited for her at the top.

"Do you think I should give Wayne a chance?" she asked the cat as they walked down the hall.

Hank jumped up on her bed once they were in her room and blinked his eyes at her.

"Is that a yes or a no?" Tena left him long enough to brush her teeth, and then she changed into her nightgown before climbing into bed. Hank took his usual spot, curled up at her feet.

Tena stared at the ceiling and considered her great-aunt's offer. Could she move to Bird-in-Hand?

But was she ready to risk her heart with Wayne? She wanted to trust him, but how would she survive another breakup when her soul was already so fragile?

CHAPTER 7

"N eed some help?"

Wayne looked up from mucking a stall in the barn and found his father watching him. "I thought you said you had some new customers coming today, *Dat*. Wednesday, right?"

"They're not coming for another couple of hours. They left a message saying they got a late start." *Dat* grabbed a pitchfork and started on the next stall. "How are things going at Emma's?"

"They're going well. The harvest has been fantastic, and we've raised a lot of money for the Bird-in-Hand Shelter." Wayne swiped his arm across his sweaty brow before returning to his task.

"That's great. I was talking to the bishop the other day, and he said he's proud of what you all have done. Not only have you helped Emma, but you've helped others in the community."

"*Danki*." Wayne's thoughts turned to Tena. "*Dat*, when you were dating *Mamm*, how did you know for sure she was the one God intended you to marry?"

Dat appeared in Wayne's stall, his blue eyes wide as a smile crept across his face. "Have you met someone?"

Wayne nodded. "*Ya*, I have. I really care about Emma's greatniece, Tena. We've become *gut freinden*, but she's been closed off. I finally got her to open up to me Saturday night, but when I told her I cared about her, she said she wasn't ready to date again. She was engaged back in Indiana, and her fiancé broke her heart. I don't want to lose her, but I also don't want to come on too strong and scare her away."

Dat leaned on his pitchfork. "Well, to answer your question, I just knew with your *mamm*. It was as if God had put it in my heart that she was the one for me. If you feel that, then Tena's most likely the one. If she's not ready, though, I think you should just concentrate on being her *freind* and follow her lead. She'll let you know when she's ready to date."

"Okay." Wayne nodded, and hope rose in his chest. If he was patient, maybe, just maybe, she'd eventually realize he would never hurt her and give him a chance to prove she deserved true love. He just hoped she would love him too someday.

He stilled. Love? Did he love Tena?

He did—with his whole heart.

"How has Alex worked out?" *Dat* asked as he walked back to the stall next to Wayne's.

Wayne took a deep breath and brushed some straw from his shirtfront. "He's been doing a great job. He helps with the weeding as we agreed, and he also helps Emma and Tena around their *haus*. He told me he's thankful we're letting him help us." He turned back to his stall.

"That's *wunderbaar*. I think you've helped that man see he can be a productive member of the community. All he needed was a chance."

"You know, I think we should do more for him. Maybe we can help him find a place of his own and a better job."

"That's a fantastic idea. If you feel like God wants you to help Alex in those ways, you should pray about it and then talk to your *freinden*."

"*Danki, Dat*," Wayne called over to him. "I think I'll do that."

He smiled as ideas began to form in his head. Now, if only Tena would agree to help Alex even more.

~

Tena hung one of her great-aunt's dresses on the clothesline that stretched from the back porch to a large oak tree. As she moved the line, she gazed toward the garden, where Wayne and some of his friends were loading pumpkins into wheelbarrows. Alex was with them.

As she methodically hung her clothes, *Aenti* Emma's clothes, and Alex's clothes to dry in the fall sunshine, her thoughts moved to her conversation with Wayne a week ago.

When Wayne brought up Alex, and she said she was still uncomfortable around him, she was sure he was about to tell her the man had nothing to do with Kendra. Fortunately, he dropped the subject. Maybe Wayne would have been right, but she wasn't ready to tell him what an *Englisher* had done to Micah. She'd been emotional enough just telling him about Lewis. And no matter what, she still couldn't discard her resentment toward *Englishers*, Alex included.

She'd avoided the man as much as possible the whole time he'd been here, ignoring what could be merely a veneer of good, still amazed that her great-aunt and friends welcomed his presence.

She was about to carry the empty clothes basket into the house when Alex called her name from the bottom of the porch steps.

"I have to go for supplies, and your aunt's driver is here. Do you need anything from the store?" he asked.

She'd been so deep in thought she'd never noticed the van's arrival. "No, *danki*." All she could manage with Alex was politeness.

"Okay."

Alex walked away, and Tena went inside, puzzled. Her

great-aunt and Mandy were washing heads of lettuce at the kitchen sink. "*Aenti* Emma, did you ask Alex to go to the store for you?"

"*Ya.* Why?" *Aenti* Emma turned toward her.

"Nothing. I was just wondering." Tena slipped into the utility room, where Hank sat on the floor beside the wringer washer. She looked at him as she set the basket on the floor. "Maybe Alex *is* a *gut* help around here. Still . . ."

Hank responded with a yawn before collapsing onto his side and closing his eyes.

Tena joined the two women in the kitchen. "May I help you?"

"Oh, *ya.* Please." Mandy pointed to the several heads of lettuce clogging up the counter. "Would you please put those in plastic bags and then price them?" She pointed to the stickers on the kitchen table.

"Sure." Tena set to work while her mind spun with thoughts of Indiana. She'd spoken to her parents a few days ago, and they were doing well. Still, she missed seeing them daily, and she missed her friends back home. How would she cope with leaving them all behind if she stayed with *Aenti* Emma permanently?

The women had worked for nearly an hour, washing, bagging, and preparing today's harvest of vegetables for storage and sale, when Alex walked into the kitchen carrying three bags.

"I got all the groceries you put on the list, and also a few things from the hardware store." Alex handed *Aenti* Emma a few bills and coins. "Here's your change."

"Thank you so much." *Aenti* Emma slipped the money into her apron pocket.

"You're welcome." Alex put the bags on the table, nodded at them, and then disappeared through the mudroom.

Tena looked over at her great-aunt. "Has he gone for groceries for you before?"

Aenti Emma shook her head. "No, but he offered, so I thought

I would let him go. He seems to like helping, and we can certainly use it."

Tena nodded slowly. "*Ya*, I guess that's true." Had she misjudged Alex all along? Had avoiding him so much kept her from knowing him as well as everyone else did?

"Alex is a great help." Mandy stepped over to Tena. "And he's been a complete gentleman since he came here."

Tena divided a look between them as she considered their words. "He doesn't make you *naerfich*?" she asked Mandy.

"Alex make me nervous?" Mandy gave a little laugh. "Are you joking? Not at all. He reminds me of Ephraim and Chris. He works harder than half the young people out there in the garden. They're all taking breaks and chatting, but he's still carrying pumpkins." She pointed to the window. "You should take a look."

"I believe you." Confusion wafted over her as she began loading the lettuce into a plastic container. No one else felt the same fear she did when Alex was around. Had she been wrong about him from the first time he walked up to their stand?

Maybe, but she had more reason to be cautious than anyone else.

"Tena, listen to me." *Aenti* Emma rested her hand on Tena's back. "You're going to miss out on a lot of *wunderbaar* friendships being so distrustful of people who are different from you."

Tena kept her eyes focused on her work as guilt crept in. Maybe her great-aunt was right, but she still couldn't forget what that *Englisher* did to Micah.

Wayne waved at Tena as he guided his horse past the roadside stand. She was working with Clara, and some *Englishers* were checking out their pumpkins and the apples from the small orchard Emma told them Henry planted long ago. And of course, the baked goods.

Tena waved in response before turning her attention back to a customer.

A chilly breeze seeped through Wayne's light jacket, and he regretted not grabbing a warmer one when he left the house. For the past two weeks the days had grown shorter and the nights were colder. Now the chill seemed to permeate the air from morning to night. Fall had descended upon Lancaster County.

He frowned as he drove up Emma's driveway to her barn. Thanksgiving was only a month away, which meant he had only a month to convince Tena to stay.

When Wayne reached the barn, he hopped out of the buggy, unhitched his mare, and led it to the pasture. Then he headed toward where Ephraim, Chris, and Jerry were leaning on the pasture fence.

"Well, look who decided to show up today." Ephraim smirked as he gave Wayne's shoulder a light punch. "We were just talking about you."

"Oh *ya*?" Wayne grinned. "What were you saying?"

Jerry pointed to Ephraim. "He was saying he imagined you were sleeping in today while we were doing all the work."

"First of all," Wayne began, holding up his pointer finger, "I never get to sleep in. The chores don't end on *mei dat*'s farm. And second, what exactly kind of work is this?" He gestured toward them. "You're all standing here talking. I wouldn't call that work."

"We just finished carrying more pumpkins down to the road." Chris jammed his thumb toward the driveway. "Since the *Englishers* will celebrate Halloween next week, we can't seem to keep the pumpkins stocked at the stand."

"We're almost out, actually." Jerry nodded toward the garden. "We should plant more next year."

"That's a *gut* idea." Chris nodded. "I'll tell Katie Ann to write that down. She and Mandy are keeping a list of ideas."

"I have an idea I want to run by you all." Wayne leaned back against the fence.

"Uh-oh." Ephraim rolled his eyes with a grin.

"Keep your comments to yourself, Blank," Wayne said, and Ephraim laughed. "I've been thinking about how hard Alex has been working, and I want to do more for him."

"What do you mean?" Jerry asked.

"I keep feeling that God wants us to help him more. I talked to *mei dat* about it a couple of weeks ago, and he suggested I pray about it. So I have been, and I keep coming up with the same answer."

"What answer?" Chris asked.

"That we should help him find a permanent place to live and a real job that pays money. He can keep working here"—Wayne pointed to where Alex was helping harvest apples—"and we'll give him some of the money from our sales to find an apartment. We can support him until he finds a decent-paying job. Maybe we can ask everyone who volunteers here if they know of someone who might hire him. He'd be a fantastic handyman, or he could work at a nursery. He seems to love to be outside working with the crops."

"I think it's a *wunderbaar* idea." Chris held up his hands. "You've all told me the purpose of the garden is to help people."

"Exactly." Wayne nodded. "*Mei dat* said the bishop has been impressed with our work here. He even said he was proud of us."

"Wow." Jerry's eyes widened. "You should bring it up at the meeting tomorrow to see what everyone else thinks."

"I think so too." Ephraim patted Wayne's shoulder. "It's a great idea. It will help us take this project to a new level. Not only will we still be supporting the Bird-in-Hand Shelter, but we'll be helping someone we know get back on their feet."

"Exactly." Wayne's stomach constricted with some worry, though. Would Tena understand?

⌒

Tena shivered and hugged her quilt closer to her body as the bon-fire snapped and crackled in front of her. A large group of young people had gathered at the back of her great-aunt's property for a bonfire and singing tonight.

Couples huddled together as they sang hymns and laughed under the stars. Sad, Tena scanned the happy pairs in the warm glow of the fire. She could still recall how she and Lewis enjoyed attending singings together. They would talk and laugh and enjoy the company of other couples. Would she ever find that happiness again?

"What's on your mind?"

She looked up at Wayne sitting beside her and shrugged. "I was just thinking about how cold it's gotten."

"It has." He pulled his quilt closer. "October has flown by and brought the cold with it."

"*Ya.*" She looked out at the bonfire again.

The group began singing again, and Tena joined in. After a couple more hymns, the group started to break up. A few of the young men used buckets of water to douse the fire, and soon most everyone was heading home.

"Would you walk me to my buggy?" Wayne asked after they'd lingered under the stars a while longer.

"Of course. Let's just take the quilts to the *haus.*" Tena folded up their quilts, and he carried them. They left the quilts on the porch steps, and then she walked with him to his buggy.

"I had fun tonight," he said, holding up a lantern to guide their way.

"I did too." She smiled up at him.

"Tena, I know it's been weeks ago, but I want to apologize for coming on too strong the night I told you how I felt about you." He paused and looked up at the sky before meeting her gaze again. "Your friendship is important to me, and I never want to lose it."

"You haven't." Her stomach fluttered as if on the wings of a thousand hummingbirds as she looked up into his gorgeous blue eyes. "I'm sorry for being so skittish. You're important to me too. I just don't think I'm ready to jump into another relationship."

"I understand." He leaned back against the buggy. "Is there anything I can say to convince you to stay after Thanksgiving?"

She smiled. "I've been thinking about it."

"Really?" His face lit up in a brilliant smile.

"*Ya.*" She hugged her jacket to her body. "I'm just not sure how my parents would take the news."

"Maybe you could stay until Christmas?"

She scrunched her nose. "I'm not sure my parents would agree to that."

"What if we were snowed in at Thanksgiving, like we were last Christmas Eve?" He pointed to the house as a grin turned up the corners of his mouth. "If you were snowed in, you couldn't catch a bus back to Indiana."

She laughed as she touched his arm. "You have all kinds of devious plans, don't you?"

"I do." He cupped his hand to her cheek. "I really like you, Tena." His voice sounded low and husky, sending a ripple of excitement through her body. She shivered.

"I really like you too." Her smile faded as his gaze became intense, stealing the air from her lungs.

He leaned down, and she felt his warm breath on her ear. "I hope you stay," he whispered before brushing his lips across her cheek. She sucked in a breath at the contact.

"I should get going," he said. "I'll see you at church tomorrow. *Gut nacht.*"

"*Gut nacht.*" Her voice was barely a whisper as her body vibrated with anticipation.

He climbed into his buggy, and she waved as he guided the horse toward the road.

Then she ran into the house, locked the back door, grabbed a lantern, and rushed up to her room. After brushing her teeth, she changed into her nightgown and flopped onto her bed. Her head was swimming with both confusion and exhilaration. She moved her hand over her cheek as she remembered the soft caress of Wayne's kiss.

She had enjoyed it! Her heart danced at the possibility of having a relationship with him. But that would mean she'd have to stay in Bird-in-Hand. Would her parents agree to her staying? Did she want to stay?

She covered her face with her hands and stifled a happy yelp. Her cheeks felt as if they would burst into flames.

When she felt something warm and soft against her arm, she opened her eyes and found Hank rubbing his head against her as he purred.

"*Danki.*" She opened her arms to him.

As Hank snuggled with her, Tena tried to imagine a life with Wayne. But how could she think about a future with him when her heart still ached whenever she thought about Lewis's betrayal?

"Please, God," she whispered. "Heal my heart."

CHAPTER 8

"Here's what I want to propose," Wayne began during the meeting the following afternoon. "I think we should take our assistance to Alex one step further."

Tena glanced around the table in confusion and shock as Wayne explained his plan. She studied each of her friends' expressions, waiting for someone to show any sign of disagreement. But they all seemed to nod or smile. She gripped the edge of the table as she tried to wrap her head around Wayne's idea.

"So I think we can help him by paying his rent and seeing if anyone in the community has any leads on a job for him," Wayne concluded.

"What do you all think?" Ephraim asked, looking around the table. "We should discuss it and then vote."

"I love it." Clara tapped the table. "In fact, I'm going to talk to *mei onkel*. He owns a nursery, and he might have a job for Alex."

"Really?" Katie Ann smiled. "That would be great if your *onkel* gives him a job." She turned toward Wayne. "I love the idea too. I support helping him find an apartment. We've been making money since April, and although we've donated most of it to the shelter, we've also saved some of it for any needs that came up. I wouldn't be surprised if we have enough to pay a deposit and a couple of months of rent, as long as it's for a modest apartment."

"I agree," Chris said.

"Me too," Mandy echoed.

"Wait a minute." Tena held up her hands, and she saw Wayne's posture go rigid beside her. "Does anyone disagree?"

The kitchen fell silent, and no one responded.

"Everyone thinks this is a great idea?" Tena asked.

A murmur sounded as they all nodded.

"I'm not sure I think it's a *gut* idea," Tena continued as she noticed Wayne slumping back on his chair.

"Why not?" Mandy gave her a palms up.

"I don't think it's a *gut* use of our money," Tena explained. "I think Alex should use the resources available to him, such as the homeless shelter, to find help. We should just keep donating money to the shelter."

"Isn't it the same thing, though, to help Alex?" Clara asked.

"*Ya*, I agree." Katie Ann nodded. "In fact, this feels more meaningful to me."

"I think so too," Biena said.

"When Wayne shared this with me," Ephraim began, "I told him this feels like we're taking our community service to a new level." He pointed at Wayne. "Tell Tena what the bishop told your *dat*."

Wayne turned to Tena, and she saw pain in his eyes.

"The bishop told me *Dat* said he was proud of us and what we're doing for the community." His voice was soft as if he were pleading with her to agree with him.

But she couldn't agree with him. Still, remorse for stating her opinion so strongly came fast and hard, stealing her words for a moment.

"I think the bishop would be really impressed with this idea too," Jerry added.

"*Ya*," Clara said.

Humiliation dug its claws into Tena's back as she scanned her friends' faces once more. None of them agreed with her. None of them understood how she felt. She was completely alone, and she felt her face flush with embarrassment. She had to get away before she drowned in it.

"I'm sorry." Tena pushed back her chair and stood. "I don't agree with you all, but I don't want to hold you back. Do what you feel is right with the money." She spun and hurried out of the kitchen and up the stairs, ignoring her friends' calls to come back.

When she reached her bedroom, she sank onto the edge of her bed and hugged her pillow to her chest. She'd never felt so alone and ostracized.

Wayne glanced around the table as silence fell over the kitchen. Defeat bulldozed over him, and his throat felt thick. He'd been afraid Tena might not understand his heart about this, but he never imagined she would react this way. He'd been certain their relationship had grown by leaps and bounds after their conversation last night, and she hadn't recoiled from his kiss on her cheek. But he was wrong. They still didn't see eye to eye about Alex. His shoulders slumped with the weight of his disappointment.

"What happened?" Emma appeared in the doorway holding a book in her hand.

Wayne explained his idea. "We voted to do it, but Tena disagreed." Wayne shook his head as both dismay and regret warred in his gut. "She got upset and left. We called her to come back, but she just kept going up the stairs."

Emma set her book on the end of the counter. "I'll go talk to her."

"*Danki*," Wayne said.

Mandy pushed back her chair and stood. "Tell her we're going to eat now, and she should join us."

"I will."

⌒

Tena rolled onto her side and stared out the window as she heard footfalls echoing in the stairwell. When a knock sounded on her doorframe, she looked over her shoulder at *Aenti* Emma.

"Tena, do you want to talk about this?"

"No."

"All right. But you should be with your *freinden*. They're all concerned about you."

"I'll come down later," Tena said, hoping it would appease her.

"But you should have something to eat," *Aenti* Emma said.

"No, *danki*." Tena turned her attention back to the window.

"Mandy brought buffalo ranch chicken casserole."

"I'd rather just be alone." She held her breath, waiting for her great-aunt to move away. She heard her sigh.

"Don't stay up here too long. There might not be any food left. You know how much those *buwe* eat," *Aenti* Emma said. And then her footsteps echoed in the hallway and down the stairwell.

Tena was so tired.

She closed her eyes and listened to the murmur of conversations through the floor while she waited for sleep to take her. She'd hoped Hank would join her, but he must be enjoying being with her friends too much to keep her company.

When the *clip-clop* of horse hooves and hum of buggy wheels on the rock driveway woke her, she sat up, smoothed the wrinkles in her dress, and then patted loose strands of hair back under her prayer covering. She was surprised she felt hungry, and she hoped *Aenti* Emma had saved a plate of casserole for her.

She headed down the stairs to the kitchen and stopped short when she found Wayne standing at the counter with *Aenti* Emma.

When his eyes locked with hers, the whisper of awareness swept over her skin.

"I thought you'd be gone," Tena said.

"I didn't want to leave until I had a chance to talk to you."

Aenti Emma patted his shoulder. "I'll give you two some privacy." She crossed the kitchen floor and gave Tena an encouraging expression. "I'll be in my room if you need me." Hank trotted after her.

"Why did you run out and hide upstairs?" Wayne asked.

Tena shrugged and then sat down in the closest kitchen chair. "No one agreed with me. I was embarrassed, and I felt like the odd person out. I was all alone in the discussion, so I figured it was best if I left."

"No one wanted you to leave." He sat down across from her, a frown forming on his face. "You ran off like a coward."

A coward?

"What was I supposed to do? Everyone was looking at me like I was *narrisch*."

"No one thinks you're *narrisch*." He studied her. "I don't understand how you can be so cold toward Alex after all he's done, though. He's become like one of us, working hard to keep the garden going. Why can't you agree that he's worthy of our help?"

"Wayne, I've told you how I feel, over and over. If you don't understand it by now, there's nothing left to stay." She stood.

"I disagree. I have plenty more to say." He stood as well, his eyes fierce and his tone icy. "Alex may not be Amish, but he is a child of God. Jesus said, 'A new command I give you: Love one another. As I have loved you, so you must love one another. By this everyone will know that you are my disciples, if you love one another.'"

She took a step back as if his words bit her.

"We're called to help one another," he continued, "and Alex deserves our help. I don't understand you. Frankly, I'm disappointed in you for not supporting me and the rest of our *freinden* with this new aspect of our project."

Tena sniffed as her confidence crumbled. "I never meant to disappoint you."

"Just the other day I was thinking about what kind of future you and I could have together." His voice rose. "I was thinking we could date, and then I would ask you to marry me after a few months. *Mei dat* has always said I can build a *haus* on his farm, so I would build whatever size *haus* you'd like. Then we would live there and, with God's blessing, raise a family together."

She swallowed against her arid throat as she looked up at him.

His scowl deepened. "But I can't plan a future with someone who believes anyone who isn't Amish isn't a child of God. You aren't the *maedel* I thought you were."

She opened her mouth to protest, but a sob choked off her words.

"*Gut nacht*, Tena." Turning on his heel, he marched out of the house, the back door slamming in his wake.

Tena stared at the doorway to the mudroom as tears cascaded down her hot cheeks.

"What happened?"

Tena swiveled to face her great-aunt. "Wayne said he thought he could have a future with me, but now he can't because I refuse to accept that Alex is a child of God and deserves our help."

"Let me make some tea, and we'll talk about this. I've kept your casserole warm in the oven." *Aenti* Emma filled the kettle and set it on the stove. Then she took two mugs and tea bags from a cabinet and brought them to the table. "Sit."

Tena sat down and rested her chin on one palm as heartache threatened to suffocate her.

When the water was ready, *Aenti* Emma filled their mugs and brought Tena's supper to the table. They sat in silence for a few minutes, the ticking of the clock the only sound as Tena took a few bites of her food while contemplating her confusing feelings and breaking heart.

She jumped with a start when Hank suddenly appeared on the chair beside her. She scratched his ear.

"Do you care about Wayne?" *Aenti* Emma finally asked.

"*Ya*, I do." Tena kept her focus on the cat as she nodded. "I care about him a lot."

"Is what Lewis did to you the source of your bitterness?"

"My bitterness?" Tena faced her great-aunt. "You think I'm bitter?"

Aenti Emma cupped her mug in her hands. "When you were little, you loved going to the market. You once told me you enjoyed seeing the *English* women and their different hairstyles. You used to talk to them while we stood in line to pay for our food." She chuckled. "One time you asked a lady why the ends of her hair were yellow but the top of her hair was black."

"No!" Tena gasped. "What did she say?"

"She just laughed and said it was because the blond was fake and the dark was her real color." *Aenti* Emma's smile faded. "Back then you enjoyed seeing people who were different from us, and you weren't afraid of them. Now I see resentment in your eyes when you're around Alex. You're even still afraid of him, aren't you?"

Tena wiped her eyes with a paper napkin as her tears began to flow again. "It's true. I am afraid of him because of how that *Englisher* hurt Micah."

Aenti Emma clicked her tongue, a sure sign she didn't like what she was hearing. "Have you told Wayne what happened to Micah?"

Tena shook her head.

"If you told him, he'd understand your point of view, why you struggle with your feelings toward Alex."

Tena sniffed. Why hadn't she told Wayne before? It wouldn't be easy, but he'd been so understanding when she told him about Lewis. Would he be that understanding about how Micah's attack affected her?

"I know Lewis hurt you, and I know you're still healing from what Micah went through." *Aenti* Emma leaned over and squeezed her hand. "I'm sorry for your heartache, but you can't let bitterness define the rest of your life. Lewis has moved on, and Micah has healed from his injuries and returned to a normal life. Now you need to do the same. Live the life God has given you."

Tena wiped her eyes again as regret clamped down on her chest. "Maybe it's time for me to go home."

"Do you really think that's true? Or are you just trying to run away from your problems?"

Tena was dumbstruck by the question and the piercing look in her great-aunt's eyes.

"Pray about it, Tena, and then do what seems right." *Aenti* Emma lowered her eyes and sipped her tea.

Tena stared down at her plate as her thoughts continued to spin like a weathervane in a windstorm. She needed to trust Wayne with the truth about Micah, and she needed to see the truth about Alex, whatever it was. She *would* pray. Only God could help her trust again despite her fears.

CHAPTER 9

G uilt and disappointment bogged Wayne's steps as he made his
way toward where Alex was working near the garden. He was
exhausted after not sleeping more than an hour or so last night.

Every time he closed his eyes, he saw the pain etched on Tena's
face when he'd said he was disappointed in her. He'd hoped they
could have a future, but he couldn't spend the rest of his life with
someone as selfish and cold as she had been toward Alex.

Still, it hurt to the depth of his soul to have to push her away
and abandon his dreams. It was as if he'd broken up with her even
though they'd never dated, and his heart felt as though it had
cracked down the middle.

"Wayne." Alex turned from raking leaves. "Are you all right?
You look like you had a rough night."

"You could say that." Wayne lifted his straw hat and pushed his
hand through his thick hair. "I was wondering if we could talk."

"Of course." Alex dropped the rake and wiped his hands down
his jeans. "What's on your mind?"

"I proposed an idea to the group last night, and they all agreed.
We'd like to help you get set up in an apartment and find a better
job, maybe in a nursery. That way you can get on your feet—have
a place of your own and a steady income."

Alex gaped. "Are you serious?"

"*Ya*. What do you say?"

Alex clamped his hand over his chest. "I don't know what to say. This is an answered prayer, a dream come true. I don't know how to thank you."

"You don't have to thank me." Wayne nodded toward his buggy. "I picked up a newspaper on my way over here so we could look for furnished apartments. We can't afford anything fancy, but we can at least get you something decent."

"I don't need fancy. I just want a place to call my own."

"That's what we'd like to find for you." Wayne nodded toward the buggy. "I'll go get the newspaper. Why don't you take a break, and we'll go through the ads."

"Great. Thank you, Wayne."

"You're welcome."

When he thought he felt someone watching him as he headed to his buggy, he looked up toward the porch, and his gaze tangled with Tena's. Even from this distance he could tell she had dark circles under her eyes. Maybe she hadn't slept much either. An ache opened in his chest and spread through him. While he longed to apologize to her, his head told him to keep walking.

Wayne turned away from her, and as his feet picked up their pace, his ache deepened with each step.

~

"I have an announcement to make," Clara said as they all sat around Emma's table the following Sunday afternoon. "I talked to *mei onkel*, and I told him how hard Alex works here in the garden. I told him he loves the work and he's also a great handyman." Her face lit up. "*Mei onkel* wants to interview Alex for a job."

Everyone clapped.

Tena smiled. She was grateful to hear Alex had the possibility of a job. Though it had taken some courage and much prayer, throughout the week she'd made new efforts to talk to him. Slowly, she realized he truly was a good man. God showed her she'd avoided and misjudged him because of the fear of *Englishers* she developed after her brother's attack, and because of her resentment toward Kendra Ramsey.

She'd asked God to heal her heart the day Wayne proposed they help Alex with an apartment. But she hadn't been willing to really let go. Now, with God's help, she'd realized she could love and trust *Englishers* just as she loved and trusted those who were Amish. She didn't need to fear them.

She glanced across the table at Wayne. He met her gaze but then quickly looked away. Her smile fell. She'd tried to talk to Wayne the day before, but he'd found a way to dismiss her. Sorrow squeezed at her heart. How she wanted to tell him she'd changed.

She missed him. She missed their special friendship, but she'd ruined it all with her selfishness.

"That's *wunderbaar*," Jerry said.

"I know." Clara picked up her glass of water.

"We have an announcement too," Ephraim said as he looked at Mandy.

Mandy blushed and looked down at the table. Ephraim leaned over and whispered something in her ear, and she nodded.

"What is it?" Katie Ann asked, her smile growing.

Did Katie Ann know what their announcement was?

"Mandy and I are getting married in December," Ephraim said, and Mandy's face seemed to glow.

While everyone applauded, Tena looked at Wayne again. He met her gaze, but this time he held it. What looked like sadness and regret filled his eyes. She stared at him, and her pulse thumped as tears welled. She longed to be a part of his life. In fact, she loved him. She loved him with her whole heart, and she missed him so much that she felt as if a hole had been punched in her chest.

For a moment she couldn't breathe, and her anguish felt as if it might smother her. She couldn't give up on him! She had to apologize. She had to convince him to give her another chance.

Wayne looked away, and the loss of the connection knocked Tena off balance for a moment.

"Did I hear someone is engaged?" *Aenti* Emma appeared in the doorway.

"*Ya*, we are." Mandy pointed to Ephraim.

"What fantastic news!" *Aenti* Emma exclaimed. "I'm so *froh* for you both!"

"Come and join us for supper, Emma." Biena gestured for *Aenti* Emma to sit beside her.

When Tena heard a chair scrape across the floor, she looked up to see Wayne heading out of the kitchen toward the mudroom. Alarm gripped her as she heard the back door open and close.

No, no, no! This can't be over!

She jumped up and raced out the back door without grabbing her coat. A wall of coldness slammed into her as her feet hit the back porch. She reached the railing just as Wayne started down the path toward his horse and buggy.

"Wait!" she called after him. "Wayne, please! Wait!"

He spun to face her, his handsome face twisted into a deep frown.

She flew down the steps and caught up to him, shivering as the chilly air seeped through her dress. "I'm sorry. I was wrong, I was selfish, and I was hateful. Please forgive me."

His frown relaxed slightly as he stared down at her.

"You—you were right about Alex. I was so wrapped up in my resentment toward *Englishers* that I didn't realize I had let it change me and turn me into someone I don't want to be."

He opened his mouth to speak, but she drew a deep breath and took the plunge she'd been fighting. "There's something I never told you. Two years ago, my older *bruder*, Micah, was walking down the street in town when an *Englisher* high on drugs beat him with a baseball bat. He almost died. He spent months in the hospital and rehab, first fighting for his life and then to recover."

Wayne gasped as his eyes searched hers. "Why didn't you tell me?"

"I should have. But talking about it has always been so painful." She gestured toward the barn. "I was distrustful of Alex because of what happened to Micah, and I was wrong. Alex *is* a child of God, and he *does* deserve our help. We're called to be helpers, and it's our duty to do what we can for people like him. I'm sorry I didn't realize sooner that I was being so sinful and hateful, so closed to the truth, so unwilling to let go."

She took another deep breath. "But I know one thing for certain. Losing your friendship is my greatest fear. The idea of not having you in my life scares me to death. I miss you. And I would do anything to convince you to give me another chance."

She closed the distance between them and reached up, cupping her hand to his cheek. "I love you with my whole heart, Wayne. I want to stay here in Bird-in-Hand. I want us to date, and I hope someday we'll marry and build a life together. I want to see what God has in store for us. So, please, Wayne, please forgive me."

A strangled noise escaped his throat, and his blue eyes glistened. "I thought I'd never hear you say that."

His placed his lips on hers, sending an electric heat roaring from her toes to her cheeks. She closed her eyes and then felt herself relax. He wrapped his arms around her, and she lost herself in the feel of his touch. She felt safe, protected, and cherished. This was what true love felt like.

"*Ich liebe dich*," he whispered against her ear. "I would be honored to be your boyfriend."

Tena smiled as she looked up at him. "You'll have to ask *mei dat*, but I'm pretty sure he'll say yes. *Aenti* Emma will tell him what a *wunderbaar* man you are."

Wayne laughed and trailed the tip of his finger down her cheek.

⁓

Tena and Wayne sat on the glider on *Aenti* Emma's back porch with a quilt wrapped around their shoulders, sipping hot chocolate.

Tena smiled as she looked up at the stars twinkling in the sky above them. It had been a wonderful afternoon. After their talk outside, they'd joined their friends for *Aenti* Emma's amazing chili, and everyone seemed thrilled to see they'd repaired their friendship. Alex was there, too, and he had a smile on his face when he caught her eye.

Now she and Wayne were enjoying quiet time alone.

"This is the best hot chocolate I've ever had," Wayne said as he cradled his mug in his hands and looked into her eyes. "You've truly spoiled me with your expertise. I don't think I'll ever enjoy anyone's cooking as much as I enjoy yours."

Tena giggled as she bumped her shoulder against his. "You're just saying that so I'll keep cooking and baking for you—especially anything with peanut butter."

"*Ya*, that sounds *gut*." He smiled down at her and then sighed. "I love sitting out here, but pretty soon it will be way too cold."

"We'll just have to visit in the *schtupp*, then. We'll be nice and warm in there."

"When are you going to call your parents?"

"Tomorrow night. I don't want to wait, do you?"

Wayne shook his head, and her stomach fluttered at the thought of telling *Mamm* and *Dat* she wanted to stay in Bird-in-Hand. "Why don't you come over for supper? Then we can call them together, and you can ask *mei dat*'s permission to date me after I explain everything to them. After all, you're the main reason I want to stay here with *Aenti* Emma."

He took her mug and set it and his on a nearby table. Then he turned and brushed his lips against hers, sending her emotions into a wild swirl. "I love you, Tena."

"I love you too."

She rested her head on his shoulder and smiled. She'd allowed fear to shut out the truth for too long, but she was so grateful God had taught her to trust again.

And now? Now she looked forward to seeing her love for Wayne and his love for her grow like the crops in Henry's garden, nourishing them both with a lifetime of happy memories.

Discussion Questions

1. Tena doesn't want to use some of the proceeds from the garden to help Alex because she believes it's not her or her friends' responsibility to help an *Englisher*. Do you agree with her point of view?
2. Tena left her community to try to escape the heartache of her breakup with her fiancé. Have you ever tried to escape a bad situation by moving away? If so, how did this turn out for you? Share this with the group.
3. Wayne is convinced God has called him to help Alex. Do you agree with his point of view and determination to help Alex?
4. Which character can you identify with the most? Which character seemed to carry the most emotional stake in the story? Was it Tena, Wayne, Alex, or someone else?
5. Alex is down on his luck when he happens upon the roadside stand. He has no idea he's found people who truly want to help him. He's overwhelmed by their willingness to give him a chance to prove he can contribute to their community. Have you participated in any volunteer programs to help the homeless at your

church or elsewhere? If so, how did you help them? Did
you find your efforts rewarding?

6. At the end of the story, Tena realizes she had been so
embroiled in her bitterness after her breakup and brother's
attack that she allowed it to change her point of view
about God's call to help others. What do you think caused
her to change her point of view throughout the story?

Acknowledgments

As always, I'm grateful for my loving family, including my mother, Lola Goebelbecker; my husband, Joe; and my sons, Zac and Matt.

Special thanks to my mother and my dear friend Becky Biddy, who graciously proofread the draft and corrected my hilarious typos.

I'm also grateful for my special Amish friend who patiently answers my endless stream of questions. You're a blessing in my life.

Thank you to my wonderful church family at Morning Star Lutheran in Matthews, North Carolina, for your encouragement, prayers, love, and friendship. You all mean so much to my family and me.

Thank you to Zac Weikal and the fabulous members of my Bakery Bunch! I'm so grateful for your friendship and your excitement about my books. You all are awesome!

To my agent, Natasha Kern—I can't thank you enough for your guidance, advice, and friendship. You are a tremendous blessing in my life.

Thank you to my amazing editor, Jocelyn Bailey, for your friendship and guidance. I'm grateful to each and every person at HarperCollins Christian Publishing who helped make this book a reality.

Acknowledgments

I'm grateful to editor Jean Bloom, who helped me polish and refine the story. Jean, you are a master at connecting the dots and filling in the gaps. I'm so happy we can continue to work together!

Thank you most of all to God—for giving me the inspiration and the words to glorify you. I'm grateful and humbled you've chosen this path for me.

WINTER BLESSINGS

With love and appreciation for Zac Weikal
and the members of my Bakery Bunch

Glossary

ach: oh
aenti: aunt
appeditlich: delicious
bedauerlich: sad
boppli: baby
brot: bread
bruder: brother
bruders: brothers
bruderskinner: nieces/nephews
bu: boy
buwe: boys
daadi: grandfather
danki: thank you
dat: dad
dochder: daughter
dochdern: daughters
Dummle!: Hurry!
fraa: wife
freind: friend
freinden: friends

froh: happy
gegisch: silly
gern gschehne: you're welcome
Gude mariye: Good morning
gut: good
Gut nacht: Good night
haus: house
Ich liebe dich: I love you
kaffi: coffee
kapp: prayer covering or cap
kichli: cookie
kichlin: cookies
kinner: children
krank: ill
kuche: cake
kuchen: cakes
kumm: come
liewe: love, a term of endearment
maed: young women, girls
maedel: young woman
mamm: mom
mammi: grandmother
mei: my
naerfich: nervous
narrisch: crazy
oncle: uncle
schee: pretty
schmaert: smart
schtupp: family room
schweschder: sister
schweschdere: sisters
sohn: son

Was iss letz?: What's wrong?

Wie geht's: How do you do? or Good day!

wunderbaar: wonderful

ya: yes

FAMILY TREE

Featuring *The Christmas Cat* novella characters from
the collection *An Amish Christmas Love.*

Thelma m. Alfred Bender

Mandy   Rhoda

Leona m. Marlin Blank

Darlene m. Uria Swarey   Ephraim   Katie Ann

Emma m. Henry (deceased) Bontrager

Hank the Cat

Darlene m. Uria Swarey

Savannah   Rebekah

Marietta m. Roman Hertzler

Clara

Gertrude m. Elvin King

Wayne

Feenie m. Jeptha Lantz

Arlan   Christian

Saloma m. Floyd Petersheim

Jerry   Biena

CHAPTER 1

"S orry I'm late! But I brought a chicken and rice casserole." Mandy Bender gave a little laugh as she rushed into Emma Bontrager's kitchen carrying a Pyrex portable container.

"Oh, Mandy! That casserole sounds *appeditlich!*" Emma clapped her hands. Although Emma was old enough to be Mandy's grandmother, her dark-brown hair and nearly wrinkle-free skin made her look much younger than her late sixties.

"*Danki.* I hope it tastes as *gut* as it sounds." Mandy looked down at Emma's large, fat, orange tabby cat as he rubbed her leg and blinked up at her. "Hi, Hank. Do you want to try some chicken casserole?"

"He'd probably love that." Emma held out her hand. "Give me your coat, and I'll hang it in the mudroom."

Clara Hertzler walked over to the counter. "What's in the container Ephraim's carrying?"

"A salad." Mandy spun to face her fiancé, Ephraim Blank.

"The casserole does sound *wunderbaar.*" Clara took the salad from Ephraim and set it on the counter. "We were just concluding our meeting."

"Oh no. I was afraid of that." Mandy frowned as she set the casserole next to the stove. Unfortunately, her mother let someone borrow both their insulated carryalls, so she had to warm up the casserole.

"You can tell us what we missed," Ephraim said. "I can't wait to have some of that casserole. My stomach growled all the way here just thinking about it."

Mandy smiled up at him. She loved how he towered over her by nearly one whole foot. Of course, since she was only five feet two, most of her friends were taller than she was. But it wasn't just Ephraim's height that had attracted her. With his light-brown hair that turned golden in the summer, his kind honey-brown eyes, his strong jaw, and his bright, inviting smile, he was the most handsome man she'd never known.

"Are you going to turn on the oven?" He grinned at her.

"Oh, right!" Mandy gave a little giggle as she flipped the dial to preheat, and then she looked toward the table where her group of friends all sat. She knew they'd been discussing the community garden they'd started on Emma's property in memory of her late husband, Henry, just like they did every Sunday afternoon. Along with baked goods and, now, Emma's orchard apples, they sold the fruits and vegetables they grew at a roadside stand in front of Emma's house. Then they donated most of the profits to the Bird-in-Hand Shelter for the homeless, Henry's favorite charity. The rest they saved for any other needs.

"So. What did we miss?" Ephraim asked.

"Let's see." Katie Ann, his younger sister, tapped her lip as she looked down at a notebook. "We were just discussing closing the stand for the winter. Since it's getting colder and our only offerings now are winter squash from the garden and Emma's apples, we should probably do it no later than the weekend before Thanksgiving. We have some vegetables left, but Emma, Tena, and Mandy plan to can them this week for Emma and Tena to use all winter."

"I agree," Christian Lantz said with a nod. He'd been Katie Ann's boyfriend for a while now, and Mandy was thrilled for her best friend.

"I do too," Jerry Petersheim chimed in. He'd recently returned to the church, and he and Clara had the chance to rekindle their attraction for each other because of Henry's garden. They planned to date as soon as he was baptized.

Oh, how this project was bringing couples together!

"What do you think?" Katie Ann met Mandy's gaze.

"*Ya*, of course." Mandy shrugged. "Whatever you all decide is fine with me." She watched Ephraim cross the floor to the kitchen table and sink into a chair between Wayne King and Chris.

"We were talking about Alex too," Clara said, referring to Alex McCormack, a homeless veteran who'd helped them manage the garden during the fall. She pulled a stack of paper plates from Emma's cabinet. "I gave everyone some news about him."

"Oh?" Mandy took the stack of plates and delivered them to the table. "What news?"

"*Mei onkel* interviewed Alex for a job at his nursery and hired him. Also, he offered Alex the suite in the back of his office until he finds an apartment. It has a bedroom, bathroom, and kitchenette, and he's going to move out of Emma's barn tomorrow."

"Really?" Mandy smiled. "That's great news. It has to be getting cold at night in your barn, Emma."

"*Ya*, it is," she said. "This comes just in time!"

"Are we still going to help him with his security deposit and a couple months' rent?" Ephraim asked.

"*Ya*." Clara nodded. "But *mei onkel* says there's no hurry."

"That's fantastic," Mandy said.

"I'm glad we were able to help him," Wayne added.

"I agree." Tena Speicher, Emma's great-niece, smiled at him. They were dating now too.

Another "garden variety" pair.

She put the casserole in the oven to warm.

"So when do we eat?" Ephraim said as Clara carried the container of salad to the table.

"Patience," Mandy said. She followed Clara with disposable bowls, and Tena brought utensils. "Emma, I assumed you'd have some of your fantastic homemade salad dressing. I hope I wasn't wrong."

Emma moved to the refrigerator. "You know I always have some made up. I'll get it."

"I'll get the glasses and a pitcher of water." Katie Ann hopped up and made a couple of trips before she and everyone else sat down.

After a silent prayer, they all filled their bowls with salad and conversation broke out around the table. Mandy smiled as Katie Ann shared a funny story about a customer who'd stopped by the stand yesterday, but although she did her best to seem cheerful and interested, she couldn't stop thinking about everything she had to do for her December wedding. She had only a little more than a month to finish making the dresses, and she also had to plan the menu and make the table decorations.

How was she going to get everything done in only six weeks? It wasn't that she'd waited too long to get started. Ephraim had proposed only two weeks ago!

She had to stop worrying, though. She and Ephraim had so much to look forward to! She'd get it all done somehow.

When everyone had finished eating their salad, Mandy gathered the bowls and tossed them.

"The casserole should be ready now." She flipped off the oven and grabbed two pot holders. "It just needed to be warmed up a bit." She opened the oven, and a wall of warmth hit her face. She hefted the dish onto the counter.

"All right." Mandy smiled at her friends as she carried the

casserole to the table. "This is *mei mammi*'s recipe. I hope you like it."

"It looks amazing." Tena rubbed her hands together.

"*Danki.*" Mandy grinned as she set the platter in the center of the table. Then she sat down beside Ephraim. He gave her a nod, and then scooped some casserole onto his plate.

Mandy sat back in her chair as her friends all filled their plates. The room fell silent as they dug in. When Mandy felt something touch her thigh, she found Hank standing on his back legs with his paws on her lap.

"So you *do* wish you could have some of this food too?" Mandy touched his nose.

"Oh, Mandy!" Tena gushed. "This is fantastic."

"It's great." Ephraim leaned close to her, his voice low in her ear, sending a flutter low in her belly. "*Wunderbaar.*"

"*Danki.*" Mandy's chest swelled with warmth as the rest of her friends joined in with praise. "I'm so glad you like it. I made this meal special for us."

Mandy smiled. Sunday nights were her favorite times with her best friends.

Ephraim folded his arms over his heavy coat as he sat on a rocking chair on Emma's back porch and looked toward the garden he and his friends had planted in the spring. His life had changed so much since he'd asked Mandy to be his girlfriend eleven months ago. It was as if their relationship had grown and blossomed like the fruits and vegetables they'd sold at the roadside stand all season long.

He smiled to himself as he imagined her beautiful face, her bright-blue eyes, and her sweet laugh. He'd always considered Mandy to be just another young girl who came over to bake and giggle with his sister. But then one day he saw her in a new light. It was as if she had grown up overnight. Before long she was also his friend, and he wanted to know her better.

Along with Katie Ann, Mandy, and Wayne, he'd visited Emma last Christmas Eve, and his world seemed to shift just as sure as they'd been snowed in. That night he realized he wanted to be more than Mandy's friend. A few days later, he asked her to be his girlfriend, and then two weeks ago he worked up the courage to ask her father's permission to propose. Mandy had said yes, and neither of them wanted to wait for marriage any longer than necessary.

In six weeks, Mandy would be his wife, and they would start a new journey together. His heart thumped as he pictured their bright future. He was blessed to have Mandy in his life, and he would cherish her and take care of her to the best of his ability.

"So you're going to be a married man in less than two months." Wayne, his best friend, patted his shoulder from the rocking chair beside him. "How does that feel?"

"Amazing." Ephraim grinned and glanced at Wayne. "I'm ready."

"You know, you're making the rest of us look bad," Chris teased.

"How so?"

"Now the other *maed* will want us to propose," Chris said, turning his palms up. "Now they'll all want to get married—soon."

"Not Clara." Jerry smirked. "I can't propose until after I'm baptized next fall, so I'm off the hook for now." He pointed his index fingers at Wayne and Chris. "But you two, well, that's a different story."

Chris groaned. "I don't think I'm ready yet."

"I admit I'm not either," Wayne said. "Tena and I are just getting to know each other better." Then he smiled. "But I'm *froh* for you." He gave Ephraim a nudge. "You and Mandy will have a *wunderbaar* life together."

"*Danki.*" Ephraim smiled. He couldn't wait to see what God had in store for him with the woman he loved.

~

"The casserole was *appeditlich.*" Emma gave Mandy a warm smile as she held up her clean Pyrex dish.

"*Danki.*" Mandy buttoned her coat and then took the dish. "I'm so glad you liked it."

"Are you ready?" Ephraim asked as he lifted the salad container from the counter.

"*Ya.*" Mandy said good-bye to her friends, and then she followed Ephraim to his waiting horse and buggy. She shivered as she looked up at the clear sky, taking in the bright stars twinkling above her. "It's such a *schee* night for early November."

"*Ya.*" Ephraim opened the buggy door for her and took the Pyrex dish out of her hands. "It is."

As she climbed into the buggy, she smiled. She'd known Ephraim nearly all her life. Mandy and Katie Ann had declared each other best friends on their first day of school when they were seven years old. Mandy still recalled seeing Ephraim on the playground that first day. He was two years older than she was, and he caught her eye the moment he smiled at her. She'd always had a crush on him, and she never imagined he'd ever see her as more than his little sister's friend.

But everything changed last fall. He seemed to linger and talk to her more often when she visited Katie Ann at their farm. Then he seemed to seek her out at church and at youth group events. He finally asked her to date him shortly after Christmas last year, and her father had readily agreed.

Two weeks ago, he'd proposed, surprising her, and she couldn't contain her happiness! She couldn't wait to take his name and move in with his family until his father built them a house on his dairy farm.

"Can you believe we'll be married in six weeks?" Mandy heard her voice lift with excitement as he handed her the dish and container to hold on her lap. "It's coming so quickly!"

"It is." He closed the door and jogged around to the driver's side.

"But I have so much to do. I still have to finish making my dress. Then I have to make the dress for *mei schweschder*. She has enough to do helping *Mamm* with her sewing business." She angled her body toward his. "And I have to plan the menu with *mei mamm* and *schweschder*."

"It will all come together." He gave a slight nod as he kept his eyes trained on the windshield while guiding the horse toward the road.

"What do you think about having lasagna and garlic bread for our wedding supper?" she asked. "*Mamm* thought it might be a *gut* idea since we can prepare the lasagna pans ahead of time."

He gave a shrug. "Anything will be great."

She tilted her head as she studied his profile. "It's just so much. I'm overwhelmed."

"Don't worry. It will all get done."

But how? she wanted to ask him. Not only did she still have responsibilities to her family at home, but she hadn't realized planning and executing a wedding took so much work. That was probably because she was the first to marry among her friends. Maybe her mother had some idea, but Mandy knew she would never want to be anything but optimistic about their plans.

She turned toward Ephraim, who still stared straight ahead without another word. The buggy was filled with the sound of wheels scraping on the road, the *clip-clop* of the horse's hooves, and the roar of passing traffic. Still, it was too quiet for her, allowing the list of wedding tasks to once again roll inside her head.

"What are you thinking about for table decorations?" Ephraim's voice broke through her thoughts.

"What?" She spun to face him.

"I asked what you're thinking about for table decorations."

"Oh." She forced a smile. "*Mamm* and I think we should go with a blue candle that matches the dresses, and maybe a little baby's breath. That will be simple but elegant."

"Sounds perfect."

"*Ya.*" She blew out a sigh.

"What was that sigh for?"

"The truth is I just don't see how I can accomplish everything I need to do for the wedding in six weeks." She threw up her hands, almost spilling the stack of kitchenware on her lap to the floor.

"Well, both of our *schweschdere* will help you. Your *mamm*, too, right?"

"I know, but still, it's hardly enough time." Her shoulders tightened as she awaited his response, even though she wasn't sure what she wanted him to say.

He halted the horse at a red light and faced her. "Would you feel better if we went by to see *mei mamm*? Maybe she can help make the decorations."

"Really?" Hope lit in Mandy's chest.

"Sure." He smiled. "I bet she'll be thrilled to help."

"Great." She gripped the stack on her lap. If Ephraim's mother agreed to help, surely some of the stress plaguing her would ease.

CHAPTER 2

After Mandy placed the dish and container on the floor of the buggy, Ephraim held out his hand as she climbed out. "Everything will be fine. I promise you."

"*Danki.*" She laced her fingers with his and enjoyed the reassurance his hand entangled with hers always gave her.

She allowed him to steer her through the cold air up the path and to the back porch. As they entered the home's back door, voices sounded from the kitchen.

"Do your parents have guests?" she asked Ephraim as she pulled off her coat.

"I wasn't expecting any." Ephraim took her coat and hung it on a peg next to his.

Mandy followed him into the kitchen, where they found Ephraim's parents sitting with his older sister, Darlene. Her husband, Uria, and their young daughters, Savannah and Rebekah, were there too.

"Darlene!" Ephraim said as they walked in. He greeted Uria and the girls. "How are you all doing?"

"Hi, Mandy!" Savannah waved. Seven years old, she had her mother's light-brown hair and honey-brown eyes, so like Ephraim's as well.

"Hi." Mandy waved hello to all of them and then took a seat in the empty chair by Rebekah. She was nine and had the same coloring her sister had. Mandy glanced around the table and took in the adults' expressions.

Something was wrong. Didn't Ephraim notice? His parents' faces looked serious, and Uria looked upset. Had his sister been crying?

"Would you like some *kaffi*?" Ephraim's mother held up a carafe.

"*Ya. Danki*, Leona." Mandy pushed back her chair.

"Sit. I'll get you a mug." Ephraim retrieved two mugs from a cabinet. "I didn't know you all were coming. I would have stayed home from the meeting at Emma's if I'd known. What brought you here today, Darlene?"

Mandy noticed a look pass between Darlene and her mother, and Darlene dabbed her eyes. What was going on?

Ephraim filled the mugs with coffee before setting one in front of Mandy. After he sat down next to Uria, she saw him take a good look at his parents and then his sister. "What am I missing?"

"I lost my job," Uria said.

"What? When?" Ephraim's handsome face clouded with a scowl.

"Back in August." Uria blew out a deep sigh. "The construction company closed. I've been doing odd jobs and looking for something permanent, but nothing has panned out."

"I'm so sorry to hear that," Ephraim said. "Why didn't you tell us sooner?"

"We were hoping something else would come along," Darlene said. "We hated to burden you all with our problems."

"Do you have a plan?" Ephraim asked.

Mandy sipped her coffee. When she felt something touch her arm, she turned and found Rebekah holding up a chocolate chip cookie.

"*Danki*," Mandy whispered as she took the cookie and bit into it.

"We came to ask for help." Darlene looked at her husband and rubbed his arm. "We can't pay our rent anymore, and we've gone through our savings. We have nowhere else to go."

"They're going to move in with us!" Ephraim's father said. "Uria will help Ephraim and me run the dairy farm, and we'll get to spend more time with our granddaughters."

Mandy was glad to hear his cheerful tone. Yet knowing his daughter and her family had come to this point had to be difficult.

Mandy took another drink as she tried to catch Ephraim's eye. The stress in the room was palpable. This felt like a private family discussion. If Ephraim would just look at her, she could motion for him to take her home.

Mandy felt a tug on her sleeve. She turned as Rebekah held out another cookie. While her parents were trying to find stability, the girls just seemed happy to be eating cookies.

"*Danki*," Mandy said again as she took the cookie and placed it on a napkin next to her half-eaten first one.

The back door opened and clicked shut, and Katie Ann appeared in the doorway.

"Darlene!" She went to her sister and hugged her. "I didn't know you were coming today. Rebekah! Savannah!" She hugged her nieces next. "What's the occasion?" She sat down next to Savannah and took a cookie from the little girl's plate with a grin.

Darlene cleared her throat. "Well, Uria lost his job in August, and he hasn't found anything permanent. Since then we've depleted our savings."

Katie Ann looked around the table. "Are you moving in, then?"

"*Ya*," Leona said. "They are. We were just discussing that. Uria is going to work on the farm with your *dat* and Ephraim."

"Darlene and Uria can take the sewing room," *Dat* said.

"And the *maed* can stay with me." Katie Ann turned to her nieces. "Would you like that? One of you can sleep in my big bed. And we'll get a cot for the other."

"Yay!" Rebekah clapped her hands. "We can stay with *Aenti* Katie Ann."

"Can I bring my dolls?" Savannah's tone seemed hesitant.

"Of course you can." Katie Ann poised to take a bite of her cookie. "I'll clear some of my shelves. You can both bring your special things."

Savannah seemed satisfied with that.

"Are you really okay with this?" Darlene's eyes glistened.

Katie Ann rubbed Savannah's arm. "I always have room for my favorite nieces."

"We're your only nieces," Rebekah said, and Katie Ann laughed.

"I really appreciate it," Darlene said. "We just don't know what else to do."

"We'll make it work for now." Marlin reached across the table and touched Darlene's hand. "I'll build you all a *haus* in the spring. We'll just be a little cramped in this *haus* until then."

"*Danki, Dat.* We hate to be a burden."

"Family is never a burden, *mei liewe*," Marlin insisted.

"Would it be all right if we move in this week?" Uria asked. "We have to be out of our rental as soon as possible."

"*Ya*, of course. We can help you move tomorrow." Marlin turned to Ephraim and Katie Ann. "Right?"

They both nodded.

Mandy shifted on her chair. This conversation felt so personal. She shouldn't be here. She turned to Ephraim, who had finally looked at her. He raised his eyebrows in question. "Why don't you take me home?"

"Okay." Ephraim pushed back his chair.

"It was nice seeing you all," Mandy said.

They all said good-bye, and she followed Ephraim into the mudroom. After they pulled on their coats, they headed into the cold and climbed into his buggy.

They rode in silence as he guided the horse away from the house. Mandy contemplated the family's discussion. The Blanks were facing some big changes. Her heart broke a little as she recalled the sadness on Darlene's face.

"Why didn't Uria tell us when he lost his job?" Ephraim's question broke through their silence. "He and Darlene should have known we wouldn't consider knowing about their troubles a burden."

"Maybe he was embarrassed. I'm sure he feels responsible for taking care of his family, and he never expected to find himself in such dire straits."

"But my parents could have helped them months ago." Ephraim gave her a sideways glance.

"Uria probably thought a job was going to come through." Mandy bit her bottom lip as she suddenly saw her future shifting. How could Marlin build a house for Darlene and her family next spring and build one for Ephraim and Mandy at the same time? It wasn't possible. And how could the family manage with so many people in the house all winter, including her? She wouldn't be a blessing. Even though she knew they'd never think so, she'd be a burden!

Only one solution made sense.

"It will be different having Darlene and her family living with us," Ephraim said, his voice pleasant as he looked out the windshield. "But it will be nice to see my nieces every day."

"The *haus* will be cramped," Mandy said.

"Cramped?" Ephraim shrugged. "*Ya*, I suppose so, but we'll make do." He smiled at her. "Just wait until you move in. Then it will really be chaotic."

"You don't honestly think I should still move in?"

"What do you mean?" He halted the horse at a red light and turned toward her. "Why wouldn't you move in?"

She angled her body toward him. "The last thing your parents will need is another mouth to feed. You're already going to have eight people in the *haus*."

"Exactly. That's why it won't make a difference if there's a ninth."

"No." Mandy shook her head. "We need to delay the wedding. Not just because it will be crowded with me there, but to give your family the time they need to adjust. It won't hurt us to wait a few months."

His eyes went wide. "You don't want to marry me as soon as possible?"

"Of course I do. But I think we should delay the wedding for your family's sake. Besides, I'm stressed because I don't have enough time to get everything done. An eight-week engagement has turned out to be too short."

"We have plenty of time," he said, insisting.

"No, we don't. And now your parents have more important things to worry about."

A horn behind them tooted, and Ephraim guided the horse through the intersection.

A heavy silence fell between them, and Mandy racked her brain for how to make Ephraim understand her point of view. Wasn't it obvious that this wasn't the best time to get married?

"Ephraim, please hear me out," she began. "Your parents are under a lot of stress right now. The wedding is the last thing they need to worry about. They need to be concerned about Darlene and her family first."

"I disagree," Ephraim said. "They love you, and they want you to be part of our family."

"I know that," Mandy kept her words measured. "I love your family, too, but things will be better in a few months. Let's wait until everything settles down. We'll still have to wait for our *haus*, but at least—"

"No." He interrupted her. "I don't want to wait."

Mandy pinched the bridge of her nose. "There's no reason to rush."

"There's no reason to wait," he said, challenging her.

She blew out a frustrated sigh and looked out at the passing traffic.

"You're having doubts, aren't you?" he spat. "That's the real reason you want to put off the wedding. You were going to use the excuse that you had too much to do, but now Darlene has given you an even better excuse."

"What?" She spun to face him. "That's ridiculous!"

"Then why won't you marry me now?"

"I've already explained my reasoning. Why can't you wait a few months?" she said. "What's the hurry? We've been engaged only two weeks. Let's take our time and enjoy our engagement."

"You've known me nearly your whole life. We don't need a long engagement."

She scrunched her eyes shut. "Why are you being so stubborn about this?"

He turned back toward the windshield and stared at the road ahead. A muscle ticked in his tense jaw.

Mandy folded her arms over her chest and sat up straight. They were at a stalemate. She couldn't think of any way to sway him.

They sat in silence as her family's house came into view. If only she could cut the tension pulsing between them.

"Ephraim," she said when they stopped behind her house, "I've loved you since I was a little girl. I always dreamt that someday you would see me as more than Katie Ann's best friend, and that dream came true last Christmas. Then another dream came true when you asked me to be your *fraa*."

She turned to face him and found him staring at his lap. "I do want to marry you, but I think we need to wait a few months. Your family is in turmoil now. Your parents will most likely be relieved if they hear we're going to delay the wedding. That will give your family time to adjust to this new situation without my adding to the crowded conditions, and, yes, it will give me time to prepare for the wedding."

"We'll have my room."

"And four women would be sharing the kitchen instead of three. I think that will be too much for all of us. We'll trip over each other. We didn't even plan for three, since we thought we'd have our own *haus* next spring. Now your *schweschder* and her family need one instead."

"I think you've changed your mind about marrying me, but you won't admit it."

"That's not true! I've just realized it's too soon for our wedding, especially since your family is dealing with a crisis. It would be selfish for us to get married now."

"Selfish?"

"*Ya*, selfish. You need to think about your *schweschder* and her family. You have to move them in and help rearrange the *haus*. How can you even think about our wedding when they need your help?"

"So you think I'm selfish." He leaned back against the buggy door. "What else do you think about me?"

"You're twisting my words." She threw up her hands and nearly dropped the dish and container still on her lap. "I don't understand why we're arguing about this."

"Maybe we should just break up."

"What?" Her eyes stung, threatening tears. "You want to break up with me just because I want to delay our wedding?" She fought a sob as tears welled.

"Even if you do still want to marry me, you don't seem to want to deal with my family's problems because you'll be inconvenienced. Not just with what you consider a crowd, but because we won't have our own *haus* as soon as we thought. So maybe we should just forget our plans."

"Ephraim, you're overreacting. Stop and listen to what you're saying."

"I know what I'm saying. My family has a hard time, so you choose to distance yourself."

"I don't want to break up. You're blowing this way out of proportion!" Her voice shook as fear spiraled through her. But she was frustrated too. "Maybe you're too stubborn to think someone else might have a *gut* idea. You always have to be in control. You always have to make the decisions in our relationship. My opinion matters too!"

"Is that so?" he snapped. "So you think I'm selfish, bossy, *and* controlling?"

"*Ya*, I do!"

"Maybe this relationship won't work, then."

"I never said that!"

"We need some space." He turned to stare out the windshield.

"What does that mean?"

"That means we should take a break and talk about this again some other time."

"So you *are* breaking up with me?" Her voice shook.

"I don't know." Ephraim scrubbed his hand down his face. "This is too much to take in. It's been a crazy night."

"I know." She nodded as her hands trembled. "But I love you. I don't want to take a break. I just want to slow down."

He shook his head. "Well, I do need a break. I'll talk to you tomorrow."

"But you're moving your *schweschder* and her family tomorrow."

"So we'll talk another day."

Was she dreaming? This felt like a nightmare!

"We'll talk another day," she repeated, trying to make sense of his words. "You just told me you need a break, and you don't know when you want to work it out." Her stomach tightened with growing panic.

"I'm sorry."

"No, Ephraim, I'm sorry." She scooped up the container and dish with one arm, flung open the buggy door, and ran up the path to the back porch. Once in the mudroom, she dropped the containers on the bench, shucked her coat, and hung it on a peg on the wall. Then she sank to the floor, covered her face with her hands, and dissolved into gasping sobs.

CHAPTER 3

M andy!" *Mamm*'s voice sounded close by.

Mandy tried in vain to get hold of her raging emotions, but her tears continued to fall, rolling down her cheeks, darkening her black apron and the skirt of her favorite green dress. She removed her hands from her face and found her mother squatting in front of her. *Mamm* pushed back a stray tendril of Mandy's hair that had escaped her prayer covering.

"*Was iss letz?*" *Mamm*'s sky-blue eyes were warm and kind, causing more tears to fill Mandy's eyes. *Mamm* clicked her tongue. "*Ach, mei liewe.* What could possibly have upset you so much?"

"I think it's over," Mandy managed.

"What's over?" *Mamm*'s eyes searched hers.

"Eph—" Mandy couldn't say the words aloud. Had Ephraim truly broken their engagement? Wasn't she dreaming? But her broken heart was real—so real she thought she could feel the shards cutting her inside.

"Rhoda!" *Mamm* called. "Grab a box of tissues and bring it to the mudroom. *Dummle!*" Then she turned back to Mandy and placed her hands on her arms. "Whatever it is, I promise it's going to be okay. We'll get through this together."

Mandy shook her head. No, she'd never get over this. Never.

"What happened?" Rhoda appeared in the doorway holding a box of tissues. At sixteen, her sister was petite like Mandy, and she'd also inherited their mother's same sunshine-colored hair and bright-blue eyes. Those eyes widened as she kneeled beside *Mamm*.

Mandy took deep, shuddering breaths, trying to stem her sobs.

"Shh." *Mamm* mopped up her tears with a tissue. "Just calm down and talk to us. We can help you if you tell us what happened."

"I'll put on tea." Rhoda popped up and hurried into the kitchen.

"*Gut* idea." *Mamm* held out her hand to Mandy. "*Kumm.*"

Mandy took her mother's extended hand and let her guide her into the kitchen.

"Sit." *Mamm* nodded to Mandy's usual spot at the table.

Mandy sat down and swiped a few tissues across her face. How had this happened?

Tears filled her eyes anew.

"Mandy." *Mamm* sat down beside her and took her hands. "Talk to me."

Mandy sucked in a deep breath. "I think Ephraim broke up with me."

"What?" Rhoda came to stand behind their mother.

"We had an argument on the way home from his parents' *haus*. I told him I thought we should delay the wedding. He got upset and accused me of things that aren't true." As she explained everything, it was hard to keep her voice steady, but she managed to keep her tears at bay. "I can't believe it. I just asked to delay the wedding, but he made all kinds of assumptions and blew everything I said out of proportion."

The kettle whistled, and Rhoda poured water over tea bags in three mugs and carried them to the table.

"*Danki.*" Mandy wrapped her hands around her mug and stared into the hot liquid.

Rhoda sat down across from her and shook her head. "I don't know what to say, except I know Ephraim loves you. I can tell every time he looks at you. Maybe he needs a day to think about everything, and then he'll realize you're right."

"But I don't understand why he's so upset. What's wrong with waiting a few months until his family has adjusted to their new situation? What's wrong with giving me enough time to get ready? As I thought about both needs, it dawned on me that delaying the wedding made sense. What do you think, *Mamm*?" Mandy looked over at her mother. Surely she would have some words of wisdom to make everything better.

Mamm took a sip of her tea and then set down her mug. "I think you're right."

"So how do I convince Ephraim?"

Mamm tapped her finger against her chin. "What if you propose a new plan to him?"

"What do you mean?"

"I don't think Ephraim realizes how much Darlene's needs change everything for his family. I'd take your concern about moving into Marlin's house further. Even if you delay your wedding for a few months, you still won't have your own *haus* for some time. Maybe years. And I've always thought privacy is best for a young couple. It's not selfish to want that.

"What if after the wedding Ephraim moved into our home? The one drawback is that he'd no longer be on-site to work on his father's dairy farm, but he could work for your *dat*'s brickmasonry company. Then I'm sure your *dat* would want to build a *haus* for you here."

Mandy blinked. "That's a brilliant idea!" She leaned forward. "Do you think *Dat* would agree to it?"

"Would I agree to what?"

Mandy turned to find her father stepping into the kitchen.

With his light-brown hair and gray-blue eyes, Mandy had always thought he was the most handsome older man she knew.

"Ephraim's older *schweschder* and her family have fallen on hard times, and they're moving in with Ephraim's parents," Mandy began. "Their *haus* will be crowded now, and I suggested we delay our wedding, at least until Marlin builds a house for Darlene and her family next spring. Now Ephraim is upset with me."

Dat took a seat across from her at the table. "I don't see why he should be upset. It sounds like a mature idea to me."

"*Danki.*" Mandy cupped her hands around her warm mug. "This also means Ephraim and I won't have our own *haus* for some time. *Mamm* came up with an idea to make this whole situation a little easier on everybody. What if Ephraim moved in here after we're married and went to work for you?"

Dat nodded as he touched his beard. "Of course. Your husband would always be welcome to live here until you find a place, and I've been thinking about hiring someone else." He looked at *Mamm*. "We could also build them a *haus* here. We have plenty of land."

"*Ya.*" *Mamm* nodded and smiled. "I thought you'd say that."

"Do you both think Ephraim will agree to this plan?" The question leapt from Mandy's lips before she could stop it.

Mamm ran her fingers over her mug as she nodded. "I think it's a possibility. If Uria and Darlene are going to live there, and Uria will help run the dairy, then his becoming a brickmason is a great plan for him and for you."

Dat's smile was warm and encouraging. "I'd love to have him as my apprentice."

"I think it's a great idea," Rhoda chimed in.

"You and Ephraim need to calm down and talk this out, though." *Mamm*'s voice was gentle but firm. "You can't make this decision for him. Really listen to each other and think about your future."

Mandy's lower lip began to tremble, and she held her breath. She wanted to marry Ephraim, raise a family with him, and grow old with him. But she wanted to get married when the time was right. Would he change his mind? Would he even consider living with her family and changing his vocation for her?

"What are you thinking, *mei liewe*?" *Mamm* rubbed her arm. "I hate to see you so troubled."

"I'm still confused, and anxious." Mandy slumped back in her chair. "It seemed like everything was perfect two weeks ago when Ephraim proposed to me. But now I don't understand why he can't see things from my point of view. Tonight it felt like God was saying we should slow down. But when I suggested it, Ephraim accused me of using Darlene's circumstances as an excuse. He said maybe I'm having doubts about marrying him. Then he said I was just feeling inconvenienced because Marlin's *haus* would be crowded, plus we wouldn't have our own *haus* next spring. Why is he making these things up? Why is he so defensive?"

Dat leaned back in his chair. "Probably because all these changes are out of his control. He feels like he should be able to provide a better life for you, but he can't right now. He's doubting himself, not you. Just give him time to think and calm down. Even if he's not willing to move here and work with me, he'll realize delaying the wedding makes *gut* sense."

"How long do you think that will take?" Mandy rubbed the back of her tightening neck as she waited for her father to calm her worries.

"I think Ephraim can be a bit stubborn," *Dat* said. "Am I right?"

"*Ya.*" Mandy nodded. "He can be very stubborn."

"He might need a few days, but I believe he'll come around." *Dat* smiled. "Trust God."

"Exactly," *Mamm* said. "Just pray about it, and then talk to Ephraim. God will lead you both to the right answer."

"*Ya, Mamm* is right." Rhoda nodded, and the ties to her prayer covering fluttered around her slight shoulders.

"I will." Mandy picked up her mug and took a long sip. She silently prayed her family was right, that Ephraim would agree to delay the wedding rather than throw away their love. But she had to admit, she also hoped he'd be willing to alter their plans and live with her family. That just seemed like the best idea for everyone.

~

"*Dat?*" Ephraim's entire body shook as he walked toward the light he saw glowing near the back of his father's largest barn. "*Dat*, are you in here?"

"Ephraim?" *Dat* walked toward him, carrying a lantern. "Are you all right?"

"No, I need to talk to you. Are you alone?" Ephraim set his lantern on the ground. Then he lifted his straw hat and pushed his hand through his thick hair.

"*Ya*, I'm alone. I was just checking on the animals." He pointed toward the stalls. "Darlene, Uria, and the *maed* went home. What's going on?"

"I think Mandy and I may have just broken up."

"What?" *Dat*'s dark eyes widened. "Why would you break up? You seemed fine earlier when she stopped by with you."

"*Ya*." Ephraim scowled and looked toward the barn doors as confusion swamped him. Had he made a mistake? None of this made any sense.

"Why?"

"We argued on the way to her *haus*. She wants to delay the wedding. She thinks she doesn't have enough time to get ready. She also thinks our family has too much going on with Darlene and her family moving in, and if she moves in, the *haus* will be too crowded." Ephraim rubbed at a knot on his shoulder. "I got upset. I don't want to wait a few months to get married. I think we have plenty of time to get ready, and I'm okay if the *haus* is a little crowded. She disagrees with me. We argued, and we said some horrible things. I told her we both needed some space. I guess we kind of broke up." He grimaced as doubt edged his words.

Dat touched his beard and looked past Ephraim.

"What, *Dat*?" Ephraim touched his father's arm. "Tell me what you're thinking."

"I'm surprised. You two seemed so *froh*. Do you really want to break up over this?"

"I don't know." Ephraim sat down on a hay bale. "There's more. I accused her of making excuses to delay the wedding because she's having doubts about our relationship, and because she's feeling inconvenienced by the prospect of sharing a *haus* with so many of us. Unless that's true, I just don't understand why she wants to delay the wedding. Her excuses don't make sense to me."

Dat sat down beside him. "Maybe she really does just want to wait for things to settle down."

"Maybe, and maybe she does still want to marry me. But this feels like she doubts the strength of our relationship." Ephraim kicked a stone with his shoe. "Then she said I'm stubborn and bossy and controlling, and that makes me doubt our relationship." He pinched the bridge of his nose, where a headache brewed. "I've been looking forward to starting our life together, but now . . . How did you know when it was time to marry *Mamm*?"

"Well, your *mamm* and I had known each other for years, like you and Mandy have," *Dat* began. "We started dating when we were in our early twenties, and then I just knew when it was time."

"You never had any doubts?" Ephraim held his breath in anticipation of the response.

Dat grimaced, and Ephraim groaned, covering his face with his hands.

Ephraim rubbed his eyes as doubt and heartache pummeled his chest. The pain in Mandy's beautiful face and eyes kept replaying in his mind.

Had he just made the biggest mistake of his life?

He thought he heard hay crunch, but he kept his face covered. It must have been one of the horses moving in a nearby stall.

"Talk to me, Ephraim," *Dat* said. "Holding in your emotions isn't healthy."

"If she means what she says, I think Mandy's overreacting. Her family, our family, and her *freinden* will help her with wedding preparations." He looked up at his father. "You're going to build a *haus* for Darlene in the spring, right?"

Dat sighed. "I'm going to have to."

"Will you still build our *haus* next?"

Dat hesitated. "*Ya*, but it might be a few years before I can afford it."

"That's what I thought. But we can live with you and *Mamm* until then, right?"

"*Ya*, you can. It's going to be chaotic for a while, though."

"Why isn't that *gut* enough for Mandy?" Ephraim's voice echoed in the barn.

"You need to respect her point of view, even if you don't understand it yet," *Dat* said. "You've just broken Mandy's heart by breaking your engagement. If you try to apologize now, she may not forgive you. Even if she does forgive you, she might not agree to marry you."

"You broke your engagement?" Katie Ann's voice called from nearby.

Ephraim spun to face his sister. She gaped at him, and he knew his father would elect to stay out of this confrontation. He'd always let his children sort out their own conflicts.

"How could you do that? She loves you."

"It's a long story." Ephraim was suddenly exhausted. All the fight had drained out of him, and he was certain his bed was calling him. "I'll tell you tomorrow."

"No." Katie Ann shook her head. "You'll tell me now." She pointed to the barn floor. "Mandy is my best friend. She adores you. How could you hurt her like that?"

"And I'm your *bruder*," Ephraim snapped. "What about my feelings?"

"You loved her yesterday!" Katie Ann pointed at him. "What could she have possibly done to make you break your engagement?"

"It's complicated. We had an argument after we left here earlier. She wants to delay our wedding, and I got upset." Ephraim let his arms fall to his sides. "I'm going to bed." He tried to walk past her, but she blocked his way. "Katie Ann, please let me by."

"Not until you tell me everything that happened." She looked up at him, her eyes looking as if they might spark with her anger.

"It's none of your business." Ephraim picked up his lantern and then slipped past her before stalking toward the house.

"Wait!" Katie Ann rushed after him. "You have to tell me what's going on."

"I don't have to tell you anything." Ephraim marched up the back-porch steps and into the house, where he took off his coat and hung it on a peg. He hung his hat next to it and then carried his lantern into the kitchen.

"Why are you acting like this?" Katie Ann trailed after him. "What's wrong with you?"

He spun to face her. "All I told her is we need a few days to cool off. But I guess she considers that a broken engagement. This is between us. Stay out of it, Katie Ann."

She opened her mouth and then closed it, her face lined with confusion.

Ephraim took a step back. "I'm going to bed. Tomorrow is going to be a long day. We have to move Darlene and her family here. It's going to be exhausting, and we both need rest. *Gut nacht.*"

Before his sister could respond, he jogged up the stairs and into his bedroom, and then he dropped onto his bed as his mind spun with questions.

All he knew for sure was that his heart was breaking. Right now, though, he needed sleep. He'd figure out his problems with Mandy tomorrow.

CHAPTER 4

I'll get it!" Mandy rushed to the back door the following evening, praying the knock she'd heard was Ephraim's. She'd spent all day thinking about him and worrying that their relationship was truly over.

When she pulled open the door, her worries evaporated. Her handsome fiancé stood on the porch, holding a lantern.

"Hi." She pushed the door open wide.

"Hi." Ephraim spun his straw hat in his hands. "Can we talk?"

"*Ya.* Just let me get my coat."

Once outside, she pointed to the glider where they'd spent hours talking. It seemed like just yesterday Ephraim had asked her to be his girlfriend, and now they were facing a crossroads in their relationship—delaying their wedding or calling it off. Her chest constricted at the possibility of losing his love forever.

"How was your day?" she asked. They both sank onto the cool, wooden glider, and then she gave it a gentle push with her toe.

"Long and exhausting." He set his elbow on the arm of the glider and then rested his head on his hand. "Katie Ann helped Uria and Darlene pack at their rental while *Dat* and I made space for their belongings at our *haus*. Then two men *Dat* hired met me at the rental while *Dat* stayed behind to take care of the cows. We had to load it all into their truck, and then unload it." He paused and cupped his hand over his mouth to shield a yawn.

"We had to carry a lot of it up the stairs. We set up Uria and Darlene in the former sewing room, and we got the girls situated in Katie Ann's room. They'll have to finish unpacking all their stuff during the week. We put a lot of boxes in the attic and basement, and what extra furniture didn't fit in the attic or basement had to be transported to one of the barns." He rubbed his eyes and then yawned again. "I think every muscle in my body hurts."

"*Ach*, Ephraim. You should have gone to bed, then, instead of coming over here." She rubbed his shoulder.

"No." He looked at her, and the intensity in his eyes sent a tremor through her. "I couldn't leave things unsettled between us."

She held her breath, and her pulse tripped.

"You were right. Our *haus* is not just crowded, but chaotic. But we're family." He swiveled toward her. "I love you, and I can't wait to start the rest of my life with you, to make you part of my family. There's room for you, too, even before *mei dat* builds Darlene a *haus*. He can't guarantee when he can build our *haus*, but I don't care where we live. I just want to be with you, Mandy."

She swallowed against a swelling ball of emotion. "If you don't care where we live, then I have an idea for us."

"What?" His expression seemed skeptical.

"What if we lived here instead of at your parents' *haus*?" She pointed to the porch. "There's plenty of room, and *mei dat* said—"

"Wait a minute." He held up his hand, silencing her. "I can't live here and work for *mei dat*. It would take me too long to get there for the morning milking, and I'd have to make too many trips back and forth."

"I understand. I have a solution to that too. *Mei dat* says you can come work for him at his brickmasonry business. You could be his apprentice." When Ephraim looked unconvinced, she spoke faster. "*Dat* said he'd love to have you work for him, and he would even build us a *haus* here."

"No." Ephraim's voice was so forceful that she jumped.

"Why not?"

"I don't want to be a brickmason. I want to be a farmer like *mei dat* and his *dat* before him. That land has been in our family for generations, and it's my birthright to live on that land and raise my family there. If I have a *sohn*, he'll inherit that land and run it."

Mandy's shoulders wilted. "You won't even consider another plan for us?"

"That's not what I want," he insisted.

She pointed to her chest. "What about what I want?"

He lifted his hat and held it, leaning forward as if ready to leap up and leave. "So we're back to this again."

"What does that mean?" Her voice vibrated with frustration. "This is a *gut* plan. We can delay the wedding, and—"

"So not only do you want to still delay the wedding, but you also want to change our plan to live with my family on *mei dat*'s farm and change my vocation?" He gestured widely. "Why does everything have to change? Why isn't our original plan *gut* enough for you, even if Darlene and her family are moving in?"

She shook her head as angry tears filled her eyes. "It's not a question of being *gut* enough for me. It's a question of what makes sense for us. Your *dat*'s *haus* is too full of people now, and even though that's temporary, you just said he has no idea when we can build a *haus* of our own."

She motioned toward the back door. "We have plenty of space here, and room to build another *haus*. *Mei dat*'s business is thriving. Why wouldn't you want to work for him, especially now that your *dat* has Uria's help? Being a brickmason is *gut* work. Is it not *gut* enough for you?" She pointed to him.

He snorted. "You're just spoiled."

"What?" She stood up and faced him. "How am I spoiled?"

"Your *haus* is bigger than mine, and your *dat's* business is more successful than *mei dat's* farm. I'll never be able to satisfy you with the life I can offer you as a farmer. My family isn't *gut* enough for you. Maybe that's what this is really about." He picked up his lantern, stood, and started toward the porch steps. "Let's just forget it all."

"Wait!" She lurched forward, grabbed his arm, and spun him to face her. "How did we wind up here?" She gestured between them. "I want to marry you. I want to raise a family with you and grow old with you. That has never changed. All I did was suggest we wait a while—"

"And then change *all* our plans." His expression crumbled into a frown. "It's like I'm not the man you want or need anymore."

"That's not true." She cupped her hand to his cheek. "I want to be your *fraa*, but I think it might not be best for us to live on your *dat's* farm. Circumstances have changed. Why is that so difficult for you to see?"

"Because this is who I am." He pointed to his chest. "If that's not what you want, then it's over."

"So that's it." She took a step back and hugged her arms to her chest as if to shield her crumbling heart. "You want to just break our engagement and end it all because I suggested living here and your working for *mei dat*?"

He shrugged. "I guess so."

Mandy sniffed as her tears broke free. "I'll miss you."

"I'll miss you too." He spun and walked down the steps toward his waiting horse and buggy.

Mandy choked on a sob before stumbling into the house and the family room. Her parents and sister were sitting in their usual spots, reading.

"Mandy?" *Mamm* set her book on the end table and leaned forward. "Was that Ephraim?"

"*Ya.*" Mandy dropped onto the sofa beside Rhoda, her coat still on. "It's really over this time. He doesn't want to delay the wedding, he doesn't want to live here, and he doesn't want to work for *Dat.* He said if their *haus* and life on his *dat*'s farm isn't *gut* enough for me, it's over. He's going to throw it all away because I suggested a different life for us."

Mandy succumbed to sobs as despondency whipped through her. She covered her face with her hands, and her lungs felt as if they would burst with her grief. How could things go so badly so quickly? It felt as if she were stuck in a nightmare!

"*Ach,* Mandy." Rhoda's voice was close to her ear as she rubbed her back. "It's not over yet."

"*Ya,* it is." Mandy's words were muffled by her hands. "It's really over. I don't know what I'm going to do. I was so certain he'd agree to live here. He said it didn't matter where we live, but he meant where we live on his farm. He said he can't abandon his family's land. He has to be a farmer like his *dat* and his *daadi.* Shouldn't it only matter that we're together?" She tried to swallow back more tears, but her sobs overwhelmed her.

"Shh." *Mamm* appeared beside her and rubbed her shoulder. "Everything will be okay."

"No, it won't." Mandy looked up as *Dat* sat down on a footstool in front of her and handed her some tissues. She swiped them over her eyes and nose. "Nothing can fix this."

"That's not true." *Dat* glanced at *Mamm,* and they shared knowing expressions. "Your *mamm* and I had a bad argument shortly before we married."

"Really?" Rhoda asked.

"You never told us that." Mandy tossed the crumpled tissues on her lap and shrugged out of her coat.

"We had a few disagreements, and we broke up for a couple of weeks," *Dat* said. "We took some time to cool off and realized our pride was standing in our way."

"That's true," *Mamm* agreed. "But then one night your *dat* came to see me, and we talked for a couple of hours. Then he proposed again, and we were married a couple of months later."

Dat smiled at her, and the love in his eyes made Mandy's chest ache. Would Ephraim ever look at her like that again?

"I realized I wanted to be with your *mamm* more than I wanted to feel as if I were right about everything." *Dat* touched Mandy's cheek. "Your *mamm* and I had to talk it through. I think you need to find out why Ephraim is so upset. There must be more to it. Ask him to share more about how he feels, and listen to him."

"Your *dat* is right," *Mamm* chimed in. "You might have hurt his feelings without realizing it."

"What if he won't talk to me?" Mandy felt the tremble in her voice.

"I'm sure he will. You just need to gently push him." *Dat* brushed a tear from her face. "You and Ephraim love each other, but marriage is a lot of work. You both need to learn how to listen and to respect each other's opinions and feelings. That's a vital part of marriage."

"It's a tough lesson, but it will help you work through any problems you face." *Mamm* touched her hand.

"Okay." Mandy shuddered as more tears filled her eyes. "I just can't imagine my life without him. I don't want to lose him."

"You won't lose him if you show him you care," *Mamm* said.

"And take a *gut* look at what you've said to see if you've accidentally hurt him," *Dat* said. "You can work this out together if you're both willing to be honest."

Mandy leaned against her mother and hoped her parents were right.

Ephraim felt as if exhaustion and grief might drown him as he made his way from the barn to the house. He was grateful no one was in the barn when he stowed his horse and buggy. Now he just had to make it to his bedroom without a family member questioning him. He wanted to be alone with his confusing and agonizing thoughts.

After hanging his coat and hat in the mudroom, he breathed a sigh of relief. The kitchen and family room were both empty.

As he climbed the stairs, he heard voices echoing from the bedrooms above him. When he hit the second-floor hallway, he slipped into his own bedroom, closed the door, and set his lantern on his dresser. He sank onto the corner of his bed and covered his face with his hands.

He'd never imagined his day would end with truly breaking up with Mandy. As he'd headed to her house, he envisioned they'd repair their relationship and agree to the original plan to marry in six weeks. He'd tell her they could ask some of their friends and other family members to help her with the wedding preparations, and she'd realize it didn't matter if his father's house was crowded for a while or how long it would be before they had a house of their own. Instead, their conversation had gone completely off the rails.

How would he go on without her? She'd been his life, his future, and his heart for almost a year. Now he was left with nothing, alone. His eyes burned.

A knock on his door startled him. He sat up straight and cleared his throat.

"Come in." He hoped his voice sounded stronger than he felt.

The door opened, revealing *Mamm* standing in the doorway.

"I thought I heard you come home." She stepped inside. "Did you go see Mandy?"

"*Ya.*" He tried to sound causal.

"How is she?" *Mamm* studied him with what looked like suspicion.

"Fine." Ephraim rubbed at the stubble on his chin. "Why?"

Mamm closed the door and leaned against his dresser. "We both know why."

Ephraim blew out a deep sigh. "Did *Dat* tell you or Katie Ann?"

"They're both concerned." *Mamm*'s eyes filled with concern too. "Did you work things out with her?"

Ephraim shook his head as a messy knot of grief choked back his words.

Mamm sank onto the bed beside him and looped her arm over his shoulders. "What happened?"

"We broke up for *gut*." He tried in vain to clear his throat. "The wedding is off."

"But you two were so in love, and you had such a strong relationship."

"Everything fell apart." He wiped at his eyes, hoping to keep his emotions at bay until after his mother left. But that was difficult as he told her about Mandy's latest suggestions. "That's not what I want. I don't want to live with her parents, and I don't want to be a brickmason. We argued, and then we broke up."

He paused as he tried to analyze his raging feelings. "I feel like she thinks our life here isn't *gut* enough for her, as if being a farmer's *fraa* isn't as *gut* as being a brickmason's *fraa*. Or maybe it's not her. Maybe I'm worried that our life on the farm is too humble, and I'm projecting that onto her."

"You have no reason to be embarrassed by our life, Ephraim, and I doubt Mandy wouldn't be *froh* living here. I think you're both reeling from all the changes our family is facing with Darlene's problems, and I'm sure planning a wedding so fast is stressful for her." *Mamm* shook her head. "I'm sorry all your plans are in question because of your *schweschder*'s problems."

"It's not your fault or Darlene's fault. It just happened, and Mandy can't adapt to it. That means we're not supposed to be together."

Mamm cringed.

"What?"

"You're permitted to change your plans," *Mamm* said. "You can become a brickmason if you want."

He shook his head. "No. I told you. That's not what I want. I'm supposed to be here. That's what *Dat* and *Daadi* said when I was a *bu*, and I'm going to stick to that plan."

Mamm gave him a sideways hug. "No one said you couldn't change your plans. We didn't plan for Uria and Darlene to come here, but we're *froh* to have them. If you want to build a life with Mandy working for her *dat*, then your *dat* and I will support you. This is your life, Ephraim. Your *dat* and I aren't going to dictate it for you. We pray our *kinner* are healthy, *froh*, and that they stay in the church and follow God. The rest is up to all of you. These are your lives."

Ephraim contemplated his mother's words and then shook his head. "That's another thing. God wants me here, too, doesn't he? I'm to honor *mei dat*. If Mandy can't live with me on this farm, she can't be *mei fraa*."

"Ephraim," *Mamm* began, "you need to pray about that. I think you're misinterpreting what I said."

"I'm not." He swiped the back of his hand over his eyes. "I'm certain of it."

Mamm nodded. "If that's what you believe, but I think you need to keep talking to God." She seemed to study him. "Are you all right?"

He gestured toward his pillow. "I just need some sleep."

Mamm stood and faced him. "I'm here if you want to talk more."

"Danki, Mamm."

"*Gut nacht.*" She walked into the hallway, gently closing the door behind her.

Ephraim changed into shorts and a T-shirt, and then he climbed into bed. As he stared up at the ceiling, he recalled the pain in Mandy's beautiful face, and grief swelled inside him once again.

He missed her so much his heart ached, but he couldn't allow himself to change his roots for her. If his grandfather's farm wasn't good enough for Mandy, then how could he satisfy her for the rest of their lives? Nothing he could ever give her would be good enough.

Was he just self-conscious about the humble life he and Mandy would have on the farm and projecting that onto her? Was he so immersed in his own hurt that he wasn't thinking clearly?

He groaned and covered his eyes with his forearm. He only knew he missed Mandy and he grieved for the bright future that was at his fingertips a few days ago. It was as if their future had wilted and died like the leftover summer crops faltered when the cold weather invaded Henry's garden. Was it too late to save their relationship, or would it wither as the ground grew colder?

Rolling to his side, he sucked in a deep breath and waited for sleep to find him.

CHAPTER 5

"Do you need help?"

Mandy looked at the far end of the porch as Katie Ann walked toward her the following morning. "What are you doing here?"

"Well, that's a nice hello." Katie Ann rested her hands on her hips.

"I'm sorry." Mandy sighed as she hung another pair of her father's trousers on the clothesline that stretched from the porch to the barn. "*Gude mariye.*" She frowned. "I didn't get much sleep last night."

"I'm sure you didn't." Katie Ann joined her at the laundry basket, picked up another pair of trousers, and handed them to her. "I'm sorry about what happened. *Mei mamm* told me the news. Ephraim won't talk to me, but he's talked to both *Mamm* and *Dat*, so I know what's been going on. Despite *mei bruder* telling me to stay out of this, I would have come to offer you my support yesterday. But we had to move Darlene and her family to our *haus.*"

"I know. *Danki.*" Mandy's bottom lip quivered as she hung the trousers on the clothesline. "I don't understand it. I thought my solutions made sense, but he got so upset, he broke up with me. As of today, I'm single again, and all my wedding plans were a waste."

"*Mei bruder* is stubborn, pigheaded, ridiculous, or whatever word you want to use to describe him." Katie Ann handed her the last pair of trousers. "Just give him time to understand what he's done."

Mandy hung the trousers on the line. "He was adamant that he'd never consider living here and working as a brickmason, and then he said I think I'm too *gut* to be a farmer's *fraa*." She looked down at the empty laundry basket and then at the full clothesline. "That's not true. I can't deny I'd like living here, but that doesn't mean I wouldn't like living with your family. I just thought we had an option for giving you all a less stressful life."

"I believe you, Mandy," Katie Ann said.

"But I also keep thinking maybe this isn't just him. It takes two for a relationship to work. Maybe I made a mistake, but if I did, I don't know how to fix it. If I hurt him by accident, how do I fix what's broken between us? My parents say I should talk to him and really listen, but I don't know when he'll be ready. I've never seen him like this."

"Why don't we go inside and have tea?" Katie Ann rubbed Mandy's arm.

"Okay." Mandy lifted the laundry basket and followed Katie Ann into the house.

After storing the basket in the utility room, Mandy filled the kettle and set it on the stove while Katie Ann took mugs and tea bags out of a cabinet. From upstairs her mother's sewing machine chattered, telling her *Mamm* and Rhoda were busy working on projects for their customers. She set a container of iced oatmeal cookies on the counter and then pulled out sweetener and milk. Once the kettle whistled, Katie Ann filled the mugs and brought them to the table.

They sipped their tea and ate cookies in silence for a few minutes. Mandy lost herself in regret, analyzing what she'd said, wondering what she could have said to Ephraim that might have changed the outcome of their conversation the night before.

Katie Ann's voice broke through Mandy's mental gymnastics. "*Mei mamm* said Ephraim was really upset last night. She talked to him when he got home. He was heartbroken, so I think he's going to realize he made a huge mistake."

Mandy fought the tears filling her eyes. "If he regretted it, why didn't he come back to see me last night and make things right? He said some terrible things to me. He even called me spoiled because *mei haus* is bigger than yours." Mandy wiped her eyes with her fingertips. "He was really mean. It was like he became another person."

Katie Ann pressed her lips together. "He's always had a terrible temper. Do you want me to talk to him? I can try to make him realize how ridiculous he's being."

Mandy shook her head. "I don't think so. He'll think I asked you to, and it might make things worse."

"I don't think it could get any worse." Katie Ann picked up another cookie and took a bite.

"I just don't understand it. I thought I was suggesting great ideas." Mandy waved a cookie around for emphasis as her eyes stung with fresh tears. "Why does it matter where we live if we truly love each other?"

"You're exactly right. I understand he's always wanted to be a farmer, but *mei bruder* is being a dolt. He's letting his pride get in the way." Katie Ann shook her head as she scowled.

Mandy took a sip of tea. "How is your family adjusting now that Darlene and her family have moved in?"

"It's noisy." Katie Ann crumpled a paper napkin as she spoke. "And it's a little tight in my room with the girls there." She smiled. "But we did a lot of giggling last night. It will take some time to get used to having two people with me, along with two more dressers and a cot. Thankfully, my room is fairly large." She smoothed out the napkin again. "*Mei dat* said he'll get started on their *haus* as soon as he can in the spring. This will be temporary. I love *mei bruderskinner.* It's just an adjustment."

"Just like it would be for Ephraim and me if he'd consider what I suggested." Mandy rested her chin on her palm as guilt rained down on her. Maybe she'd made a mistake by suggesting they take another path. Had she not taken everything Ephraim might be feeling into consideration?

She had to find a way to talk to him.

⁓

"Hello." Mandy stepped into Emma's kitchen and set a container of lemon bars on the counter. "I brought you a special snack."

"Mandy!" Emma moved across the room's expanse to meet her. "It's so *gut* to see you. How are you?"

She shrugged as she touched the container. "I've been baking a lot. *Mei schweschder* says it's a coping mechanism."

"A coping mechanism?" Emma opened the container. "Oh my! Look at those lemon bars."

"Have one. They're pretty *gut.*" Mandy leaned back against the counter. "I'm going to try a similar recipe later when I get home. I'll bring you some."

Emma picked up a bar and then looked at Mandy. "What's going on?"

"You haven't heard?" Mandy asked. When a meow sounded, she looked down. Hank was walking back and forth, rubbing against her shins. "Hi, Hank."

"I haven't heard what?" Emma asked.

"Ephraim and I broke up." Mandy went to the table and sat down in a chair. "It's been two days. I feel like I'm going out of my mind. I'm baking to stay busy."

Emma gasped as she sat down across from her. "What happened?"

Mandy told her the entire story while drawing imaginary circles on the tabletop with her fingertip. When she finished, she looked up and found Hank sitting next to her, his attention focused on her.

"What do you think, Hank?" Mandy rubbed the cat's ear, and he tilted his head toward her and purred.

"Hank and I think you shouldn't give up." Emma smiled at her. "The issues may be deeper than what you're seeing on the surface. I think you're feeling overwhelmed, and Ephraim is doubting the wisdom of marrying you because your suggestions may have made him feel less-than. If you take a step back and look at the whole picture, you might agree with me."

"So it's all my fault?" Mandy felt as if the breath rushed out of her lungs at the possibility that she caused the breakup.

"No, no, no." Emma reached for her hands. "Your suggestions are mature. I commend you for wanting to slow down and not rush your wedding. Many young women are so obsessed with the wedding that they lose sight of what's really important—their marriage. That's your future. Taking your time and doing what's right is a grown-up decision. But you also need to look at this from Ephraim's perspective. He loves you so much he doesn't want to wait to marry you. But he comes from a line of farmers. He might have taken your suggestions as an insult to the way of life his family has lived for many generations."

"So I need to forget the idea of living with my parents? And I was wrong to suggest that he learn a new trade?" Mandy's heart ached as she recalled the pain and anger lining Ephraim's handsome face when he told her their relationship was over.

Emma touched one ribbon of her prayer covering and paused as if contemplating the correct response. "No, I don't think you were wrong, but I believe he reacted out of hurt. Married to Henry, I learned I had to take his feelings into consideration, no matter how certain I was that my point of view was right. Two people make a marriage, and the only way it will work is if those two people listen to each other and compromise. Together you and Ephraim can find a solution. Just like our crops in Henry's garden needed both sun and water, you two need to work together to nourish and grow your relationship."

"Oh." Mandy's thoughts were spinning so fast she thought she might pass out. Guilt and shame wrapped around her chest, squeezing at her lungs. "I was selfish and pushy when I insisted he consider my ideas, let alone just go along with them. I didn't consider how he might feel." Her bottom lip trembled. "What if he doesn't forgive me?"

"Everything will be fine, Mandy. You just need to talk to him, calmly." Emma stood and retrieved the lemon bars from the counter. "These are positively scrumptious. *Danki* for sharing them with me." She set the container in the center of the table and took another bar. "Talk to Ephraim and discuss your options. Also pray for him. Ask God to help him see that you do love him and want to marry him." She smiled at Mandy. "Don't give up hope. You and Ephraim can work it out, but you can only do it together."

"Okay." If their hearts could get past the hurt.

"Now, are we going to get started on canning today?"

"*Ya*, I'm ready. And Katie Ann and Clara plan to be here a bit later." Soon she and Emma were gathering supplies, and Tena came downstairs to join them. It felt good to talk and even laugh as they started canning the last of the beans, carrots, and corn they'd grown in the garden.

When the back door opened and then clicked closed, Mandy turned her attention to the mudroom doorway.

"Do I smell lemon bars?" Wayne asked.

"*Ya*, Mandy made them," Tena told him. "Come have one."

Wayne stepped into the kitchen, and Mandy's stomach seemed to drop when Ephraim appeared behind him. He froze in the doorway as his striking brown eyes focused on hers. Then his lips formed a thin line, but his eyes seemed to plead with her. Did he want to fix things between them? Or did he want her to leave? She longed to read his mind as the intensity in his gaze sent goose bumps ripping up her arms.

Wayne took a lemon bar from the container and took a big bite. After swallowing, he turned to Ephraim. "These are fantastic." He held up his half-eaten bar. "You need to try one."

Ephraim took one from the container, bit into it, and nodded at Mandy. "It's *appeditlich*."

"*Danki*." Mandy cleared her throat as she tried to hide the sadness his formal tone caused her.

Ephraim looked at Wayne. "We should get outside and start on our project."

"What project?" Tena asked.

Wayne swiped another bar from the container. "We're going to replace some of the boards on the shed doors. I want to get this done before it gets any colder."

When Mandy felt Ephraim's stare burning into her, she kept her focus on Emma. "Why don't we go through your cookbooks, Emma? We could find something fun to make when we're finished canning."

"*Wunderbaar*." Emma stood and turned to Wayne. "*Danki* for fixing the shed doors. Let me know what I owe you for supplies."

"It's no problem." Wayne held up his hand. Then he winked at Tena. "See you soon."

"*Ya*, you will." Tena grinned at him, and the love that passed between them made Mandy's heart crumble even more.

Ephraim gave Mandy a brief glance and then walked out the back door with Wayne.

"Am I missing something?" Tena asked Mandy after the men disappeared outside. "You and Ephraim were a bit cold to each other."

"I'll tell you while we work."

~

"You're telling me you broke up with Mandy because she suggested you wait a few months to get married, then move in with her parents, build a house on her *dat*'s land, and have the chance for a new career?" Wayne asked as they removed the old shed door from the hinges.

"*Ya*, I guess that sums it up." Ephraim shrugged.

"Don't you think you overreacted?" Wayne turned toward him.

"No, I don't." Ephraim looked down at the rotten wood to avoid Wayne's accusing stare. By this morning, he'd decided he hadn't made a mistake. No matter what she said, deep down, Mandy was having doubts about their relationship. He was sure of it, but he didn't want to tell Wayne that. "She knows I've always planned to be a farmer and take over *mei dat*'s farm someday."

"But plans can change," Wayne said. "Isn't being together the most important plan of all?"

"Why don't we stay focused on this repair instead of my breakup?" He pointed to the door.

"Hey," Jerry said as he and Chris approached. "Are we ready to work on the shed today?"

Ephraim looked past them to where Katie Ann and Clara climbed the porch steps and headed into the house. Why didn't his sister mention this was the canning day at Emma's? In a matter of minutes, all the women would know he and Mandy had broken their engagement and ended their nearly one-year relationship.

Why should he let Wayne make him feel guilty? Mandy was

the one who suggested they change their plans. She was the one who was changing her mind about him. This was her fault, not his!

But then why did he lie awake at night, analyzing their argument over and over? Why did he find himself contemplating what life would be like if he became a brickmason?

"Ephraim?"

"What?" He looked up at Jerry.

"What has you so distracted?" Jerry asked, a grin tugging at his lips.

"You haven't heard?" Wayne asked. "Ephraim and Mandy broke up on Tuesday."

Ephraim swallowed a groan. *Here we go. Now they'll all analyze my life and tell me what I've done wrong.*

"Are you serious?" Jerry asked. "Katie Ann didn't say anything on the ride over here."

"Katie Ann told me yesterday." Chris frowned at Ephraim. "You're honestly going to let her get away because you're too stubborn to even consider living with her parents and working for her *dat*?"

"That's why you broke up?" Jerry asked.

"Worse," Wayne told him. "This all started just because Mandy suggested they delay the wedding a few months. She had *gut* reasons too."

"Look. This is my business." Ephraim held up his hands. "I really don't need your opinions."

"That's too bad." Jerry sat down on a plastic crate and looked up at him. "You're going to get our opinions, so take them like a man." His other friends mumbled their agreement. "Don't you love her?"

"*Ya*." Ephraim leaned back against the shed. "Of course I do."

"Then why are you letting a little change of plans ruin your future with the *maedel* you love?"

"A little change of plans?" Ephraim gestured widely. "Are you kidding me? Moving off my parents' farm would be a huge change. And what do I know about being a brickmason?"

"So you're afraid to learn a new trade?" Jerry snorted. "Do you think I knew anything about being a plumber when I first went to work for *mei onkel*? Now I'm his assistant manager and working my way up to being his partner. You might like a career change."

"This farm has been in my family for generations. How can I walk away from that?" Ephraim demanded.

"Darlene and her family moved in, and Uria can help run the farm now," Chris said as he sat down beside Jerry. "It's okay to learn a new trade, Ephraim. It's all about finding stability for you and Mandy, and from what I hear, considering what might be best for your parents and older *schweschder* and her family too. Besides, you could take over her *dat*'s business someday. He has two *dochdern*, and you'll be his first *sohn*."

"He's right." Wayne shrugged. "You need to think about what you're gaining, not what you're losing."

"That's enough." Ephraim threw down his tool. "I didn't come here today for a lecture. I came here to work on this shed."

"And you wanted to see your ex-fiancée," Wayne muttered.

Ephraim spun and kicked the side of the shed, sending searing pain radiating from his toe up to his shin. "I didn't know she'd be here today."

"I don't think breaking your foot is going to fix things between you and Mandy," Wayne quipped.

"He's right, Ephraim," Jerry added. "You need to relax."

"Can we please fix these shed doors and stop analyzing my life?" He needed them to stop bugging him. How could he share the truth? He was afraid Mandy just didn't love him enough to live on the farm with him, that she didn't think he was worth what she considered a sacrifice. He didn't want to admit how much that possibility hurt.

"Fine, fine." Jerry picked up a hammer. "Let's give Ephraim a break."

As Ephraim turned his attention to the shed, his mind spun with his friends' words and unsolicited advice. He looked toward the house and imagined Mandy sitting at the kitchen table, telling her friends about their breakup. Were they also giving her unsolicited advice? He tried to redirect his thoughts to the task at hand, but his mind lingered on Mandy and the pain he'd seen in her eyes this morning. Did she miss him as much as he missed her?

Then why wouldn't she just agree that their original plan to marry in December and live with his family was best?

He shoved away the thoughts. She was the one who wanted to change their plans. This breakup was *her* fault.

Still, his heart yearned for her.

"Do you need a ride home?" Katie Ann asked Mandy as they pulled on their coats that afternoon.

"*Ya*, I guess so. It would save me some money." Mandy buttoned her coat. "*Mei dat* paid his driver to drop me off since he needed his horse and buggy today."

"You can ride with Chris and me." Katie Ann gestured for Mandy to follow her.

Mandy said good-bye to Emma, Clara, and Tena and then headed outside with Katie Ann. As they walked down the path to the waiting buggies, Mandy slowed her steps when she spotted Ephraim standing with Chris, remembering how uncomfortable he'd made everyone feel as they all gathered around Emma's table for lunch.

"It's okay." Katie Ann took Mandy's arm and guided her toward the buggy. "You don't have to feel awkward around him."

Mandy walked over to Chris's buggy and climbed into the back.

"I'll see you later," Chris told Ephraim.

"All right." Ephraim hesitated, but then he looked into the buggy.

Mandy sucked in a breath as she took in his stoic expression. She lifted her hand to wave to him.

With a frown, Ephraim nodded at her and then walked to his own horse and buggy.

Mandy released the breath she'd been holding and then settled into the back of the buggy as Katie Ann and Chris climbed onto the bench seat in front of her.

As Chris guided the buggy toward the road, she hugged her arms to her chest and recalled her conversation with her friends while they finished canning the vegetables. While they had all offered her kind encouragement and told her to pray and ask God to guide her heart, their words felt empty of hope. Of course she would pray, but she still felt like a third wheel sitting in the back of her best friend's buggy while her ex-fiancé rode home alone. And Ephraim showed no signs of wanting to talk.

Holding back tears, Mandy closed her eyes and asked God to somehow heal their broken relationship. She couldn't do it by herself.

CHAPTER 6

A s conversations swirled around him at the breakfast table
Saturday morning, Ephraim scooped home fries onto his
plate and then forked a few into his mouth.

"*Onkel* Ephraim?"

He looked to his left, where Rebekah sat. "*Ya?*"

"Do you like potatoes?"

"I do." He couldn't stop a grin as he pointed to his plate. "This
is my second pile of home fries."

"Oh." Rebekah scrunched her nose and then looked back at
her eggs.

"Why do you look so disgusted?" he asked.

"Savannah says home fries are gross because potatoes grow in
the ground and are dirty," Rebekah said.

"I didn't say that!" Savannah exclaimed from across the table.

"Savannah!" Darlene scolded. "No yelling in the *haus*."

"I never said that," Savannah hissed.

"*Ya*, you did," Rebekah retorted.

"You know, your *mammi* washes the potatoes before she makes
the home fries, so the potatoes aren't dirty when we eat them."
Ephraim tried in vain to hide his smile.

"Oh." Rebekah tapped her finger against her chin as she considered this. "So they aren't yucky when you eat them?"

"No, they aren't." Ephraim scooped another mouthful onto his fork.

"May I please have some?" Rebekah pushed her plate toward Ephraim.

"Of course." Ephraim shifted some onto her plate and then smiled at Darlene.

"*Maed.*" Darlene rolled her eyes and then smiled at Uria.

Ephraim stopped chewing as he watched his older sister and brother-in-law grin at each other. The adoration sparking between them stole his breath for a moment. Could he have had that same deep love and affection in marriage with Mandy? The thought felt like a bucket of frigid water drenching him after a long, hot shower.

He turned his attention to his nieces. Would he and Mandy have had children? Would they have had daughters who were as beautiful as Mandy with her golden hair and stunning blue eyes? The potatoes soured in his mouth. How could he have let her slip through his fingers?

"Ephraim, are you going to Emma's today?" Katie Ann's question cut through his thoughts and swelling regret.

"Maybe later." He lifted his glass of orange juice. "I have chores to do first."

"Chris is going to pick me up in about an hour," Katie Ann said. "Maybe I'll see you there."

Ephraim nodded. Part of him wanted to avoid Emma's so he didn't have to see Mandy, but another part of him wanted to go to Emma's every day to sneak a glimpse at Mandy. When would he stop feeling so confused?

When he was finished with his meal, he carried his dishes to the counter. Then he pulled on his hat, coat, and boots in the mudroom and headed out to the barn.

He did his best to push thoughts of Mandy out of his head as he began to muck the horse stalls, but her gorgeous smile crept back in. The muscles in his arms and back burned as he worked harder and harder, trying to erase her from his mind's eye. But she lingered there, taunting him as he raked with all his strength.

"You're going to break that pitchfork in half."

Ephraim turned and found his father standing at the end of the stall. He leaned the pitchfork against the wall and swiped his sleeve over his sweaty brow.

"How are you?" *Dat*'s dark eyes seemed to study him.

"I'm okay." Ephraim shrugged and picked up the pitchfork again. "I have a lot of work to do."

"Do you miss her?" *Dat*'s question caught him off guard.

Ephraim froze. Was it that obvious? He returned to work in hopes his father would walk away.

"If you do, maybe you should try talking to her."

Ephraim stopped working and looked at his father. "I've tried talking to her, but we want different things."

"That's the thing about marriage," *Dat* began as he leaned on the stall door. "It only works if you compromise."

"We're not married." Ephraim shook his head.

"And you never will be if you don't start thinking like a couple."

"What does that mean?"

"When you marry, you become one, but you can't behave as if you're not. Take a step back and think about her point of view. Be careful not to jump to any conclusions about her intentions. Your *mamm* told me you're afraid Mandy doesn't want to be a farmer's *fraa*. You could be completely wrong about that. Don't fall into the trap of projecting your insecurities onto her. You need to talk this out."

Dat tapped the stall door. "Let me know if you want to talk more about it."

Ephraim watched his father walk away as his words marinated in his mind. Maybe he had misinterpreted Mandy's reasons for suggesting they change their plans. He did owe it to her to try to talk this out, but what if her words just hurt him more? He was still reeling from their last discussion.

His father made it sound so easy, but how could Ephraim even consider just walking away from his family's legacy and starting a new life when it felt so wrong?

Still, he couldn't deny that he missed Mandy, and as much as he tried, he couldn't erase her beautiful face from his mind.

Mandy searched her bedroom as panic dug into her shoulders. Where was her purse? She'd seen it just last night, but it wasn't on her dresser where she always left it. She looked on the floor, under her bed, and on her windowsill. Had she left it downstairs somewhere?

She stepped out into the hallway and into the sewing room, where she spotted her purse on the sewing table. She didn't even recall walking in here yesterday. When she crossed the room and picked up her purse, her eyes focused on the half-finished, baby-blue dress on the table. She froze, cemented in place.

Her wedding dress.

Tears stung her eyes as she ran her fingers over the material. Beside it was a bolt of material to make the dress for Rhoda.

But now the dresses would never be finished. The wedding would never happen.

Mandy wiped away a tear. How she missed Ephraim. She missed his smile, his boisterous laugh, their long talks, their friendship.

"Is there anything I can do to fix it?" She whispered the question as if someone would answer.

Then an idea sparked in her brain. What if she took his favorite cookies—peanut butter—to Emma's today? If he came, she could use them to try to encourage him to talk to her. She'd baked some last night. Baking seemed to be her only solace during this unending and unbearable heartbreak.

Had she subconsciously made the peanut butter cookies because she missed him? Probably.

"Mandy!" *Mamm*'s voice sounded from downstairs. "Katie Ann is here!"

"Coming!" Mandy touched the dress one last time, and then she hurried down to the kitchen, where she said hello to her friend.

After she grabbed the container of peanut butter cookies and put on her coat, she and Katie Ann stepped outside and she climbed into the back of Chris's buggy.

"*Danki* for picking me up," Mandy told Chris after she was settled.

"*Gern gschehne,*" Chris said.

Katie Ann turned around and pointed to the container. "What are those?"

"*Kichlin.*"

"What kind?"

"Peanut butter."

"Oh. Are they for *mei bruder?*"

"Maybe." Mandy tried to sound casual. "How is he?"

"Grumpy and mopey." Katie Ann rolled her eyes. "It's so obvious he misses you. If he wasn't so stubborn, you'd be back together already."

Mandy hugged the cookies to her chest. Would they be enough to encourage him to talk through their problems so they could work out a compromise?

"How are you doing, Mandy?" Chris asked.

"I'm getting by. I'm baking a lot." Mandy ran her fingers over the top of the container. "*Mei mamm* said we should open a bake stand at the *haus*." She gave a little laugh, but it didn't warm her troubled soul.

"Don't give up on Ephraim, okay?" Chris asked.

Mandy nodded.

"We're all working on him," Chris continued.

"You are?" Mandy leaned forward. "What do you mean?"

"Just trust us." Katie Ann smiled at her.

Ephraim leaned on Emma's fence as Jerry told him and Wayne about a plumbing job at a rich *Englisher*'s house. When a horse and buggy appeared in the driveway, Ephraim stood up straight, and his pulse picked up.

Chris and Katie Ann climbed out, and then Mandy did before turning and removing a large container from the back seat. As she and Katie Ann walked toward the house, Ephraim admired her from afar. He'd always enjoyed seeing her in blue.

Mandy turned toward him, smiled, and lifted her hand in a wave. His heartbeat thumped as he returned the gesture before she disappeared into the house.

"Why don't you go talk to her instead of staring at her like a stalker?" Wayne gave Ephraim a shove.

"Why don't you mind your own business?"

"Who are you trying to kid?" Jerry chimed in. "You still love her, and you miss her. So why are you standing here with us?"

Ephraim scowled. "Why don't you worry about your own relationship?"

"Give it a rest, Blank," Chris added as he came to stand with the rest of them. "Just go talk to Mandy. We're all tired of your moods."

Ephraim divided a look among his friends as they all pointed toward the house. He hated to admit it, but maybe they were right. Perhaps it was time to talk through their problems. "Fine."

They applauded as he walked toward the house, and Ephraim rolled his eyes. Despite the cold weather, his hands began to sweat. What if Mandy refused to talk to him? But she'd waved and smiled at him just now, so that was a good sign. She must still care for him.

Ephraim squared his shoulders as he entered the kitchen, where Mandy stood with Clara and Tena. Her friends turned to look at him, and their eyes rounded.

"Tena," Clara said, "why don't we set up the stand?" They both gripped the handles of two big bags of apples.

"*Gut* idea." Tena hurried out the back door with Clara close behind.

He glanced at the table, where Katie Ann and Emma weren't even pretending they weren't watching him. Mandy picked up the container he'd seen her carrying and held it up to him. "I brought peanut butter *kichlin*."

"You did?" Warmth filled his chest as he walked over to her. Mandy nodded. "Your favorite."

"Do you mean you made them for me?"

"*Ya*, I guess so." She removed the lid. "Try one."

"*Danki*." He took a cookie, and when their hands brushed, he felt electricity spark in the air around them. It suddenly felt as if they were the only two people in the room. He lost himself in the depth of her blue eyes as he bit into the cookie and savored the sweet peanut-buttery taste.

"Do you like them?" Mandy's expression seemed hopeful.

He nodded as he swallowed. "*Ya*, I do. Can we talk?" He heard the thread of hope in his voice.

Her eyes glistened, and she nodded toward the doorway. "Let's go into the *schtupp*."

Mandy set the container of cookies on the counter, and she and Katie Ann shared a knowing look before they headed out of the room. Were Mandy and his younger sister planning something? The thought sent suspicion curling through him.

He followed Mandy into the family room, where Hank slept curled up in a ball on what used to be Henry's chair. Ephraim shook his head at the cat and then sat down on the sofa.

Mandy lowered herself into a chair across from him. "How's your family?"

"Okay." Ephraim shrugged. "I guess we're all getting used to each other. I have to make a strategic plan to get into the bathroom first in the morning." He gave her a sheepish grin, and she laughed. How he'd missed that sweet lilt. "How are you?"

"I'm surviving." She folded her hands in her lap. "I miss you. I miss us."

"Can't we make this work?" He leaned forward. "We could still get married in December."

Her expression changed. She'd seemed so open, but now she looked . . . determined.

"No. December is still too soon. I walked into the sewing room this morning, and I saw my wedding dress. It's not even half done. I've been telling you I don't have time. Why won't you believe me?"

"I'll get you help. And *mei dat* thinks Darlene and her family will be in their *haus* by late spring. The *haus* would be crowded only for a few months."

"Ephraim, you're not listening to me."

All his hope dissolved as he stared at her. "So you miss me, but you're not willing to compromise?"

She pointed to her chest. "I'm not willing to compromise?" Then she pointed at him. "No, you're the one who isn't willing to compromise. You're just saying we should follow through with the original plan. You won't even consider how I feel and my proposals for our future. You're the one who's stubborn and stuck on only one plan."

He stood. She didn't love him. At least not enough. "This is a waste of time."

"Really, Ephraim?" She stood and jammed her hands on her small hips. "That's how you see me? I'm a waste of time? Do you even love me?"

"Does it matter?" he said, challenging her.

"*Ya*, it does matter." She lifted her chin. "I want to marry you and build a life together, but you're too obstinate to even consider delaying the wedding, let alone my other suggestions. This can never work if you don't respect my opinions."

He stared at her as his father's words echoed in his mind. Was she right? Did he have to bend to her for their relationship to work?

But Ephraim was a farmer. He came from a line of farmers. How could he abandon his heritage for her? And he still thought delaying the wedding was her way of letting him know she wasn't sure they were right for each other, even if she didn't realize it. Even if she said she loved him.

"Forget it." He waved her off and marched out the front door, the muscles in his back aching with growing frustration, his heart breaking again.

Mandy wilted as Ephraim stalked out of the house.

Meow?

Hank stood on his back legs and rested his front paws on her thigh. She wiped away her tears. "He's incorrigible, Hank. I have to face the fact that it's over." She rubbed the cat's chin, and he responded with a purr.

But was it truly all Ephraim's fault? She'd been so incensed when he asked her to stick with the original plan that she hadn't even asked him why he'd been so upset. She hadn't followed Emma's or her parents' suggestions of listening to him and then respecting his opinion. Maybe he wasn't the only one to blame for their problems.

"Don't say it's over." Katie Ann's expression was fierce as she stood in the doorway to the kitchen. "I'll talk to him tonight. I'll tell him he needs to give your relationship another chance."

Mandy nodded, but in her heart, she was certain Katie Ann's efforts would be wasted.

~

Ephraim walked up his family's back-porch steps later and saw Katie Ann sitting on the glider. He set his lantern on the railing and then leaned against it. "Isn't it late for you to be outside in the cold?"

"I've been waiting for you ever since Chris brought me home." She pushed the glider into motion as she looked up at him. "Where have you been?"

"I took a drive. Why?"

"We need to talk." She pointed at him. "Why are you being such an imbecile?"

"Excuse me?" Irritation colored his words.

"If you keep pushing Mandy away, you'll eventually lose her forever." Katie Ann stood and wagged a finger at him. "You're going to regret it when you realize how stupid you've been."

"I think you need to mind your own business." He picked up the lantern and moved toward the back door.

"It's kind of hard to mind my own business when I care about both of you and want you both to be *froh*. Everyone can see how much you love each other. Why can't you take a step back and listen to what Mandy has to say?"

He spun to face her. "I have listened, and we want different things. That's why it can't work between us."

Katie Ann threw up her hands. "Why does it matter so much where you live or where you work?"

"Because I'm a Blank!" He pointed to the ground. "I belong *here*. And *mei* future *kinner* belong here. I don't want to live with Mandy's parents or become a brickmason."

"Do you think Uria wanted to give up working construction to become a dairy farmer?" Katie Ann crossed the porch and stood in front of him. "Darlene and Uria are making the best of a tough situation. Why can't you and Mandy do the same for the sake of your love for each other?"

Ephraim stilled as Katie Ann's words rolled over him, but he didn't want to talk anymore. "*Gut nacht.*"

Yet as he climbed the stairs, he wondered if his sister could be right. *Mamm* said she and *Dat* would support whatever he decided. But would he dishonor his grandfather if he abandoned the farm that had sustained and defined his family for generations? He had to think about that too.

CHAPTER 7

"H ave you talked to Ephraim?" Tena asked as Mandy entered Emma's kitchen Monday afternoon.

"No. He wouldn't even look at me at church yesterday, and you know he didn't come to our garden meeting." Mandy sat down at the table across from Tena and Emma and set a container in the center. "I can't believe we've been apart for more than a week now. It feels like an eternity." She sighed. "I came so you could try my cheesecake. I baked all morning, and even Rhoda and *Dat* are saying they can't eat it all."

"*Ach, mei liewe.*" Emma shook her head. "It's only been eight days. Don't give up yet."

"It's difficult not to. After our argument on Saturday, I've kind of lost hope." Mandy removed the lid from the cake saver, and the sweet smell of the cake filled the kitchen.

"All the guys are trying to make him realize he's made a huge mistake by being so prideful." Tena stood and crossed to the counter, where she took plates from a cabinet and forks from a drawer.

"They're still trying to get through to him?" Mandy heard the thread of hope in her voice.

"Oh *ya*." Tena brought the plates and forks to the table and then returned to the counter. "Even Katie Ann said she's working on him."

"I know." Mandy frowned as her hope deflated like a balloon. "She told me Saturday she was going to talk to him. I was hoping he'd show up at *mei haus* and ask to talk to me last night. I was imagining us sitting on the back-porch glider despite the cold, working out all our issues. Then he'd propose to me again. But he didn't come. It's just a *gegisch* dream."

"Don't give up on that dream." Tena brought a knife and cake server to the table. "Someone will get through his stubborn head."

"I hope so." Mandy stared at the cake. "I'll run out of baking supplies."

Emma and Tena laughed, and Mandy felt the corner of her lips turn up into a smile.

"I think that cake is too *schee* to eat," Emma said.

"No." Tena shook her head. "It's too *schee* to waste."

As Tena cut into the cake, Mandy smiled. Despite her overwhelming sadness over losing Ephraim, she was so grateful for her wonderful friends.

~

Ephraim shivered as he walked out to the pasture fence. His father stood looking up as the sunset soaked the sky with shades of orange and yellow. The horizon was like a brilliant watercolor painting.

"*Mamm* was looking for you." Ephraim stood beside him and leaned on the fence. "What are you doing?"

"Enjoying the sunset." *Dat* gave him a sideways glance. "Sometimes you have to stop and enjoy the beauty of God's creation."

Ephraim set his foot on the bottom rung of the split-rail fence. Then he rested his chin on his palm and his thoughts turned to Mandy for the hundredth time today. Was she watching the sunset too? He slammed his eyes shut. Why did she invade all his thoughts?

"When your *mamm* and I first married, we argued nearly all the time."

Ephraim turned toward his father, curious. "Why?"

Dat shrugged. "I think most newlyweds go through a similar phase. You're trying to get used to living together, and you're adjusting to each other's moods. *Mei dat* used to say love is blind and marriage is the eye-opener." His loud belly laugh echoed throughout the pasture, and Ephraim couldn't stop a smile.

"*Daadi* really said that?"

"All the time." *Dat* wiped at his eyes. "Your *mamm* and I were young, and we had a lot of growing up to do. We didn't have a *haus*, and we didn't have any money. Your bedroom was our bedroom until your *mammi* and *daadi* retired and moved into the *daadihaus* on *mei bruder's* land." He pointed across the pasture toward his younger brother's farm, nearly twenty acres away from them.

"I didn't know that." Ephraim studied his father. "I thought you and *mamm* moved into this *haus* after my grandparents retired."

"Sometimes your plans aren't what you expect, but love and faith will get you through." *Dat* patted Ephraim's shoulder. "Like your *mamm* told you last week, it's okay if you decide to move off this land. You can decide to learn a new kind of work. Your *mamm* and I will support you no matter what you decide to do, and I know your *daadi* would have too. He always cared more about family than he cared about this land. Just don't let your stubborn pride stand in the way of your future with Mandy."

Ephraim stilled as his father's words washed over him. Despite their wisdom, he still had no idea what path he should choose.

He suddenly felt an overwhelming need for God's love and support through all his crushing confusion. Why hadn't he sought that more? As he looked toward the sunset, he opened his heart and silently began to pray.

God, please lead me on the path you've chosen for me. I love Mandy with all my heart, but I'm confused. Am I supposed to be with her? If so, am I supposed to abandon my dream of running mei dat's *farm and become a brickmason? Please send me a sign.*

~

Mandy leaned her head against the doorframe as the sewing machine hummed while her sister worked. Her eyes moved to the unfinished wedding dress on the table, and renewed regret surged through her.

Rhoda stopped and looked up at her. "How long have you been staring at me?"

"Just a few minutes." Mandy stepped into the room and sat down on a chair next to her. "What are you making?"

"Just a dress." Rhoda held up the light-blue frock. "I thought it would be *schee* for church."

"It's lovely." Mandy touched the material and then looked again at her unfinished wedding dress. "You should make something out of that. I'll never wear it."

"Stop." Rhoda frowned. "You're giving up too easily."

Mandy tilted her head as she crossed one leg over the other. Maybe she had given up too easily. Maybe she'd been too prideful.

"I think you're right," Mandy whispered.

"Give Ephraim another chance." Rhoda touched Mandy's arm. "And always have faith."

Mandy touched the unfinished dress. Would she ever wear it? Or would it just remain half sewn, sitting patiently on the table, collecting dust? If her sister was right, there was still a chance she and Ephraim could work things out. A tiny seed of hope took root in her chest, but she didn't know where to begin when Ephraim was so angry with her.

～

Mandy folded her hands as she sat between Katie Ann and Rhoda at church the following Sunday. She stared down at the lap of her pink dress while the bishop preached from the book of John.

She glanced to the far side of the barn where Ephraim sat between Wayne and Jerry. She took in his handsome face with its strong chiseled jaw and his long, thin nose. He was the most handsome man she knew.

When the bishop announced it was time for the fifteen-minute kneeling prayer, she knelt facing the bench and leaned forward on it. Then she opened her heart.

God, I was blessed when Ephraim asked me to be his girlfriend almost a year ago. I had never been so froh *in my life. When he proposed, I felt blessed beyond measure. Please help Ephraim and me find our relationship again. I believe he still loves me, and I know to the depth of my soul that I still love him. Help us find a compromise for our future. Please lead him back to me. Only you can help us mend our broken relationship.*

Mandy opened her eyes and felt warmth encircle her like a loving hug. It was as if God were comforting her. She knew then that, somehow, everything was going to be okay. Maybe she could find a way to let Ephraim know she still cared.

～

"Have you talked to Mandy?" Jerry asked Ephraim as he sat across from him during lunch.

"No." Ephraim stared at the lunch meat and bread on his plate. Mandy looked beautiful today. He'd tried to keep from staring at her across the barn during the service, but his eyes betrayed him.

At one point, their gazes collided, and heat crawled up his neck to his cheeks. Had she felt the same heat when she looked at him?

"Why are you avoiding her?" Wayne asked. "Why are you letting her slip through your fingers?"

"Don't you want to work it out?" Jerry added.

"Quit ganging up on me. It's my business." Ephraim looked up as Mandy approached with a carafe.

He swallowed as that familiar heat began traveling up his neck. She was the most beautiful woman in their district, if not the entire state of Pennsylvania. Her pink dress complemented her rosy complexion, and her gorgeous blue eyes sparkled as she filled a man's cup and smiled. How he longed to touch her face and tell her how much she meant to him. He still loved her. He was certain of that.

His father's advice tumbled through his mind. But how could they work out their problems if they didn't agree on their future together?

Mandy filled his friends' cups and then turned to him.

"*Kaffi?*" Her gaze met his as she held up the carafe.

"*Ya.* Please." He lifted his cup and she filled it. "*Danki.*"

"*Gern gschehne.*" She lingered for a moment, and he was certain the world had stopped turning just for them.

I love you, Mandy.

If only he could say the words aloud. Would she say them back to him?

"Could I have some *kaffi*?" A man called from nearby, breaking through their trance.

"Excuse me." Mandy cleared her throat and moved on to the neighboring table.

"You need to talk to her." Jerry's voice was close to Ephraim's ear. "How would you feel if she fell in love with someone else while you were still stuck obsessing about where you want to live? Don't you think you'd feel like a moron for not seeing where God was trying to lead you?"

"It's too late now." Ephraim shook his head. "I think I've missed my chance with her. We've said some horrible things to each other."

"You know that's not true. I saw the way she just looked at you." Wayne's expression was serious. "Listen, I said terrible things to Tena when we argued, and she still forgave me. We all say terrible things out of anger. That's part of being human. We're all taught to forgive, and Mandy will forgive you if you ask her to."

Ephraim picked up his cup, wondering if Wayne could be right, wondering if everyone had been right. Wondering if God would send him that sign. Until he had one, he didn't know what to do.

CHAPTER 8

"I can't believe Thanksgiving is this Thursday," Clara said as she sat next to Mandy at Emma's table the following Sunday afternoon. "November has flown by."

Mandy glanced across the table at Ephraim as he sat slumped in his chair between Katie Ann and Wayne. She felt awkward and uncomfortable not sitting beside him. He seemed to feel uncomfortable just being in her presence.

After the intense stare they'd shared after the church service last week, she'd convinced herself he'd appear on her porch one night and beg her to work out their differences. But another week had gone by, and he'd given her only halfhearted hellos and goodbyes when they passed each other at Emma's house. All her hopes for their future had evaporated. It was officially over between them. Too many obstacles stood in their way.

"It has flown by," Jerry said. "We took down the roadside stand this morning, and it's stowed in Emma's barn. The garden is closed for the season."

"It's been a great season," Katie Ann chimed in. "We've raised quite a bit of money for the Bird-in-Hand Shelter in memory of Henry." She looked at Emma. "We're so grateful you allowed us to do this."

"No, thank you all. I'm so honored that you want to keep Henry's memory alive in such a *wunderbaar* way that helps our community." Emma began to clap, and everyone joined in.

Mandy looked over at Ephraim, and he met her gaze. She sucked in a breath as he nodded at her. She returned the nod and then looked down at the table. Would looking into his eyes be painful for the rest of her life? She dreaded the possibility as her chest tightened with grief.

"Should we talk about what we want to plant next year?" Clara asked. "I can get the seeds from *mei onkel* again."

"That's a *gut* idea." Katie Ann turned to a fresh page in her notebook. "Let's talk about lessons learned. What worked and didn't work this year?"

For the next hour, Mandy tried to focus on her friends' discussion about the garden's future, but she kept losing herself in thoughts of Ephraim. She breathed a sigh of relief when Tena declared the meeting over and then brought out turkey tetrazzini casserole for supper.

Mandy picked at her food and kept her focus on her plate as everyone ate. The conversations swirled around her, but she responded only when someone said her name. After they had brownies for dessert, she helped the other women clean the kitchen while the men talked in the family room.

"Are you ready to go?" Katie Ann asked Mandy when they were done.

Mandy nodded. "*Ya.*"

"*Was iss letz?*" Emma asked as she joined them.

Mandy looked past Katie Ann to where Ephraim now stood in the kitchen, talking to Wayne. When he turned toward her, she looked away. "I'm just tired."

"I have something for you." Emma pulled a piece of paper out of her apron pocket and slipped it into Mandy's hand. "I found it when I was going through *mei mamm's* favorite cookbook. I think it might help you."

"What is it?" Mandy opened the paper and found a recipe for peanut butter pie. She looked up at Emma. "I don't understand."

Emma smiled. "The way to a man's heart—"

"Is through his stomach." Katie Ann finished the statement with a grin.

"Did you two work up this plan together?" Mandy pointed at each of them, and they nodded.

"It was my idea to find a recipe Ephraim might like." Katie Ann pointed to the paper. "If you're not ready to give up, then here's an idea for a conversation opener. He's crazy about peanut butter, so I'm sure he'll love this."

Mandy glanced over at Ephraim, and she felt new hope sprouting like a cornstalk. Maybe this was just what she needed to loosen the tension between them!

Wrapped in his warmest jacket, Ephraim sat on his parents' glider and stared out toward the pasture. He shivered as he pushed it back and forth and watched his father's cows lounge in the pasture.

The back door opened and then clicked closed.

"Happy Thanksgiving."

Ephraim glanced at Uria as he approached. "Happy Thanksgiving."

"May I join you?" Uria pointed to the rocker beside him.

"Of course."

Uria sat down and pushed his chair into motion. They sat in amiable silence as the hum of the rocker and glider filled the air.

"I felt like I was in the way in there," Uria finally said. "All the women are scurrying around the kitchen, barking orders at everyone. And the girls are so excited I can't corral them."

"*Ya.*" Ephraim smiled, but it wasn't the chaos of the house that had driven him outside. It was Mandy's absence. They'd planned for her to join his family today, but that plan died along with their breakup. Without her company, the house felt too small, too cold, too dreary. Even with his nieces' laughter.

"How are you doing?" Uria asked.

"Fine. How are you?"

Uria lifted a dark eyebrow as he brought the rocking chair to a halt. "You're fine? Really?"

Ephraim shifted his weight on the glider.

"You miss her." Uria's words were simple, but their meaning ran deep in Ephraim's soul.

He looked straight ahead to avoid his brother-in-law's stare.

"Sometimes our plans for ourselves are different than God's plans," Uria said. "I never imagined I would lose my job and have to uproot my family. But Darlene and I love each other, and we'll always support each other no matter what."

Uria paused for a moment as if gathering his thoughts. "My parents died a long time ago, and I don't have any other family members to lean on. I'm grateful for your family and what you've done for us. And with our love for each other and our family and our faith in God, Darlene and I will get through this and anything else we have to face."

Ephraim rubbed his face as his eyes stung.

Uria leaned toward him. "If your love for Mandy is strong enough, you'll find a way to make things right with her. I know it's none of my business, but I can see how much this breakup is hurting you. It doesn't have to be this difficult, Ephraim. Just let your love for Mandy guide your heart, and you'll find your solution."

Ephraim swallowed against his suddenly dry throat. Did he and Mandy love each other enough to endure all the trials they would face as a couple? Enough to resolve the conflict separating them now?

Suddenly it all clicked in place in his mind. Uria's words were the sign he'd been waiting for! This was what God had been trying to tell him all along. If their love was strong enough—and he believed it was—he and Mandy could make it through any trial or tribulation they encountered. It didn't matter when they married, where they lived, or what he did for a living as long as they had God's blessing and loved each other. The rest would fall into place.

Ephraim leapt to his feet. "I have to go."

"What?" Uria looked up at him.

"I need to go talk to her now."

Uria waved him off with a smile. "Go. I'll tell your parents where you've gone."

"*Danki!*" Ephraim ran to the barn, praying Mandy would forgive him.

"Are we expecting company?" Rhoda called as she started for the mudroom to answer the back door.

"No." Mandy looked at her mother.

Mamm shrugged. "Not that I know of." She pointed to the stove. "Would you please check the turkey?"

"*Ya.*" Mandy opened the oven door, and the succulent aroma of turkey caused her stomach to grumble in delight. How she loved Thanksgiving!

"Mandy."

Mandy turned and gasped as she found Rhoda standing in the doorway with Ephraim close behind her.

"You have a guest." Rhoda smiled and stepped aside, and Ephraim came into full view.

Mandy stilled, confused. She'd planned to ask her father if she could borrow his horse and buggy to visit Ephraim later this afternoon and deliver the pie. She'd never expected him to surprise her with a visit instead.

"Go." *Mamm* gave Mandy's shoulder a gentle nudge. "I'll take care of the turkey."

Mandy stepped over to Ephraim as Rhoda slipped past her. "Hi."

"Happy Thanksgiving." He fingered the zipper on his jacket, and then he pointed to the back door. "Do you have a moment to spare?"

"Of course." Mandy turned toward the refrigerator. "And I have a gift for you."

"A gift?" His eyebrows lifted.

"*Ya.*" She retrieved the peanut butter pie. "I was going to take this to you later."

He took the pie, lifted the plastic wrap, and breathed in its sweetness. "Peanut butter?" He grinned. "You made this for me?"

"*Ya.* It was Emma and Katie Ann's idea. They said the way to a man's heart is through his stomach, so they suggested I make it for you."

He leaned his head back as laughter burst from his mouth. She joined in, and soon they were laughing together. She didn't know why he was here, but hope took center stage in her heart.

Mamm appeared beside her. "Let me put the pie away so you two can go talk alone."

"*Danki,*" Mandy said.

Mamm winked at her before turning away.

As Mandy walked into the mudroom and pulled on her coat, her pulse galloped. Had her prayers been answered? Would God help them mend their relationship? She held her breath as they moved to the porch and sat down on the glider.

Ephraim angled his body toward her. "Uria said something to me today that made me realize how wrong I've been."

"Oh?" Her heartbeat spiked.

"He said all that matters is that he and Darlene are together." He took a deep breath. "He said they support each other no matter what. I finally realized it doesn't matter when you and I are married, where we live, or what I do for a living as long as I have you by my side. These weeks without you have been pure torture, and I can't stand it anymore. I miss you. I love you, Mandy. I want to be with you, no matter where God leads us. And I do think he's leading us, if we'll only listen."

She took a deep breath as well. "I love you, too, but I owe you an apology. I was so overwhelmed with wedding plans and sure I was right about what we needed to do that I didn't take your feelings into consideration. I never meant to try to force you to do what I thought would work best. I never meant to make you doubt how much I love you and want to marry you." She touched his cheek. "I love you with my whole heart, and I never wanted to hurt you. I don't care where we live or what you do for a living. I never meant to appear spoiled. I could be *froh* whether I'm a farmer's *fraa* or a brickmason's *fraa*."

She paused and took a shuddering breath. "Please forgive me for hurting your feelings and pride. You're the man I want to spend my life with. You're the man I believe God has chosen for me. All that matters is that we're together."

A small sound escaped his throat as his eyes glittered. "*Danki.*"

She sucked in a breath as tears filled her eyes. "Let's find a way to work this out, Ephraim. I can't stand this distance between us anymore. I'm ready to listen to you and respect your feelings."

"And I'm sorry for letting our disagreement go on for so long. I want to make up for lost time." He traced his fingertip down her cheek, and she felt a tingling in her chest. "Will you please forgive me?"

"*Ya*, of course, I will."

He leaned forward, and when his lips brushed hers, her heart took on wings. "Will you marry me when you're ready?"

"*Ya.*" She nodded. "I will."

He took her hands in his. "I'll live anywhere you want to live. We can build a *haus* here on this farm, and we can raise our *kinner* here if that's what's best. I just want you to be *mei fraa.* I want to take care of you, and I want to spend the rest of my life with you."

As he kissed her again, she closed her eyes and savored the feeling of his lips against hers.

FOUR MONTHS LATER

Mandy smiled as she threaded her fingers with Ephraim's and walked with him from her father's barn to the back porch. She shivered as the cool March air kissed her cheeks, and she pulled her sweater over her baby-blue dress with her free hand. Then she looked up at her husband as happiness fluttered in her chest. They'd had such a wonderful engagement all winter, but now the time was right for marriage.

Mandy reflected on their perfect day. The three-hour ceremony was held in her father's large barn, beginning with the congregation singing hymns from the Amish hymnal, the *Ausbund*, while she and Ephraim met with the minister.

Then as she and Ephraim sat at the front of the congregation after the meeting, along with their attendants, Rhoda and Wayne, she'd been so grateful her sister had helped her finish the dresses. She thought they were beautiful, and Rhoda looked stunning in that shade of baby blue. Ephraim and Wayne were both handsome in their traditional black Sunday suits and white shirts, but her challenge was keeping her eyes off Ephraim.

She loved him so.

When the ceremony was over, the men began rearranging furniture while some of the women set out the wedding dinner—lasagna and garlic bread, with bountiful desserts.

The tables were decorated with the blue candles and baby's breath decorations Mandy and her friends made. She was so thankful all the plans had come together. Their wedding was exactly as she'd dreamt it would be.

"It's a *schee* day." She peeked up at the clear blue sky once again.

"It's the *perfect* day." Ephraim stopped and faced her. "Because you're finally *mei fraa*."

"*Danki* for waiting for me."

"You were worth the wait."

She smiled as she touched his cheek. "You're going to be even more handsome with a beard." Then she turned toward the porch where their friends all sat. "Everyone looks so *froh*." She grinned as all the "garden couples" laughed together. "I wonder who will be the next to get married."

"I guess we'll see what God has in store for them." Ephraim looped his arm over her shoulders and turned toward the pasture. "I think we're going to start framing this week. The foundation is in."

Excited, she gazed at where their *haus* would be. "You and *Dat* did a great job. You're a *wunderbaar* brickmason."

"I still have a lot to learn." He smiled down at her. "But your *dat* is a great teacher, and I do like the work. It helps to know Uria and *Dat* are doing so well at the farm."

"Ephraim! Mandy!" Katie Ann called from the porch. "Come here!"

"Let's go join our *freinden*." Ephraim gave her hand a gentle tug, and they started down the path.

As they climbed the steps to join their friends, she felt so grateful that Henry's garden had brought them all together. Love had grown throughout the seasons, especially for her and Ephraim. She closed her eyes for a moment and thanked God, not just for today's dream come true, but for the winter blessings he'd brought them.

Discussion Questions

1. Mandy feels overwhelmed with her wedding to Ephraim only six weeks away. When she learns his family is facing a challenge, she feels even more hesitant about rushing their wedding. She suggests they delay it. Do you think her feelings are valid?

2. Ephraim thinks Mandy's complaining about how little time she has to plan the wedding and then her suggesting they delay it is an indication she's doubting their plans to marry. Why do you think he jumps to that conclusion?

3. Mandy is crushed when Ephraim breaks up with her. Have you ever felt utter heartbreak and loss? If so, where did you find your strength to go on? What Bible verses helped you?

4. After the breakup, Mandy finds solace in baking. Have you ever faced a difficult situation? If so, where did you find comfort during that time?

5. Which character can you identify with the most? Which character seemed to carry the most emotional stake in the story? Was it Mandy, Ephraim, or someone else?

6. At the end of the story, Uria shares with Ephraim what he and Darlene have endured in their marriage, and how.

Why do you think his story changed Ephraim's ideas about sacrifice and compromise, especially in marriage?

7. How did Henry's garden play a role in all the relationships in this novella collection?

ACKNOWLEDGMENTS

As always, I'm grateful for my loving family, including my mother, Lola Goebelbecker; my husband, Joe; and my sons, Zac and Matt.

Special thanks to my mother and my dear friend Becky Biddy, who graciously proofread the draft and corrected my hilarious typos.

I'm also grateful for my special Amish friend who patiently answers my endless stream of questions. You're a blessing in my life.

Thank you to my wonderful church family at Morning Star Lutheran in Matthews, North Carolina, for your encouragement, prayers, love, and friendship. You all mean so much to my family and me.

Thank you to Zac Weikal and the fabulous members of my Bakery Bunch! I'm so grateful for your friendship and your excitement about my books. You all are awesome!

To my agent, Natasha Kern—I can't thank you enough for your guidance, advice, and friendship. You are a tremendous blessing in my life.

Thank you to my amazing editor, Jocelyn Bailey, for your friendship and guidance. I'm grateful to each and every person at HarperCollins Christian Publishing who helped make this book a reality.

I'm grateful to editor Jean Bloom, who helped me polish and refine the story. Jean, you are a master at connecting the dots and filling in the gaps. I'm so happy we can continue to work together!

Thank you most of all to God—for giving me the inspiration and the words to glorify you. I'm grateful and humbled you've chosen this path for me.

ABOUT THE AUTHOR

Dan Davis Photography

Amy Clipston is the award-winning and bestselling author of the Amish Heirloom series and the Kauffman Amish Bakery series. She has sold more than one million books. Her novels have hit multiple bestseller lists, including CBD, CBA, and ECPA. Amy holds a degree in communications from Virginia Wesleyan University and works full-time for the City of Charlotte, North Carolina. Amy lives in North Carolina with her husband, two sons, mom, and three spoiled-rotten cats.

Visit her online at amyclipston.com
Facebook: AmyClipstonBooks
Twitter: @AmyClipston
Instagram: @amy_clipston